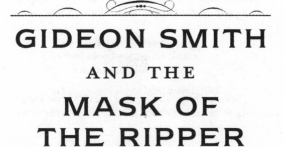

GIDEON SMITH
AND THE
MASK OF
THE RIPPER

David Barnett

SNOWBOOKS

Proudly published in the UK by Snowbooks

Copyright © 2015 David Barnett
David Barnett asserts the moral right to be identified
as the author of this work. All rights reserved.

Snowbooks Ltd
email: info@snowbooks.com
www.snowbooks.com

British Library Cataloguing in Publication Data.
A catalogue record for this book is available from the British Library.

First published September 2015

Printed by Nørhaven, Denmark

Ebook: 9781909679757
Paperback: 9781909679559

- Also available from Snowbooks -

Gideon Smith and the Mechanical Girl Paperback 9781907777974
Gideon Smith and the Mechanical Girl Hardback 9781909679061
Gideon Smith and the Mechanical Girl Ebook 9781909679160

Gideon Smith and the Brass Dragon Hardback 9781909679313
Gideon Smith and the Brass Dragon Paperback 9781909679337
Gideon Smith and the Brass Dragon Ebook 9781909679320

Gideon Smith and the Mask of the Ripper Ebook 9781909679757

This one's for Malcolm Barnett,
the best dad in the world.

ACKNOWLEDGMENTS

Writing a book, for me, means long hours at the keyboard, generally in very unsociable hours. It also means long hours staring into space, *thinking* about writing a book. And that can make for a very unsociable time, as well. So I'd like to thank my wife, Claire, and my children, Alice and Charlie, for putting up with me when my eyes glaze over and I adopt that thousand-word stare, drifting into Gideon's world trying to find out just what he and his compatriots are up to.

Writing might be a solitary business, but the production of a book isn't. It's a team effort, and I'm proud to be part of the fantastic team that's responsible for this, the third Gideon Smith adventure, being released into the world. That team includes, of course, my agent, first reader, and friend John Jarrold, without whom none of this would be happening. Huge thanks must also go to the wonderful Tor books team—my editor Claire Eddy, Bess Cozby, Desirae Friesen, Leah Withers, Irene Gallo, Patrick Nielsen Hayden, and anyone, anywhere at Fifth Avenue who's had a hand in these books coming to fruition. A big tip of the hat to cover artist extraordinaire Nekro for his wonderful work on the covers not only of the books but the short stories on Tor.com set in Gideon's world. And big thanks to Emma Barnes and the team at Snowbooks, UK publishers of Gideon, for all their support and help along the way.

But most of all, thanks to the many, many readers who've picked up Gideon and Co. and taken them to their hearts. There really is nothing more satisfying and humbling than getting an e-mail or message from someone you've never met saying they stayed up all night finishing your book. Really, when that's the case, can I do any less?

Bring me some midnight oil. I got books to write. . . .

David Barnett
England, 2015

"The doer" is merely a fiction added to the
deed—the deed is everything.

—FRIEDRICH NIETZSCHE,
On the Genealogy of Morality, 1887

1 CALIFORNIAN MEIJI
2 FREE STATES OF
  AMERICA
3 BRITISH AMERICA
4 NEW SPAIN
5 FRENCH LOUISIANA

6 THE CONFEDERACY
7 FREE FLORIDA
8 *Nyu Edo*
9 *Uvalde*
10 *San Antonio/Steamtown*
11 *New Jerusalem*

12 *Blackfoot land*
13 *Rooseville*
14 *Ciudad Cortes*
15 *New York*
16 *Fort York*

BRITISH
CANADA

Atlantic

Ocean

MASON-DIXON
WALL

Pacific

EQUATOR

Ocean

Atlantic

Ocean

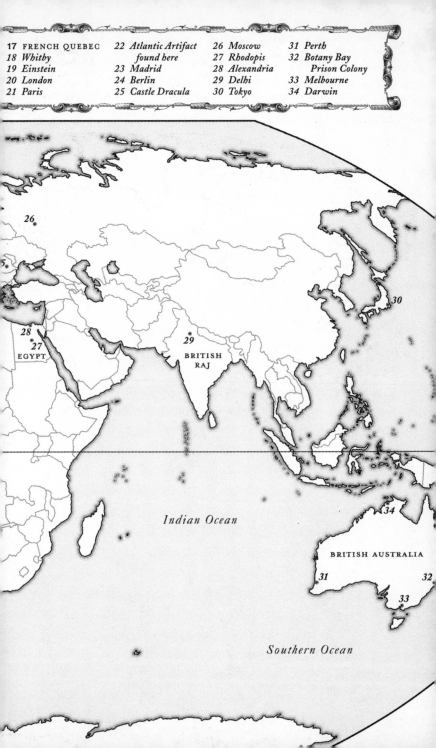

26

5

30

28
27
EGYPT

29
BRITISH RAJ

Indian Ocean

34
BRITISH AUSTRALIA

31
32
33

Southern Ocean

GIDEON SMITH
AND THE
MASK OF
THE RIPPER

1

DECEMBER 1887

Captain James Palmer held the wheel steady as the *Lady Jane* lurched into a trough between gunmetal waves taller than Big Ben. There was a volley of shouts from the deck and a crack of splintering wood; Palmer ignored it, concentrating on keeping his vessel upright on the storm-ravaged sea. It would be that damned cargo, swinging around on the gantry and crashing into midships. He didn't care how much the bloody thing had cost or whether there would be hell to pay; if it threatened to drag the *Lady Jane* over he would order it cut loose, and hang the consequences.

The door to the bridge banged open, letting in the howling Atlantic gale and a spray of seawater. Cursing, Palmer reached one hand out for the papers the wind tried to snatch up, the wheel skidding a half-turn, the ship shuddering and dipping in the storm.

"Our status, please, Mr. Devonshire," called Palmer without turning around, shoving the papers into his oilskin and returning his full weight to keeping the wheel immobile.

"Never seen anything like it," gasped the first mate, throwing himself at the door to force it shut against the sodden wind. "It's bloody hell out there."

"It *is* December, and it *is* the Atlantic," said Palmer. "You were perhaps expecting sunshine and lily pads, Mr. Devonshire?" Not waiting for the first mate to answer, Palmer went on, "Here, take the wheel. I need to look at these charts again."

Devonshire, his woolen sweater drenched, his gray hair plastered to his head, applied his meaty forearms to wrestling the wheel into submission. A sudden lull allowed Palmer to place himself at the bolted-down table and withdraw the papers from his coat.

"How are our guests taking this bit of weather?" asked Palmer mildly.

Devonshire gave him a gap-toothed grin. "They're Royal Navy, so they'd never let on. But I can tell they're shit-scared."

Palmer grunted with satisfaction. "Good. Perhaps teach them not to try to lord it over us on our own ship."

Us, of course, was a bone of contention for Captain Palmer— of the *Lady Jane*'s regular crew, only himself and Mr. Devonshire were on board. If the ever-mysterious Mr. Walsingham'd had his way, it would have been Palmer only, but the captain had drawn the line there. He was an experienced seaman who had done his fair share of work for the Crown on enterprises that were not always aboveboard, and very often beyond the ken of ordinary folk. When Walsingham had come to visit him at Portsmouth he'd outlined the mission, named his price, and laid down the terms: a journey to Gibraltar to pick up a secret cargo, three Royal Navy officers, and a civilian. There Palmer was to give his regular men shore leave and pick up a casual crew from the sailors who hung around the place they called the Rock, paying them in coin and telling them nothing of the next leg of the journey—a specific spot some 150 miles west by southwest of the Faroes, just about midway between Scotland's northernmost tip and the arse-end of Iceland.

"No," Palmer had said. "My crew goes with me."

"Not this time," said Walsingham, watching him intently with those hawkish eyes. "Not if they want to live."

Palmer had leaned forward, his elbows on the table in the shadowy quayside pub where he liked to do business, and filled the bowl of his pipe with tobacco. "Suicide mission, is it?"

"Not for you, Captain. But dangerous. Very, very dangerous. And most secret."

"You wouldn't be here otherwise," said Palmer, stroking his beard.

He'd negotiated his trusted first mate, Mr. Devonshire, on board but had eventually capitulated on the rest, of course, taking Walsingham's handsome purse and granting the rest of his men a week's paid furlough on Gibraltar. He'd picked up five new crewmen easy enough; once word got out that Captain James Palmer was hiring, they were lining up to sign on. His reputation preceded him, and it was one of adventure and—more often than not—riches. There were two Spaniards, a Frenchman, a mulatto built like a brick outhouse with tribal tattoos on his face and a silent way about him, and an Irishman from Cork. Like all sailors-for-hire who hung around the Gibraltar ports, they had a slightly desperate air about them: They were men who had nothing to lose because they'd already lost it, travelers with no ties who went whichever way the winds—or the steam-engines—took them. Gibraltar was a Royal Navy base these days, but still the Rock drew the flotsam and jetsam of the merchantman trade as a way station between Europe and Africa and a place to hear stories, listen to gossip, pick up rumors, and sign on for the next voyage. It was a melting pot, which was why Captain Palmer had both Spaniard and Frenchman on board without—as yet—any bloodshed. Even with grog in them and their blood up, land-bound enmities were put aside in favor of the brotherhood conferred by a life on the sea. The ocean was a constantly shifting, ever-changing territory, but still men such as those he had hired on Gibraltar considered it home more than they did any land-locked state.

Palmer spread the papers out on the table. He had been given them by Walsingham, who had insisted that he was to show them to no one else, nor copy them in any way, and that they were to be returned at the close of the venture. They were excerpts of a larger work that Walsingham termed the *Hallendrup Manuscript*, dating back to Denmark sometime in the 1650s, but the hawkish representative of the Crown had not elaborated further. The hand-copied pages given to Palmer seemed to detail the journey of a Norse longship in the late tenth century, which had met some calamity in the Atlantic Ocean. The clumsy translation suggested the ship had fallen victim to what the original manuscript called *hafgufa*, which seemed to translate as "sea mist." The *Lady Jane* lurched again, the wind howling around the cabin, lashing the windows with thick rain that hinted at fledgling ice. Palmer shook his head. A ferocious sea mist, to send a Viking longship to the bottom of the sea. But that name . . . *hafgufa*. He was sure he'd heard it before, or something like it, but in a much different context than a sea mist. He shook his head. A sailor of his years heard a lot of things. He checked the coordinates on the notes against his own charts and rolled up the sheets of paper again, secreting them in his oilskins.

"We're here," he said to Devonshire. "I'll take the wheel; go tell the Corkman to kill the engines and inform the navy boys that they can start getting their little toy ready."

"Better them than me," sniffed Devonshire.

Palmer gazed out at the storm-lashed sea again. "And me, Mr. Devonshire. And me."

The three Royal Navy officers were dressed in regulation yellow oilskins, two of them hanging on to the tarpaulin that covered the bulky cargo dangling on chains from the gantry that had been bolted to the *Lady Jane*'s deck while the third, Commodore Peter Leadbeater, stood with his fists on his hips, riding the bucking and rolling of the deck with the consummate ease of the seasoned seaman. The fourth man was gray haired and steely eyed, but wiry and fit, and the tossing of the deck didn't seem to bother him overmuch. Dr. John Reed he was called, and despite his lack of military title the navy men—including Leadbeater—seemed to defer to his quiet authority. Devonshire emerged from belowdecks as the steady thrum of the engines ceased and the ship danced freely on the storm-tossed waves, the Corkman behind him.

"Captain Palmer," acknowledged Leadbeater, his waxed mustache standing proud despite the weather. The sky above the ship boiled blackly, the last trails of smoke drifting from the *Lady Jane*'s chimneys to add to the gloom, and the deck was slick with rain and the seawater that crashed against the hull.

"We have reached our coordinates," shouted Palmer above the storm. "Are you sure you want to do this? It seems folly to me."

Leadbeater smiled crookedly. "Once we're down there, the weather won't trouble us, Captain." He nodded to the two lieutenants, who began to untie the tarpaulin from the object slung beneath the gantry.

What emerged was a sleek, cigar-shaped object, twenty feet in length and the height of a man, with a hatch fitted into the side and a glass dome at what Palmer assumed was the fore of the vessel. At the aft was a propeller, and flexible cables as thick as a man's arm were attached to the top. The whole thing was plated in steel, riveted tightly together. The hull bore the legend *HMS Proteus*.

"Tell me you're not getting into the water in *that* thing," said Devonshire, agog.

"That we are, Mr. Devonshire," said Leadbeater proudly. "This is a submersible, an underwater ship. The first of the Royal Navy's new fleet. Experimental, admittedly, and highly secret, naturally."

Palmer raised an eyebrow; Leadbeater was being remarkably loose lipped with a crew of casual sailors culled from the Gibraltar dives. Palmer said, "Steam?"

One of the lieutenants had opened the hatch and unfurled a rope ladder. He began to clamber inside the cramped space and Leadbeater said, "Yes, with a gear-driven backup. We take in water as ballast in a chamber beneath the submersible and expel it when we want to rise. The cables you see attached to the top will connect us to an air pump up here on the deck of the *Lady Jane*."

Palmer pursed his lips. "And what are you looking for down there, Commodore? I presume you *are* looking for something?

We haven't come all this way to carry out mere testing of your experimental underwater ship?"

Finally Reed spoke up, fixing Palmer with his stare. "I'm afraid that is *above* top secret, Captain Palmer."

Palmer returned his gaze. "What exactly is your role in all this, Doctor? You have been awfully quiet the whole journey."

Reed smiled. "You don't need to know, Captain. You don't *want* to know." He turned to Leadbeater. "I think you boys should get ready."

The commodore saluted and followed his lieutenants into the cramped submersible, clanging the hatch closed behind them. Palmer nodded to Devonshire, who rallied the hodge-podge of a crew to begin hauling on the ropes that swung the gantry's twin arms, the *Proteus* suspended between them, over the rising gray waves.

"Better them than me," said Devonshire again.

"Unlikely to be you, Mr. Devonshire," said Palmer as the sailors lowered the submersible into the sea, where it immediately began to sink. He glanced at Reed, who leaned on the railings, watching the operation. "Above top secret, and all that. Not for the likes of you and me."

The coils of thick rope fixed to the deck began to unspool as the *Proteus* dropped out of sight beneath the cold Atlantic, and Devonshire nodded for the Irishman to begin working the bellows that pumped fresh air through the pipe that was similarly coiled on a giant bobbin.

"How deep do you think they'll go in that thing?" asked Devonshire.

Palmer shrugged, tightening his oilskin around him as the freezing wind tore across the deck with seemingly renewed vigor. "Until they find what they are looking for, whatever that might be. Perhaps Dr. Reed can enlighten us."

Instead, a crack of thunder clapped overhead, and Reed said, "They used to say not far from here that storms were called up by the thunder god, Thor, when he was angry."

Palmer raised an eyebrow. "Perhaps your mission does not have the blessing of the gods, Doctor."

They waited an hour on the storm-battered deck, until the wind and rain seemed to drop slightly, though there was no respite from the oppressive gray clouds overhead. One of the Spaniards shouted in alarm as the thick rope still connected to the aft of the *Proteus* went suddenly slack. Palmer raised an eyebrow; were the navy boys in trouble? He joined Devonshire at the starboard side and peered into the brine.

"Wind those ropes," he ordered the sailors, nudging Devonshire in the ribs. "Look."

Beneath them a dark shape that could have been a small whale or even a shark shimmered in the deep, rising until half a dozen yards off the starboard bow the *Proteus* surfaced with a splash, seawater coursing off its brass panels, the ropes slack on the sea's surface. The hatch sprang open and Leadbeater, grinning broadly, waved.

"Captain Palmer! Dr. Reed! Would you be so good as to wind us in?"

The mission had been a success then, given the smile on the commodore's face. Reed nodded, evidently satisfied. Devonshire put a man on each winding coil and they began to haul the ropes taut, dragging the *Proteus* back toward the *Lady Jane*. Palmer turned to go to his cabin to get a bottle of rum; it was customary to toast a successful expedition, and he trusted the navy chaps wouldn't spurn his hospitality.

"Captain!" Palmer was only halfway to the bridge when Devonshire's cry rang out, followed by a volley of shouts and screams. He turned to see the ropes tighten, just as the deck bucked beneath him, almost throwing him off his feet. The *Proteus* seemed to be making steam, trying to dive again. What on earth was that fool Leadbeater—?

Then, as he reached to steady himself on the rail, he saw a brown mass seeping over the submersible—it appeared to be brown fronds of seaweed, but massive, creeping over the brass hull.

No, not seaweed. Tentacles. One yellow eye opened and seemed to regard Palmer directly, balefully, as the slick, bulbous shape fully twenty feet across wrapped itself around the *Proteus* and emerged from the iron-gray waves.

Palmer swore. Suddenly he remembered where he'd heard that word before, *hafgufa*. Sea mist his foot. An old Danish sailor, always the worse for ale, used to burble the word all the time in one of the pubs in Portsmouth. He was an old drunk, not to be trusted with even the most menial jobs on board any ship. He was white haired, which he said had happened through sheer terror, after coming face-to-face with the most terrible of creatures that roamed the oceans.

Hafgufa.

"The kraken," said Reed at his side, drawing a revolver from his belt.

Leadbeater poked his head out of the hatch, looking around at the source of the commotion, and his eyes widened as one of the kraken's tentacles swung by his head. Palmer stood transfixed; he had never thought to see such a beast, never really believed they existed. Then the deck lurched again; the kraken was determined to take the *Proteus* down—and it threatened to take the *Lady Jane* with it.

"I'm going to have to cut you free!" roared Palmer at Leadbeater. "The thing's going to pull us over!"

The commodore disappeared beneath the hull for a moment then returned, hauling an oilskin bag with him. "Doctor Reed, take this!"

He tossed the bag over the three yards between the *Proteus* and the *Lady Jane,* and it skidded to a halt at Reed's feet. Devonshire had at least had the foresight to take out his gun, and he was emptying the chamber into the thick hide of the beast that tugged and tugged at the submersible. Reed was firing, too, and Leadbeater took out his own pistol and began to fire at close quarters, gore and slime spraying up from the kraken's eye as the commodore's bullets found their mark.

On the deck, the bag had spilled out something remarkable.

Almost like a glass bowl. Palmer stooped to pick it up. It seemed to be made of something much harder than glass, opaque with a yellowish tinge. He hefted it; it was perhaps three pounds in weight, the curved side bisected by a slight indentation, the underside peppered with symmetrically spaced holes and one large aperture, an inch in diameter. It seemed both incredibly old and fantastically *other* at the same time. A shout brought Palmer back to his senses.

"Cut the ropes!" he ordered, then headed to the bridge, still clutching the glass artifact. He stowed it in his deep desk drawer and broke out his rifle, feeling the *Lady Jane* right herself as the *Proteus* was cut loose. Loading the rifle, he headed back out on deck, to see the submersible and the vast kraken wheeling away in the waves. He raised the weapon and blasted at the beast, ripping a huge wound in its flank. Leadbeater had crawled out onto the hull of the *Proteus*, stabbing at one of the kraken's leathery tentacles with a knife. The man was not short on bravery, Palmer had to give him that.

Another of the navy crew had appeared at the hatch, firing at the kraken's other eye. By accident or design, the monster swung a tentacle at him, curling it around the sailor and lifting him, screaming, into the air. Palmer reloaded and fired again, but the kraken plunged the navy man deep into the water with a forceful finality.

It seemed to be loosening its grip, sliding backward off the *Proteus*, whose air-filled cells were proving more than the beast had bargained for. Reed cupped his hand to his mouth and called, "Leadbeater! Swim for it, now the beast is injured!"

The commodore nodded and shouted into the submersible. The surviving lieutenant climbed out and the two men dove into the choppy waters. Palmer ordered the two Spaniards to throw them lines; that water was freezing and they wouldn't last long. As they were dragged toward the *Lady Jane*, Palmer raised his rifle to his shoulder and took careful aim. The thing was built like an octopus, and he hoped its brain was in the same place. He aimed for the bulge above its stricken eyes and fired. The kraken uttered its first sound, a high-pitched shriek, and slid from the submersible and under the waves. As Leadbeater and his surviving lieutenant were pulled aboard by the mulatto and the Irishman, the *Proteus*, evidently greatly damaged by the encounter, spun once, upended, and sank stern first out of sight.

"I'm sorry we lost your ship," said Palmer. "But at least we saved the—"

"Captain!" said Devonshire.

"What now, Mr. Devonshire?" asked Palmer, turning to where the first mate was pointing. One of the *Lady Jane*'s lifeboats, only a slender affair, had been put out to sea off the port side. Two figures were in it, and a quick head count identified them as the Frenchman and one of the Spaniards. The oilskin bag that Leadbeater had tossed aboard was gone.

Leadbeater glanced at Reed then closed his eyes. "Curses. We've lost the *Proteus* and the—oh, bollocks."

With a swift coldness that surprised even Palmer, Reed took his pistol and put a bullet each into the remaining Spaniard, the mulatto, and the Irishman before they even had time to realize what was happening.

"That was my crew," said Palmer, stunned.

"You were told to leave your crew at home," said Reed wearily. "This is why. Throw them overboard."

Palmer looked into the distant sea, the lifeboat lost to sight. "What of the other two?"

"Spies," sighed Reed. There were a couple items scattered on the deck, leftovers from the bag. Reed picked them up and held to the dim light a ruby of fantastic size, suspended on a gold chain. He stared into its depths for a moment then pocketed it.

"A Spaniard and a Frenchman? Working together?" said Palmer incredulously.

"Apparently so." Reed puffed out his cheeks and exhaled. "Bother. Bloody bollocking bother." He looked up at Palmer. "Don't suppose you have any rum, do you?"

Palmer led Reed and Leadbeater to the bridge while Devonshire and the navy lieutenant disposed of the Gibraltar sailors. "You going to be in trouble when we dock?" Palmer asked.

"A world of trouble." Leadbeater nodded.

"But at least you got something," said Palmer. "That ruby I saw you pocket, Dr. Reed."

"A trinket," said Reed. "Not what we came for."

Palmer opened his desk drawer and took out a bottle of rum, pouring two generous measures. He sipped his and watched Leadbeater throw his drink back in one swallow, then refilled his glass.

"Good job I saved you this, then," Palmer said, taking out the strange glass object.

Reed's eyes widened, then he broke out into a wide grin.

Palmer said, "Don't suppose there's much point in me asking what it is."

"This," said Reed, taking the artifact from Palmer and holding it reverently, "really *is* above top secret. Well done, Captain Palmer. Now I'd be gratified if you could take us all home."

2

DECEMBER 1890

Inspector George Lestrade was having a bad day, and it wasn't yet ten o'clock. Through the frosted glass of his office door he could see a thin, wiry figure, ridiculous deerstalker hat on its head, performing what appeared to be a series of jiglike dance movements. He refocused his attention on the man across the beeswaxed desk from him, on the walruslike mustache hiding his mouth as he clutched the brim of his bowler hat in both hands; he sat upright in the tall-backed chair, speckles of snow slowly melting on his hunched shoulders within his heavy overcoat.

"Doctor," said Lestrade wearily. "Just what *is* that maniac doing out there?"

"That is what we are here to talk about," said the man, wringing his hat excitedly. "My colleague believes he has a unique insight into the activities of Jack the—"

Lestrade held up a hand. He could feel a headache building behind his eyes, like the roiling waters of a dam that was about to burst. "Doctor, when I said *maniac* I was not talking about the mass murderer whom I refuse to honor with that ridiculous appellation the gutter press have conferred upon him. Rather, I am talking about your *patient*, cavorting out there in the corridor and thus bringing disturbance and yes, chaos, sir, to the Commercial Road police station over which I am trying to preside with some measure of order and discipline."

"Oh," said the man, and huffed a long sigh through the curtains of his mustache. "Inspector . . . George."

Lestrade matched the sigh with one of his own. He needed a pot of coffee to drive away the headache. He sucked in another breath and said more gently, "John. How long are you going to . . . to encourage him in this delusional fallacy? Can you really believe pandering to his fancies does your patient any degree of service?"

"I prefer to call him my colleague rather than my patient," said the other man. "And it is my firm belief that forcing him to deny the fantasy world he has built for himself will cause more harm than good. That would be like taking a sledgehammer to the wall that he has built around his own fragile mind; what is required is to take down that wall, slowly, brick by brick. And perpetuating his delusion is the only way I can get through to him."

"The Great Detective," said Lestrade witheringly. He looked out the window at the sleet that battered the glass. It had barely managed to get light out there, between the infernal, snow-laden clouds that had hung over London for three days now and the smog that lurked at street level as the capital stoked its fires and burned its gas lamps with abandon to ward off the foul winter that had settled in like a house guest with no intention of leaving. *The Great Detective.* In the window Lestrade caught his own reflection, his face sallow for want of sunshine, his eyes black pinpricks. Like a rat's, they said unkindly when they described him in the newspapers, which was becoming more and more frequent these days as he failed to bring to book the man who was slicing up prostitutes in the East End. The top brass had dressed it up as some kind of temporary promotion when they transferred him from Scotland Yard down to the Commercial Road to head up what even his bosses were now calling "the Ripper inquiry." *Do a good job with this,* they'd said, and who knows? *Maybe there'll be chief inspector in it for you, Lestrade.*

Or maybe he had been set up to fail. Maybe there was no room for old-fashioned coppers like George Lestrade these days at Scotland Yard, where they gasped with wonder and amazement at the latest technological marvel that they were sure was going to make the job of the bobby on the beat even easier. Hydraulic truncheons that expanded from a foot long to the height of a man at the push of a button. Electric machines that tapped out a man's heartbeat in inky lines that leaped and danced if he told a lie. Clockwork dogs that could follow a scent through even Billingsgate fish market.

George Lestrade didn't need any of that. Good detective work was what was needed to close a case, and failing that, five minutes and a couple of burly coppers in a locked room normally extracted a confession from even the hardiest crook. His record attested to the number of successful prosecutions that had resulted from his single-minded pursuit of justice and application of the law. By rights, the newspapers should be calling *him* the Great Detective, not John Watson's capering cretin.

"I want him away from anything to do with the Ripper case," said Lestrade finally, the word "Ripper" curdling on his tongue. But how else could he describe the man who was slicing the tops of the heads off London's whores, when that was how the rest of the country—the rest of the Empire, even—referred to him? "Seriously, John. He's hindering my investigations. And with Christmas coming up, I'm going to be short on manpower as it is without tripping over him."

"You won't even listen to what he has to say?"

"No. Keep him out of my way. I'd say lock him up, but I know you won't do that. Can't you at least cook something up to distract him?"

The doctor stroked his mustache thoughtfully. "There is something I can . . . refocus his efforts on, perhaps. My colleague's reputation is growing, and a man came to us in Baker Street with a story about a gem, a carbuncle I think, he'd found inside the carcass of a goose . . ."

"Sounds harmless enough," said Lestrade. "Let him loose on that mystery if you want. Just keep him out of Whitechapel."

Lestrade called for a constable to show the doctor out and bring him a pot of coffee. The coffee came back quickly, but also with a less edifying side order.

"Someone to see you, guvnor," said the constable apologetically as a shape, as rotund and monstrous as the doctor's patient had been thin and reedlike, hove into view in the doorway. "Sir, I do know you are aware of the regulations governing unauthorized access to—"

"Yes, yes, Ayres," said Lestrade. "Who—?"

"Lestrade, best of the effing season to you!" boomed a voice.

Lestrade pinched his nose, closed his eyes, and counted slowly to ten. "Aloysius Bent," he breathed, opening one eye to glare at the man who cheerfully described his own face as not unlike a stocking full of porridge. "To what do I owe this intense pleasure?"

The vast man, who was bearing his rumpled suit as a rock might sport a covering of moss rather than actually wearing it with any sort of style, sank heavily into the chair so recently vacated by the doctor and belched loudly. He reached over and helped himself to the single cup that the constable had brought and poured himself some coffee from the pot. "Don't mind, do you? It's colder than a witch's tit out there. Thought I'd come and see you. Been a while."

"Yes, I think the last time we met was when you vomited copious amounts of spicy sausage on my shoes."

Bent belched again. "Got to love an effing sausage, now and again. That was . . . let's see . . . Frances Coles, wasn't it? Back in July? Ripper did for her behind that tripe shop on Lomas Street."

Lestrade opened his desk drawer and found an old tin cup and poured himself some coffee. "That was the last Ripper story you did for the *Argus*, wasn't it? Shortly afterward you were transferred to the penny dreadful? *World Marvels & Wonders*?"

Bent cackled. "Don't pretend you don't know, George. I'm an effing hero, I am. Went to bloody Egypt and fought mummies, then there was all that malarkey with the brass dragon. You wouldn't believe what I've done since then. Dinosaurs, George, big as an effing house. Giant metal men. Warlords with steam-powered arms. Red Indians!"

Lestrade forced a smile. "Ah, yes. You are now the official chronicler of the adventures of Gideon Smith, the Hero of the Empire." He cocked his head, much like a ferret—a description frequently applied to Lestrade by Bent's ilk in Fleet Street. "I must say, Mr. Bent, I never had you down as the adventurous type."

Bent shrugged and poured more coffee. "A change is as good as a rest, George. Between you and me, I wasn't pleased when they told me I'd have to go off gallivanting around the effing world with young Smith, but it's been quite an invigorating experience, all told." He paused and raised one vast cheek to let loose a hissing fart. "Aside from nearly getting killed once or twice, of course."

"Heaven forbid," said Lestrade, though without much conviction. He watched Bent slurping coffee for a moment, then said, "Well, as gratified as I am that you bullishly elbowed your way into my office for no apparent reason, I'm very much afraid that I am a busy man and—"

Bent banged the cup down on the desk. "Ah ha! That's why I'm here, George old chap. Going to lighten your effing load a bit." He winked. "Give you more time to spend with that chickadee I heard you was knocking about with. Very unorthodox, so's I was told."

Lestrade raised an eyebrow. "Mr. Bent, I fail to see—"

Bent waved him away and nodded enthusiastically. "Don't worry, I don't go in for that sort of yellow journalism no more. Bigger fish to fry, Lestrade. Going to solve your bloody Jack the Ripper mystery for you, ain't I?"

Lestrade felt something wither and die inside him. The slim hope that today was going to be anything other than dreadful, he surmised. "I don't think that will be necessary."

"Oh, but it will, George," said Bent. "Necessary indeed. You see, Mr. Gideon Smith has been charged by his employers, in other words the Crown, to get to the bottom of this Ripper malarkey once and for all."

Lestrade fixed his ratlike eyes on Bent. "You jest, of course."

The journalist put a fat hand on his crumpled shirtfront. "Jest, George? About something as serious as this? Not an effing chance, big man." His eyes narrowed. "And not when I happen to be the foremost expert on Jack the Ripper in the whole of effing London."

There was a moment's silence while Lestrade tried to marshal his response into something coherent, which was broken by the constable lumbering into the office. Didn't anyone bother to knock anymore? Was an inspector in Her Majesty's Constabulary not worth even the merest ounce of respect?

"Early editions of the rags, sir," said the constable, his arms full of the midmorning newspapers. "Something in the *Argus* I thought you might want to see."

"Unlikely," sniffed Bent. "They haven't had a story I'd wipe my effing arse on since I got booted on to the penny dreadful."

Lestrade took the *Argus* from the constable and peered at the front page, surrounded by advertisements for gentlemen's outfitters offering the latest styles, Bird's Crystal Jelly, the medicinal effects of chewing tobacco, steam-powered rug cleaners and clothes washers, airship trips to Paris for Christmas. The lead story was about the suggestions to build some kind of underground steam railway beneath the streets of London to alleviate the traffic problems in the choked streets. Lestrade thought that was inviting trouble; tunnels crisscrossing the capital would be a boon to thieves and crooks of all kinds. Bent, trying to read it upside down across the desk, swore and dragged it off him.

"Effing hell. This has to be some sort of joke."

Lestrade glared and tugged the newspaper back. It was not the story about Parliament's imminent debating of the underground railway matter that was the cause of concern, but a piece below with the headline "Ruined Women" of Whitechapel Withdraw Services with Regard to Increasing Activities of Jack the Ripper. A secondary deck of type declared:

OPEN LETTER FROM LIZZIE STRUTTER, A HARLOT OF
THE EAST END, DELIVERED TO THE OFFICES OF THE
ILLUSTRATED LONDON ARGUS LATE LAST NIGHT.

The failure of the police to have any measure of success with
regard to the apprehension of the killer known colloquially
as Jack the Ripper has prompted the ladies of the night who
ply their disgraceful trade on the streets and byways of the
East End to take matters into their own hands.

A letter received late last night at the offices of this
newspaper from one Lizzie Strutter and signed (in many
cases with a simple X as the "ruined women" of Whitechapel are not known for their extensive education) by
what purports to be a phalanx of some 1,127 streetwalkers
has announced that those who pursue the vocation of
prostitute in the East End have withdrawn from their chosen occupation.

WIVES REJOICE!

Mrs. Strutter, who is considered to be one of the most mili-
tant and—according to those "in the know"—influential
prostitutes in Whitechapel, has apparently organized her fellow streetwalkers into some kind of union for the purposes
of self-preservation.

Her letter (written upon paper of a very low grade, and
in handwriting that has most certainly not been the product of any finishing school of London or beyond) states: "We
the undersigned are sick and tired of the police failing to
catch Jack the Ripper what is slicing up good honest working girls in Whitechapel & surrounding parishes.

"Until such time as Jack the Ripper is brought to justice
there will be no business entertained on the streets of Whitechapel.

"Any girl who is caught touting for custom will be properly dealt with."

WHITHER THE PEELERS?

Mrs. Strutter (though this newspaper has been unable to establish whether she is in fact a married woman) furthermore claims that our constabulary has systematically failed to make any inroads into the capture of Jack the Ripper, who (sensitive readers may wish to turn the page) is renowned for cutting the tops of the skulls of his victims—all young women who have been found on the streets of Whitechapel and the East End.

Indeed, she surmises that the police are in actual fact supportive of the actions of Jack the Ripper and wish him to wipe out the entire population of Whitechapel's "ruined women."

SCOOPED OUT THEIR BRAINS

No one is certain of Jack the Ripper's motives for his killing spree, which is about to mark its third Christmas. It is said that the monster scoops out his victims' brains with a wooden spoon and eats them as one might porridge.

The letter from the prostitutes of Whitechapel leaves no doubt that the sordid business of "favors for sale" on the public streets of the East End is now—albeit temporarily—in abeyance.

Well, that was some good news at least, thought Lestrade. The latest Metropolitan Police report had the number of prostitutes across London at something like ten thousand, and a quarter of those were in the boroughs of Spitalfields, Houndsditch, and Whitechapel. One of his biggest headaches was managing the sheer volume of streetwalkers and the associated crime that they brought to his corner of the East End. He couldn't suppress a smile, and Bent noticed.

"What the eff are you grinning about, George?"

Lestrade waved his hand at the *Argus*. "One less headache, Mr. Bent."

Bent stared at him, incredulous. "You're having a laugh, right? You think this is a *good* thing? You're off your effing rocker, Inspector Lestrade. Prostitutes are the oil that keeps Whitechapel moving. And now they're having an effing *strike*? Think about it, George. There'll be the devil to pay. Wouldn't surprise me if you had an effing riot on your hands in a day or two."

Lestrade opened his mouth to retort, then closed it again and harrumphed. "You really think so?"

"I bloody know so, and I'm speaking from experience," said Bent. "I mean, George, look at me. You think I can get a woman without paying for it? I don't get my leg over for a few days, I start to get cranky. Worst I might do, though, is kick a dog on my way back to Grosvenor Square, where I'll wank myself to sleep."

Lestrade made a face, but Bent went on. "Think about some of the characters you've got out there, George. What happens when they can't get a tumble? Some of 'em'll get their kicks in other ways. Some of 'em'll take it whether it's on offer or not. And some of 'em'll blame *you*, George. Old Jack the Ripper's been slicing up whores since the summer of '88. It's Christmas 1890. That's two and a half years. And how close have you come to catching him?"

"We've made good progress," mumbled Lestrade, but he knew as well as anyone that that was a lie.

Bent nodded. "Thought so. You're going to have to pull out all the stops, George. Because it might be snowing out there, but Whitechapel's suddenly a tinderbox of pent-up frustration. And it won't take much for it to go up, just like that."

Bent snapped his thumb and fingers, and Lestrade jumped, startled out of the reverie brought on by the sudden, dreadful realization that Aloysius Bent was exactly right. He groaned and put his head in his hands.

"Cheer up, though, George," said Bent, standing up and re-arranging his groin in the folds of his creased trousers. "At least now you've got me and Gideon Smith on the case. We'll have this sorted out in no time. I'll see myself out."

After Bent had departed, George Lestrade sat for a long time in welcome silence, reading and rereading the story in the *Illustrated London Argus*. A prostitutes' strike. And how long before it spread, how long before they got word out to Bethnal Green, Mile End, and Blackwall? Lambeth and Blackfriars? Southwark, Bermondsey, and Rotherhithe? Because though it was a Whitechapel problem just now, Lestrade knew of Lizzie Strutter by reputation very well indeed. She ruled the whores of the borough with an iron fist, and what she said went. Even the gangs were scared of Lizzie Strutter. Once the punters starved of sex in Whitechapel started drifting out to the other areas, she was going to clamp down on them as well. This thing could go across London. And when the judges and Members of Parliament and captains of industry couldn't get their illicit tumbles, then the trouble would *really* begin.

Bent's words came back to haunt him mockingly. *Whitechapel's suddenly a tinderbox of pent-up frustration. And it won't take much for it to go up, just like that. And some of 'em'll blame you, George.*

He reached for the coffeepot, but Bent had drained it dry. He looked up expectantly as Constable Ayres bobbed his head around the door. At least he could get more coffee. At least the day couldn't get any worse.

Then he saw the look on the constable's face.

"Bad news, sir," he said apologetically. "There's been another one."

Lestrade rubbed his eyes and frowned. "Another *what*, Constable?"

"Jack the Ripper, sir," said Ayres. "He's struck again."

Intermedio:
Very Far from Home

He was very far from home, yet he walked the streets of London with an unerring sense of direction and purpose, as though the sluggish black waters of the Thames coursed in his veins, as if the smog that hung oppressively over the rooftops filled his lungs. His heart was as black as the smoke-stained walls of the towering ziggurats and tumbledown tenements, and as hard as the cobbles coated with the dirty snow beneath the heels of his boots.

He was very far from home, but the shrill cries and guttural shouts gave him some comfort; the swell of the filthy bodies of the damned toward a narrow alleyway and the faint but unmistakable smell of blood on the cold, damp air went some way toward alleviating the homesickness that crouched like a black toad in his soul. He fell in with the masses, hanging back at the corner of the alley as they surged forward to get a better look. He had already seen it, and more like it besides, but still he came, and craned his neck to look.

To look at the scene of the crime.

He felt his black, stone-hard heart quicken as he caught a glimpse of the victim, her face darkened by a dried curtain of blood, before the police officers began to push the crowd back as more uniformed coppers brought out barricades to preserve the scene for the detectives. *He* would be coming, ferret-eyed Lestrade, rubbing his thin mustache and pondering the body laid against the wall, knowing with a sinking stomach what was already passing through the crowd like the pox.

Jack the Ripper. Jack the Ripper had struck again.

He allowed himself a smile and turned away, walking against the ghoulish Londoners who flocked to the mouth of the alley still, walking away from the tumult. The true work had been done; there was nothing to see but the aftermath. Art had been committed, black art, the truest and only kind of art there was. Besides, he had seen enough, and more than the great unwashed masses who jostled for a glimpse of torn flesh and rusted blood.

He had seen the ghost of the girl, pale and diffuse, almost invisible against the snow. She didn't exist, of course, because although he knew there were more things in heaven and earth, Horatio, than were dreamed of in all but the philosophy of a select few, he could distinguish phantoms of the mind from more outré occurrences. The ghost was a product of his mind, a stain on his soul, a message from deep within himself.

The ghost was encouragement that he was on the right path, as dark as the woods that the trail crept through. She was blood and blackness, set free from inside him. For when he killed, he was not merely spilling the blood of his victims. He was bloodletting his own conscience, easing his own soul lest it consume him completely, trepanning the pressure that built up inside his skull not through self-mutilation, but by the vicious injuries he dealt to others.

The ghost was also a warning.

Not enough, she had mouthed at him. *Not enough*.

3

JACK THE BLOODY RIPPER

George Lestrade was resigned: The day was only going to get worse. Three immediate pieces of evidence in support of his hypothesis were present in the snowdrifts that had gathered in the narrow alley off Commercial Street, where the constables had set up a cordon of police bunting to keep the gathering crowd of onlookers back from the crime scene.

One, it was definitely a Ripper. Slumped against the soot-blackened brick wall, a smear of red painting the brickwork behind her, was the victim, her eyes glassily, shockingly open, curtains of dried blood down her face, bisected by her nose. The top of her head had been severed, the cap of her skull peeled back as though it were nothing more than the lid of a jam jar. Lestrade knew that tests in the morgue would reveal that an initial cut across the forehead by an incredibly sharp, thin blade had been supplemented with a rough, jagged incision by something more powerful and crude, in the manner of an implement that might be used to remove the top of a tin can. That was the *modus operandi* of the man the gutter press insisted on referring to as Jack the Ripper. Beneath the pried-apart skull, the brains of the victim glistened like gray jelly.

Two, despite his stern words of less than an hour ago, that prancing fool who Dr. Watson was supposed to be keeping as far from Lestrade as possible was here, his keeper wringing his leather-gloved hands behind him as the thin, wiry figure seemed to be performing some kind of dance, just inside the cordon. Lestrade glared at Watson until the doctor felt the weight of his stare and glanced over guiltily. *Get him out of here,*

Lestrade mouthed. His head was pounding fit to burst, as though Jack the bloody Ripper had done a number on him, too.

Three—and, Lestrade fervently hoped, finally—Aloysius Bent was standing at the front of the crowd at the top of the alley, stuffing a steaming pasty into his mouth and waving cheerfully at Lestrade.

The inspector pinched his nose and closed his eyes tightly, imagining he was still in his bed and today had just been a nightmare from which he was about to wake. When he opened them again, it was all just the same, save for a young constable who had appeared by his side and was staring expectantly at him.

"Sir? I thought you might—"

"First things first, Constable," said Lestrade. "One, get that bloody idiot detective away from here. Two, increase the cordon and do not say a word to that fat man over there, Aloysius Bent. Not even 'good morning,' do you understand?"

Constable Ayres was a bright young chap, if a little too taken with rules and regulations in Lestrade's opinion, and he nodded. "Thirdly, if there is any chance of a pot of coffee, it would benefit your promotion prospects greatly."

Ayres smiled enthusiastically. "I shall get right on it, sir."

Lestrade held up his hand. "Before you go . . . you had something to tell me? Do we know who this doxy is?"

The young constable produced his notebook with a flourish. "That's just it, sir. She isn't a prostitute at all. We've hardly had any on the streets this last evening, what with all the malarkey in the papers, Lizzie Strutter—"

"I am aware of that, Constable. Not a prostitute, you say? Then we have a positive identification?"

"Yes, sir. Party of the name of Emily Dawson. She is housekeeper to Professor Stanford Rubicon, the Professor of Adventure, sir. He has a laboratory and office not far from here, on Bishopsgate."

Lestrade closed his eyes again. Professor Rubicon had

friends in high places. This was not good, at all, insofar as any young woman with her head half sliced off, slumped against a wall on his beat, could ever be described as *good*. But this was particularly not good. He chanced opening one beady eye and said, "And what was she doing in this insalubrious neighborhood?"

"One possibility, sir, is that she was on her way to the Empirical Geographic Club on Threadneedle Street, where Professor Rubicon is known to be a member. He reported a burglary just this morning at his premises on Bishopsgate; he had been at his club last night and had not ventured to his laboratory until this morning. His housekeeper—Miss Dawson—was the last person there and would normally have locked up after her cleaning shift. A constable has been to the laboratory and noted that the entire premises had been cleaned apart from one room, where the burglary had taken place. Cleaning products appeared to have been dropped at the door, as though Miss Dawson had just seen the wrecked room. There was a considerable amount of dried blood there, suggesting the burglary happened yesterday evening rather than in the small hours. It's possible that she discovered the burglary and set off on foot to Threadneedle Street to raise the alarm. . . ."

"You seem to have a fondness for *possibles*, Constable. I prefer to deal in *definites*. Do you have any definites for me?"

Ayres flicked over the pages of his notebook, which were rapidly dampening in the renewed snowfall that dusted the shoulders of his black overcoat. "Yesterday evening, sir, at around seven o'clock, Miss Dawson was seen hurrying along Commercial Street. There is a public house, sir, you will know of it—the Golden Ball. We interviewed the regular drinkers there this morning, and one who was at the hostelry last night reports that a woman matching Miss Dawson's description came in for some unwelcome attention from two men who were drinking outside. Not regulars, said the man; rough types. Apparently some of the lower classes are casting their nets quite wide looking for prostitutes who might not be caught up in this strike business, sir."

"Then perhaps this is not Jack the Ripper at all," mused Lestrade. Both he and the constable glanced toward the body of Emily Dawson, which was finally being covered against the hungry glances of the crowd with a large white sheet. Unlikely, obviously, but as Lestrade had already pointed out, he dealt in *definites*. "Have someone track down these two men; as of now they are suspects in a murder inquiry."

"Very good, sir," said Ayres. He closed his notepad and glanced up. "Now . . . get rid of the Great Detective, don't speak to Aloysius Bent, and coffee."

"Just the coffee, Constable," said Lestrade wearily. "I'll attend to the others myself."

※

"Doctor Watson," said Lestrade. The Great Detective was hopping from foot to foot, lunging forward, pulling his thin frame back, dancing around as though taken with the mania. "Perhaps I dreamed our conversation in my office just this morning. The one in which I could have sworn I expressly forbade you from allowing your patient to have anything to do with any criminal investigations in Whitechapel or its immediate environs."

Watson wrung his hands again, as the hook-nosed detective glanced over sharply at Lestrade's use of the word "patient." "Please, inspector," whispered the doctor. "His continued well-being relies—"

"His continued well-being relies upon you getting him the blazes out of my crime scene before he contaminates it and I roll up my sleeves and evict him myself!" roared Lestrade. There was a momentary silence as everyone glanced over at the uncharacteristic outburst, then continued with their activities. Lestrade coughed. "Just . . . just get him away, John. Stop him dancing like that. What is he doing, anyway?"

"I have an insight!" announced the Great Detective imperiously. "Inspector . . . you see those footprints?"

Lestrade peered at the ground before the cloth-covered
body of Emily Dawson. There were indeed scuffed boot-
prints, rapidly filling up with fresh snowfall. He hadn't noticed
them, as a matter of fact, but if one of his constables hadn't already gotten drawings of them there'd be the devil to pay.

"Watch," instructed the detective, and began to dance and
prance again.

Lestrade glared at Watson. "Away. Now."

"Come along, old chap," said Watson gently, leading his
charge by the bony elbow back toward the bunting cordon. As
a constable lifted it for them to pass, another figure bustled
through, a large man with a bushy beard and a thick fur coat
that gave him the appearance of a bear. A particularly angry
bear, at that.

"Who is in charge here?" bellowed the bear, casting around.
Several fingers pointed in Lestrade's direction and the man
stalked down the alley toward him, glancing at the sheet covering the body and faltering. "Oh! Oh, tell me that is not—?"

Lestrade rapidly went to meet trouble halfway, glancing at
Aloysius Bent at the top of the alley. The journalist seemed to
be enjoying himself immensely, availing himself of what appeared to be another pasty and a small bottle of what looked
like gin.

"I am Inspector Lestrade of the Commercial Road police
station. I am in charge of this investigation. And you are . . . ?"

"Professor Stanford Rubicon," rumbled the man, taking
Lestrade's proffered hand and squeezing the life out of it. "Is
that . . . is that Emily, my housekeeper?"

Lestrade took the professor's elbow and steered him away
from the cordon. "I'd be grateful if you could give us a positive identification, Professor Rubicon, but I am sorry to say that
it appears so, from papers about her person. Can you tell me
when you saw her last yesterday?"

"Didn't see her at all yesterday," said Rubicon, rubbing his
beard. "I'd gone off to my club before she came to clean the
Bishopsgate rooms."

"And you will certainly have people who can vouch for you at the club?"

Rubicon glared at him. "Sir, are you suggesting I did for my own cleaning lady?"

"Just to eliminate you from our inquiries," said Lestrade soothingly. He changed tack. "I believe there had been a burglary . . ."

Rubicon nodded. "Found it when I came to open up early this morning. One of the laboratories . . . wrecked. Your boys have already been round." His eyes narrowed. "You think it might have something to do with . . . ?" He nodded his head toward the body.

"What was taken, Professor?"

Rubicon rubbed his beard again with a big hand. "Looks like damage, more than anything. I had a few . . . scientific samples there. Not completely sure what's gone missing, all told."

Lestrade nodded. The professor was suddenly shifty about something. He said as conversationally as he could, "What is the nature of your current work?"

Rubicon tugged more forcefully at his full beard. "Much of it's top secret, Lestrade. You know. Government work. Catching up, a lot of it, after . . . well, you read the papers, no doubt."

Lestrade did read the papers, and knew that only three months ago Rubicon had been saved from a shipwreck on some lost island in the Pacific, where he had been marooned for half a year with Charles Darwin. Saved by Gideon Smith and Aloysius Bent, he remembered, casting another glance over at the journalist at the fluttering cordon.

"My constable mentioned a quantity of blood present at the laboratory," said Lestrade.

"Emily's?" asked Rubicon, almost tugging the hair from his beard. Lestrade made a mental note. *Pulls at facial hair when uncertain . . . or lying, perhaps?*

"We don't think so. There don't appear to be injuries other

than . . . well. Perhaps if you go with my constable to formally identify the body, we can discuss it later?"

Constable Ayres had appeared at Lestrade's elbow again, with a small flask of coffee. And yet another newcomer, tramping through the crime scene. Lestrade looked at him with as much of his weariness as he could manage hidden behind his ferrety eyes.

"Sir, this is . . ." Ayres glanced at the man, neatly bearded and with sad eyes in the shadow of his hat brim, an expensive-looking woolen overcoat keeping the snow off his immaculate black suit.

"Friedrich Miescher," said the man in a clipped accent, inclining his head.

"German?" asked Lestrade.

"Swiss." Miescher dug into the inside pocket of his overcoat. "I have a letter of introduction from Sir Edward Bradford . . . ?"

That made Lestrade perk up a little. A letter from the Commissioner of the Metropolitan Police? Who *was* this Miescher? Lestrade took the folded vellum from the man—noting it had been opened and re-folded several times recently—and read from it. Miescher was some kind of scientist, and he had been given free rein to blunder into any murder investigation in London as he saw fit, the gorier the better from what Lestrade read. He handed back the letter.

"I came as soon as I heard," said Miescher, pocketing his folded paper. "Is it true . . . ? Is this a Jack the Ripper killing . . . ?"

"Not so loud, sir," admonished Lestrade. "The gutter press is out in force behind the cordon. What exactly are you looking for here?"

"I apologize," said Miescher, tapping his ear. "I am somewhat deaf from a boyhood attack of typhus. As to what I am looking for, Inspector Lestrade . . . blood."

Rubicon uttered an oath, and Lestrade murmured to Ayres,

"Take the professor to formally identify the body, would you? Give me a minute with Miescher."

When Rubicon had been led to the sheet covering Emily Dawson, Miescher said, "What do you know of nuclein, Inspector?"

"Less than I know about the moon, Miescher. I've seen the moon umpteen times; never heard of your . . . what did you call it?"

"Nuclein," said the Swiss, rubbing his hands together. Lestrade had the sinking feeling the man was warming to a subject that was about to shoot right over his head.

Miescher said, "As a doctor I was worried my deafness would inhibit my profession, so I chose to study the things that we are all made of, the cells and their nuclei. Can you imagine the nucleus of a single cell, Inspector? Imagine how minuscule it is?"

"I am well used to finding needles in haystacks, Dr. Miescher, so I suppose I can."

Miescher nodded. "I began my research into lymphocytes but found them difficult to obtain, so switched to leukocytes—"

"You've lost me already, Doctor," said Lestrade. "And I really must be getting on . . . I have a murder investigation—"

Miescher raised his hand. "Forgive me. They are both types of white blood cell but the latter is somewhat easier to obtain . . . I used bandages from the hospital and was able to isolate leukocytes from the pus stains."

Lestrade made a face. "I still don't—"

"I will cut my story short, Inspector Lestrade. Suffice to say, my research has thrown up some fascinating results. From the nuclei of the white blood cells I managed to extract and study what I call nuclein. We all carry nuclein in our bodies, Inspector, in wonderful spirals that would take your breath away were you to behold them through the lenses of my powerful microscopes. Beautiful . . . and every single one is different. As different as our fingerprints."

Lestrade opened his mouth to dismiss the Swiss physician once and for all and then paused, screwing up his eyes. "Different, you say?"

"Like a signature buried deep inside our most microscopic parts." Miescher nodded enthusiastically. "So you see . . ."

Lestrade rubbed his chin. "So the blood of poor old Emily Dawson could be proved to be different to mine, or yours. I still don't see what this has to do with me."

Miescher's eyes widened. "I could help you, Inspector. I could help you catch Jack the Ripper. If only there is a single white blood cell . . ."

"There is plenty of blood, Doctor, but I fear it belongs to his victim."

"Ah, but perhaps she fought back, Inspector. Perhaps she raked her nails along his face. Perhaps there is a tiny fleck of blood beneath those nails, or perhaps a few flakes of skin."

Finally, the penny dropped. "So with this . . . this blood signature, you could identify the killer?"

"We could if we can match it with another sample," agreed Miescher.

Lestrade sighed, deflated. "You do know how many people there are in London, Doctor Miescher? Are you proposing we go and—what? Obtain blood samples from all of 'em?"

"The process is in its infancy," admitted the doctor. "But from what I read in the newspapers this morning . . . you can use all the help you can get, eh?"

Lestrade stared at the body for a long moment as Ayres and Rubicon began to walk back toward him down the alley. Finally he said, "All right, but not here. Don't want to give the vultures too much to crow about. We'll transfer the body to the morgue when we have finished here, and you can do your trickery there. In the meantime . . ." An idea had struck Lestrade, one that almost made him smile.

"Constable Ayres," he said. "I believe your earlier report was of a quantity of blood at Professor Rubicon's laboratories."

"That's right, sir."

"Constable, please take Professor Rubicon and Doctor Miescher to Bishopsgate, where our Swiss friend will be very interested in those blood stains. And Ayres . . . make sure you talk about this as loudly as possible as you pass Mr. Aloysius Bent."

"But sir, I thought you said—"

"I know what I said, Constable, but I've changed my mind."

Lestrade watched the three of them head off through the thickening snow toward the mouth of the alley. That should keep them all from getting under his feet for a while, all the scientists and adventurers and journalists. He turned back to regard the sheet-covered body of Emily Dawson. Get them all away, let him do what he did best without interference: good, old-fashioned police work.

4

"YOU'RE THE HERO OF THE EMPIRE, MR. SMITH"

Aloysius Bent declined the well-telegraphed offer to follow Professor Rubicon, the young constable, and the earnest bearded fellow from the scene of the crime, opting instead for a quick gin in the Golden Ball and a steam-cab back to Grosvenor Square. He would visit Rubicon, of course, but at his convenience, thank you very much, and not following the clumsy trail set by Lestrade and his boys as though he were some hound to be set after a rabbit.

Besides, he thought as paid the driver, *I've had enough of standing out freezing my effing balls off for one morning, especially after the morning's news.* The snow was all well and good if you could find a nice, warm pair of titties to bury your cold nose in, for the price of a couple of farthings. This prostitutes' strike . . . he didn't quite know what to make of it, nor where his next tumble was going to come from.

It was then he noticed the man, tall, in a heavy overcoat and with a bowler on his head, furtively lurking around the gate to the house.

"Oi," Bent shouted. "What you after?"

The man, still a dozen yards away, looked up and squinted at Bent through the snow, then turned on his heel and hurried away. Some autograph hunter, no doubt, or a snooping reporter Bent didn't know. He let himself into the house, stamping his feet on the rough mat and closing the door against the flurries of snow. As he unwound the muffler from around his bullish neck, Bent sniffed the air. Smelled like the housekeeper, Mrs. Cadwallader, had been baking. He could just taste one of her dainty little cakes—or maybe three or four, washed down with a gallon of tea. Or ale. He rubbed some feeling back into his spadelike hands. Oh yes, a big pitcher of ale, a plate of cakes, and his feet up in the study in front of a roaring fire, to mull over the events of the morning.

"Mrs. C!" roared Bent from the beeswaxed, wood-paneled hallway. "Where's young Gideon? And is Miss Maria back yet?"

Mrs. Cadwallader, all bustle and apron and starched white blouse keeping her vast bosom in check, emerged from the door to the kitchen like the ruddy-faced figurehead of some proud ship, the sails of her skirts buoyed by the warm scent of freshly baked cinnamon cakes. Not for the first time, Bent thanked his lucky stars for the way he'd fallen on his feet the way he had. He wouldn't have fancied another winter in the hovel in the East End where he'd spent the last ten years—wasn't sure, to be honest, he'd have survived it. This little place, though . . . never in his wildest dreams had Aloysius Bent thought he'd ever have a Mayfair address. The place had belonged to Captain Lucian Trigger and Doctor John Reed, and as they were a pair of poofters, there'd been no family for it to pass on to once they took a dive off the top of that brass dragon hovering above Hyde Park, ready to rain fiery death upon Buckingham Palace and all in it. Bent found it hard to believe all that business—hooking up with Gideon and the mysterious mechanical girl, Maria, scrapping with mummies on the Embankment, discovering lost pyramids in the shifting sands of Egypt—was only five months ago. A lot had happened since July, and the best of it was when they all moved into the Grosvenor Square house, so that young Gideon was fully able to succeed that old fraud Trigger as the official Hero of the Empire.

"By God, Sally, that smells effing good," said Bent, taking off his battered derby and placing it on the coat stand beside his faithful pith helmet, the one he'd bought in the souk in Alexandria. Only one previous owner, with the bullet hole to prove it. He'd be dead without it, after that pyramid collapsed right on his head, instead of just being unable to say his favorite word. He tried every day, of course, as though they were exercises and physical jerks to be done every morning, in the hope he might regain the power. But no. "Eff. Eff. Efffffff." Not a *fuck* to be had. He grinned to himself. Bit like the streets of Whitechapel.

Mrs. Cadwallader put a finger to her lips. "Not so loud and brash, Mr. Bent. Miss Maria is not yet back from whatever they have her doing with that infernal dragon, and Mr. Smith is in the parlor with guests. The Elmwoods. They have come seeking his assistance and seem most distressed."

"Oh, yes, the ones with the missing daughter. I told him not to bother with it. Job for the police. I'll take myself off to the study, I think. Is there a fire lit?"

"There is, Mr. Bent. And you have a visitor of your own in there."

Bent's eyes narrowed. "Not Big Henry, is it? I told him we was square. You know what these crooks are like, though, Sally. You think you've paid 'em off . . ."

"It's Mr. Walsingham," she whispered, as though saying his name too loud would attract his unwelcome attention from within the closed door of the study.

Bent blew a raspberry. "Oh, eff. What does *he* want? Did you tell him Gideon's otherwise engaged?"

She nodded. "I did. But he wants to see *you*."

"Double eff," said Bent. He dug in his pocket for his flask and took a slug of rum. "Better get this over with, then."

There was indeed a fire crackling merrily in the hearth of the study, but any joy it might have offered seemed to be sucked out of the room by the brooding presence of Mr. Walsingham. He was sitting upright like a black crow in one of the easy chairs, his back to the glass cabinets bearing the trophies from John Reed and Lucian Trigger's adventures: the claw of the Exeter Werewolf, Lord Dexter's Top Hat, the Golden Apple of Shangri-La. They were supplemented by trophies Gideon had assembled to carry on the tradition: poor old Louis Cockayne's pearl-handled revolvers, a piece of steel from the giant steam-powered mechanical man they had fought in Nyu Edo, a lump of clay from the Golem of Manchester, the hair of a mermaid from St. Ives. Walsingham looked up sharply as Bent entered, fixing him with his piercing eyes, the neat white mustache beneath his hawklike nose twitching as though with mild distaste. Few people in the country knew Walsingham's name, but the power he wielded was almost without boundary. Bent sometimes doubted that even Robert Gascoyne-Cecil, the Prime Minister, knew of Walsingham and just how far his tendrils reached. Walsingham had both leather-gloved hands resting on the silver head of his cane, his black suit immaculate and cut to perfection.

"What brings you out on such a foul day?" asked Bent, closing the door behind him. "The smell of Mrs. Cadwallader's baking?"

"Nothing so pleasant," said Walsingham, indicating with a curt nod that Bent should sit in the armchair opposite.

Bent flopped down and sighed. "Been on me bloody feet all effing day."

"So I believe," said Walsingham mildly. "Whitechapel, I understand."

"Had your spies out this morning?" asked Bent. "What else did they tell you?"

"They tell me that you presented yourself at the office of Inspector George Lestrade at the Commercial Road police station and informed him that Mr. Gideon Smith and yourself had been assigned to solve the murders that your erstwhile colleagues in the gutter press have attributed to one Jack the Ripper."

"Ah," said Bent.

"Ah indeed, Mr. Bent," said Walsingham, raising one eyebrow. "An assignment I certainly do not recall authorizing."

Bent leaned forward. "Thing is, Walsingham old chap, I thought, well, what with Christmas coming up, and things probably being a bit quiet on the old Hero of the Empire front, why not put my—that is, Gideon's—talents to good use here in London, give the coppers a bit of a leg up with all this unpleasantness."

"And this would have nothing to do with the Jack the Ripper crimes being something of a hobbyhorse of yours, Mr. Bent? Need I remind you that you are no longer a reporter with the *Illustrated London Argus*?"

Bent didn't need reminding at all. He had been more than happy on the *Argus*. A hack, but so what? What was it old Samuel Johnson had said? No man but a blockhead ever wrote, except for money. He'd earned a living wage and enjoyed his work. Then after all the business last summer Walsingham had gone and had him moved to the penny dreadful, *World Marvels & Wonders*, all the better to officially chronicle the adventures of Gideon Smith, Hero of the Empire, for a sensation-hungry public.

As if reading his mind, Walsingham looked around the study and asked, "Are you enjoying living here, Mr. Bent?"

Bent narrowed his eyes. "Is that a threat, Walsingham? Letting me know you can have me back on the *Argus* and living in the Fulwood Rents quicker than I can fart?"

Walsingham shrugged then tapped his chin thoughtfully with one long forefinger. "However . . . there is perhaps some conjunction of the crimes of this Jack the Ripper and the *raison d'être* of Mr. Gideon Smith's situation. And you are one of the foremost authorities in London on the Ripper murders. . . ."

"*The* foremost authority, I think you'll find," said Bent, jabbing a pudgy thumb into his chest. "You're talking about Maria, ain't you? And what's in her head? And the fact that whoever Jack the Ripper is, he's slicing off the tops of whores' heads *as though he's looking for something where the brain should be.*"

"Succinctly put, Mr. Bent. The work of Professor Hermann

Einstein with the item code named the Atlantic Artifact is, of course, entirely top secret. . . ."

"Stow it, Walsingham, I read the diaries that Gideon filched from the old boy's house. We all know now that you gave him this Atlantic Artifact, which you found in some sunken Viking longship, and that when he asked for a human brain to experiment on you handed him the gray matter of poor old Annie Crook, who you had done in just because she fell in love with the Duke of Clarence. And that's the brain he put in the automaton we all now know and love as Maria."

Walsingham smiled thinly. "It must be a huge source of frustration to you, Mr. Bent, a journalist sitting on a story of such magnitude yet unable to publish it."

Bent sighed. "Who'd believe it anyway, Walsingham? You've got me over a barrel. Anyway, the point is that unless these murders really are the random work of some lunatic, *someone* seems to know what they're looking for in the heads of East End whores, and that could well be the Atlantic Artifact. And if they know of its existence, they know what it can do. And if they know what it can do, then they must have been speaking to the only bloke in the world who has that information, and that'd be Hermann Einstein, missing now for, what, nearly a year? So the chances are . . ."

Walsingham leaned on his cane and stood. "The chances are, if we unmask Jack the Ripper, we may well be able to find Hermann Einstein, who is so terribly important to the work of the Empire. I am delighted that we seem to understand each other, Mr. Bent. So carry on. I'm glad we had this little chat. I'll see myself out."

Bent watched him go, not a little confounded by it all. He let rip with a long, thoughtful fart, then went off to find Mrs. Cadwallader and her cakes in the kitchen. He paused at the door, watching the housekeeper for a moment as she bent forward to pull a tray of steaming cakes from the oven.

She was a damned handsome woman, was Sally Cadwallader. He was almost surprised he hadn't noticed it before.

"Oh, Mr. Bent!" she said, standing and turning, the tray held in a pair of thick oven gloves. "You quite startled me, standing there. Has *he* gone?"

"He has," said Bent.

"Good. I never liked him, not when he was bossing poor old Captain Trigger and Dr. Reed around, and not now." She laid the tray down on the wooden work surface and lowered her voice. "It was him who sent Dr. Reed over the edge, I'm sure of it. Him and his . . . his *machinations*."

Mrs. Cadwallader raised an eyebrow expectantly, as Bent continued to stare thoughtfully in silence.

"Mr. Bent? Did you want me to bring you some ale to the study?"

"No," he said slowly. "No. I think I'll just pop out for a moment. Tell Gideon I'll be back soon."

⁂

Gideon poured tea into the china cups on the small table in front of the Elmwoods and sat back. Henry Elmwood was stiff and frowning, his collar high and tightly buttoned, his gray suit expensive and neatly tailored. His hair was parted in the center and brilliantined, reflecting the gaslights in the sconces fizzing and popping over the fireplace. Martha Elmwood was small and mouselike with a huge bonnet hiding her face, staring down at her fingers, which she constantly knitted and unfastened, speaking rarely and with a tiny, childlike voice when she did.

"We appreciate you seeing us, Mr. Smith," said Mr. Elmwood.

Gideon sat back in the chair, putting his left boot on the right knee of his serge trousers, tugging at the open collar of his plain white shirt. It was warm in the parlor, warm in the entire house, with every fire blazing at Mrs. Cadwallader's insistence. He ran a hand through his thick, black curls and said, "I was very touched by your letter. I'm just not that sure what I can do."

Mrs. Elmwood looked up, her eyes brimming with tears. "But you're the Hero of the Empire, Mr. Smith," she almost whispered.

Yes, the Hero of the Empire. Charged by none other than Queen Victoria to keep Britain and her interests safe from threats at home and abroad. Dinosaurs and metal men and Texan warlords that were more machine than human, mummies and vampires and things that screamed in the night. Villains and monsters were Gideon's bread and butter. But not . . .

"Not missing persons, I'm afraid," he said as gently as he could. "This is really a matter for the police . . ."

"Pah, we've tried them," said Elmwood with disgust. "Can't do a thing for us. It was my wife's idea writing to you. I told her, I said, *He's the Hero of the Empire, he won't be bothering with the likes of us.*"

Elmwood made to stand, but Gideon held up his hand. "Wait." He had the Elmwoods' letter in front of him. Their daughter, Charlotte, had been missing for three days now. It was indeed, he would have thought, a matter for the Metropolitan Police. Aside from one thing.

"Your letter mentions Markus Mesmer," he said. "Perhaps you had better start from the beginning."

⚅

Gideon knew the name Markus Mesmer well, though not from firsthand experience. He had been a regular in Captain Trigger's adventures in *World Marvels & Wonders*—adventures that Gideon, when he read them as a callow youth, had no way of knowing were actually the escapades of Dr. John Reed, disguised as the travails of Captain Trigger to present a more heroic digest of events for the reading public and to preserve Dr. Reed's covert operations.

Gideon could, even now, remember the words in the story "Escape from Bedlam," from the April 1887 issue. *My tale picks up where last month's ended. You will recall that I had confronted*

Markus Mesmer, the criminal mastermind and grandson of the much gentler pioneer of "animal magnetism," who had been controlling, through hypnosis, the minds of members of polite London society in order to fleece them of their valuables. . . .

It was the central tale in a triptych of stories featuring the dastardly German, beginning with "The Mind-Forged Manacles of Markus Mesmer" and ending with the thrilling "The Final Battle." Mesmer was one of the most exciting recurring villains in the Captain Trigger adventures, though that final story had concluded with Trigger turning Mesmer's own Hypno-Array upon him and convincing the crook that he was actually a force for good.

Of course, as Gideon had swiftly found out upon meeting Trigger earlier that year, the adventures did not often live up to the lofty claim that began each story: *This adventure, as always, is utterly true, and faithfully retold by my good friend, Doctor John Reed.—Captain Lucian Trigger*

With a start, Gideon realized Mr. Elmwood was speaking to him, and not for the first time reprimanded himself: He was no longer a mere fan of Captain Trigger's adventures. Now he was *living* them.

※

"Our daughter Charlotte has just turned twenty-one," said Henry Elmwood. "She is a very beautiful girl, though you would perhaps expect a father to say that. Beautiful and vulnerable. I confess, Mr. Smith, that I have tried to protect Charlotte from the worst excesses of this world as much as possible, but there comes a time . . . well. You cannot keep them cosseted forever. My wife thought it would be a good idea to have Charlotte mix more with girls her own age, so a year ago we enrolled her in a finishing school in Holborn. Last Sunday one of the girls who attends her classes held a birthday party, to which Charlotte was invited. The entertainment was provided by Markus Mesmer."

"After all that has been written about Mesmer, someone

thought him a suitable choice for a young woman's party?" asked Gideon.

Elmwood frowned. "I understood the stories in that penny dreadful were mere fantasies . . . but yes, Mesmer was the entertainment. We attended, of course, as chaperones. Mesmer put on quite a show, and hypnotized the girls to perform a variety of comical tasks. One quacked like a duck, and another danced around as though she were an African savage. Then, with a snap of his fingers, they were back to normal."

Gideon shook his head. Elmwood said, "Mr. Mesmer seemed to take an inordinate interest in Charlotte. . . . He seemed very taken with her blond hair. He asked us many questions about ourselves, and seemed rather peeved at our responses. When it came to Charlotte's turn to be hypnotized . . ."

Elmwood coughed and glanced at his wife. "I am sorry, Mr. Smith, but this is very delicate, and there is no easy way to tell you. Mesmer hypnotized her into believing she was nothing more than a common whore."

A small, strangled cry escaped Mrs. Elmwood's lips, and her shoulders began to shake. Elmwood placed a hand on her and said softly, "Control yourself, Martha."

"It was a terrible sight!" Mrs. Elmwood blurted out. "She cavorted around the room, approaching all the fathers of the other girls and propositioning them! We shall never show our faces in society again!"

"But did Mesmer not fix the hypnosis?"

"The scoundrel claimed his so-called Hypno-Array was suddenly broken!" said Elmwood with barely contained fury. "A scaffold of lights and lenses which he wore upon his head. He took me into the corridor and said that it would be costly to fix, and he would require funds to be able to return Charlotte to herself."

"You refused?"

"He wanted five thousands guineas, the villain!" spat Elmwood.

There was an uncomfortable silence, then Gideon said, "So . . . ?"

"Mesmer left and gave me a card with the name of the hotel in which he was staying should we change our minds. We took Charlotte home, of course, and locked her in her room—she made overtures to the cab driver and even our butler. She was like . . . like an alley cat, Mr. Smith! Our beautiful, sweet daughter, swearing like a dockworker and—and rubbing herself against any man she met!"

"You consulted a doctor?"

"Several. They could do nothing. We went to the police, but would you believe there is no crime on the statute books that deals with hypnosis? It is something I shall be writing to my MP to have him remedy at the earliest opportunity."

"And Charlotte . . . ?"

"On Wednesday," said Mrs. Elmwood tremulously, "she slipped out of her room when the maid forgot to lock it behind her. She hasn't been seen since."

"Obviously, given her state of mind, she could be . . . well, anything could happen to her," said Mr. Elmwood. His wife sobbed wildly, and he looked imploringly at Gideon. "Please, Mr. Smith. Can you help?"

Gideon felt at a loss. If the police couldn't intervene, then what could he do? He said carefully, "You will appreciate that this is not my usual purview, Mr. Elmwood. I have no jurisdiction greater than the Metropolitan Police, and—"

"I have brought a photograph of Charlotte," said Mr. Elmwood quietly, the fight seeming to have gone out of him. "Perhaps if you will just look at it . . ."

Gideon took the picture and said, "I still cannot . . . oh."

He stared at the photograph: Charlotte Elmwood in her Sunday best, holding a parasol in a photographer's studio, a painted backdrop of a sun-drenched park behind her. He stared at it for a very long time.

"Mr. Smith?" asked Mr. Elmwood.

"Yes," said Gideon eventually. "Yes, I'll help you."

He held the photograph in his hands and could not stop them from shaking.

Charlotte Elmwood, said her parents.

But the photograph was the image of Maria. The *living image* of his beloved Maria.

INTERMEDIO:
NOT ENOUGH, NOT ENOUGH

 He sat in candlelight in his rooms, the leather bag on the table, its clasp shut tight. Beside it was a newspaper, freshly bought.

JACK THE RIPPER STRIKES AGAIN! screamed the black ink. It was the late edition, detailing in lavish, grotesque language the scene in the alley where he had stood earlier that day. The victim had a name: Emily Dawson, a young woman in the employment of Professor Stanford Rubicon. He shrugged.

He was bored already. And so was the blackness in his soul. Where once he—and it—had thrilled at such murders, now they were old hat.

Not enough, the imaginary ghost had said. *Not enough*.

Familiarity breeds contempt. Man cannot live on bread alone. Variety is the spice of life.

He reached forward and unfastened the bag, the candlelight glinting off the metal that scraped and shrieked together as he lifted the leather case onto his lap. One by one he took out the items.

His hungry soul received no succor anymore from the clean, clinical swipe across the forehead. It thirsted for sweeter blood, that which was torn with greater violence and passion from its host. It had to be fed, lest the blackness grow and consume him from the inside. It had to be quieted.

He turned the saw, which had tiny, vicious teeth and a wooden handle, this way and that, the dancing candlelight glancing off its wide blade. For the severing of bones. He laid it on the table and took out a pair of long-handled tongs, each of the jointed grips ending in a rusting spike. To spear and hold slippery internal organs that needed to be removed. A wooden-handled corkscrew ending in a sharp-edged tube, for swiftly slicing a circle of flesh, fat, and muscle to allow access to the abdomen. And so on, each one more cruel and exciting than the last.

Instruments with which to create a symphony of pain.

Not enough, had said the ghost, which he now recognized as his own black soul, not the departed spirit of a murdered girl at all.

It wanted more. It wanted sweeter blood. He would provide.

He picked up the newspaper. He was so very far from home, from the heat where his black soul was birthed. London shivered beneath snow, and he found it hateful and frozen, a sluggish dead thing, almost. It was fear that iced London's heart as well, fear of Jack the Ripper. The lurid description of the latest killing elbowed out all other news, as though there were only London and its dead in the entire world.

And what a world. He turned the page, and his attention was snared by a report on Freedom, the fledgling township rising from the blood and dust of the savage lands controlled by the slaver-warlords in Texas. An escapade involving the Crown's hero, Gideon Smith, had resulted in San Antonio, popularly known as Steamtown, being blown to smithereens. A brass dragon was mentioned—whether it was the same as that which had attacked London that summer, or of a similar design, the newspaper could not hazard a guess. But there was some connection, the editors were sure, and if Mr. Gideon Smith was on the case, then there was surely little to fear. This town called Freedom, though . . . the newspaper writer confessed to some misgivings about this evidently burgeoning settlement somewhere in the wilds of Texas and not far from the border with New Spain. Was there room for yet another faction in much-fractured America? Where would their loyalties lie? With England's interests on the East Coast? New Spain to the south? The Californian Meiji? Or would they be conquered by one of the Texan warlords eager to take the now-destroyed Steamtown's slice of the pie?

He laid the newspaper down. He was thinking of Spain, of a family holiday to Madrid when he was a very small boy. His mother had insisted they all go to watch a play, an earnest, boring affair that lasted all day and into the night. He had lost track of the dull story almost immediately, and would have fallen asleep but for the *intermedio,* a series of brash and energetic short musical productions that filled the gaps between the acts of the main play. They were designed to allow the theatergoers to stretch their legs, visit the bathrooms, or buy food; he had been rapt with delight, coming alive for those brief intervals, rousing from his torpor at the loud music and hilarity.

He picked up the saw again. Intermedio. He studied its cruel teeth. Life was like the play, long and boring and interminable.

But there were flashes of clarity, shrieking music, splashes of red.

He smiled. It was time for another intermedio. . . .

5

THE GRAVITY OF THE SITUATION

Apep burst through the layer of low, gray cloud that hung over Bodmin Moor into a spotless blue sky flooded with brilliant sunshine. Maria heard noisy, messy vomiting behind her and allowed herself the smallest of self-satisfied smiles, before pulling the brass dragon into an even steeper ascent. Above her she could see the ghostly imprint of the moon. It was said that Queen Victoria wanted to put an Englishman on the moon and claim the satellite for the British Empire. Others said it was impossible, it was too far, man could not fly so high. And beyond the moon . . . why, beyond was the black emptiness of the universe. She felt something inside her subtly shift, like tiny cogs fitting together, bearings settling snugly, rods and pistons smoothly aligning. But she knew, distantly, that it was something more than that. Those were the only reference points she had, the mechanical marvels that Professor Einstein had used to assemble her body, greater than the sum of her parts. The shift was in that part of her shrouded in mystery, that which she doubted she would ever fully understand. Her human brain.

"Maria."

Moisture formed and then rolled off the glass windows in front of her—the circular "eyes" of the crocodilian brass dragon—as she pushed Apep on, and up. White trails whistled from the batlike wings and on the long snout in front of the windows, and beautiful, treelike ice formations began to crawl along the brass nose. She studied them as they advanced. *Dendritic*, that was the word.

"M-Maria! In the name of God, you're going to kill us!"

Ah. Yes. The formation of ice on the nose of the brass

dragon meant that the temperature was falling. She hadn't felt it, but it was good that Doctor Augustus had managed to stop vomiting long enough to point it out to her. The brain inside her head had put up with a lot—she had been dragged across half the world underwater, and lived, as much as the word "lived" could be applied to one like her—but she had not yet subjected herself to extremes of temperature that would kill a normal human being. She brought Apep to an abrupt halt, waiting as Doctor Augustus first thumped against the ceiling of the cramped cockpit then flopped to the floor, groaning to indicate he was still conscious.

"Down, down," he begged. "S-so cold . . . how high are we?"

Maria cocked her head to one side and considered. "36,798 feet. And a few inches."

She glanced over her shoulder at Doctor Augustus, a ruddy-faced man with a bulbous nose and a shock of white hair that protruded from beneath the leather flying helmet he was wearing. Over his white laboratory coat he had zipped up a leather and shearling jacket. She always found him a somewhat comical figure, but now she paused. Were his eyes bulging more than usual?

"Thirty-thir-thir . . . ," he said. Maria tittered slightly. "Imposs-imp-imp . . ."

Suddenly, Doctor Augustus keeled over, his hands scrabbling at his throat. Oh, dear. Perhaps there was such a thing as too high, after all. She turned Apep in the bright blue sky, enjoying the way the unfettered sunlight glinted off its wings and snaking, jointed brass tail, then began to descend in a tight spiral toward the carpet of cloud far below.

✦

Bodmin Moor had been subtly cordoned off for an area of around sixty square miles centered on a cluster of temporary huts and tents at the foot of Rough Tor. Soldiers, police officers, and agents of the crown had quietly been keeping anyone from entering the area for the past week. Maria had been given quarters in a small building made of curved metal, with the most basic of comforts; whether this was because they considered her not quite human, or because luxurious living was not high on their agendas, she wasn't sure. It was in her quarters—windowless, and lit by oil lamps—that Doctor Augustus found her, sitting on her bed and placing the last of her personal effects into her valise.

"You are packed already," he said, his white hair standing upright now that it was freed from the confines of the flying helmet. He had kept the jacket on, though. It was terribly cold on the moor.

"It is Saturday," said Maria. "My time here is thankfully at an end. And you, Doctor, seem much recovered."

"A spot of . . . well, I suppose we should call it altitude sickness. At least we know man's limits now, Maria." He chuckled. "Always nice to make a fresh scientific discovery."

He paused as Maria closed the valise. She smoothed her skirts and said, "I suppose I should apologize, Doctor. I didn't intend to fly quite so high. I certainly didn't mean to cause you harm."

Doctor Augustus flexed his muscles beneath the lab coat and jacket. "No lasting harm done. Next time I think we'll perhaps rig up some kind of breathing apparatus, such as the divers wear."

She arched an eyebrow. "Next time?"

Gideon had been dead set against her coming, of course. But Mr. Walsingham had been most insistent. He still considered Maria and Apep to be what he termed "assets" of the British Empire, and there were many questions to be answered about the brass dragon, Maria's control over it, and just what it was capable of. Besides, she burned to know the answers to those questions herself. There was much of Maria's existence that was a mystery, not least her unique relationship with a brass dragon forged in the furnaces of ancient Egypt. Unfortunately, answers seemed to be in short supply—either because the assembly of scientists, engineers, and doctors who had spent the week examining her, examining Apep, and examining her and

Apep at the same time were keeping their findings to themselves, or because, as she suspected, they just did not have
the first clue about what they were dealing with.

"There is much still to learn, Maria," said Doctor Augustus gently. "We have barely scratched the surface of Apep's—
your—capabilities. Every problem solved raises a hundred
more questions. I would relish the opportunity to work with
you again."

"I suppose that will be up to Mr. Walsingham, and I doubt
he will take my feelings on the matter into account," she said,
standing up. "How am I to return to London?"

"I will accompany you," he said. "We have a Fleet Air Arm
aerostat on standby to fly us to Highgate Aerodrome. I just
need to get my things." He paused at the door to her hut. "The
pilot says it is snowing in London, my dear. You might want a
shawl . . . ?"

Maria smiled. "As we have already established, Doctor Augustus, I do not feel the cold as much as you do."

The R-202-class 'stat was a personnel carrier that the Fleet
Air Arm considered somewhat zippy in the air, but to Maria it
felt sluggish and hellishly ground-hugging as it conveyed her
and Doctor Augustus to London. Apep was kept under wraps
at Bodmin Moor, shortly to be moved to a secret, secure fac-
ility somewhere else. When they had returned from America
in September she had felt stricken at being parted from the
brass dragon, as though she were leaving a part of herself
behind. But today the wrench was less pronounced, a symp-
tom of the subtle changes she had felt continually working
within her ever since the crash in the Texas desert.

As she stared out the porthole at the gray skies, the thrum
of the gear-driven engines propelling them eastward, she put
herself back in the cockpit of Apep, rapidly losing awareness
as she spiraled toward the ground, Louis Cockayne yelling in
surprise behind her. When she had awakened she had put it
down to exhaustion, having flown straight across the Atlantic
after being hijacked by Cockayne, but later reflection had

convinced her that something had occurred, something had changed.

Her control over Apep had strengthened, become more instinctive after the crash. She no longer required the brass pipe plugging directly into the aperture at the small of her back to connect to the dragon; she seemed to do it naturally, with the power of her mind. She had no name for the sensation she had experienced just before the crash. The nearest comparison she had was when the haphazard electrical wiring in Professor Einstein's crooked house had occasionally buzzed angrily, causing the lightbulbs to flare brightly then explode in a shower of tinkling glass. Whatever had given Maria more mastery over Apep, it had also enabled her to operate without the constant winding of the key in the small of her back. She had been granted independence of movement, more control over her own body.

It was almost as if, by degrees, she was becoming more *alive*.

When she had awoken from the crash it had been thanks to the kiss of Gideon Smith, in that torchlit cavern where the Yaqui had taken her prisoner. She had not told anyone that, not even the engineers or doctors at Rough Tor. They were men of science and mathematics, and such *fairy tales* of princesses awoken by their true love's kiss . . . well.

But the fact remained that something had shifted and altered within her at Gideon's kiss, something had come together, like the pieces of a puzzle. Before coming awake she had felt as though she were a fish, down in the black depths of a pond, and that out there in the impossible distance a fisherman of sorts was casting around for her. The kiss from her own fisherman, lovely, handsome, brave Gideon Smith, had been the hook that connected lost Maria to whatever it was that looked for her.

She shook her head. It was all nonsense, all a jumble of things that she had no names for. All she knew for sure was that above the snow-heavy clouds that hung oppressively over the countryside was the bright blue sky, and beyond the sky was an infinity that seemed to reach out to her.

Her heart ached, and she did not know whether it was for Gideon Smith or for the exhilarating rush of freedom she had experienced as she had pushed Apep on and on and on through the thinning air toward the mysteries of the beyond.

Gideon was picking over some cold meat in the kitchen while Mrs. Cadwallader poked with a knife at a chicken she had roasting in the oven when Bent announced his presence with a cough. Gideon looked up to see the journalist holding a bunch of flowers wrapped in newspaper.

"Ah, these are for you, Sally. Mrs. Cadwallader."

There was a silence in the kitchen as the housekeeper stared at the loosely wrapped bouquet then exchanged a puzzled glance with Gideon.

"For me? Why?"

Bent shrugged. "I just thought . . . well. You know. I probably don't appreciate you enough."

Mrs. Cadwallader wiped her hands on her apron but didn't move from the oven. "I get my wages, Mr. Bent. That is my appreciation."

"Still . . ." He flapped the flowers at her. "Do you want 'em, or not?"

Mrs. Cadwallader sighed and walked across the kitchen to take them from him. "Camellia, honeysuckle, hellebore . . . well, I'm not sure what to say, Mr. Bent. They are beautiful."

"No more so than you, Mrs. Cadwallader," Bent mumbled.

Gideon almost choked on his mouthful of food. Mrs. Cadwallader raised an eyebrow and laid the flowers on the worktop. "Well. I'll go and find a vase for these. There's one in the study, I think."

When she'd gone Gideon asked, "Are you feeling all right, Aloysius?"

"Effing hell, can't a man buy his housekeeper some flowers? Anyway, what happened with the Elmwoods? Did you tell them we don't do missing persons and they should call the police?"

Gideon nodded, retrieving a buff envelope from beneath his plate. "I did. They haven't had much luck with the police."

Bent pulled up a stool and took a piece of ham from Gideon's plate, sniffing it suspiciously before cramming it into his mouth. "Not really our thing, though, is it?"

"I didn't think so, but for two reasons. One, Markus Mesmer is involved."

Bent shook his head and said through his half-chewed food, "No, no, we don't get involved with Markus Mesmer."

"I know Lucian and John had run-ins with him, but that doesn't mean—"

Bent held up a hand to cut him off. "Not because of that. Well, sort of. Mesmer's a canny old soul; Trigger and Reed did indeed cross his path a number of times, but he keeps his nose clean. After the last adventure Trigger wrote up, Mesmer's lawyers called at *World Marvels & Wonders* and demanded to see some hard evidence of the villainy they'd accused him of. Of course, there was none, not that'd stand up in court. If he'd sued for defamation he could have closed the paper down. As it was, they settled out of court, for a sizeable amount, so's I understand. But since then Mesmer's been off-limits."

"But he's obviously a crook," protested Gideon.

"That's as may be," said Bent, selecting another cold cut from the plate. "But unless he's a *provable* crook, we steer clear." He paused and chewed reflectively. "You said two reasons?"

Gideon slid the picture from the envelope and handed it to Bent, who glanced at it and said, "Nice portrait of Maria. When did she have this done? And what does it have to do with anything?"

"It isn't Maria. It's Charlotte Elmwood. The missing girl."

Bent took a longer look. "Effing hell. It's the spitting image of her." He handed the picture back. "You going to tell Maria about this when she gets back?"

"I thought not, for now," said Gideon. "According to the newspaper, Mesmer has a show tonight, at a theater in Hoxton. I thought I might go along, just to watch his act."

Bent raised an eyebrow. "On the night Maria comes home?"

"I'll only be gone two hours, three at most. But you have to agree there's a mystery here, Aloysius."

They contemplated in silence for a moment, then Bent said quietly, "There's something I was going to mention, Gideon. We've been back from America . . . what, three months? And I notice Maria still has her own room."

"What of it?"

"Well, I thought . . . look, you two are hardly the most orthodox couple in Mayfair. I just can't see why you aren't . . . you know. Sharing a room."

Gideon looked down at the photograph and Bent asked softly, "Have you . . . you know?"

"I don't see that it's any of your business, Aloysius!"

Bent shrugged. "Thought you might like a bit of advice, you know."

Gideon laughed. "From you?"

Bent thumbed his nose at Gideon. "Don't get like that. I wasn't always the sack of horseshit you see in front of you. I was quite a catch when I was a younger man. Just let myself go a bit, that's all." He paused and said more gently, "Look, Gideon, I know it must be hard for you, losing your old man like you did. I just want you to know that if you need someone to talk to, I'm here."

Gideon felt oddly touched. Then Bent said, "You do know how to do it, don't you? Get the barge into the dock, and all that? Make the beast with two backs? Rumpy-pumpy? Give the dog a bone?"

The doorbell sounded, and Mrs. Cadwallader called, "I'll get it—I'm in the hall."

Bent stood up. "Think on it, anyway. It's time you two stopped being so coy, if you're going to make a go of it. I think I'll go and draw a bath."

Gideon stared at him. "A bath? You, Aloysius?"

He winked. "It is nearly Christmas, after all."

"Mr. Bent!" roared Mrs. Cadwallader.

Bent and Gideon exchanged glances. "Uh oh."

"Mr. Newby of the Grosvenor Square Residents' Commit-
tee is at the door, inquiring if we know anything about the theft
of flowers from the communal gardens . . ."

"I need the outhouse," said Bent. "Toss him a couple of
coins for the flowers, eh, Gideon?"

Gideon laughed and nodded as Bent stole out of the kitchen
as silently and swiftly as he could. He watched the journalist
go. Perhaps he was right. Gideon had thought of little else since
Maria moved into Grosvenor Square, and he had spent tortured
nights lying in his bed, knowing she was just down the hall.
He would ask her tonight, he decided. He would say that he
wished for them to share a room. To be together, properly together. Gideon glanced at the clock. He couldn't wait for
Maria to come home.

※

After escorting Maria to a steam-cab and paying her fare to
Grosvenor Square, Doctor Clement Augustus hailed one himself and told the driver to take him to Whitehall, where after
passing through the interminable gatekeepers he finally found
himself in the office of Mr. Walsingham just as darkness fell
over snow-bound London.

"Thank you for coming, Doctor," said Walsingham as Augustus sloughed off his overcoat and shook the snow from its
shoulders. "Did you have a fruitful week?"

Augustus laid several thick binders on the desk between
them. "Here are the reports by myself and the staff at Rough
Tor," he said. "They should make for interesting reading."

Walsingham sat back and steepled his fingers beneath his
chin. "A précis, if you please."

Augustus ran a hand through his shock of white hair and
sighed. "We have run Maria and Apep through a battery of
tests. In summary, together they have reached speeds in

excess of one hundred miles an hour. I suspect Maria could probably push the dragon faster, but we would need a more remote location with a wider test area to find out."

"And the fireballs?"

Augustus shook his head. "The dragon can seemingly fire an infinite amount of them. We have no idea how the energy is generated. The fireballs seem to have a consistent adiabatic temperature—that is, they don't lose their heat until they hit a target and explode—of 1,949 degrees Celsius, roughly equivalent to that of burning methane. As for altitude . . . just this morning I almost died, Walsingham, accompanying Maria to a height in excess of thirty-six thousand feet. That's higher than any man has flown before. And the terrifying thing? She could have gone farther."

Walsingham smiled. "Excellent. That is rather the point, Doctor. And your experiments with duplicating the Apep mechanisms?"

"Useless. Without Maria it is simply a very ornate pile of brass. When she joins with Apep, by means that thus far elude explanation, they become something wondrous. Something . . ." He hesitated, and Walsingham bade him go on with an inclination of his head. He murmured, "Something magical."

Walsingham said, "Magic is just science we cannot yet explain, Doctor Augustus. So it is not the dragon that flies, it is Maria. Specifically, it is the Atlantic Artifact within her head."

Augustus nodded. "We need Hermann Einstein if we are to fully understand it, Walsingham. I've read the notes you obtained from his house, of course, but his methodology . . . it was so haphazard, as was his notation. However he created Maria and what he learned from doing so, he's kept it up here." Augustus tapped his forehead with a thick forefinger.

Walsingham mused for a moment, then said, "Then we must redouble our efforts to find Hermann Einstein. And failing that, if we cannot get into the good professor's head, then I fear we must seriously consider getting into Maria's."

Augustus frowned. "You mean . . . ?"

"Yes. What Einstein did must be able to be replicated. He is an asset of the British Crown, and if it turns out he is lost for good, then I will reclaim another British asset, the Atlantic Artifact."

"That would kill her, you know that."

Walsingham chuckled and shook his head. "Oh, you are so sentimental for a man of science, Doctor Augustus. Kill her? She isn't even *alive*."

The steam-cab let Maria out on to the crisp snow blanketing the sidewalks in Grosvenor Square. She stood for a moment in the pool of light cast by the gas lamp outside number twenty-three, feeling the soft kisses of the snowflakes on her face.

Yes, feeling. She marveled at how her pale leather skin could detect the soft moisture as it alit and melted into nothingness on her. She'd had no use for feelings in the House of Einstein, especially not after the man she considered her father had left and she had been at the mercy of his debased housekeeper, Crowe. But since Gideon had rescued her a heightened sensitivity had come, and she delighted in brushing leaves with her fingertips and experiencing the thick pile of carpet beneath her bare feet; she longed for the gentle caress of Gideon on her skin.

Inside her, something welled up, something she could not rightly explain as being the proper, normal function of the pipes, pistons, rods, and gears that powered her. Gideon. Her mechanical heart beat fit to burst.

She was home. She looked up to where the clouds had thinned and slightly parted, to allow a glimpse of black sky and twinkling stars.

Home.

6

THE VISITATION

It had taken Rowena Fanshawe the best part of four months to find the place, and she wasn't much impressed by what she saw. Compared to Healwood, the new hospital—MIDGRAVE PRIVATE SANATORIUM, said the peeling paint of the weathered sign, somewhat ominously—looked cramped and dark, the soot-blackened walls that reached up to gothic spires at each corner of the squat building seeming particularly foreboding. The grounds were much smaller than Healwood, too, overgrown and unkempt. She could just pick out paths snaking between the lawns, but snow covered all. No footprints. No exercise for the patients, not today at any rate.

A much less expensive place. Not that it necessarily meant the care was of any lower quality but . . . Rowena rattled the locked gate, black paint flaking off in her gloved hands. It seemed more of a prison than a hospital. She looked either way down the dirt track, the scent of the river from nearby Southwark washing down the deserted road. Not what you might call a desirable area, but at least there was no one around for now. She grasped the gate and put her boot into the ironwork, hauling herself swiftly and silently up and over the dulled spikes and dropping to the snow on the other side. She slid to the tall wall that bounded the sanatorium and hid behind the bony branches of a row of spindly birch trees. Rowena reached into her leather jacket and withdrew the piece of paper that had cost her an eye-watering amount of money to obtain. People often thought that she, as the much-vaunted Belle of the Airways from *World Marvels & Wonders*, must be rich beyond the dreams of avarice. She smirked in the dying light of the cold afternoon.

If only. That was why she spent her days between distant adventures with Gideon Smith (and before him, Lucian Trigger and John Reed) on more prosaic concerns. Cargo runs between London and the Continent, the occasional trans-Atlantic journey to British American territories, more often domestic journeys. She had just returned from collecting a cargo of cheese from Amsterdam. Oh yes, life was one long adventure, and she whiled away her time counting her money . . . then shivering through this bloody winter under four blankets in the back room of the offices of Fanshawe Aeronautical Endeavors at Highgate Aerodrome. It annoyed her, suddenly, that Gideon had never asked where she lived. At least she had her Conspicuous Gallantry medal from Queen Victoria to keep her warm. That and the four blankets, and the oil heater that she fired up when finances allowed.

There would be no oil for the heater until the next batch of invoices was paid, that was for sure. She unfolded the paper that bore the address of the Midgrave Sanatorium and, most crucially, a room number on the third floor. The room was—according to the deliveryman she had accosted before dawn that morning, and whom she had paid handsomely for the information—at the rear of the dark building. The light was falling rapidly, and dim gas lamps were flaring in the dirty windows. Rowena stuffed the paper back into her jacket and edged around the boundary wall to the back of Midgrave.

The window was barred, as she had expected, but there was a solid growth of ivy up the back of the building, and a small window in the center of the third floor without a grate. Rowena expertly pulled herself up the ivy, and by the time she reached the window, despite the cold and flurries of snow that spun around her, she was sweating beneath her thick leather jacket and jodhpurs. She took a moment to pull off her leather flying helmet, tucking it into her jacket and running a glove through her short auburn hair. Then she peered through the small window, into a deserted corridor dimly lit by candles in the sconces set into the wood paneling. Quickly, before she changed her mind, she pressed against the glass until it cracked, then broke, and reached in to unlatch the window and pull it open, sliding headfirst through the gap and pulling herself to the threadbare carpet.

Rowena crouched on the floor, but no one came to investigate the sound. She picked up the pieces of glass and threw them through the broken pane, then pulled the tattered lace curtain across the window. It wouldn't fool anyone for long, not the way the icy wind sent it billowing into the corridor, but she had the feeling that no one would be up here before the evening meal was served in any case. And that would not be for another hour, if the staff stuck to the routines she had observed from her surreptitious scrutiny of Midgrave over the past two days.

The room she wanted was the last one down the corridor to her left, a simple wooden door. She rattled the handle: latched, but only with the simplest of locks. A matter of a few seconds' work with her lockpicks, and the chambers clicked. Cautiously, Rowena opened the door and looked inside.

The room was lit by a single gaslight and dominated by a metal-framed bed. The walls were whitewashed and grimy, and there was a simple wooden bedside cabinet, a rickety chair, and a large wardrobe, scuffed and hanging with cobwebs. Beneath the bed frame a chamber pot lurked. Rowena wrinkled her nose. A chamber pot in need of emptying.

"Hello?"

The figure in the bed was so thin, so tiny, that Rowena had hardly registered it was there at all, sticklike beneath the blankets, propped up on lumpy pillows. A woman, looking twice as old as the fifty years Rowena knew her to be, her skin almost translucent, her white hair as insubstantial as dandelion clocks, her face engraved with tragedy and loss.

Her voice came again, the exhalation of a dry tomb, as pale as her body.

"Hello? Nurse?"

Rowena quietly closed the door behind her. "Hello," she said.

The woman's eyes flickered and she began to shake alarmingly, putting her hands together as though in prayer until the tremors passed. "Is it time for my medication?"

"Not yet," said Rowena, crossing the bare floorboards and perching on the end of the chair. "How are you?"

The woman blinked, as though the question were meaningless. "How am I? I . . . I have no idea. *Are* you a nurse?"

"How are you liking it here?" asked Rowena, looking around. It wasn't dirty, so much as half-abandoned. Unloved. Uncared for. She looked at the woman and felt a sudden stab to her heart.

"It isn't as nice as the other place," sighed the woman. "They don't speak very much. Just bring me my medication and my food." She smiled, and Rowena suddenly feared her face might tear from the effort. "But you're here. You're nice."

Rowena fought back sudden tears. "Do you know what day it is?"

The woman seemed to weigh more heavily on the bed, on her pillows. "Yes," she whispered, barely audible. "Yes, I do. It's the day my daughter died, isn't it?"

Rowena said nothing, and the woman's spidery hand felt for hers, trembling and shaking as it moved across the blanket. "You came to see me before, didn't you? At the other place?"

"Yes. A year ago. Do you know how long ago it was that your daughter died?"

The woman turned her head. "My daughter is dead? Jane is dead?"

"Ten years ago," said Rowena, taking off her glove and clasping the woman's hand. "Ten years ago today."

A single tear rolled down the woman's cheek, as though it was all her desiccated body could summon. She said, as dry as sandpaper, "I don't like it here."

Then Rowena felt wetness on her own cheeks, and a sob building within her that threatened to be torn forth. She swallowed it down and wiped her cuff across her face.

"I know. I know," she said soothingly.

The woman took her hand back and held it at her breast, trembling with those terrible shakes again, her eyes suddenly wide. "Are you a ghost?"

Rowena opened her mouth to speak, then stopped. Was that the sound of footsteps in the corridor? But the nurses weren't due for . . . She stood up suddenly, at the voices that rang out clearly beyond the door.

"I'm terribly sorry, Mr. Gaunt. I can't think how the window was smashed. It must have been children. . . ."

"I'm not sure I pay you for this sort of service," rumbled a lower voice. "We might have to think about renegotiating our contract."

Rowena stood there, frozen. It was him.

Gaunt.

And she was trapped.

Keys jangled and slotted into the lock, then there was a pause.

"Is there another problem, nurse?"

"I could have sworn . . . this door . . . oh, ah, nothing, Mr. Gaunt."

The door opened inward, and a small nurse in a plain white apron and a cap pinned to her dark hair entered first, followed by a man clutching a stovepipe hat and a cane, a waistcoat fastened across his bulging stomach, his muttonchops twitching as he glared around the room with pinprick eyes.

Through the crack she had left in the door to the wardrobe, where she crouched amid rows of thick coats—none of them belonging to the woman, she guessed—that stank of mothballs and damp, Rowena watched the man glare with undisguised loathing at the woman in the bed.

At his wife. Edward Gaunt, evidently no stranger to luxury,

given the cut of his suit and the polish to his boots, and his half-dead wife, Catherine, all but forgotten in this misbegotten waiting room for the afterlife.

Rowena could have shot him dead where he stood.

Instead, she did nothing, just watched through the crack in the door as Gaunt dismissed the nurse and stood at the foot of the bed, regarding his wife who looked, in age and infirmity, more like his mother.

"How are you?" he asked eventually, with effort.

"Edward? I don't like it here. No one ever comes."

"Well, I'm here, aren't I?" he snapped. He paused, as though reeling in his temper. "You know it's for the best, Catherine. With your condition. You know you are a danger to yourself. You need constant care, and I simply cannot provide it, not with the amount of time the business takes."

"Do you know what day it is, Edward?"

"I'd be surprised if you do," he muttered, and Rowena had to stop herself from bursting out of the wardrobe and strangling him.

"It's the day Jane died."

That seemed to stop him in his tracks, and he frowned, his sideburns bristling. "Ah, yes, well. I suppose it is. Best not to think about that, eh, Catherine?" He rubbed his chin. "Perhaps I'll have a word with that nurse, get them to look again at your dosage. No good will come of getting yourself upset."

"A ghost came to see me, Edward."

"What are you talking about, woman?" He frowned.

"A ghost. I thought she was a nurse, but she was a ghost."

He shook his head. "See? This is why you have to be here, Catherine." He dug into his overcoat. "I need you to sign these checks. For the business. I've been trying to get all your assets formally signed over to me, Catherine, but you wouldn't believe the bloody hoops a man has to jump through."

He shook his head and pushed a pen into her hand. "Bloody ridiculous. If they could only see you, rambling on about ghosts.

Sign here. And here. It doesn't matter, Catherine, keep your hand still and just make a bloody mark! And here."

"Are you staying, Edward? I get so terribly lonely."

Gaunt pocketed the checks. "I am insufferably busy, I am afraid, Catherine. I will come to see you after Christmas, if the business allows. You concentrate on getting well."

"Then I might come home?" she asked tremulously, hopefully.

He smiled, not a pleasant thing to see. "We'll see, Catherine. But don't hold your breath. At least, not until I have full authority over your finances." He felt in his pocket. "I have brought you some medicine. To help you get well."

Rowena leaned forward as far as she dared, watching Gaunt unstopper a small bottle and waft it for a long moment under Catherine's nose. "Breathe deeply, my dear. It will hasten your recovery."

When he seemed satisfied that she had inhaled enough, he replaced the stopper. "And now, I am afraid I must depart."

"Please don't go, Edward," she said, holding out a bonelike arm. "Please."

"Perhaps your ghost will come back to keep you company, Catherine."

He rapped on the door and the nurse appeared in short order, and Gaunt left without a backward glance.

"Hello? Nurse?"

Rowena let herself out of the wardrobe and sat down by Catherine Gaunt. "No, it's me again."

The woman shied away. "The ghost."

"Yes," said Rowena. "The ghost. But it's not the dead you must be wary of, it's the living. Why has he locked you up in this place?"

"Edward? He has my best interests at heart. He tells me so."

"What is that medicine he gives you? Do the nurses know?

It seems to me he keeps you drugged and complacent, little more than a prisoner," said Rowena. "While he spends your money."

"He is my husband," said Catherine Gaunt simply.

Rowena stood. "I have to go. I'm sorry. I can't just stand by and let this happen."

Catherine looked up hopefully. "Will you come again?"

Rowena nodded. "Yes. I will."

Catherine sank back into the pillows. "Fifteen years. Fifteen years to the day. Poor Jane. Poor, poor Jane."

"Jane is beyond pity," said Rowena. "It's yourself you should worry about."

Quietly, she let herself out of the room and locked the door behind her.

Gaunt must have been haranguing the nurses or arguing over the bills for his wife's care, because he still had not emerged from Midgrave by the time Rowena had climbed down the ivy, stolen across the lawns, and climbed over the iron gates to where his brougham waited. The driver poured himself hot drinks from a flask while the team of two horses steamed and stamped in the freezing night air, flurries of snow battering at the windows of the red-liveried cab.

The driver was parked a little way up the track and did not see Rowena letting herself quietly down from the gates. She heard voices from Midgrave and through the wrought iron saw a rectangle of light as the door was opened and the shape of Gaunt, flanked by nurses, emerged. The carriage driver glanced over the wall from his perch and then leaned forward to pat the horses.

There was Rowena's chance, and she stole it. Bent double, she ran for the rear of the brougham, swinging herself under the chassis and bracing her feet against the front axle, her arms against the rear. She heard the iron gates swing open and the driver climb down; staring at his boots, she immediately regretted her recklessness. She could already feel the cold steel of the axle through her thick gloves, and the awkward starfish position was beginning to give her cramps in her leg muscles.

Idiot, she chastised herself. *What are you thinking? What are you doing?*

But the brougham was already lurching as Gaunt climbed inside and the driver pulled himself up to the front, and the carriage lurched forward as the driver gave the whip to the horses. Edward Gaunt was going home, and for better or worse, Rowena Fanshawe was going with him.

It was slow going through the snow-packed streets, for which Rowena was alternately thankful and miserable. Thankful because the roads the carriage took were potholed and pitted, and more than once she was almost rattled loose; any faster and she would certainly have lost her grip. Miserable because the cold was intense and the wheels threw up freezing slush and, once, a slurry of horse dung. But just as she felt she could hold on no longer, the driver reined in the horses and the brougham pulled up on a well-paved street lined, as far as she could see from beneath the carriage, with plane trees and hedges bordering long gardens.

Before Gaunt could descend from the carriage she dropped down to the road and crawled out from the back of the brougham, rising to a crouch and running for the nearest of the trees. She stood behind it, shivering and wet, and tried to get her bearings. From the location of such landmarks as she could make out in the misty, snowbound night—the distant crown of the Lady of Liberty flood barrier, the tall ziggurats of the financial district—she surmised they had traveled west from Southwark, and the grand facades of the houses put her, she thought, somewhere around Kennington.

Edward Gaunt had not done badly for himself while his wife languished in Midgrave. Not badly at all.

Rowena watched Gaunt arguing with the brougham driver

over the fare, then stomping off through the snow toward a tall gate garlanded with climbing evergreens, beyond which lay a mid-terraced house with the lights burning, well tended and most desirable. After he let himself in and the carriage departed, Rowena risked slipping from behind the tree and following Gaunt's tracks. He had let himself into the house by the time she reached the gate and she stood there, hands on the ironwork, watching his silhouette pass through the hallway and into the parlor.

She hated him as she had hated no human being ever before in her life.

Something settled in her gut, something hard and cold, like the iron she grasped. It would be but a moment's work. . . . She could be in there and teach Gaunt a lesson. A proper lesson. Finally, after all this time . . .

She was idly playing with the latch when there was a cough from beside her. Rowena looked around to see a girl, aged no more than ten or twelve, swaddled in a muffler and a thick coat.

"It's you, isn't it?"

Rowena blinked. "Sorry?"

The girl took a deep breath. "Sorry. That was rude. You're Rowena Fanshawe. The Belle of the Airways." In her gloved hand she held a copy of *World Marvels & Wonders*, damp from the snow. "I read about you all the time. I just saw you and couldn't believe it. But it's you."

Rowena stared at the girl, then at the periodical. She asked, "What's your name?"

"Maud, Miss Fanshawe. You're my favorite. I mean, Gideon Smith is all right, but . . . well. I can't be Gideon Smith when I grow up." She put her face down shyly. "But I could be Rowena Fanshawe."

The weight in her belly turned out not to be iron after all. It was ice. And it was thawing. She crouched down in front of the girl. "Maud. Maud, you can be whatever you want to be. I promise. And thank you."

"What for, miss?"

Rowena stood up, gazing back at Gaunt's house. "I couldn't put it into words, Maud. But thank you. Now you run along home, yes? It's cold and dark, Maud. Yes, so very cold and dark."

She hardly noticed the girl, clutching her magazine, running off through the snow, so intent was she on the black shape of Edward Gaunt in the parlor of his Kennington house.

7

IDENTITY CRISIS

 What are you?

Maria studied her reflection in the mirror on her dressing table. She had brushed her hair and applied a little perfume to her neck. She had selected a long silk night-gown that tied at her breast with a soft bow. She looked like a woman. A beautiful young woman.

She considered the words dispassionately, without pride or vanity. "Beautiful." "Young." "Woman." Was she any of these things? By the standards of other women she supposed she was beautiful; her features were symmetrical, her hair blond and straight, her lips full, her eyes clear. Gideon told her she was beautiful, and she caught the surreptitious glances of other men when she walked in London's streets. But if she pressed her stomach *just so* her torso would open up, miraculously, revealing the secrets within: pistons and gears, rods and wheels, copper tubes and glass pipes through which pumped viscous, dark liquids. And in her head sat the brain of a murdered woman, poor Annie Crook, killed for the crime of loving above her station.

Young? From the notebook left behind by her errant creator, Professor Hermann Einstein, Maria knew it had been a mere three years since the brain of Annie Crook, the mysterious Atlantic Artifact, and the hitherto mechanical yet lifelike automaton Professor Einstein had created for his own amusement had been brought together to create Maria.

And . . . a woman? "I refer you to my previous answers," she muttered, tugging the brush viciously through her yielding hair. *Was* she a woman? Did she deserve to sit here, in these pretty night things, with scented skin—skin made of the

finest kid leather!—and dare to hope that a man like Gideon
Smith could love her?

Maria picked up the book from the dressing table that
Mrs. Cadwallader had lent to her. *Hints on Etiquette and the Us-
ages of Society; With a Glance at Bad Habits.* The page she had
kept with an embroidered bookmark began, "Ladies of good
taste seldom wear jewelry in the morning; and when they do,
they confine themselves to trinkets of gold, or those in which
opaque stones only are introduced. Ornaments with brilliant
stones are unsuited for a morning costume."

She tossed the book on her bed in despair. There were four
more like it on her shelves, and she had been dipping into them
with increasing frustration. There was so much to learn about
being a lady, and she'd had such little conscious existence in
which to practice. How could she truly hope to be a proper
woman? Besides, she had developed a dark suspicion that the
rules in these books—which, she noticed, were largely written
by men—were nonsensically constraining. Even if she could
memorize them all, did she *want* to?

Maria needed to speak to someone. Someone who wasn't
Gideon or—bless him!—Aloysius Bent. Rowena Fanshawe had
shown her friendship, but Rowena was not here in Grosvenor
Square. There was no one.

However . . . from the floor below drifted rousing sounds,
music that seemed to lift the floorboards with energy and
passion.

Passion. That was what was expected of her now, wasn't it?
Somewhere in her breast, the wheels turned faster, the pistons
pumped harder, the gears meshed and slipped. Something fluttered there, something not explained by engineering or hard
science. Had Professor Einstein trapped a bird in her chest, or
was she more woman, more human, than she gave herself credit
for? Was Maria, really, more than the sum of her many and mysterious parts?

Slipping on a cotton dressing gown, she padded down the
carpeted staircase in search of the music. It issued from the

study, where she found Mrs. Cadwallader sitting in the armchair, nodding her head in time to the rising crescendo.

"Oh, Miss Maria!" said the housekeeper when she noticed her at the doorway. "Did the music disturb you? I was just relaxing. . . ."

"What is it?" asked Maria, stepping into the study. "The music?"

"Act three of *Die Walküre*," said Mrs. Cadwallader, nodding to the wax cylinder that turned in the corner, the dramatic sounds galloping out of the curved trumpet. "Richard Wagner. *The Ring Cycle*. Do you know it?"

"It does seem somewhat familiar," said Maria. "My . . . Professor Einstein liked his music."

"I love my opera. Used to creep the boards myself, when I was younger. Strictly amateur, of course. Think I still have some of my old props and costumes somewhere." Mrs. Cadwallader rose from the chair. "Oh, my dear, whatever's the matter?"

The thought of music at the house of Einstein had brought with it more unpleasant memories: those of Crowe, Einstein's despicable manservant, who when the professor had mysteriously disappeared a year ago had begun, cautiously at first but with increasing boldness, to fully investigate just how lifelike the inventor had made his automaton. Had Gideon not rescued her from the place that summer, she was sure that Crowe would have eventually worked up the courage to fully . . .

She pushed the thought away and brushed away the liquid that trickled down her cheeks. "Leakage from my eyes," she said absently. "It happens sometimes. A fault in my workings."

"Tosh," said Mrs. Cadwallader. "I know crying when I see it. Sit down, miss, and you tell Sally all about what's bothering you."

Maria did as she was bid, taking the armchair next to Mrs. Cadwallader's. "I just needed someone to speak to," she said softly. "Gideon has . . . oh, I can't tell you. You'll be scandalized."

Mrs. Cadwallader folded her arms beneath her ample bosom. "Miss Maria, I lived here for many years as housekeeper to Captain Trigger and Doctor Reed. Two men, as in love as any courting couple you might find promenading in front of the Taj Mahal in Hyde Park. You think anything you say can shock me?"

Maria swallowed. "Gideon has asked . . . if I would be willing to share his bed. From tonight."

Mrs. Cadwallader clapped her hands together. "Oh, Miss Maria! Well, it's about time! I was starting to wonder what was up with the boy."

"You aren't shocked?"

Mrs. Cadwallader sighed. "Look, Miss Maria, I know that polite society would have you and Gideon married before you became involved in that side of things. But these are interesting times in which we live, and I'm afraid you and Gideon aren't ever going to have what others might call a *normal* sort of relationship, are you?"

"Were you married, Mrs. Cadwallader?"

The housekeeper sat back, a faraway look in her eye. "I was. My Albert was a lovely soul, always took care of me. We never had children—well, we had two, as a matter of fact, but neither of the poor mites lived beyond a day. He was gentle but strong." She paused thoughtfully. "Like your Mr. Smith, I think." She shook her head and looked at Maria. "He was a soldier, for his sins. Died during the annexing of the Transvaal in 1877. I do miss him terribly."

"And you have been alone all this time?"

Mrs. Cadwallader laughed. "Who'd have me, miss? I'm well past my best. Whereas you . . . but . . . you won't mind me asking this, I hope. *Can* you . . . can you love a man in that way?"

"I think so," said Maria. "I . . . there was a man called Crowe. He used to abuse me most dreadfully, Mrs. Cadwallader. I know that I am designed as an exact copy of a woman, thanks to him."

"The scoundrel! And has Gideon not yet sorted him out?" said Mrs. Cadwallader stoutly. "I shall suggest he makes it his next assignment."

Maria shook her head. "I wish to forget Crowe, Mrs. Cadwallader. But while I know that I am . . . anatomically correct, I'm afraid . . ." She took the housekeeper's hand. "I don't know what to *do*, Mrs. Cadwallader!"

Mrs. Cadwallader sat forward. "Well, my dear, there's a lot of nonsense talked about what a woman should do and shouldn't do. There's a school of thought—put about by men, I should add—that says it's a woman's role to lie back and think of England, and just let the man get on with his own pleasure."

"You don't agree?"

"Do I—well, I nearly borrowed a turn of phrase from our Mr. Bent, then. No, I do not! The act of love is a partnership between a man and a woman, Miss Maria. A contract, if you will, and both sides must uphold their end of the bargain. Do you understand me?"

"Not really."

Mrs. Cadwallader patted her hand. "Not to worry. You'll know what to do when the time comes. Just bear in mind that your pleasure is as important as his." She sat back, frowning for a moment, and then said, "You are going to wait in Gideon's bed until he returns from this little investigation he has embarked upon?"

Maria nodded.

"In that case, there's no harm in . . . well, finding out what you like." Maria looked blankly at her, and Mrs. Cadwallader leaned forward, cupped her hand around Maria's ear, and whispered at length.

"Oh!" said Maria, her hand at her breast, a flush on her cheeks. "Really? That sort of thing is allowed? The books never mentioned anything like that."

Mrs. Cadwallader cackled. "My dear, there's a whole world

waiting for you to discover. And it's not all in the books!" She paused then dropped her voice to a whisper. "Well, not *all* books. I have this volume that Dr. Reed brought back from his travels . . . it's very risqué. I'm not sure I should . . ."

Maria bit her lip. "I think I should very much like to see it."

Mrs. Cadwallader smiled. "It's called the *Kama Sutra*. You go and settle down in Mr. Smith's room, and I'll go and find it and drop it in to you."

As the housekeeper went to change the cylinder on the gramophone, Maria took herself upstairs to Gideon's room. She slipped into his double bed and settled down to await his return, and some light reading from Mrs. Cadwallader.

✦

Gideon stood in the snow outside the Britannia Theater on Hoxton Road, hands jammed into the pockets of his overcoat, scrutinizing the poster pasted to the wall.

Direct from Germany! The Teutonic Marvel of the Age! Be astounded as Markus Mesmer and his amazing Hypno-Array lay bare the very secrets of THE MIND ITSELF!

A raucous crowd was already filing into the Britannia, full of gin and high spirits, young men catcalling and groups of women shouting back.

"See you after the show!" yelled one tall youth in a derby pulled over his eyes as he waved at a knot of girls, the bottoms of their dresses wet with slush.

"Not unless you're buying the drinks," riposted one of the young women.

"Eh, paying for it's not allowed anymore, even in alcohol! Haven't you read the newspapers? Lizzie Strutter'll cut off your doodle!" another man bellowed, and the crowd rang with peals of laughter.

Close by, a voice cut through the chatter, as though for his ears only. "Lost, handsome."

He hadn't noticed the woman sitting with her back to the

wall, a small folding table covered by a silk scarf in front of her. At first he thought she was old, due to the gray rat-tailed, dread-locked hair tied with bright scraps of rag. But the eyes in her coal-black face were shining and bright, the shoulders exposed to the biting cold smooth and thin.

"No, I am not lost, thank you for asking."

She smiled, a gold incisor flashing among her gleaming white teeth. "It wasn't a question, handsome. It was a tell."

She indicated the bones—rat, perhaps, or bird—scattered on the silk scarf covering the table. Gideon nodded. "You're a fortune-teller."

She shrugged those immaculate shoulders, her breasts rising from the patchwork dress she wore. "Fortunes, futures. Fates." She locked her white eyes with Gideon's. "Possibilities. All for a farthing."

Gideon sat down on the crate before the folding table, handing over the coin. The woman spirited it away and snatched up the white bones, shaking them in her cupped hands and whispering into them before casting them on the faded silk. She studied the pattern of their falling.

"A lost father dies," she announced.

Gideon smiled sadly. Too late. Arthur Smith was dead these five months, lost beneath the claws and teeth of the rampaging Children of Heqet, his bones picked clean in the caves beneath the Lythe Bank promontory near Sandsend, where Gideon and his father had lived.

"That's the past," he told the woman. "I thought you told the future."

She heaved those shoulders, that chest. "Possibilities, I said."

"Who are you?" asked Gideon.

She looked from beneath plucked brows, her eyes cold as diamonds. "Names, or at least the knowing of them, are powerful things, not to be traded lightly." He stood to go, and she said, "Be careful, Gideon Smith. Don't get lost."

Gideon was looking to the lines now heading into the theater when he wondered how she knew his name. But when he turned back she had gone, crates and table and all, disappeared into the crowd.

Gideon joined the flow into the theater and purchased a ticket for the stalls at the box office, ignoring the woman with a basket of rotten fruit for sale, three items for a ha'penny to throw at acts that didn't come up to scratch. The performance was due to finish at nine thirty; plenty of time for him to get back to Grosvenor Square and . . .

And what? His approach to Maria after her return from Bodmin Moor had been clumsy and awkward, and had Bent witnessed it he would have put his head in his hands. Eventually, Gideon had managed to stammer that he wished Maria and himself to have a *closer* relationship, and that although he had to go out on business he would not be *averse* to returning to find her in his bed, should she think such a thing was *appropriate* or indeed *desirable,* the latter being something that he himself considered her to be. Eventually he had brought his anguish to an end and fled to his room to prepare for the evening, being careful to clear away any errant clothing, tidy the bedside cabinet, and put on the gas lamps at their lowest setting.

He filed into the theater, pushing through the throng to get as close to the front of the stalls as he could manage. The crowd was noisy and restless, and the heavy stage curtains were still drawn, with an easel in front bearing the same playbill as was displayed outside the building. Gideon intended only to get a look at Mesmer, at his methods, and then decide what course of action to take regarding Charlotte Elmwood. Her disappearance, of course, was a source of concern to her parents, but it was in her eerie likeness to Maria that the real mystery lay.

The lights dimmed as Gideon found a seat and the curtains swung back, a stagehand removing the easel. The stage was bare, and a voice boomed, "Ladies and gentlemen, please allow yourselves to be amazed at the neurological gymnastics of the legendary master of mental manipulation, Markus Mesmer. . . ."

There were a few whistles and catcalls, and then the crowd quieted as a figure walked stiffly from the wings to the center of the stage. He was tall and thin, clothed in a gray serge suit and a waistcoat buttoned up to a silk cravat. His hair was parted down the middle and greased flat, his cheekbones sharp enough to catch the lights above as dazzlingly as his well-polished shoes, his eyes as steely and gray as his clothes. He carried a cloth bag that bulged with something the shape of a decent-sized cabbage.

At the center of the stage Mesmer stopped and turned sharply to face the audience, his heels clicking. One eyebrow raised, he surveyed them, the working classes of East London, then began to speak in clipped, modulated English.

"My great-grandfather Franz Mesmer postulated that there was an invisible yet irresistible force, an energy transference that occurred between all objects. This he termed animal magnetism. Since his theories were published there have been many who have followed in the study of hypnosis and the suggestion and control of the human mind."

He paused, casting his arched gaze around the hushed auditorium. "But only I, Markus Mesmer, have perfected my great-grandfather's early hypothesis and experimentation."

Mesmer dug into the bag and emerged with what appeared to be a complicated skeletal structure with a series of lenses, magnifying glasses, and colored glass circles held tightly within moveable brass orbits arranged at one side. He held it up, casting the cloth bag away.

"Behold, the Hypno-Array! The ultimate marriage of animal magnetism and man's technological ingenuity!"

Mesmer held the device reverently up for the audience to consider, then placed it on his head, the cage fitting snugly to his skull, the lenses arranged around his eyes. "Now," he said. "A volunteer, if you please."

There was a reticent murmuring at first, then a rangy youth

stood up to applause and whistles. He gave a gap-toothed grin to the crowd and bowed to laughter. Gideon recognized him as the young man who had shouted at the girls outside. Fixing his derby on his head, he shuffled out of his row and sauntered down the aisle to where Mesmer's aides, hidden in the darkness of the orchestra pit, helped him up onto the stage.

"A brave volunteer," said Mesmer, lightly putting his hands together to encourage more applause. "What is your name, sir?"

"Walter Longridge," he said, grinning again and waving at his mates in the crowd. "I work down at the docks."

"At the docks," mused Mesmer, steepling his fingers. "And you will work with fish at the docks, yes?"

"Crates of 'em!" Longridge laughed, then frowned. "'Ere, you're not saying I stink of fish, are you?"

The crowd roared with laughter again, and Longridge smiled broadly, waving at them. Mesmer said, "How would you like to *be* a fish, Herr Longridge?"

The young man sniffed. "Not so much. Why?"

Gideon leaned forward as Mesmer manipulated a switch or mechanism on his Hypno-Array, and the wheels began to turn, the lenses rotated, and a sharp light from what Gideon surmised must be tiny electrical bulbs implanted in the array shone through the colored glass circles as they moved in an elliptical orbit around the structure, casting multi-hued lights on the surprised face of Walter Longridge.

Mesmer was murmuring something, but Gideon couldn't make out what. Longridge seemed to relax and stared into the Hypno-Array, his shoulders slumping, his jaw slackening. The crowd remained silent, then Longridge crouched down and began to make exaggerated swimming motions with his long arms, his eyes bulging out and his cheeks puffed with air as he opened and closed his mouth, moving slowly as though through rushing water around Mesmer.

"Behold!" said the German with a tight smile. "The man is now the fish!"

When the uproarious applause and laughter had died down, Mesmer switched off his Hypno-Array, clapped his hands, and sent the befuddled Longridge back to his seat on a wave of applause. Over the next two hours, Gideon watched members of the audience fall over themselves to allow Mesmer to humiliate them by making them think they were chickens, horses, and ballerinas. To the delight of the audience he hypnotized two burly bricklayers into behaving like a coquettish courting young couple.

When the curtain finally fell, Gideon stayed in his seat for a moment, considering. From what he had seen it was quite plausible that Mesmer had hypnotized Charlotte Elmwood into behaving in quite an unbecoming manner, and it did seem that Mesmer had to deliberately end the mind control before the subject returned to normal. But what to do about it? As he moved to join the lines of the crowd filing out of the auditorium, he was before he realized it sliding away from the flow and making toward the stairs that led backstage, where a uniformed theater employee stood guard by a velvet rope.

"Mr. Mesmer don't want no autograph hunters," said the man.

Gideon showed him the card that identified him and his affiliation with the Crown. "He'll see me."

"Mr. Smith. Very good, sir," said the man, unhooking the rope and ushering Gideon through.

Gideon tapped his nose. "Not a word, though."

The man winked. "Of course. Top secret, sir."

The staircase led to a corridor at the end of which was a door marked ARTISTES. Gideon paused outside it for a moment, glancing back along the deserted corridor. He could hear voices from within—including Mesmer's Teutonic accent, raised in controlled anger.

"Where is he? How is it that we cannot find the swordsman? Am I surrounded by assholes?"

Another voice answered, *"Je suis désolé, l' homme à épée n' habite pas où je le croyais."*

"In English, you cretin!" yelled Mesmer. "It is the one bloody language we are all supposed to share!"

"I am sorry," said the voice again, more haltingly. "The swordsman is not living where we thought."

"God," said Mesmer. "You do not think he has found out about the outbreak of typhus in New Orleans that has claimed his wife and daughters? That he has gone rogue, abandoned his mission?" There were some noncommittal murmurs and Mesmer sighed raggedly. "It was a rhetorical question, you buffoons. You, Alfonso. What news of the whore?"

A deeper voice came. "It is difficult, Señor Mesmer. *La puta*, they are . . . how they say? On strike. Finding this girl on the streets . . . it is like a needle in a haystack."

Gideon frowned. Mesmer had Spaniards and Frenchmen working for him? It was normally the case that they were at each other's throats if in the same room for more than five minutes. And what were they talking about? Swordsman? And whores? He pulled back from the door thoughtfully. There was certainly something—

Too late he heard the padding of footsteps on the carpet, and he had barely turned to see the grim faces of two unshaven men in big coats before something hard hit him at the back of the head, and he slumped to the floor.

⚙

When Gideon awoke he was bound with thin rope to a high-backed chair, his head throbbing. Markus Mesmer was in front of him, perched on the edge of a dressing table, smoking a cigarette and coolly regarding him. Gideon's wallet was on the dressing table, and Mesmer held his card in his hand.

"So you are Gideon Smith," he said. "I must say, I was quite saddened to hear of the deaths of Reed and his catamite Trigger." He smirked unpleasantly. "They were a great source of income for me with their slanderous lies."

Mesmer flicked the card over his shoulder and stood. "You do not look much like your likeness in *World Marvels & Wonders*, Herr Smith."

"They take some measure of artistic license with the illustrations," said Gideon, his mouth dry. "So as not to impede my passage and my work."

"Ah yes, your work," said Mesmer. "The Hero of the Empire! How very grand. And you imagine I am up to villainy, Herr Smith?"

Gideon met his stare. "I have been knocked unconscious and tied to a chair. So yes, I fear some villainy at work."

Mesmer spread his hands, his face a picture of innocence. "You were eavesdropping at my door, Herr Smith. My employees quite naturally suspected *you* of villainy."

"Why are you blackmailing the Elmwoods, Mesmer?" asked Gideon.

Mesmer smiled. "Ah. Direct. I like that, Herr Smith. But . . . blackmail? Libel, Herr Smith. Defamation. You seek to continue the good work of Lucian Trigger and fill my pockets with settlements from your employers?"

Gideon narrowed his eyes. "What are you up to? Who is the *swordsman*?"

Mesmer nodded. "I see you heard much at our door. Perhaps this is the moment when I lay bare all my plans, safe in the knowledge that you are my prisoner. But then you escape, Herr Smith! You foil my dastardly machinations! I am undone! You see, I am very much familiar with the formulaic plots of your cretinous story papers."

Gideon glanced around the room. There were five other men apart from Mesmer, rough looking and muscular. At least two of them were Spanish in appearance. He said, "A rather . . . *international* team you have. You are to be commended for bringing old enemies together."

Mesmer smiled. "They serve neither the Emperor of France nor the Queen of Spain. Like me, they have other loyalties, Herr Smith. We have pledged fealty to an older king."

Gideon tugged at his bonds and asked, "What are you doing here, Mesmer? Surely you are not just in London to perform for East End crowds."

Mesmer sat on the dressing table again and lit another cigarette. "What are *you* doing here, Herr Smith? Playing the hero?" He paused for a moment. "But what is a hero? A man who does as he is told, or who finds his own way? And are heroes born or made, Herr Smith? Shall we find out?"

One of the Frenchmen handed the Hypno-Array to Mesmer, and he fitted it to his head. Gideon closed his eyes tightly but felt his head gripped by strong hands that pried his eyelids open. The light from the contraption blinded him momentarily, colored shapes swimming in front of his eyes, as Mesmer began to murmur.

"Yes, Herr Smith. Are heroes born or made? What if we took away all your heroic doings? What if we wiped the slate clean? What if I convinced you that you were not the Hero of the Empire, but the *enemy* of Britain? Would you be able to fight that?"

Gideon no longer struggled against his captors, but simply stared at the lights and shapes rotating and spinning in the Hypno-Array, and let Mesmer's honeyed words flow over him until he felt sleepy, so very sleepy, and his eyelids began to flicker and droop.

He awoke, cold and with a thudding headache, crouched in a doorway, snow falling heavily from the night sky. He pinched his nose and tried to remember how he'd gotten there. The doorway was on a narrow street of shuttered shops and pale gaslights, and far away he could hear the brittle shouts of revelers. Where was he? He climbed unsteadily to his feet and staggered out of the doorway into the street, turning his face to the soft kisses of the snow. He looked down at his boots, his trousers, his overcoat, and blinked. Nothing seemed to make sense to him. He looked at his hands as though it were the first time he had seen them. There was something big that he should have known, but he didn't, and he couldn't even give a name to it. He turned and peered in the darkened glass of a comestibles store, at the shadowy reflection that looked back at him, and suddenly the question was given form. Now he realized what it was he didn't know. He stared for a very long time at the face in the window.

Who are you?

INTERMEDIO:
THE SHAPE OF THE NIGHT

The shape of the night was this: a tunnel that snaked from wherever he was to wherever he wanted to be. That was how he saw the night: for his benefit, his convenience. For his protection and security. For his hungers and desires.

He wasn't sure whether the night had created him, or he had created the night. Or whether, in some small way, they had birthed each other. And walking through the tunnel of night, clothed in darkness, armored in blackness as black as his soul, he was put in mind of Ouroboros, the serpent that devours itself, and wondered if in some small way he and the night destroyed each other, too.

His tunnel of night had brought him to bright lights in the chill air, and a mass of humanity he found repulsive. Like a single, many-headed beast they flowed and oozed on the sidewalk outside the theater, their collective voices gathering in a multi-pitched scream, their stench rising like a cloud. A many-headed beast, with barely a grain of free will between them. A dullard hydra, beaten into submission. And, like a hydra, cut one head off, and another grew in its place, for the many-headed beast rutted and pawed itself, perpetuating its own existence.

Still, no reason not to slice a head off, every now and then, to remind the beast that for all its ubiquity and presence, it did not rule the night.

He saw her, skin shining darkly in the gas and oil lamps, gray hair in rat-tails hanging over her bony shoulders, a gold tooth finding the pale, lost light of the moon for a moment as the blanket of smog and cloud parted; the tooth glinted as though signaling to him. He hefted the leather bag, felt the instruments within shift heavily and clank dully together.

Yes. She was the one. She sat at a makeshift table, the crowd flowing around her as though she were a rock in a river. She was looking up at a man he could not see, but he heard a snatch of her words on the air as the hydra-crowd moved it around with its incessant surging motion.

"Names are power."

He hesitated for a moment, and her eyes, like miniature twin moons, met his.

Names are power.

He faltered, then, felt the intermedio fade, felt the tunnel crumble, as if all his carefully constructed safeguards were for nothing.

Her eyes continued to burn into his until he tore his gaze away. He looked up a moment later, and she was gone: completely gone, the crowd flowing over where she once had sat.

He knew it was impossible that she could know him, but he felt out of sorts, rattled enough that he could not conceive of killing tonight. The intermedio was over. Names are power. He had been brought, quick and hard, back to the play.

8

RULE OF LAW

Bent took breakfast alone in the dining room, a rela-
tively light—for him—repast of bacon, eggs, black pud-
ding, and fried tomatoes. He avoided stuffing himself on
Sundays, when Mrs. Cadwallader liked to do a nice side of
beef. As she brought a pot of coffee in to him, he said, "Why
don't you sit down, take the weight off? Have something to
eat with me."

"I had my breakfast hours ago, Mr. Bent," she said. The
housekeeper paused and looked at him quizzically. "Mr. Bent,
there's something different about you. Have you cut your
hair . . . ?"

He ran a thick hand over his head. "Had a good soak last
night, didn't I."

She nodded. "Ah. I wondered what that black tide mark was
around the bath." She glanced upward at the sound of a creaking floorboard from upstairs. "That'll be Miss Maria, or
Mr. Smith."

Bent chuckled. "I must say, I didn't hear much noise last
night. Gideon must have well-oiled bedsprings."

"Mr. Bent!" said Mrs. Cadwallader, a hand on her breast.
"I would thank you not to make such inappropriate comments
over breakfast. And on a Sunday!"

He shrugged, pushing a sausage into his mouth. "Sunday's
as good a day as any for being inappropriate in my book, Sally.
We're none of us what you might call staunch churchgoers." He
chewed reflectively and glanced at her sidelong. "Been a while
since this place has resounded to the noise of squeaking bedsprings. Long overdue."

She shook her head and glared at him to be quiet as the

door opened and Maria let herself in, sitting herself quietly at the far end of the long table and staring—somewhat morosely for a girl who'd just had a night of bedtime athleticism with the Hero of the Empire, in Bent's opinion—at her hands.

"Gideon having another half an hour?" said Bent, winking at Mrs. Cadwallader, who shot him another warning look.

"I'm sure I have no idea what Mr. Smith is doing with his Sunday morning," said Maria.

Bent chuckled. "No need to be so coy, girl."

"Oh, leave her be, Mr. Bent," said Mrs. Cadwallader, studying Maria. "Miss Maria? Is something the matter? You're . . . your eyes are leaking again."

Maria looked up. "Oh, Mrs. Cadwallader. Gideon didn't come to me last night. I waited until after one in the morning, and there was no sign. So I took myself off to my own room. He obviously had better things to do."

"Better things to do?" said Bent, wiping his mouth with his napkin. "We'll soon see about that. Effing idiot."

"Oh, please, Mr. Bent, do not cause a scene," said Maria anxiously, but Bent was already stalking out of the dining room and heading for the staircase.

Maria and Mrs. Cadwallader had caught up to him by the time he huffed up to Gideon's room, rapping on the door. "Open up, Gideon. It's Aloysius." He turned to the women. "This is man's talk. Leave us to it."

"There's no answer," said Mrs. Cadwallader. "Do you think he's ill? Where did he go last night, anyway?"

"Off to find Markus Mesmer," said Bent, knocking on the door again. "To do with this missing Elmwood girl. I told him it wasn't our business, but after that portrait . . ." He glanced at Maria. "Well. You know what he's like. Gideon! Are you in there?"

Bent rattled the handle and opened the door. The room was empty. He said, "Did you make the bed up after you left, Maria?"

She nodded.

"And this was after one?" Bent rubbed his chin. "Then Gideon hasn't slept here. He didn't come home."

"I was a fool to think—" began Maria, but Bent held up his hand.

"If he didn't come home, it can't be for any good reason. He must have gone off half-cocked with Mesmer. Effing hell."

From downstairs, a bell sounded. Mrs. Cadwallader said, "The front door."

"It might be Gideon!" said Maria.

"Lost his keys and home with the milk cart," said Bent, but didn't sound convinced even to himself.

They trooped down the staircase and Mrs. Cadwallader opened the door to a smart young man in green livery. "Telegram for Mr. Gideon Smith," he announced, waving a brown envelope.

"He's not here," said Bent. The man checked a small notebook. "Then I am to hand it to Mr. Aloysius Bent, Miss Maria, or Mrs. Cadwallader." He looked up. "I take it that's you three?"

As Mrs. Cadwallader closed the door against the snow, which had fallen all night and made a blank, frozen landscape of Grosvenor Square, Bent ripped open the envelope.

"Is it from Gideon?" said Maria.

"No," he said, reading. "It's from Rowena Fanshawe."

"Rowena? What does she say?"

Bent blinked, read it again, and looked at the others. "She's been arrested," he said slowly. "On a charge of murder."

⁂

Bent had been to Holloway Prison many times, but only to watch murderers hang. He tried to push the thought away as he stood in the ankle-deep snowdrifts outside the prison, hammering with his gloved fist on the wooden door set into the huge gate that fronted the crenellated fortifications. He couldn't think for a minute what Rowena was doing locked up in there. Her telegram had been brief: ARRESTED FOR MURDER STOP HOLLOWAY INCARCERATED STOP HELP STOP

It's a funny old world, he considered as he continued to bang on the door. *It's quite acceptable to crisscross the globe killing folk hither and thither on old Walsingham's orders, but do it on your own time back in the home country and you find yourself clapped in irons in Holloway.*

"Come effing on!" roared Bent, kicking the door. He'd get to the bottom of it all as soon as these effers opened the door and let him see Rowena. Holloway had been a mixed prison up till recently—with a nice little consecrated yard where they buried those who had to undergo the long drop—but had just become women-only. A thought flitted across his mind: He wouldn't mind being locked in there for a night himself, given what was shaking down in Whitechapel. Then the door swung begrudgingly open and a sour-faced guard with a drooping mustache peered out through the crack.

"I want to see Rowena Fanshawe," bellowed Bent. "What have you been doing in there, anyway? Playing effing chess?"

"No visiting on Sundays," said Droopy, forcing shut the door.

Bent shoved his foot in the crack. "Hold your horses. I'm Aloysius Bent of *World Marvels & Wonders.* Companion to Mr. Gideon Smith, Hero of the Empire. Now let me in and take me to Rowena Fanshawe!"

Droopy smirked. "No visiting on Sundays, and no visiting at all for her on account of she's facing a capital charge of some severity. Certified defense solicitor only at this stage, Mr. Bent of wherever you're from, companion to whoever and whatnot."

Bent glared at him. "So who's her certified effing defense solicitor?"

Droopy sniffed. "No need for language like that. She's arraigned to appear before the Central Criminal Court at ten o'clock tomorrow morning. She'll probably be given a lawyer then."

The guard kicked Bent's foot out of the door and slammed it shut. He looked up at the thick walls of Holloway. The Old Bailey at ten. He had no idea whether Rowena had a lawyer she could call on nor, now he came to think of it, whether she could afford a decent one. If she couldn't, the courts would assign her one and she could get legal assistance *in forma pauperis*. But the Belle of the Airways deserved better than that. She'd been decorated by Queen effing Victoria! Perhaps it was time to go to the top.

Naturally—two steam-omnibuses that made painfully slow progress through the snow-crippled city and a heart-bursting hike on foot later—Bent arrived at the building that housed Walsingham's offices to find the door resolutely shut. There was a pull bell, which he hung on for some minutes, gathering his breath and hoping Rowena Fanshawe was going to be happy when he was found dead of a heart attack for her benefit. Eventually a thin man with blank eyes slid open a hatch in the door and inquired what he thought he was doing, ringing the bell at Crown offices on the Sabbath.

"Get me Walsingham," gasped Bent. "Matter of great urgency. Christ, I need an effing cigarette."

As Bent patted his pockets for his tobacco, the man said, "No Walsingham here, I'm afraid. Be off with you."

"Don't play silly buggers with me," said Bent, eventually locating his tin of rolling papers and tobacco. "Mr. Walsingham—face like a hawk, eyes like a shark. Above top secret and all that. I know him and you know him, so let's cut out all the malarkey and you go and get him. Tell him it's Aloysius Bent."

The hatch slid shut, and ten minutes later the man opened the door and showed Bent in, taking him up three flights of a staircase that knocked out of him the breath he'd only just recovered.

"Christ, I need to get effing fit," muttered Bent as the man rapped on the door.

"Enter," said the unmistakable voice of Walsingham, and Bent elbowed past his guide and barged in.

Walsingham was sitting at his desk, reading through a sheaf of papers that he slid into a tray. "Mr. Bent. We meet again, twice in two days. To what do I owe the pleasure of your return visit?"

"Don't you ever go home, Walsingham? Ain't there a Mrs. Walsingham at home, warming your bed?"

"Not that my domestic arrangements are the slightest concern of yours, Mr. Bent, but no. I consider myself married to my job. Was that it? Now you have established that, is your visit at an end? I have much to do. . . ."

Bent sat down heavily across from Walsingham. "You know full well why I'm here. Rowena's been arrested on a murder charge."

Walsingham steepled his fingers beneath his chin. "Yes, I had heard. Most unfortunate."

Bent leaned forward. "So what are you going to do about it?"

"What would you have me do about it, Mr. Bent?"

"Get her out of Holloway, for starters," said Bent, counting off on his nicotine-stained fingers. "Get the charges dropped. Find out why she's been locked up."

Walsingham shook his head. "I am very sorry, Mr. Bent. Britain is built upon the rule of law, and Miss Fanshawe is as bound by it as anyone. There is nothing I can do to interfere with the judicial process."

"Effing bollocks." Bent snorted. "You only have to fart and you could call off this kangaroo court. After all she's done for you, for the Empire, it's the least you could do."

Walsingham leaned back and considered Bent for a long moment. "Miss Fanshawe is what my department would term a "deniable asset," Mr. Bent. Any involvement she has had in official Crown business has been through subcontracted commissions from Mr. Gideon Smith, and Reed and Trigger before him. She is not, has never been and—sad to say, it seems—will never be an employee of the Crown. It may seem harsh, Mr. Bent, but she is nothing to us. Especially if she is convicted of a capital offense."

"The Queen gave her an effing medal!" said Bent.

Walsingham nodded. "And if you look at the charge sheet at the Old Bailey tomorrow, it will read *Regina v Fanshawe*. It is the Crown that brings prosecutions, Mr. Bent. I'm sorry. There's nothing I can do."

Bent knew he was right. "I'll see myself out," he said.

Out on Whitehall Street, he lit another cigarette and inhaled deeply. He was damned if he was going to let Rowena face this charge with some court-appointed lawyer who didn't give a shit for her. It was time to call in a debt.

※

"Shine a light, Bent! It's bloody Sunday!"

The tall man with unruly hair and a beak of a nose glared with wild eyes at Bent from the doorway of the ramshackle property in Holborn, before peering around the courtyard at the windows where his fellow practitioners of the law lived when they were not working at the city's courts or the chamber offices that dominated the oppressive little square.

Bent glanced at the towel the man had wrapped around his scrawny middle. "Get some clothes on, Siddell. I'm here to collect."

"Ah," said Siddell, glancing back up the dark staircase and scratching at the mustache that flapped under his impressive nose. "Yes. I owe you ten guineas, don't I? Thing is . . ."

"Willy?" drifted a voice down the stairs. "Willy, come back to bed. . . ."

"Thing is, you've spent the money you owe me wining and dining some doxie," said Bent. "But there are other ways you can pay me back."

William Siddell's quarters comprised a bedroom, on which he hastily shut the door, a tiny living-room-cum-study, and a washroom in which a cat would have had trouble swinging a mouse. As Siddell climbed into his trousers, he said, "What's to do, Aloysius?"

"Got a job for you. Tomorrow morning. Old Bailey at ten."

Siddell stared at him. "Old Bailey? Shine a light! What is it?"

"Rowena Fanshawe. You heard of her?"

"Of course I have," said Siddell, shoving his shirt into his trousers. "Belle of the Airways and all that. I heard you was running around with that mob now, heroes and pilots and what-not. What's up with her?"

"Got herself on an effing charge. I want you to defend her."

Siddell paused, his eyes narrowing. "Well, then . . . you see, that sort of representation don't come cheap, Aloysius. I'll have to shuffle cases around and—"

"You'll be paid," cut in Bent. "And I'll wipe out the debt. You'll be there tomorrow, yes?"

Siddell shrugged. "I suppose. What's she up for? Flying too high? Smuggling?"

Bent picked up a wrinkled pear from a dusty bowl in the living room, rubbed off the mold, and bit into it. As good a time as any to start eating more healthily.

"Murder," he said.

He knew he was in London. He knew Queen Victoria was on the throne. He knew it was the year 1890, that the shapes that steamed overhead in the thick cloud were dirigibles, that Britannia ruled the waves and the air, that New York and Boston were British and Nyu Edo on the West Coast of America was Japanese. He knew it was a Sunday, and he knew that the couples who walked arm in arm were lovers.

He knew all this. He wasn't an idiot.

But he had no idea who he was, or his name, or why he was walking the streets of the East End. He had no wallet, no identification, not a penny in his pockets.

He also knew he was cold, and scared, and tired, and hungry.

Above all, he was hungry.

He'd walked all night and all morning, knowing he was somewhere in Whitechapel, surrounded by soot-blackened slums and filth washing through the streets. There was a young man with a small barrow selling fruit and fish. He sidled up to it with the flow of the shabby, dirty folk who populated the thoroughfare, his stomach rumbling at the sight of the food.

Stealing was wrong; he knew that. It was the law of the land.

But starving was worse. And surely there was a rule of law that was higher than the law of the land, a rule of law that said a man was entitled to have clothes on his back and food in his belly. That counted more than the profit the barrow boy would put in his pocket, surely?

Life and death versus profit and loss.

To his mind there was no contest. He strolled past the barrow, snatched two apples in each hand, and began to pelt through the slush and mud with the barrow boy's cries of "Thief! Thief!" ringing in his ears.

He wolfed down the apples in the shadows of an alleyway in the stews of Whitechapel. The tenements reared up all around him, blocking out what thin light penetrated the oppressive white clouds now darkening with the late afternoon. The snow had stopped falling, for which he was grateful, but he shivered in his overcoat, and the slush had soaked his boots and chilled his feet.

The narrow street he found himself on seemed almost supernaturally quiet. The windows of the cramped, tumbledown buildings were shuttered against the harsh winter, no pedestrians fought their way along the filthy track between the rotten rows, no steam-cabs lumbered through nor horse-drawn carriages clattered by.

It was as if the world had ended, somehow, and he was the last man on Earth. Across from where he lurked, stamping his feet and rubbing his frozen hands, there was a closed hardware store, bars running down the windows. Above there was a sign in peeling paint. ALBERT SMITH & SONS.

Smith.

It was as though a dim sunbeam penetrated the clouds above. Smith.

He blinked and caught a fluttering black shape on the periphery of his vision. Walking down the street was a woman in dirty, ragged skirts and a shawl pulled about her shoulders. She wore no bonnet and her blond hair hung about her shoulders, framing the most beautiful face he had ever seen.

Smith, he thought to himself. *I know that name.*

And I know her.

He extracted himself from the shadows to get a better look, and she paused as she saw him, putting her hands on her hips and giving him a long stare.

Eventually she said, "Well? You just going to look or do you want to spend some money?"

He stepped into the muddy track. "Spend some money? Who are you?"

She smiled. "Name's Lottie, dear. It's cold. Want to share some body heat down that alley of yours?"

He felt a lurch in his trousers as the wanton woman began to stride purposefully across the road. Lottie. That didn't seem right. But with every step she took her beauty captivated him more and more, and by the time she reached him, winding her body sinuously against his like a cat, he could think of nothing other than—

"Oi!"

The shout rang out from the streets that had been empty before, but now funneled toward them a group of men—half a dozen, maybe more—who marched with purpose and malice. They carried sticks, and knives, and exuded menace in their stony faces.

The girl—Lottie? Though that still didn't feel right— seemed to melt away, and he was alone, dithering, not knowing whether to run or protest his innocence of whatever crime he was sure the men suspected of him. But it was too late; they closed the gap and grabbed him roughly, one of them with a bald head and stinking breath putting his meaty face against his and sliding a smooth stick under his chin.

"Name?" demanded the man.

He shrugged. "I don't know."

"A likely fucking story. You're not from Whitechapel, that's for sure."

"Is it him, Henry?" asked another as they began to haul him through the slush and dirt, gripping his arms and dragging him along the street until it opened out into a tight square lit by gas lamps.

"Are you him?" said Henry.

"Who?"

"Jack the fucking Ripper, that's who."

Then he noticed the lampposts, and what was hanging from them. At first he thought they were sacks, or tangled rags. It was only when he felt a rough ring of rope slid over his head that he recognized them for what they were: bodies, suspended from the arched iron.

"I'm not . . . I'm not . . . ," he began, but Henry slapped him, hard.

"Don't fucking matter. You're on the street when you've no right to be." He grinned savagely as they began to lead him toward the nearest post, and he finally began to fight. "Better safe than sorry, eh?"

9

LIZZIE STRUTTER

Lizzie Strutter's boarding house was situated in Walden Street, a well-appointed Whitechapel slum. Well-appointed because it was a stone's throw from the Lord Clyde public house on one side and the Wycliffe Congregational Chapel on the other—one a source of custom and the other a supply of girls, fallen women who threw themselves upon the mercy of the church and, when God was found wanting for the provision of clothing, money, and food, made their way down to Lizzie Strutter's to seek gainful employment.

Not that there was much in the normal way of work occurring this grim Sunday afternoon, though Lizzie Strutter reflected that she had no one to blame but herself. Still, a stand was a stand; she'd organized a strike of all the whores in Whitechapel, and that meant no business for her girls, whether on their backs or on their knees. They were in quite jolly spirits about it at the moment—after all, which of them actually *wanted* those sweating, stinking, rotten-toothed hulks thrusting and grinding on top of them?—but the strike was only a day old. When the novelty wore off, and the money stopped coming in, then she might have a problem keeping them reined in, especially the streetwalkers and the other madams who had tacitly agreed to the action.

By then, though, they might have caught Jack the Ripper. And Lizzie Strutter would be the toast of the East End. And the girls could get back to work, earning some honest coin.

Lizzie considered her reflection in the cracked mirror in her boudoir. There were those—like that rat-faced inspector at the Commercial Road police station—who would laugh at that, honest coin. But was there a purer and more honest transaction than that which occurred between her girls and their johns? A fixed price for a fuck. Everybody knew what they were getting; no one was disappointed. Could the costermongers on Tottenham Court Road or the fancy shops in Oxford Street say the same?

She called it a boudoir, but that was just her little joke, of course. Lizzie's room was as dark and damp and cockroach infested as the rest of them, her best sheets gray and tattered, her worst ones grimy-black and torn. But she had a lock on the door, a pot to piss in, and the fearful regard of half of the East End. And, underneath her bed, by the chamber pot, a loose floorboard beneath which was hidden the immoral earnings of her girls. Lizzie Strutter's escape route. Because one day she was going to make enough to leave this behind, raise her situation, and have a proper boudoir, with red silk sheets and thick drapes, a mirror that wasn't mottled and spiderwebbed with cracks, and gas lamps rather than candles—perhaps even electrification!

Lizzie Strutter stared at herself in the mirror as she tied her dry hair up in a bun. She was past her best; that was true. Four babies—all dead now—and more abortions than she could count, thanks to old Mrs. Weatherbottom's hot baths, gin, and knitting needles, had taken their toll on her body. Her titties were heading toward her belly and her cunt'd had more pricks than the round board they liked to throw iron darts at in that new game at the Lord Clyde. She didn't turn tricks anymore—well, only for her favorites. She was thirty-eight, but she reckoned she could scrub up nicely, once her ship came in and she made it good up west.

There was a cautious tap at her door, and Lizzie shouted for whoever it was to come in. It was Rachel, a pretty little thing, save for that nasty scar down her left cheek. They liked that, some of the punters. Liked a girl who looked like she'd been in the wars. Got excited by some strange things, did some men.

"Mum?" asked Rachel, loitering in the doorway. Lizzie liked all her girls to call her that. One big, happy family at Lizzie Strutter's bawdy house.

"What is it, girl?" she asked, turning away from the mirror, hefting up her drooping breasts in the tatty corset.

"Me and the girls, Mum, we was getting hungry. Wondered if we might go and get some pie and mash or something."

Lizzie dug into her little purse and tossed a couple of coins at the girl. "Go over to Frank on Fordham Street," she said. "And don't go alone. I don't want you getting attacked by some sex-crazed lunatic."

Rachel nodded but didn't leave. Lizzie said, "What's up with you? I thought you was all starving down there."

"Me and some of the other girls, Mum, we saw a girl down round Holly Street. Working."

Lizzie frowned. She'd gotten the agreement of all the other madams on this. "One of Lushing Loo's?" If anybody was going to break the accord, it was that gin-soaked old tart.

Rachel shook her head. "Don't think so, Mum. Never seen her before. And she's awful pretty. Like, really, really pretty. And she looks well fed and—"

Lizzie shot her a look. "You saying you ain't?"

"Not that, Mum. It's just . . . she's *clean*, Mum. Got all her own teeth."

Lizzie scratched her head, nipping a flea between the cracked nails of her thumb and forefinger. She'd threatened that she was going to get the rich sluts up west and north of the river involved in the strike, but hadn't made any inroads yet. Why was some doxie slumming it in Whitechapel? If anything, she thought the johns would be pooling their pennies and heading out to the richer areas, where they wouldn't even be able to afford the price of a wank.

"You think you can take me to where you saw her?" asked Lizzie. The girl nodded. "I think we need to have a word with Little Miss Got-All-Her-Own-Fucking-Teeth, then."

"Is Gideon not back yet?" asked Bent as he stamped the ice from his boots on the mat. "At least it's stopped effing snowing out there."

"No sign of him yet," said Mrs. Cadwallader, waggling her eyebrows toward Maria, who looked quite bereft.

Bent consulted his fob watch. "Hmm. It's getting on for five. I think we might have to assume that he isn't keeping away of his own volition."

Maria wrung her hands. "You think harm has befallen him?"

"'Course not!" said Bent with a forced joviality that rang insincere even to himself. "He's the Hero of the bloody Empire, ain't he?"

"Perhaps we should call the police?" asked Maria.

"Thing is, Miss Maria, what would they say?" said Bent gently. "He's not been gone a whole twenty-four hours yet. He's a strapping lad of twenty-four, and a hero to boot. Come on, now, he's got to have a good reason for staying away."

"What news of Miss Fanshawe?" asked Mrs. Cadwallader, by way of changing the subject.

"Not good," said Bent, unwinding his muffler from about his neck. "She's in Holloway and due up before the courts tomorrow morning. They wouldn't let me see her. Walsingham was no help, so I've procured the services of a lawyer acquaintance of mine, William Siddell. I'll get to the Old Bailey at cock-crow tomorrow, and we'll have to take it from there."

"I'll make some tea," said Mrs. Cadwallader. That was her answer to everything. Bent would have preferred gin.

"Where has Gideon gone?" asked Maria. "Aloysius? Where was he going?"

Bent bit his lip. Gideon hadn't wanted to tell her about the Elmwood girl, but things had taken something of a turn. He didn't really want to turn up at court tomorrow and have to tell Rowena that Gideon was missing, but he didn't see how he was going to find the fool boy himself before then. "Let's take the tea in the study," he said.

While Mrs. Cadwallader poured the tea, Bent told them about the Elmwoods' visit. Then he handed over the portrait that Gideon had stashed in the bureau in the drawing room.

"Oh," said Maria, her hand at her breast. "Why that's . . . me."

"That's what I said." Bent nodded. "Apparently it's Charlotte Elmwood. The missing girl."

Maria stared at the picture for a long time before handing it back. "And this is why Gideon took the case?"

Bent shrugged. "Presumably. We don't bother with missing persons as a rule. Perhaps he thought there might be some link to your Professor Einstein."

"And where did Gideon go to observe this Markus Mesmer?"

"The Britannia, in Hoxton, I think," said Bent. "Mesmer has a short run there."

"Then I will go tonight," said Maria.

"I thought you might say that. There's no show on Sunday; I checked. If he's not back tomorrow, we'll go along after Rowena's been up in the dock."

Maria nodded, then said, "I think I will retire to my room."

When she had gone, Mrs. Cadwallader asked, "Do you think Gideon will be all right? Really?"

Bent sighed. "I'm not happy about him being out all night, but it's like I said . . . he's a grown man. We'll just have to wait it out."

"I do hope Miss Maria doesn't get any strange ideas about going out alone. . . . You *will* go with her tomorrow, Mr. Bent?"

Bent stretched his legs and waggled his toes at the fire blazing in the hearth of the parlor. "'Course I will. But you ain't seen her in action, Sally. It's easy to forget that she ain't a flesh-and-blood girl, but you ought to see her punch. . . . She laid one of them horrible Children of Heqet flat out at the Embankment, and old Louis Cockayne, God rest his soul, nearly had his jaw broken by her. She can look after herself."

Mrs. Cadwallader puttered around the parlor, turning up the gas lamps. Bent watched her for a moment and patted the sofa next to him. "Why don't you clock off, Sally? Come and sit down."

She sighed. "I wish you wouldn't be so forward, Mr. Bent. It's not appropriate for you to speak to me with such familiarity."

"Oh, tosh, Sally," said Bent. "Come on, we're both adults. We've both been around the block." He paused then said, "We're both lonely."

She raised an eyebrow in horror. "Oh, Mr. Bent! All this . . . the flowers, the baths . . . Oh, Lord. I do believe you're courting me!"

He shrugged. "What of it, Sally? You're a damned handsome woman. I have *needs*, Sally. We both do."

"Needs, Mr. Bent? I thought you sated your hunger at—oh. Oh, now it all becomes clear. You think I don't read the newspapers, Mr. Bent? Think I don't know that those harlots you frequent in the East End have withdrawn their services?"

Bent put his hand on his chest. "Sally, no, it's not that—"

She laid a frosty gaze upon him. "I believe it most certainly is, Mr. Bent. I have never been so insulted in all my life. I think I will, as you suggested, clock off now. I will be in the study, listening to some music. I trust you can see to your own *needs*, whatever they may be, for the rest of the evening. There is food in the pantry and drink in the icebox. I'm sure you can sort yourself out."

Mrs. Cadwallader slammed the door to the parlor shut as she left. Bent stared at the flames in the grate for a long moment, until the thunderous strains of Wagner struck up from the study, and then murmured, "That went well."

I'm going to die without even knowing my own name.

He struggled, of course, and gave a good account of himself, taking down at least two of the thugs with his well-placed blows. But there were more of them, and the weight of their numbers pressed on him, pulling the noose tight. One of them tossed the rope up and over the lamppost in one fluid movement. The windows of the dingy tenements looked down on him, blankly. If there was anyone watching from behind the shutters, they didn't offer any help.

"Say your prayers to whatever god you fancy," said the one called Henry.

But a sharp whistle, sounding three times, put any peace-making on hold.

"Shit, the coppers," spat one of the mob.

"Run!" yelled Henry, and the rope went slack. He pulled it loose and over his head, and without really knowing why, fled in the opposite direction from the approaching footsteps and the scattering thugs.

He didn't stop until he was back on the street where he'd met the girl, ducking into a tight alley and peering out from the shadows at the two policemen who had paused in the small square, shining their lanterns up at the bodies that hung like grisly Christmas baubles from the gas lamps.

Why had he run from the police? He had done nothing wrong. He was the victim of that fracas. But something they had said . . . Jack the Ripper. The memory bobbed tantalizingly around, just out of reach, like an apple in a barrel at a children's party. They had thought him to be Jack the Ripper. But he couldn't remember who Jack the Ripper was, or guess why Henry and his thugs would have thought he had anything to do with it.

His heart leaped as he spied, across the square and beyond the knot of policemen, an unmistakable shape framed in lamplight. That girl, Lottie. He felt a surge of something, desire and . . . more. He felt fiercely protective of her, felt as though his heart would melt at the mere sight of her. Was this love at first sight? He seemed to know her, deep inside, but she had showed no recognition of him.

And then another figure loomed behind her, thick and black, even its head, as though it was covered by a tight hood or cowl. And the dull lamplight glinted off something in its hand. A blade.

Suddenly, he remembered all about Jack the Ripper.

"He's there!" he yelled. The policemen looked up in unison, squinting through the darkness at him. He pointed frantically to the alley far behind them. "Over there! Jack the Ripper!"

Incredibly, they didn't turn to pursue the villain, but began to lumber toward him, blowing their whistles and raising their lanterns. He ducked back into the alley. Damn. Stupid, stupid idiots. Jack the Ripper was getting away, and now they were pursuing *him*. He ran back into the darkness, tripping over a metal dustbin and sending foul-smelling rubbish spilling across the alley. He picked himself up and ran on, skidding on the icy metal circle of a manhole cover, before he came up tight against a solid brick wall.

A dead end. The whistles of the policemen drew nearer, and he saw flashes from their lanterns at the end of the alley.

"Who's down there? Come out, now. No funny business," called one.

He could hear other voices, as well. Where the street had been as quiet as the grave before, people had seemingly arrived from nowhere.

"Who are the coppers after?" shouted a man.

"Only Jack the bleeding Ripper!" answered a woman.

The wall was straight and bare and hanging with sheets of ice. He would never get up it. And somehow he trusted the police about as much as he would put himself at the mercy of Henry and his mob again.

Before him, in the ground, was the manhole cover. If he couldn't climb up . . .

The footsteps were shuffling cautiously down the alley, behind the lantern light, by the time his frozen fingers finally pried the iron disc from its housing. He scraped it back and glanced into the utter darkness below. There was the sound of sluggish water and a stench so foul as to wake the dead. But the police and the mob that had assembled were picking over the rubbish he had disturbed earlier. He slung his legs over and his feet found the rungs of an iron ladder. Quickly and quietly he let himself down into the underworld, dragging the manhole cover back over him and shutting off even the meager light from above.

It is only when you are in complete darkness, he thought, *that you miss so much, even the tiniest flame.*

The odor was almost more than he could bear. Carefully he began to descend the ladder. Perhaps he would only have to wait here moments while the police search moved on. But even as he thought it, the ladder pulled away from the curved wall with a sickening lurch and a shower of brick-dust. He felt himself hanging in air for a moment, before his weight brought down the ladder and he fell heavily to a hard, filth-slicked surface, banging his head and losing consciousness.

Across the square, the girl watched the commotion with interest. Lottie. She rolled the name around her tongue. Lottie. It wasn't right. Almost, but not quite. The police were there. She half-thought that she should go to the officers, ask them for help. But help for what? She was nothing but a common prostitute! Why should she need the help of the police?

A common prostitute. Again, that didn't quite feel right. Besides, weren't prostitutes supposed to earn money? She didn't have a penny in her purse. And she was hungry. Lottie didn't remember much before Wednesday, when she'd run, run, run from that place where the mad people had locked her in a room and brought doctors and all sorts of others to look at her. Rich men, mainly, and she'd tried to come on to all of them, but none had given her the time of day.

She counted off on her fingers. Wednesday, Thursday, Friday, Saturday . . . four nights she'd been out on the streets, so that made today Sunday. She suddenly thought she should have gone to church, and that made her upset. She pushed it away. Common prostitutes didn't get upset. They were hard as nails, tough as old boots. Still, she was hungry and cold. And nobody had done with her what prostitutes do for money. People were scared. And it occurred to her, distantly, that this thing that prostitutes do . . . she wasn't quite sure what it was, exactly. But that was silly, wasn't it? She was a common prostitute. Of course she must know.

She had to get some money soon. She'd slept in doorways, glad of her thick skirts and jacket, but felt as though she might be getting a chill. She'd found a place giving soup out to homeless wretches a few streets away, and been back every day. But it hadn't been there today, probably because it was Sunday.

Lottie felt like someone was watching her. She looked around sharply, but she couldn't see anyone. But when she turned back to the square there was suddenly a face up against her that made her shriek.

"'Ello, darling," said the man. He had a big head that put Lottie in mind of a potato, his mouth full of black stumps of teeth.

She looked him up and down. A common sort. But then, so was she. "Hello yourself."

She tried not to flinch as the man took a pinch of her hair in his dirty fingers. "Pretty little miss, ain't you?"

"I get by. What's your name?"

"Henry. Henry Savage. What do they call you?"

"Lottie," she said. And even as she uttered the next words, she felt suddenly sick to her stomach. "Do you want to do the prostitute thing with me, Henry Savage? For money?"

He grinned, his warm breath washing over her. "You don't half talk funny."

He put his hands on her shoulders and pushed her back into the shadows. "Do the prostitute thing, eh, Lottie?"

And suddenly he was grasping at her skirts and pushing

himself against her. She wanted to cry out, but that wasn't what common prostitutes did, so she let him force his knee between her legs and part them roughly, while his hands crawled over her, grasping at her bosom.

"Please," she said, suddenly very afraid. "I don't—"

"Get your hand down there, Lottie," he grunted, pushing his face into her neck. "Get a good hold of that, it's all right, I'm nearly hard, just need a little . . ."

"Henry Savage, you stick that thing in that girl and I'll chop it off and shove it up your arse."

The man was off her quicker than a dog out of a trap, or so she supposed, not being sure if she'd ever seen such a thing. Behind him was a woman with a face as mean as the tarnished hatchet she was carrying, her hair piled up on top of her head, the cut of her tattered frock showing more flesh than Lottie had ever seen before. She was flanked by three other women.

"Lizzie," said the man, suddenly as meek as a kitten. "I wasn't going to pay her, 'onest."

"So you was going to *rape* her then, Henry Savage?" said the woman, crossing her arms.

"I wasn't going to do nothing," he said miserably. "It's just . . . for God's sake, Lizzie, I never had a wife. I never needed one. I always got what I wanted at your house and besides, look at me, who'd marry a face like that?" He dropped his voice to a wheedling tone unbecoming, Lottie thought, of such a big man. "I'm desperate for a fuck, Lizzie."

"Well fuck off and catch Jack the Ripper, and you can have one on the house," she sneered. "Balls, I'll do you myself if you catch him. Now skedaddle."

As Henry buttoned himself up and sidled out of the alley, the woman he'd called Lizzie looked Lottie up and down. Eventually she asked, "And what's your game, pet?"

Lottie held her head high, though she was as terrified of this woman as she had been of Henry Savage. "I'm a common prostitute, just plying my trade. Who are you?"

There was a collective intake of breath from the three women, and their leader put her face close. "I'm Lizzie fucking Strutter, my love, and you are pissing on my manor. I don't know what you're up to, but I think you and me need a friendly little chat."

INTERMEDIO:
A CESSPIT OF SUCH VILENESS AND ROT

He knew this much: He hated London. Detested it. Felt trapped, imprisoned, caged. Yes, the walls of his cell were distant; he could barely walk from the north one to the south in a single day. But it was no less a prison for that. It was only when he slipped and sank into what he had now come to always refer to as the "intermedio" that he felt somewhat unshackled, as though he had given his jailers the slip, or they were turning a blind eye to his actions, just for a few hours.

He hated London because he was submerged in it, and had been for so long. He had almost forgotten that any other place existed, could almost believe that the reports he read in the newspapers of far-off lands were mere fiction. It was as though London were the only place in the world, and sometimes that seemed the only explanation for its power, reach, and influence. How could a cesspit of such vileness and rot really rule the world?

He slipped back into the shadows to watch the grimy little passion play unfolding in front of him. The big man had been about to ravish the young woman, but now four other, harder-looking women had turned up to spoil his fun.

It was all rather entertaining, in a somewhat squalid way, for him and those like him. Those who traveled by the tunnel of night, those who clothed themselves in darkness.

He had come close, tonight, but the jagged teeth of his instruments had yet to taste blood. His black soul puckered as though blindly demanding to be fed. He turned away from the little scene at the end of the alley and carefully made his way back through the darkness, the intermedio heightening his senses, taking him unerringly onward in search of prey.

He passed out from the mouth of the alley to a brightly lit thoroughfare he would have to cross to melt into the night again. A long, soot-blackened brick wall curved to the right; on it, someone had painted foot-high white letters, a message in broad, blocky brushstrokes.

COPPERS GET JACKY T. RIPER OR WE WILL & WE DONT CARE WHO WE KILLS WILE WE DUZ IT.

He knew he was taking a risk walking the streets of White-chapel while the vigilante mobs prowled. He had already seen their handiwork, the bodies strung up from the gas lamp-posts, the freezing weather keeping them fresh and preserved, their faces frozen in the final, horrified expressions of claimed innocents.

I'm not him, they would have screamed, as men like that ravisher in the alley punched them in the stomach and slipped a noose over their necks. *I'm not Jack the Ripper!*

Of course you are not, he thought to himself as he crossed the filth-strewn road without incident and disappeared into the yawning maw of another alley, the lights in the street behind him quickly fading from view. *Of course you are not Jack the Ripper.*

Up ahead, he heard the scuff of heel on cobble, a quick step that could only belong to a woman.

There is only one Jack the Ripper.

Without breaking stride, he quietly unclipped his bag.

10

TAIT AND LYALL

 He awoke in darkness—close, choking darkness that stank to high heaven. Water lapped at his boots, and his head roared with sharp, stabbing agony. For a moment he thought something heavy lay across him, so tight was his chest, so trapped and immobile did he feel. Something bobbed up from the blackness within him, a dim memory of being carried, as a child, out of tunnels into the sunlight and gentle wash of the sea against a pebbly shore. Then he realized it was fear and panic that kept him frozen to the damp, slimy bricks.

Your fear is a lie.

He tried to latch on to the thought, but it popped like a bubble on the surface of a black lake. He tried to sit up, and something skittered on the stone beside him, claws scrabbling for purchase and a heavy black shape sliding into the sluggish river that flowed by. A rat, a big one. His eyes became more accustomed to the gloom, because it was not total blackness that surrounded him. High above he could see a tiny crescent of white light that allowed a grayness to dilute the darkness. He rubbed his head. Of course. The manhole cover, in the alley where he had fled the mob. He must be in the sewers.

With some effort, because panic still hung around him like a pall of smoke, and his head—he must have hit it when he fell—ached terribly, he rose to a crouch. Around him were the petrified remains of the ladder he had begun to descend . . . last night? That must be daylight above, so he must have knocked himself unconscious and lain there, among the rats and filth, for hours. The ladder had rusted almost to crumbs, collapsing with his weight and bringing him down onto the narrow ledge that ran on either side of the stream of effluent. He wrinkled his nose. There was no way up; the wall was too smooth and slimy for him to climb. But there must be another manhole, a ladder in better condition, farther along the curved tunnel.

As he considered the crescent of light tantalizingly out of reach, there was more chattering behind him. More rats, and he didn't have so much as a stick to defend himself. He had heard—though he didn't recall where, of course—that London's sewers were home to huge, vicious vermin which, when they gathered into packs, could kill a man. Just like the streets above.

But it was not a rat that chattered behind him. He turned to see, on the opposite ledge, a tiny figure with pinprick eyes chewing thoughtfully on a scrap of food, perhaps a nut.

It was a monkey.

The thing kept its eyes, which reflected the dim light most curiously, upon him as it tossed the fragments of its snack into the stinking water, and despite the stench he felt his stomach rumble. When had he last eaten? The monkey cocked its black and white head and scratched its arm absently. It wore a faded little red waistcoat, braided with thick gold thread, and its tail slapped, serpentlike, on the stone ledge as though it were impatient to see what he would do next.

The monkey suddenly turned its head toward the darkness. He hadn't heard anything, but . . . yes, there it was. A faint noise . . . singing? And the palest of lights, illuminating the brickwork of the curving sewer tunnel. Someone was coming.

When he looked back, the monkey had gone. But whoever was down with him was coming closer, because he heard clearer the sonorous voice, even made out the words as they drifted through the cold, fetid air.

"In Westminster not long ago | There lived a ratcatcher's daughter. | She was not born at Westminster | But on t'other side of the water. | Her father killed rats and she sold sprats | All round, and over the water | And the gentlefolks, they all bought sprats | Of the pretty ratcatcher's daughter. . . ."

He remained in a crouch as two figures rounded the bend, one of them holding a staff from which dangled an oil lamp, flooding the tunnel with welcome light. They were both dressed in leather waders that came up to their chests, one tall and thin, the other portly and no taller than the other's shoulder. The taller man had added height thanks to a battered felt top hat; the shorter wore a derby as round as his belly. Both had skin as white as paper, hair the color of snow. The hems of their thick coats dragged in the black water they strode through, pots and cutlery festooning the heavy backpacks each wore and clanking in rhythm with their stride.

"She wore no hat upon her head / Nor cap, nor dandy bonnet / Her hair of her head it hung down her neck / Like a bunch of carrots . . . oh!" The singing of the shorter man tailed off and they both stopped in the flowing filth as they sighted him.

"Well," said the taller. "What *have* we here?"

"Mud lark. Shit-hawk. Waif. Stray," said the other, counting off on fat, dirty digits that poked through frayed woolen fingerless gloves.

The taller man raised the oil lamp higher, squinting through the shadows. "Does he know we're armed?" he wondered. "We'll stick him like a pig if he tries anything."

"He does now." The fatter man nodded with satisfaction. He raised his voice. "Who are you? And what's your business here? This is our patch, don't you know?"

He straightened up, holding out his hands to show he had no weapon. "I don't mean you any harm. I fell down . . . I need to get out."

"Fell like manna from heaven," said the tall man. They resumed their sloshing walk toward him. "Wants to get out. What do you make of that?"

"I say it's a good job we found him." The short man nodded. "What do they call you, then?"

The thin one clambered up onto the ledge, holding out a long arm to haul his companion up with him.

His name? He recalled the sign on the hardware shop above,

which had plucked at something in his dim mind, like idle fingers at a loose thread.

"Smith," he said, rolling the word around his mouth. "My name is Smith."

The shorter man screwed up an eye. "Christian name or surname?"

"Not both, I hope," said the other. "Can't abide men who have names that are either-or. Remember Walter Edward? Hated him."

The short man smiled. "I found him quite palatable company."

"And Peter John. Ridiculous."

"Smith," said Smith. "It's just Smith. And you are . . . ?"

The tall man removed his top hat and bowed low. "We forget our manners. I am Mr. Tait."

The other gave a curt nod. "And I am Mr. Lyall."

"Tait and Lyall?" said Smith dubiously.

"Tait with an 'i'," said Tait, standing up straight.

"And Lyall with an 'a'. Though a man who calls himself *Smith, just Smith*, ought not to be casting nasturtiums on the appellations of gentlemen he's just met."

"It's aspersions," said Tait, replacing his hat. "Not nasturtiums. Those are flowers."

Lyall broke into song again, his deep voice echoing off the brick walls. "A flower gal by profession, I earns my smokes and drinks, I does just wot I likes, and sez just wot I finks!"

"But what are you doing down here in this dreadful place?" said Smith.

Tait looked at him aghast. "Dreadful place? My dear Smith, you are standing in one of the great engineering marvels of the modern age! Sir Joseph William Bazalgette's sewer system! The large intestine of London!"

Smith wrinkled his nose. Lyall nudged Tait in the ribs. "I bet he doesn't remember the Great Stink."

Tait nodded. "Too young, by half. The Great Stink, Smith. Summer of 'fifty-eight. London was awash with . . . well, we're all men here, aren't we? Shit, Smith. Shit. London was drowning in it."

"Dropping like flies, they were. The cholera, don't you know. That's why Sir Joseph—"

"God bless him!" shouted Lyall.

"Indeed. That's why he created the sewer system. Bloody genius."

"But what are you *doing* here?" asked Smith again.

"Doing here? This is where we earn our living, isn't that right, Mr. Lyall?"

Lyall nodded. "Correct, Mr. Tait. We're toshers, Smith, that's what we are. Toshers."

"Toshers," said Lyall as they walked down the tunnel, Smith on the ledge and the two men splashing through the filth, "provide an invaluable service to the City of London."

"It's an honorable trade," said Tait. "A profession."

"But what do you do?" asked Smith.

Tait swung his lantern wide, and a pair of rats splashed out of their way, nosing ahead of them in the water. He said, "We find that which is lost."

"Down here?"

Lyall nodded. "You wouldn't believe what ends up in the sewers. Money. Jewelry. Scrap iron. Why, once we found a whole steam-cab." He shook his head. "Heaven knows how *that* got down here."

"And you . . . salvage these lost items? Sell them?"

"That we do," said Tait. "There's a handsome living to be made as a tosher, which is why we're very particular about who we find on our patch."

"I'm not after your business," said Smith. "I just want to get out of here. Did you say there'll be another ladder . . . ?"

"Soon," said Lyall. "And yes, we sell what we find. Thing is, we tend to spend more time down here than up there, these days. Sometime we even sleep down here, me and Mr. Tait, bundled up in our blankets, under our bivouac."

"But the smell . . . ," said Smith.

Tait smiled. "I don't mind. You get used to Mr. Lyall after a spell."

"Cheeky blighter," said Lyall with good humor.

"What of the rats?"

"Quite tasty, sometimes," said Tait.

Smith gaped at him. "You eat them?"

"They have a taste of chicken." Lyall nodded. "That's not all we eat. There's hogs over in Hampstead, you know. In the sewers. They can be vicious buggers, but get one of 'em on their own . . . why, we can eat for a week. Not to mention the cats and dogs that find their way down here."

Smith felt his bile rise. "But you said you sell the things you find . . . don't you make enough money to buy food?"

They paused at a fork in the tunnels. Lyall pulled a rolled paper from his coat pocket and unfurled it; Smith glanced at what appeared to be a map of this strange subterranean world. "Left," said Lyall, then as they moved on said, "Fact is, we tend to keep more than we sell, these days. Inveterate collectors, Mr. Tait and I. Can't bear to part with some of our finds."

The tunnel they had taken widened, and the ledge grew progressively wider, for which Smith was thankful. Tait removed a pocket watch from his waistcoat and inspected it. "Lunchtime, Mr. Lyall."

"Can't that wait until we get out of here?" said Smith.

"Oh, don't be in a rush to get up top, Smith," said Tait. "It was snowing something vicious, last time I looked. No snow down here, no rain neither."

Both men climbed up onto the ledge, slipping the packs from their shoulders. As Lyall began to unpack pans and a small oilstove from his, Tait held up his lamp and squinted down the tunnel. "That's most curious, Mr. Lyall. What do you make of it?"

Smith followed the tall man's pointing finger. There was what seemed to be a doorway in the opposite ledge some distance along the tunnel, but the closer he looked the more he realized the brickwork had been smashed through to create an opening. Lyall left his stove to consult the map in the light from the oil lamp.

"Curious indeed, Mr. Tait. It seems to be a proper tunnel, but bricked up at some point. It isn't on the map. Perhaps a service tunnel, or a sewer that wasn't needed."

"I'm sure I didn't see it last time we passed this way. What was it, a week ago, perhaps?"

"Yes, a week ago. If it's Monday we're here, Tuesday over Holborn, Wednesday under Tottenham Court Road, Thursday up at Highgate . . . regular as clockwork, ain't we, Mr. Tait?"

"You have to follow a routine, Mr. Lyall. A schedule. Country'd be off to hell in a handbasket if people didn't have routines and schedules. Yes, regular as clockwork, we are."

Lyall turned his attention to lighting the small stove. Smith caught Tait glancing at him with interest. The tall man said, "How did you come to be climbing down here, Smith?"

"I was . . . escaping."

"Escaping? Escaping what? Or whom?"

"A mob," said Smith. "The police."

"Ah," said Lyall, looking up. "A wrong 'un!"

Tait caught Smith's perturbed look and said, "Don't fret, Smith, we're not about to hand you in to the authorities, whatever you've done. What happens on the surface stays on the surface. We're not interested."

"Just like what happens down here stays down here," said Lyall, eventually lighting the oilstove with his matches. "Ah. Lovely."

"What are you eating?" asked Smith. His stomach ached with hunger, but the thought of eating one of those rats, whether it tasted of chicken or not, forced his appetite to flee.

"You'll have a sweetheart who'll be missing you, a fine, strong, handsome lad like you," said Tait.

An image of that prostitute's face—Lottie's face—flitted

through his mind. There was something about that girl, something he couldn't let go of . . . but it was ridiculous. Men didn't fall in love with prostitutes, not at first glance.

"No," he said, though not sounding convinced even to himself. "No sweetheart."

"Family?"

There was an aching hole inside him at the thought of *family*. "No, no family."

There was a moment's silence in the sewer, save for the distant splashing of rats and the sluggish flow of the river of muck. Smith glanced from Tait to Lyall. Both were looking at him most curiously.

"No sweetheart," said Lyall.

"No family," said Tait.

"A wrong 'un running from the police."

Lyall reached into his bag and withdrew something that glinted in the lamplight, a long-bladed butcher's knife.

"No one to miss him at all," said Tait. "We'd be doing society a favor, Mr. Lyall. A valuable service we perform."

Lyall grinned unpleasantly and hefted the knife as Tait suddenly grabbed Smith by the scruff of the neck, the tall man's thin fingers exerting an unexpectedly ironlike grip.

"Lunchtime," said Lyall, his eyes shining, and licked his lips.

Then a deafening roar rent the thick air in the tunnel.

⁂

"Now what do you suppose *that* was, Mr. Tait?" said Lyall, his eyes narrowed, the carving knife poised in the air. "Have you ever heard the like?"

Tait looked over his shoulder, behind him down the sewer tunnel. "Can't say as I have, Mr. Lyall."

"Allegations in the sewers, do you think?"

Tait gave a thin chuckle. "I think you mean *alligators*, Mr. Lyall. And you know as well as I do that those are just stories. Rats, cats, dogs, and snakes. Pigs. A horse, once. But never alligators."

Another roar echoed around the brick tunnel, and Smith took the opportunity to wriggle free from Tait's slackening grip, throwing himself back against the curved wall. He rubbed his neck and said, "You were going to *eat* me?"

"We weren't going to eat you," corrected Lyall, raising the knife again. "We *are* going to eat you."

Tait still looked pensive. "That noise, though, Mr. Lyall. . . ."

Smith aimed a boot at the short man's arm, and the knife went flying over his shoulder, skittering away into the darkness. He pushed with both hands at the surprised Tait, causing the tall man to splash backward into the effluent, the oil lamp spinning out of his hand.

They were going to *eat* him.

In the dancing rays of the catapulting lamp, he set off into the darkness, down the tunnel that lay in front of them. Behind him, he heard curses from the two men.

"He's making a break for it, Mr. Lyall!"

"Then I propose we pursue him, Mr. Tait! We can't let him get to the surface. . . . He could bring all manner of problems down on us."

The light was fading behind him, but he heard Tait and Lyall splashing through the muck. They knew the tunnels well, while he was foundering in the dark. Even if he could outpace them, hungry and weak as he was, would he be able to make it to a ladder and force a manhole aside in time?

In the last of the gray gloom from the lamplight, Smith noticed a quick and sudden movement off to his right. He was passing the broken wall the two men had pointed out earlier, and a tiny shape bobbed up and down. A rat?

No, the monkey.

It chattered at him excitedly, waving its arms.

Was it telling him to follow?

He risked a glance back. Tait and Lyall were dim shapes in the corona of the recovered oil lamp, lurching closer. If he could get across before they fully rounded the bend . . .

Smith jumped down into the cold, thick stream, grimacing as his foot slipped on something slimy. He waded swiftly across to the other ledge and hauled himself up. The monkey jumped up and down then disappeared into the darkness, reappearing a moment later to ensure he was following.

"Stop, Smith, stop!" called a voice behind.

Without a backward glance he clambered through the damaged brickwork into blackness. A tunnel—thankfully dry—led in a gentle downward slope. He felt the sudden weight of the bricks and darkness, suffocatingly thick, but pushed the fear away.

Your fear is a lie, said the voice from the past again.

Feeling his way along the narrow walls, he followed the chattering of the unseen monkey. A distant voice called, "Smith? You down there?"

Tait and Lyall. He hadn't fooled them at all. But then another roar—closer, reverberating around his head—sounded from ahead of him. The monkey jumped up and down; he could see it now, in a dim light emanating not from the pursuing toshers but from ahead, where the tunnel was curving to the left. Smith paused, looking back. Was it better to take his chances with Tait and Lyall or face what lay ahead? But then the decision was made for him. Strong hands grabbed him, and he found himself surrounded by three or four figures melting out of the shadows who held him fast and hauled him off his feet and around the corner, into a wide brick-walled room lit by a burning brazier. A man stood with his fists on his hips in the dancing shadows, regarding him with a frown, but Smith barely gave him a glance.

His attention was somewhat diverted by the young tyrannosaur that strained at a thick chain driven into the wall and fixed him with its piercing yellow eyes, opening its vast mouth to display teeth like knives and roaring with uncontained fury.

11

REGINA V FANSHAWE

The crowd on the pavement outside the arched doors of the Central Criminal Court was so big that it was already spilling out into the Strand, much to the annoyance of the steam-omnibus and carriage drivers who were trying to negotiate the busy, slush-filled thoroughfare. *Word got out, then,* thought Aloysius Bent. He had hoped to get to the Old Bailey early and secure a seat, but so had the massed ranks of his former colleagues on a dozen London newspapers, not to mention the aficionados of the adventures in *World Marvels & Wonders* and assorted ghouls, tourists, and *tricoteuses.* Bent checked his pocket watch; it was a shade after nine. Proceedings would get underway in an hour; it was to be hoped that Siddell had been inside for some time, interviewing Rowena. If the lawyer had spent another night on the tiles and awoken late, then it would not only be the Belle of the Airways who would be up on a murder charge today.

"As I live and breathe, Aloysius Bent!" called one of the press men who were jostling behind a wooden barrier, waiting for the ushers to open up and let them into the fine gray stone Gothic building, its spires scraping the underside of a sky that hung low like paving slabs, threatening yet more snow.

"Herbert." Bent nodded, pushing through the throng until he got to the journalists. As a friend of Rowena he wasn't guaranteed a seat in court number one any more than the casual observers, but he was still a bona fide member of Her Majesty's Press, and he was going to pull every string he could.

"How's life on the penny bloods?" asked another man in a battered derby and flapping collars.

"Tolerable." Bent nodded.

"Heard you was keeping right high-falutin' company these days," sniffed Herbert, who'd worked for the *Gazette* longer than anyone—much less Herbert himself—cared to remember. "Heroes and the like. Come to slum it with your old chums?"

A man who was even fatter than Bent stuck a pockmarked nose into the conversation. "Nah, he's thick with the defendant, he is. Rowena Fanshawe. She's one of his mob."

Herbert looked at him with interest. "Oh, yes, that's right. You a witness for the defense, Bent?"

"*Witless* for the defense, more like." The fat man chuckled. Bent aimed a half-hearted cuff toward his beacon of a nose.

"Eff off out of it, Gargrave, or I'll have cause to tell your missus just where you spends your time on all those nights you claims to be working late. Unless you've already passed her a dose of the clap, and she knows full well."

Gargrave made a face at him, but he shut up. Bent felt a surge of something he'd almost forgotten, the banter and feeling of belonging that he'd always had with the press pack. He'd spent more days waiting to go into the Old Bailey with this mob than he'd had hot dinners, but not more than he'd had glasses of gin with them afterward. By God, he'd missed it. He asked, "Who's the judge?"

Herbert looked over his half-moon glasses at the court list in his gloved hand. "The Right Honorable Edwin Stanger."

Bent groaned. Stanger the Hanger. They said he had his black handkerchief permanently on his lap when sitting at the Old Bailey, couldn't wait to pass the death sentence. "What about the silk?" They'd definitely be putting up a hot-shit Queen's Counsel for this one. He crossed his pudgy fingers behind his back. Please let it not be—

"Angus Scullimore," said Herbert.

"Oh, eff," said Bent, as the huge doors began to swing inward. Scullimore. As bad as it could be. He ducked under the wooden barrier and melted in with the journalists as they be-

gan to file through the porch. Willy Siddell better'd have had
a hearty breakfast, that was all.

Bent crossed the marble floor beneath the huge, vaulted ceiling of the court foyer, weaving between knots of people hanging around the wide doors to each of the individual courtrooms.
Rowena Fanshawe, for all her fame, was just one of dozens of
defendants who would pass through the Old Bailey today. Justice was a great leveler. Or so they said. Lady Justice, arms outstretched and sword in one hand, scales in the other, providing
a handy perch for London's ragtag pigeons on the dome above
their heads, was as fallible and corruptible as any street thug,
in Bent's experience. She wore a blindfold because the law, like
love, was supposed to be blind. More like she couldn't bear to
look, half the time.

Outside the shuttered court number one Bent spied Siddell,
looking a little more harried than he would have liked. Still, at
least he'd dragged himself out of his pit on time. Bent hailed
him and pushed through the crowd to the door. There was a
handwritten notice slid into a brass frame on the wall: *Regina
v Fanshawe*.

"Siddell! Have they brought Rowena over? You been down
to see her?"

"Shit, Bent!" said Siddell. He was clad in his robes and held
his powdered wig in one hand, running the other through his
unruly hair. "I've been down in the cells since before dawn."

"Well? How is she?"

Siddell bit his lip, his eyes roving around the hall. "A
little . . . on edge, Bent. As you'd expect, given the charges laid
against her."

"Out with it, Siddell!" said Bent impatiently. "What are
they saying she's supposed to have done?"

Siddell deposited his wig haphazardly on his mop of curls
and retrieved a buff folder from where it was wedged in his
armpit. He flicked it open to the first sheet. "Murder, on

Saturday night. The victim is one Edward Gaunt, found dead at his home in Kennington. Mean anything to you?"

"Never heard of him. Should I have?"

Siddell shrugged. "Not necessarily, though it might help if you had. He was strangled with a length of rope. Found by his housekeeper, who'd come by late Saturday to drop off some milk and bread."

Bent narrowed his eyes. "Why would it help? What's Rowena saying?"

"Nothing, pretty much. Other than to say she didn't do it."

"Of course she didn't effing do it! What have they got on her, anyway?"

Siddell perused the charge sheet again. "The prosecution is planning to call five witnesses. The housekeeper, the constable who attended, a girl who saw Miss Fanshawe outside the house, a watchman who saw her return to Highgate Aerodrome two hours after the killing is said to have taken place. And some Swiss fellow . . . Miescher?"

Bent rubbed his chin. "So Rowena was at the scene? Why?"

Siddell made a face. "She won't say."

Bent stared at him. "Well, she's going to have to bloody say! You know who's sitting, I take it?"

"Stanger," said Siddell miserably. "And Scullimore for the prosecution."

Bent sighed. "Has she given you anything to go on?"

"Just that she didn't do it," said Siddell. "That she never went in the house."

Bent had heard defenses built on foundations as fragile, but he'd never heard them succeed. And not against a bulldog like Angus Scullimore. He said, "She must have given you *something*. Someone must have seen her somewhere at the time of the murder, we must be able to subpoena a witness who can vouch for her."

"She says she did go to Gaunt's home, but just watched the house. Then she went to Highgate, where she stayed all night in her office. Alone. If we're having witnesses, Bent, then they're going to have to be character witnesses. I presume your Mr. Gideon Smith is our best bet?"

He would be if he'd come home last night, Bent thought. That was a problem he'd had to stuff to the back of his cranium for the time being; young Maria was beside herself and despite Bent's forced jollity he was beginning to worry as well. Two nights without coming home, and after tackling Markus Mesmer? What the hell had Gideon gotten himself into?

"I'll make sure he's here," said Bent, though without conviction. "In the meantime, put me down as a character witness." He remembered something and shoved his hand into his overcoat pocket. "Oh, and give her this, tell her to wear it."

Siddell unwrapped the rag, and his eyes widened. "The Conspicuous Gallantry Medal!" he said.

"Yeah, Her Majesty gave Rowena one just like it, but I'll bet she ain't got it on her. She can borrow mine, might carry some weight with the jury and old Stanger."

Bent checked his pocket watch. They should be opening the court any minute. Siddell coughed and said, "I think there's someone to see you, Bent. I'll go and read through these notes once more."

Bent turned and almost farted in surprise at the thin, rangy figure standing there in an immaculate silk top hat and woolen overcoat, leaning lightly on a gold-tipped cane.

"Mr. effing Walsingham! You've changed your mind, then? Come to put a stop to this farce?"

"Would that I could, Mr. Bent," said Walsingham with a mockery of sadness that Bent found offensive. "But I did think that perhaps I should . . . observe proceedings."

"Make sure Rowena doesn't say anything to drag your name through the shit, you mean," said Bent. He tapped his chin thoughtfully. "Perhaps we should subpoena you, as a character witness for the defense."

Walsingham raised an eyebrow. "I am exempt, Mr. Bent, from such things. Besides, you don't know my name, nor where I live. I am but a ghost to the ordinary world."

"I know enough," said Bent. "I'd have it addressed to Mr. Walsingham and dropped off at your office."

"Where they would profess to ignorance of my existence. Walsingham is not so much a *name*, more a *situation*. A profession. A vocation, if you will. I exist outside the affairs of normal life."

"Got a pretty inflated effing opinion of yourself," muttered Bent.

Walsingham ignored him and looked around. "Is Mr. Smith not here? I would have thought—"

"Gideon's . . . missing," said Bent.

Walsingham arched a gray eyebrow. "Missing?"

Bent sighed. "He ain't been home for a couple of nights."

"And you are concerned? He is the Hero of the Empire, after all. And a young man in London, where there are many diversions and distractions for one of his looks and constitution."

"Perhaps," said Bent. "But for all the remarkable things he's done in the service of the Empire, he's still a country boy at heart. He's been in London for not yet six months. It's a tough city out there, Walsingham. Besides . . ."

"Besides . . . ?"

"He went to check something out with Markus Mesmer," said Bent finally.

Walsingham sighed. "Mesmer is a mountebank, a petty criminal, a con man. And a litigious one at that. If he has managed to best Gideon Smith, then perhaps Gideon Smith is not the man for the job with which he has been gifted. Why was he pursuing Mesmer?"

Bent bit his lip. Should he tell Walsingham about the Elmwood girl and her striking resemblance to Maria? Something told him to hold off for a while, not show all his cards just yet. He shrugged and said, "You know what the boy's like. Reads those old Captain Trigger adventures like they're the effing Bible. Gets all manner of stuff into his head."

Walsingham frowned, but said, "Well, please keep me informed, Mr. Bent. If Mr. Smith remains missing for very much longer, then I will have words with the Metropolitan Police."

"Why don't you have words with the Prime Minister while you're at it? I bet you could get this trial stopped just like that."

"Mr. Bent, Parliament is about to finish for the Christmas recess. There is the matter of plans for an underground railway in London to debate first; I think that the House of Commons has more on its plate than a murder charge."

Bent made a face as the doors began to open. "Even this one?" he said, nodding at the sign on the wall. "*Regina v Fanshawe*. In July the Queen gave Rowena a medal; now she's prosecuting her on some trumped-up murder charge."

"I'm sure it is nothing personal," said Walsingham. He took off his top hat and smoothed down his white hair. "Shall we?"

The Right Honorable Edwin Stanger presided over court number one like a large black bird of prey, his robes spread about him like tattered wings, his shrewd, pale eyes casting about his aerie as the press and public filed in. Stanger sat in splendid isolation and elevation, only the portrait of the queen on the oak-paneled wall behind him in a higher position than he, the empty jury benches to his right and the full-to-bursting press bench to his left, the public galleries ranged around the borders of the room, which held the subtle scent of beeswax, authority, and despair.

Directly beneath Stanger was the dock, in which Rowena Fanshawe sat, clothed in the plain gray shift and starched white bonnet that was the uniform of Holloway Prison. Bent was shocked to see her, the Belle of the Airways, sitting there with her shoulders slumped, her eyes downcast, her skin pale, her smoldering auburn hair trapped and tamed beneath the prison-regulation headwear. She looked broken already, a small and fragile thing about to be snatched up in Stanger's claws.

Before the dock were the lawyers; Siddell's small file looked rather weedy beside Angus Scullimore's stacks of ordered papers and depositions. Bent swallowed dryly. Another bad omen.

Siddell straightened his wig and made to flick through the thick sheaf of notes, while Scullimore sat back, relaxed, tamping down his pipe and regarding Rowena with his dark eyes. Scullimore had a full head of black hair, which he liked to keep brilliantined under his wig, and a list of courtroom triumphs long enough to fill a book.

Bent elbowed his way to the bench behind the lawyers, pushing Scullimore's team of grumbling clerks along with his fat behind until he had positioned himself to the rear of Siddell. Walsingham, he noticed, lost himself in the murmuring crowd.

Every available space in the large, square courtroom was taken as the black-robed ushers began to force closed the doors to a tumult of protest from those waiting outside. The clerk of the court, a large man with owlish spectacles, blinked at his papers then looked up and cleared his throat.

"Silence in court. His Honor Judge Edwin Stanger is in session."

Stanger cast his icy gaze around the room and rumbled, "A packed house today. Hardly surprising, given the defendant we have before us."

There was a murmur of agreement from the crowd and an audible scribbling from the press bench. Stanger said, "I have not yet had the jury sworn in; I am going to take representations from Mr. Scullimore, for the Crown, and Mr. . . . ." He glanced down at his papers. "Mr. Siddell, for the defense. I believe Mr. Scullimore has something of an unusual request to put before the court today."

Unusual request? Bent poked Siddell in the back, and the lawyer gave a half-turn and a shrug, his eyebrows dancing up to his wig.

"I shall take a plea from the defendant and, depending on what that is, we shall either proceed to sentence or initiate a full trial, with witnesses, before a jury of twelve men good and true, as the law of the land dictates. Mr. Astin?"

The clerk blinked again and stood. "The charges before the defendant are as follows. One, that sometime on the evening of Saturday just gone, she did willfully and with malice aforethought commit murder most foul upon the person of Mr. Edward Gaunt of Kennington in the city of London. The second charge is that she—alone or with compatriots unknown—did participate on Friday night in the burglary of premises on Bishopsgate, London, belonging to Professor Stanford Rubicon."

Rubicon? Bent leaned forward again, furiously poking Siddell in the shoulder. Siddell leaped to his feet, steadying his wig with one hand.

"Objection, Your Honor! This is the first time that I have been told of this second charge. There has been no advance disclosure from the Crown—"

Stanger raised his hand. "Thank you, Mr. Siddell. Objection sustained." He appraised Siddell with his shrewd eyes. "Well done, sir. First blood to the defense. Yes, you should have had the papers on this. Mr. Scullimore, I will require you to provide Mr. Siddell with said details this afternoon."

Siddell grinned broadly. Stanger steepled his fingers and went on. "Though burglary is a far less serious offense than murder, Mr. Siddell. Should you not have a cast-iron defense for your client, the sentence the more serious charge carries with it will render the secondary charge somewhat moot."

Rowena looked up and blinked as though seeing the crowd for the first time. Her anguished eyes briefly met Bent's, and he gave her as encouraging a smile as he could. She bit her lip and tried to return it, but her mouth trembled and her eyes filled with tears. Bent felt his heart suddenly break at the enormity of what she'd gotten herself into.

Stanger turned his attention to the Crown. "Now, Mr. Scullimore. I believe you have a rather unusual request for the court."

Scullimore stood, his bearing confident and, yes, thought

Bent, a little arrogant. He laid his pipe on the table and said, "Your Honor, I wish to call as a witness Doctor Friedrich Miescher, and to submit to the jury incontrovertible proof that places the defendant at the scene of the murder at the time of Mr. Gaunt's terrible death."

Stanger frowned. "That is somewhat your job, Mr. Scullimore. I had been led to believe there was some measure of the extraordinary about this."

Scullimore nodded. "This will be the first time that evidence of such a nature has been submitted in a criminal prosecution in the entire world."

There was a gasp from the public galleries and a renewed scratching from the press bench. Stanger sat back in his chair and picked up his gavel, tapping it into the palm of his hand. "How very exciting. You are not attempting to blind the jury with science, I hope, Mr. Scullimore?"

"Of course not, sir. Doctor Miescher has been employed by the Metropolitan Police to examine a number of crime scenes with a view to implementing what he is convinced will become a foolproof method of snaring criminals." Scullimore smiled. "You would be something of a pathfinder by allowing this evidence, Your Honor. This trial will doubtless go down in history."

"Effing arse-licker," breathed Bent. He made a face as the judge allowed himself the tiniest of smiles.

"You have something for me to consider, an explanation?" said Stanger.

"Of course," said Scullimore, selecting one of his files and handing it to the usher, who flapped over to the clerk and laid it on his desk. Mr. Astin handed it up to the judge's perch.

Stanger glanced at the folder then laid it to one side. "Let us take a plea. Mr. Astin, put the charges to the defendant."

"Stand, please," the clerk instructed Rowena. She got shakily to her feet, facing the empty jury bench and looking up to Stanger on her left.

"On the count of burglary at the premises of Professor Stanford Rubicon, on or around Friday evening at Bishopsgate, how do you plead?"

Rowena opened her mouth but only the slightest croak emerged. She swallowed, with obvious difficulty, and tried again.

"Not guilty."

Mr. Astin adjusted his spectacles and made a note on the charge sheet. "And on the count that you did murder Edward Gaunt at his home in Kennington on Saturday night, what is your plea?"

Rowena looked directly at Bent, who gave her his most winning smile.

"I didn't do it, Aloysius," she said.

"I never doubted you, girl," he called back.

Stanger banged his gavel sharply and Astin said, "Please direct your reply to the bench, Miss Fanshawe. Again, how do you plead?"

She raised her head high, something of the old Rowena shining through her eyes, thought Bent.

"Not guilty," she said clearly.

Stanger gathered his files and stood, and Astin hurriedly called for the court to rise. To the scraping of benches and the shuffling of feet, Stanger announced: "Then I shall retire to consider whether Mr. Scullimore's new evidence will be admissible. We shall sit again at nine in the morning, when a jury shall be sworn in for the trial of Miss Rowena Fanshawe."

As Stanger disappeared through the door into the chambers, the press bench as a man made for the exit, the afternoon editions to fill with the scant but doubtless sensationalized business from the morning session. Rowena managed to give Bent a small wave before she was led down to the holding cells beneath the court.

"Shine a light," said Siddell. "I've never seen anything like it. Scientific evidence? What's he talking about?"

"I don't effing know," said Bent, keeping his eyes on

Scullimore, who was talking to a short, mustachioed man
whom he presumed was the mysterious Doctor Miescher. "But
I want you to play your little heart out, Willy Siddell. Lay off
the gin, keep your tripe in your trousers, and early to bed. And
for God's sake, be on top of your effing game tomorrow like
never before."

INTERMEDIO:
A VILLAIN BIRTHED IN THEIR OWN
PRIMAL FEARS

A costermonger wheeled a barrow up and down the busy sidewalk outside the pale edifice that was the Old Bailey, the framework erected on the barrow fluttering with copies of back issues of the penny dreadfuls.

He wove through the crowd toward the man, who spied him and halted his lurching progress, pushing his half-moon spectacles up on his nose and enquiring if he would like to purchase some old adventures of Miss Rowena Fanshawe, from before she turned bad, as told in these very collectible editions of *World Marvels & Wonders*.

He took a story paper from the man, leafing through it. The man hazarded a guess that he was an aficionado of such things, and that right at the moment there was a convention of like-minded individuals gathering close to the docks, where trading in the penny dreadfuls was brisk, and even some of the writers of the adventures were present to mingle with the public.

"Dr. John Reed, perhaps?" he asked, gesturing at the adventure printed in the magazine, a tale of derring-do featuring Captain Lucian Trigger, the erstwhile Hero of the Empire, in which Rowena Fanshawe had played a not inconsiderable part. The tale, as were all the Trigger adventures, was supposedly penned by the good Captain's constant companion, Dr. Reed.

The costermonger squinted at him. "A joke in bad taste, sir. Perhaps you haven't been in London long enough to know."

He handed back the story paper. Of course he knew, as did everyone else, that Captain Trigger and Dr. Reed had died the previous summer while trying to prevent anarchists in a fabulous flying brass dragon from raining fire and destruction on Buckingham Palace.

There was a new Hero of the Empire now, Mr. Gideon Smith. He wondered what would happen to this one. Heroes died, like Captain Trigger, or were found wanting, like Rowena Fanshawe.

He looked at the colorful cover illustrations of the penny dreadfuls as the costermonger pegged the one he had flipped through back in its place. The British loved their heroes. They loved their villains almost as much, thrived on booing the pantomime antagonists as much as they enjoyed cheering on the Empire's finest.

As he watched the costermonger move away with his fluttering barrow, he wondered what they would make of *him*. Jack the Ripper was perhaps the biggest and worst villain of them all, not an external threat to England like the ridiculous grotesques Captain Trigger had faced off against every week in the pages of *World Marvels & Wonders*. Jack was one of their own, as far as they knew, a legend born in their own smog-cloaked streets, a villain birthed in their own primal fear— that of not knowing what was really out there in the dark. London teemed with humanity; its towers and ziggurats scraped the underside of heaven with an arrogance only the British could muster; new wonders and inventions sprang forth fully-formed from sweating brows every single day.

Yet still, for all this, as a new century loomed but a decade distant, they lay sleepless in their beds, fearful of one lone man who stalked the slums by night.

The costermonger gone, he could see himself reflected darkly in one of the narrow windows of the Old Bailey, his image warped and twisted, as though it showed his soul, his intermedio self, rather than what those who milled about him saw, and ignored.

He wondered what they would say if they truly knew who Jack the Ripper was.

12

AIRS AND GRACES

Gideon had not returned home, and Maria felt a dullness in her chest, as though the mechanical components that powered her had suddenly gained weight and substance. It was almost as if the mere presence of Gideon allowed her to forget her true nature, and into the vacuum left by his absence rushed keenly felt reminders that she was not, and would never be, a real woman.

Aloysius and Mrs. Cadwallader had, of course, tried to re-assure her over breakfast that Gideon would be fine, that he must have been caught up in some minor adventure or other, and he would soon be bursting through the door with a breath-less tale to tell. But Maria could see in their eyes, in Bent's particularly, that they did not really believe that.

"He can't have come to mischief," said Bent for the hun-dredth time. "He's the Hero of the Empire."

Around Maria's growing anxiety that harm had indeed be-fallen Gideon there lurked a shadow of something else. He was a young man of modest means, handsome and strong. And, as Mr. Bent had pointed out, he was the Hero of the Empire. What if it was not peril that had ensnared him, but sin? What if he had suffered second thoughts about inviting Maria to his bed and had given into the temptations of the flesh? She clenched and unclenched her hands, feeling the brass joints within her fingers extending and closing, watching the way her skin—the softest, butteriest leather, but not *true skin* after all—stretched and contracted over the fake musculature beneath.

What if he had gone out and found himself a real woman?

The only thing about Maria that could be said to be real was her brain, and that wasn't hers at all. Annie Crook, who had dared to love the grandson of Queen Victoria, had been put to death by agents of the Crown for her insolence, her brain given to Professor Hermann Einstein for his experiments with the mysterious Atlantic Artifact. When Gideon had first rescued Maria—then unaware of her true nature—from the absent Einstein's tumbledown house, she had confided in him her dreams of London, impossible dreams of a city she had never visited. Now she knew they were the residual memories of Annie Crook. She could not call even her dreams her own.

Those dreams troubled her still. She had no other memories of Annie Crook, and she fiercely believed that, whatever experiments Einstein had conducted to ally the brain with the clockwork automaton he had created for his own amusement, she was greater than the sum of her parts. She was not just a mechanical girl with a human brain, any more than Mrs. Cadwallader or Aloysius Bent or any of them were merely sacks of flesh and blood and bone.

She was Maria. She was *Maria*.

But was that enough for Gideon?

Maria stood from the sofa in the parlor and paced the rug before the blazing fire yet again. Aloysius had said he would accompany her to the theater to see if there was any clue in Markus Mesmer's performance as to Gideon's whereabouts. But who knew what demands the trial of Rowena Fanshawe would put upon Bent, and she could not just sit here all day and do *nothing*. Maria was sick and tired of waiting for the Hero of the Empire to burst in and save the day, sick and tired of being the one who was captured or menaced or required rescuing. Gideon had saved her life—she snorted a humorless laugh. Her *life*!—more times than she could count. Her feet took her to the bureau, and the letter from the Elmwoods. Maria picked up the picture of Charlotte Elmwood, suddenly hating the girl for the *life* she pulsed with in the grainy monochrome image even as she marveled at the uncanny resemblance the girl bore to her.

No, she reminded herself. *She doesn't look like me. She's the living one, the natural one. I'm the copy, the creature, the toy of an idle genius. I look like* her.

Maria glanced at the letter the Elmwoods had sent to Gideon, imploring him for help, and felt a leaden weight settle in her stomach. Perhaps he had taken the case because Charlotte Elmwood had everything that Maria had, and life besides.

She tucked the letter into her skirt pockets and went to get her jacket, muffler, and bonnet. It was time she took matters into her own hands.

❦

There was a small area where the steam-cabs gathered just off Grosvenor Square, and after a light lunch with Mrs. Cadwallader, Maria found the driver at the front vehicle shoveling coal into the furnace at the back, warming his hands at the same time. He looked at her from beneath the brim of his woolen flat cap as she approached through the slush and said, "Climb in the back, miss, and I'll be with you directly. Not half using a lot of coal, this weather is, just to keep the engine running."

When Maria had climbed into the leather seat the driver closed the door behind her and climbed into his cab, blowing on his fingers. "Devilish weather, miss. Devilish. Worst winter for years, they're saying. Where can I take you?"

"Winchmore Hill," she said, reading out the address she had copied from the Elmwoods' letter.

The driver chuckled. "That's not Winchmore Hill, strictly speaking, miss. Friends of yours?"

"No, I've never met them," she said.

The driver wrenched at the levers on his dashboard, and the cab shuffled forward in the snow. "Just on the edge of Winchmore Hill that is, miss, where the people live who want to say they live in Winchmore Hill, but can't rightly afford it. Airs and graces those sort have, miss. Like to think they're something they're not."

Like me? thought Maria. She said, "Perhaps they are merely aspirational, sir. Is there anything terribly wrong with wanting to better your situation?"

He chuckled again. "Not at all, miss. But a person shouldn't rightly say they are a thing until they properly have become it, don't you agree?"

Maria said nothing, simply looked out at the snowbound city as the cab steamed northward.

Oblivious to, or perhaps uncaring of, Maria's reflective silence as the cab negotiated the valleys of black slush that had once been the major thoroughfare of a well-to-do neighborhood, the driver continued to expound at length on all manner of topics. *One does not need to buy a newspaper every day,* thought Maria, *merely take a steam-cab ride every lunchtime to find out the happenings of the day, with a liberal* (or perhaps not so liberal, in the case of this particular driver, who had already advocated the transportation of all opium addicts to Australia, the closing of the poor houses, and several army regiments being given control of London to aid the capture of Jack the Ripper) *dose of comment and opinion.* He broke off from his tirade to heave the cab into a narrow street of semidetached two-story houses with modest front gardens, and said, "Here we are, miss. Not-quite-Winchmore Hill."

It was noticeably colder here than the squares of Mayfair, insulated by the loving embrace of affluent London, and fresh snowfall threatened, heralded by a few flurries that played around the unlit gas lamps. Maria climbed out of the cab and paid the driver.

"Do you want me to wait, miss?"

She considered then said, "If you would. I shouldn't be long."

Then, double-checking the address on the letter, she let herself into the snow-covered front garden of the nearest house by the flaking iron gate and padded up the paved path, wondering whether she had not acted somewhat rashly and pondering what she was going to say when the black-painted door ahead of her was suddenly flung open.

"I thought I saw you walking up the path!" exclaimed the

man with center-parted hair and red-rimmed eyes who hung in the doorway. "Oh, my darling daughter Charlotte, welcome home!"

Maria was still trying to find the right words as the man—Henry Elmwood, she presumed—strode out in his shirtsleeves to embrace her, calling over his shoulder, "Martha! Martha! Oh, do come! It is Charlotte, come home to us."

Awkwardly, Maria extricated herself from Elmwood's grasp as a small, neat woman came to the door and regarded her coolly.

"Martha! Are you—ah, you're here! Look! It's—"

"It's not my daughter," said Mrs. Elmwood, her eyes flicking toward her husband. "For pity's sake, you are in the view of the whole street. Remove your arms and ask yourself how you could have possibly thought this was Charlotte."

"Mr. and Mrs. Elmwood . . . ," began Maria. She suddenly felt sure she couldn't have made a bigger mistake than coming here.

Elmwood stepped back and frowned. "Not Charlotte? But . . . then who?"

"Isn't it obvious?" said Mrs. Elmwood, her lip curling. "It's that unholy creation of Professor Hermann Einstein."

⚜

Mrs. Elmwood ushered Maria away from the twitching net curtains on the narrow street and into a small parlor dressed with slightly shabby furniture and a painted portrait of their daughter on the wall that brought her up short. She perched on the edge of the worn green sofa as Mr. Elmwood stared at her, unabashed.

"It really is quite remarkable," he said, sitting down on the other sofa without taking his eyes off Maria. "Did it talk the last time we saw it? And did it look so real?"

Maria felt the oils and fluids that coursed through her body thumping in her human brain. She thought she might be about to have her first headache. She put her hand to her temple and asked, "You have seen me before?"

"No matter how real it looks, I cannot believe that for a moment you thought it was our daughter," said Mrs. Elmwood. "A mother knows these things in a heartbeat."

Elmwood placed his hands on his knees. "Old Einstein must have been working on it, improving it. I say he's done a bang-up job."

"But what is it doing here?" asked his wife. "Has the professor sent it as some kind of ghastly joke?"

Maria put her hand up and closed her eyes momentarily. "Please," she said. "Please. You know Professor Einstein?"

Elmwood shook his head wonderingly and addressed her directly. "You can properly speak? You can understand me?"

"Henry," admonished Mrs. Elmwood, "of course it can't—"

"I can!" said Maria, more sharply than she had intended. "I can. Oh, I know this must be a shock for you. But I was unaware of your daughter's existence until you came to see Gideon. I apologize for appearing on your doorstep like this, but I had to know . . ."

"Gideon Smith?" said Mr. Elmwood. "He has sent you?"

She shook her head. "I am on my own errand. I reside with Mr. Smith. I am . . ." She paused. She was *what*? "I am his compatriot," she finished. "I aid him in his endeavors."

Mrs. Elmwood sat forward. "But why did he not tell us about you, when we visited him in Mayfair?"

And why did he not tell me *about* Charlotte? thought Maria. She said, "Please, I beg of you. Professor Einstein has been missing for a year. I must know what has become of him. I thought perhaps your daughter's resemblance to myself might have been mere coincidence, but you say you know the professor . . . ?"

Mrs. Elmwood narrowed her eyes. "It is more that you have a resemblance to our daughter. And that is no accident. Some years ago my husband applied for membership at a gentlemen's club in Holborn." She shot him a glare. "Always trying to better himself, my husband. Always trying to have us move in circles beyond our class and our finances."

"Please, Martha," hissed Mr. Elmwood. "I merely wanted to improve our situation. . . ."

Mrs. Elmwood ignored him. "An occasional member of this club, when he was in town, was your Professor Hermann Einstein. After some months of Henry drinking brandy and smoking cigars he could ill afford, the professor invited us to an exhibition he had planned at the club. That was the unveiling of his latest invention."

"Me," said Maria.

"You recall?" asked Mr. Elmwood.

Maria shook her head tightly. Mrs. Elmwood smiled sourly. "I am surprised you do not, if you are as *real* as my husband seems to think you have become. You caused quite a stir. Not least among ourselves when the Professor took off that drop cloth. My daughter almost fainted."

"She saw me?" asked Maria. "Charlotte?"

"She was only seventeen at the time. The professor had met her on several occasions at social functions, and I think he had become quite taken with her." She cast a disgusted glance at her husband. "I do believe in my heart you encouraged this, Henry. And the professor with a wife and son of his own back in Germany. Was there nothing you were not willing to sacrifice to improve your standing?"

"Martha," said Mr. Elmwood, a note of warning in his voice. He took up the tale. "We were shocked, of course, but also strangely touched. The work that had gone into it . . . you . . . was quite astonishing."

"Until you ran amok," said Mrs. Elmwood, raising an eyebrow.

Maria stared at her. "Ran amok?"

"No sooner had he wound you up with that huge key—which, I must say, sickened me to my stomach to see—and instructed you to waltz with him, but you began to thrash about and made for the doors. One poor man from the club who tried to bar your way received a fractured arm for his trouble."

Maria put her hand to her mouth, eyes wide. Mrs. Elmwood

said, "They found you three hours later, on Cleveland Street, I believe. You had been terrorizing the locals."

Cleveland Street. The home of poor old Annie Crook, who had loved the queen's grandson and ended up a mutilated husk on the banks of the Thames, thanks to Gideon's paymaster Mr. Walsingham, her brain removed and dispatched to Professor Einstein, who had used it to perfect his ultimate creation. Maria. And like a dog to its vomit she had blindly found her way back to Cleveland Street, driven by the final, fading memories of tragic Annie Crook.

"I didn't see old Einstein again for a few months," said Mr. Elmwood. "He was very apologetic when he came back to the club. Said he'd ironed out a few kinks in the . . . in you. Taken it . . . taken you all to pieces and put you back together again. Said you were safe and sound, now."

So that explained why Maria had no memories of her unveiling to society and her terrifying flight to Cleveland Street. Whatever *ironing of the kinks* the Professor had done must have all but wiped the memory from the stolen brain that resided in the strange Atlantic Artifact in her head. But a trace of it must have remained, allied with the ghosts of Annie Crook's memories, that forged the stolen, fractured dreams she'd had of London in the dark days between Professor Einstein disappearing and Gideon liberating her from the country house where the old scientist performed his secret tasks for the British Government.

As if Maria's very thoughts were laid bare in her eyes, Mr. Elmwood said, "Curious, though, that you are now residing in the company of Mr. Smith, whom we petitioned for help in finding Charlotte. When you said you were associated with him I thought perhaps there might be news. . . ."

"Mr. Smith has been searching for your daughter since Friday night," said Maria. "He went out to observe Markus Mesmer's performance."

"And has he interviewed the blackguard?"

"He is following several lines of inquiry," said Maria carefully. "I am sure he is giving the matter his undivided attention."

The day had grown old outside while they were talking, and in the gloom of the Elmwoods' parlor Maria had a sudden realization. Gideon had indeed rushed out on Friday to find the girl, barely even waiting for Maria to return from her exhausting battery of tests and examinations in Cornwall.

"Why do you think Mesmer singled out Charlotte for such treatment?" asked Maria.

"Perhaps he thought we were rich," sighed Mrs. Elmwood. "The party we attended was one thrown for the daughter of one of Henry's associates from that club. He had persuaded us to enroll Charlotte in the finishing school the girl attended, another expense. I knew no good would come of us reaching so far above our station."

"So merely for a ransom, then?"

"Perhaps," said Mr. Elmwood. "But Mesmer did seem somewhat interested in Charlotte. . . . One of his attendants—a rough-looking chap, Spanish I think—had with him a notebook and drew Mesmer's attention to something within it. I saw them both looking at whatever was within and then scrutinizing Charlotte across the room. It was almost as though they were looking for someone, and thought it might be her."

"Mr. Mesmer approached us and asked us all kinds of questions about Charlotte," said Mrs. Elmwood. "I fancy he was trying to be casual, but his approach was so stiff, so . . . *Germanic* . . . well. It felt more like an interrogation."

"What kind of questions?" asked Maria.

Mrs. Elmwood shrugged. "When she was born, what she had been like as a child, which schools she had attended. It almost felt as though he could catch us out, as though we were somehow *lying* about Charlotte being our daughter." She laughed mirthlessly. "It was very strange."

They sat in silence for a moment. There was a small cloth doll with buttons for eyes and a gingham dress lying on the sofa. It had pigtails of red wool. Mrs. Elmwood fixed her eyes on Maria's. "I made that for Charlotte when she was four years old. Even before she disappeared, she loved it and carried it everywhere in the house."

Maria looked at it, suddenly feeling very sad at the thought of the girl, out there, without her dear doll. "It's beautiful."

Mrs. Elmwood continued to stare at her. "You're really Professor Einstein's invention?"

"Automaton," said Mr. Elmwood, snapping his fingers. "That's the word old Einstein used."

"Yes," said Maria. "I am Professor Einstein's automaton."

"Sitting here, talking . . . I confess that my husband is right. You are an exceptional thing. I almost forgot you weren't a real young woman."

"Are you sure you're not Charlotte, hypnotized afresh to think you're this automaton?" asked Mr. Elmwood, screwing up his eyes.

Maria smiled. "I can take off my dress and open up my chest, if you like."

"That won't be necessary," said Mrs. Elmwood briskly. "I thank you for coming to update us on Mr. Smith's progress." She stood, and Maria did the same. Mrs. Elmwood said, "I would prefer it if you did not come again. It is too distressing, while Charlotte remains missing."

Maria bowed her head. "I understand."

As they walked to the door, Mrs. Elmwood said, "It is like a story I read as a child. The fairies whisked away a human child, and left in its place a changeling."

"Martha," said Mr. Elmwood, placing a hand on her arm.

She shrugged him off and glared at Maria. "You will never replace Charlotte, do you understand? It is not a fair exchange, a beautiful young woman for an unholy thing of brass cogs and copper pipes. It should be you who is gone, gone to the scrapyard, not a living young woman like my daughter."

Maria stepped backward against the door, surprised by the sudden ferocity of Mrs. Elmwood's words, at the angry tears flowing down the woman's cheeks.

"It should be you," said Mrs. Elmwood again, but more weakly. "Who would miss you? I just want my daughter back. I want my little girl."

Mr. Elmwood began to steer his wife toward the stairs, looking over his shoulder. "I am sorry. Come on Martha, let me take you upstairs for a lie down. You can let yourself out . . . uh . . . ?"

"Maria."

"Maria. Thank you." He turned to help his sobbing wife up the stairs. "Come on, darling, it's all right. The Hero of the Empire is on the case. Mr. Gideon Smith will not let us down."

Maria quickly let herself into the cold snow flurries. A little way up the street she could make out the dark shape of her steam-cab.

It should be you who is gone.

Who would miss you?

Mr. Gideon Smith will not let us down.

The metal and glass in her chest weighing her down more heavily than any human heart could, Maria stifled a sob of her own and ran toward the waiting vehicle, the rag doll still unwittingly clutched in her hand.

13

THE MAN WHO KNEW TOO MUCH

He stared at the monster, which paced up and down in the short space that its chain tether allowed and beheld him with furious yellow eyes, saliva dripping from its teeth, until the man standing by the brazier finally spoke, wrenching his attention from the beast.

"It appears you will not have to go out into the snow after all, Deeptendu. Providence has brought us meat for our pet."

The monkey leaped onto a simple wooden stool and then to the shoulder of the man, who fed it a nut from a paper bag in his hand. He had a lined, weathered face and dark, long hair pulled into a plaited ponytail that hung over his collarbone. He was perhaps fifty years of age, lithe and athletic of build beneath a rough cotton shirt and worn leather trousers, a crudely stitched collarless jacket of tanned hide over his simple outfit. His right leg ended at the knee; beneath was a thick rod of wood, capped with tin or some other malleable metal at the foot.

"You mean to feed me to your tyrannosaur?" he said, glancing around the dimly lit cellar at the one the man had addressed as Deeptendu, one of four who had hauled him into the room. He was swarthy, too, but more obviously Indian than the one-legged man. He was tall and wore a length of black cloth wound into a turban on his head, and he regarded Smith with dark eyes that sat closely together above a hooked nose. There were three other men in turbans, one fatter than his fellows, one with a cruel-looking scar that ran from above his right eye to the left corner of his mouth, giving him a sneering expression. All four wore loose cotton trousers and long-sleeved linen shirts, their feet shod in leather sandals.

The one called Deeptendu flexed his fists in front of him, and Smith saw a thin leather thong snap tight between them. "Do not fear," said Deeptendu. "We will kill you first."

The man with the ponytail held up his hand, one eyebrow raised in his deeply tanned face. "Wait, friend." He scrutinized Smith. "Tyrannosaur, you say? You know this beast?"

Smith turned back to look at the monster, which had settled down expectantly to wait for its meal. Memories bobbed maddeningly around the periphery of his understanding. He said, "I met one, once. A little bigger, though." He smiled, despite himself. "Its mother, perhaps."

The man fed the monkey another nut and murmured to it, "Well, what a surprising thing you've led to us, Jip."

"Who are you?" asked Smith. "What are you up to, skulking in the shadows like this, with a monster chained up in the sewers?"

Before he could even register that the man had moved, the one with the scar had crossed the space between them and slapped him sharply across the face. "Do not disrespect Fereng in this way!"

Smith felt himself drop to a defensive crouch, but the turbaned man had stepped back. He put a hand to his lip and glanced at the blood coloring his fingertips. "Fereng?" he said, looking to the one-legged man. "You?"

"A name." He shrugged. "One of many I have used." He raised his head in a sharp upward nod at the scar-faced man. "Kalanath. That is no way to treat our guest."

Kalanath's face contorted unpleasantly. "Guest, Fereng? I thought he was the monster's dinner."

Smith's stomach rumbled, and he realized it was a long time since he himself had eaten. Fereng heard it, too, and said, "You are hungry? Come, sit with us. We have a little dhal simmering. Then you can tell me what you're doing down here and how you know so much about our little pet."

The tyrannosaur howled in apparent indignation at losing out on its meal. The youngest of the turbaned men, who looked

no older than Smith, sighed. "Does this mean we have to go
and find the monster food, Fereng?"

"I'm afraid so, Naakesh."

"After we ourselves have eaten, though?" asked the fatter
one. "I am famished, and it does not do to hunt on an empty
stomach." He bellowed a laugh. "You always come back with
more than you need."

Fereng laughed, too, and sat down cross-legged by the brazier, which Smith saw had a round metal pot suspended above
the licking flames. "Quite true, Phoolendu. Let us sample this
dhal you have cooked up, friend. The beast can wait a little
while longer."

Smith wiped clean the small, cracked bowl with the last of the
thin bread; he'd finished three servings of the deliciously spicy
vegetable dhal, and gratefully accepted a canteen of water from
Fereng to slake his thirst and ease the pleasant burning in his
mouth. Sitting cross-legged on a simple mat, facing the warmth
of the burning brazier, he felt as though he were thawing out
for the first time since the incident that had robbed him of his
memories and knowledge of himself. Despite the looming
presence of the tyrannosaur—which had curled up like a dog,
its reptilian tail counting out beats on the stone floor, as though
it were sulking at being robbed of its dinner—and the fact that
a scant hour before he had been about to be garroted, Smith
felt strangely safe for the first time in days. He felt suddenly
sleepy, and he stifled a yawn. "Why have you not killed me?"
he asked.

Fereng, rubbing his thigh above where it was strapped into
a leather cup from which the wooden extension protruded,
shrugged. "I don't know. I haven't yet decided that I won't."

Smith tensed, but he felt that the man was joking. He
asked, "Who are you?"

"You first," said Fereng.

Smith shrugged. "I cannot remember. Something has

robbed me of any memories save for the last few days . . . what day is it, anyway?"

Fereng said, "Naakesh? Do you still have the newspaper you procured this morning?"

The young man reached behind him. "Most of it. I used the insides to light the fire."

He passed it over to Smith. It was the *Illustrated London Argus*, and the dateline read *Monday, December 15, 1890.* "Monday," he said. "I think . . . Saturday is the first I can remember." A headline caught his eye among the dense forest of type: BELLE OF THE AIRWAYS ARRESTED ON CHARGE OF MURDER MOST FOUL, but before he could read on or work out why it gave him a sudden shudder, Fereng was speaking again.

"You remember nothing? Not even your name?"

"Smith seems to ring bells, but nothing more."

Fereng rubbed the salt-and-pepper whiskers on his chin. "Smith. Suitably anonymous. And what have you been doing since Saturday, Smith?"

He thought of the mob who had tried to string him up from the lamppost, of the shrill whistles of the policemen who had chased him into the sewers, of the bloodthirsty cries of the crowd who had believed him to be Jack the Ripper, of the gruesome toshers Tait and Lyall and the dismal end they had planned for him.

"Running away, mostly," he said.

Fereng leaned forward; the monkey, Jip, scaled his outstretched arm and settled happily on his shoulder, combing through his hair. "Running from who?"

Smith shrugged. "Everyone, it seems. The police. Criminals. Those men in the sewers . . . they were going to cook me. Even you had designs on throttling me, and I'm not yet convinced you won't."

Fereng smiled. "Don't worry, Smith. I think you are far too intriguing to feed to my pet." He reached out and squeezed Smith's bicep. "Strong, too. Evidently a gentleman of some

166   David Barnett

stripe, by the quality of your dress and grooming. And something of a fugitive. I have a feeling you could be very useful to me, Smith."

Smith met his gaze. "But who are you?" He waved his arm around. "What does all this mean?"

Fereng leaned forward, his eyes shining in the light from the brazier. "It means revenge, Smith. They say it is a dish best served cold, and my fury has been chilling for twenty years. Now, as London shivers and stokes its fires in the worst winter most can remember, ice clogs the Thames and water freezes in the standpipes." He raised his arms. "Hell has finally frozen over, Smith, which means it is time for London to finally reap the bitter seeds of wrath it sowed within me so long ago."

"Does such venomous melodrama make you want to flee, Smith?" asked Fereng. "Would you rather take your chances with cannibalistic troglodytes or pitchfork-waving mobs?"

Smith glanced at the dark tunnel that led back to the sewer system, at the dinosaur glowering at him from its corner, at the dark gazes of the four turbaned men. "I don't have much choice, do I? You aren't going to let me leave, are you?" he asked quietly. "Not now that I know about all this."

"You do present something of a problem," agreed Fereng. "You do, as they say, know too much. Which is somewhat funny for a man who knows so little. And it leaves me with a choice: either I feed you to my pet, as originally planned . . ."

"Or?"

Fereng smiled. "Or I ask you to join us."

"Join you?" said Smith, miserably staring into the brazier. "I still don't know what you are up to."

"Up to, Smith? I have already told you. I am up to vengeance." He braced his hand on the shoulder of the youngest of his men, Naakesh, and hauled himself up to stand on his good leg and his wooden stump. "But perhaps you wish to know why?"

Smith nodded. "You are English, despite your appearance. How did you come to be in the company of four Indians?"

Fereng laughed, his eyes shining. "Not mere Indians, Smith. Thuggee. Do you know what that means?"

He searched the black ocean of his memory. "Assassins," he said. "Murderers."

The four men laughed. Fereng nodded. "So the stories would have it. Roaming gangs of criminals who travel the highways of the subcontinent, falling in with travelers and insinuating themselves in their confidence until—"

There was a sudden, sharp twang that made Smith blink and jump. Deeptendu was grinning at him, the thin leather thong he had displayed earlier held taut between his fists, still resonating.

"We would strangle them!" said the fat one, Phoolendu, cheerfully licking his bowl. "Sometimes we would do it so hard that their heads would fall clean off!"

Smith looked at each of the men. "Why?"

Kalanath leaned forward, the scar tissue on his face seeming to glint in the firelight. "For money. Food. Gold. And sometimes just because we didn't like the look of them."

Smith tore his gaze from the man's scar and met his eyes. "And, presumably, you don't like me."

"Not especially."

He looked back to Fereng. "You have fallen in with murderers, then, and assassins. As I said."

"Kalanath is fooling with you, or at least not telling you the whole story. Deeptendu. Tell Smith why you kill."

Deeptendu closed his close-set eyes and placed a hand on his breast. "For every life a Thuggee takes, the return of Kali is delayed by one thousand years."

"Kali?"

"The mother goddess of time and change," said Fereng. "The consort of Shiva. The black one who is beyond time, who will dance in the ruins. Every life a Thuggee takes flows through the cosmic river of the shakti like wine through water, and appeases Kali for the blink of her eye. Which, fortunately, is a hundred lifetimes or more here on Earth."

There was a moment's silence in the dim room, save for the grunting of the tyrannosaur. Smith looked over his shoulder at it. "So how did four Thuggee assassins come to be lurking in the sewers of London? And what of *that* thing? Did you bring that from India?"

Phoolendu laughed. "Nothing like that in India. Elephants and tigers, yes. And snakes. Plenty of snakes."

As though knowing it was being talked about, the beast began to push itself up on its tiny forearms, sniffing in their direction, a rumble in its throat.

"I think we have decided that we are not going to feed you to it," said Fereng, his monkey Jip chattering on his shoulder. "Which means, I am afraid, that we are going to have to secure some meat for it. Kalanath, Naakesh, see what you can find near the markets. Be silent and invisible, like the wind. Deeptendu, you should go and search the sewers, see if there is any sign of these men who would have had Smith for lunch. I would not want them venturing too close to us."

Deeptendu looked down his hooked nose at Smith. "What of him? He may try to run, or attack you."

"Phoolendu will be here," said Fereng.

The fat Thuggee slapped his belly and pointed a warning finger at Smith. "Don't think I won't snap your neck and garrote you, Smith, because I will."

"I do not doubt it," said Smith, rising stiffly to stand beside Fereng.

"Besides," said Fereng, "where would he run to? I think Smith and I have come to an understanding, or are about to. He will be staying, and will mean us no harm. Indeed, I feel he will be a boon to us."

As the three Thuggees began to edge around the beast toward the tunnel that led to the sewers, Phoolendu called, "Oh! See if you can find some of those small round savory bread cakes, the ones with holes in the top. Oh, what are they called?"

"Crumpets?" offered Smith.

Phoolendu rose and slapped him on the shoulder. "Indeed! Crumpets!"

Kalanath sneered and said testily, "And anything else, while we are out?"

"Butter would be good," said Phoolendu. "For the crumpets. And milk, for the chai."

Kalanath glared at him and indicated with a sharp movement of his head that the others should follow him into the tunnel. When they had gone, Phoolendu gathered the dishes and took them over to a bowl in the corner, which he filled with water from a pitcher, and began to scrub them with a piece of cloth.

"Magnificent, isn't it?" said Fereng, gazing at the tyrannosaur.

The monster narrowed its yellow eyes and gave an exploratory tug with its huge neck, but the chain that shackled it to the wall remained firm.

"If it didn't come with you from India, then where?" asked Smith.

Fereng gave him a sidelong look. "Don't think I haven't considered the possibility that you might be a spy, you know, Smith."

Smith looked at him. "A spy? For whom?"

"For those who would rather I stayed as dead as they believe me to be."

"Your enemies? Who are they?"

Fereng smiled. "I will tell you, Smith, once you have proved yourself. I would be a fool if I hadn't considered the possibility that they had already found me, and sent you to infiltrate. But my gut feeling is that you are not a spy, Smith. And I have survived for twenty years on my gut feelings." He cocked his head, and the monkey began to nuzzle his ear. "I like you,

Smith. I feel some kind of kinship with you, though I have no idea why."

"Fereng is not your real name. What is it?"

"It is so long since I have used it that I have almost forgotten. Almost, but not quite. It isn't something you need to know, for now."

"But who *were* you? What took you away for twenty years? From where comes this desire for revenge?"

"Who was I . . . ?" said Fereng, a distant look in his eyes. "Why, Smith, you would hardly believe me. Who was I? Twenty years ago, Smith, I was a Hero of the Empire."

"Are you all right, Smith?"

Fereng put his hand out to steady Smith, who had suddenly staggered as though felled by a blow. He brushed off the helping hand and put his hands to his face as a memory exploded in his mind.

Are heroes born or made? What if we took away all your heroic doings? What if we wiped the slate clean? What if I convinced you that you were not the Hero of the Empire, but the enemy of Britain? Would you be able to fight that?

"You . . . what you said . . . a hero?"

Fereng helped Smith to sit down on the floor and regarded him quizzically.

"Of a fashion. Why does that affect you so?"

Smith shook his head. "I don't know. For a moment I thought . . . but it's gone." He squeezed the bridge of his nose tightly between thumb and forefinger.

"You look exhausted, Smith. When did you last sleep?"

He looked up at Fereng. "Sleep? I can't remember. Not proper sleep."

Fereng gestured at the corner opposite Phoolendu, who was whistling as he dried the bowls with a length of cloth. "There are blankets and rolls there. You should have some rest."

Smith smiled humorlessly. "And I will be garroted in my sleep, no doubt."

"You don't believe that, Smith. You are safe here. Perhaps more safe than you have been for days." Fereng fed Jip another nut. "I give you my word that no harm will befall you. Have some rest, and then we will talk again."

"You said something about proving myself. . . ."

"Later, perhaps tomorrow. I have waited a long time for my revenge, Smith, and I am not about to rush it now. I have plans to put into place."

"Your revenge . . . if you were a hero of the Empire, as you say, then you have been abandoned, or betrayed. Your revenge will be against Britain, or her government."

Fereng smiled. "You are very perceptive, Smith."

"And that thing . . . the tyrannosaur? It is the key to your vengeance?"

"I did not know that when I arrived back on these shores, but yes. I trust in providence, Smith, and providence rarely lets me down. The tyrannosaur is indeed the sword with which I shall smite my enemies. And when this is done, there shall be enough blood spilled to ensure that Kali's return is delayed for another six hundred and seventy thousand years!"

"That's very precise," said Smith, stifling a yawn.

Fereng smiled. "Neither of us shall have to worry about anything by then, in any case. Now you are exhausted, Smith. Sleep. No harm shall befall you."

He nodded and crept to the corner, laying out a roll and pulling a blanket over himself. Within moments, he had sunk into the wide, black, rolling ocean of his darkened mind.

INTERMEDIO:
PERSISTENCE OF VISION

They looked for patterns, of course. *Jack the Ripper only kills prostitutes* was the main fiction, which seemed to suit all concerned. It kept the lower classes subdued with fear; it gave some assurance to good girls that they would not be targeted, so long as they stayed away from Whitechapel—and what well-bred girl would be found in Whitechapel anyway, after dark or not?

Jack the Ripper did not only kill prostitutes. As the intermedio claimed him and he stalked the snowy streets, he considered the last girl he had killed in Whitechapel, mere yards from where the vigilante gangs patrolled. He knew she was not a prostitute because she had told him so as she begged for her life, weeping as she urged him to reconsider, telling him that she was a match girl and that she had three young ones at home.

Every woman in Whitechapel had borne children. They bred like rats. The only remarkable thing was that she had three who were still alive. It didn't save her life, though. Perhaps when her eviscerated body was discovered, her children would be put upon the mercy of the parish. They would have a better chance at life that way.

Still, they looked for patterns. If the girl was not a prostitute, they ignored her death, because murders were ten a penny in the stews and slums at the best of times. Resisting the lure of selling her flesh for coppers would, ultimately, cost her immortality. The victims of Jack the Ripper would live on through lurid newspaper reports and endlessly repeated gossip, the incandescence of their deaths on the public consciousness.

A murdered match girl with three hungry children at home was beneath anyone's notice. He almost felt sorry for her.

Death by a swift cut along the forehead was another pattern that had enthused the press and public. That was why he had been quietly experimenting with different methods of dispatching his victims, greater use of the surgical instruments. It confounded the police's search for patterns, allowed him to try new methods with murders that were sometimes ascribed to Jack the Ripper, sometimes not.

But a change was coming, he knew, and he had to be ready. He had to decide what to do, how to continue. If indeed he should continue. If indeed he was able to stop.

They saw things that weren't there; they created patterns from chaos. It was like that parlor game illusion, the thaumotrope. A distinctly different drawing on either side of a piece of stiff card, the card twirled rapidly by way of a piece of taut string. The eye was fooled, seeing something that was not there, a conglomeration of the two drawings that came together to form something else entirely. The scientists called it persistence of vision, an insistence of the eye to continue to see what was no longer there, even as it was assimilating a new thing. The eye brought them together.

Because, if there was no pattern, then what was the point? The public, and the police, were brought up on fictions, tidy and patterned. Things had to make sense, because if they didn't . . . then Jack the Ripper could be anybody. And perhaps anybody could be Jack the Ripper.

But things would change. A pattern would emerge, and it would give them the breakthrough they needed, and things would have to change.

14

THE PROFESSOR OF ADVENTURE

It was the barometers that finally brought Inspector George Lestrade's headache brimming over to a point that he thought he might have to excuse himself, take a steam-cab home, and lock himself in a darkened room until Sunday had rolled around once again.

There were dozens of barometers, perhaps even a couple hundred, littering the cellar of the house in Kennington, which had been turned into a simple makeshift workshop. A wooden table, of the kind used by decorators for pasting wallpaper, was on the side of the room facing the staircase, overflowing with barometers of all shapes, styles, and sizes. Plain copper barometers, ornate wooden ones, decorative ones carved with cats chasing mice along their edges, industrial barometers with steel casings.

All of them with their faces smashed in.

Broken glass crunched under Lestrade's boots as he paced up and down the cellar, putting him queasily in mind of walking on the backs of crushed insects. His constables had rigged up a sequence of oil lamps hanging from the low ceiling, but the light they shed gave him no inkling of what he was really looking at, save for the shattered carcasses of barometers, all smashed to smithereens, piled high on the long table and spilling onto the stone floor.

Lestrade stroked his mustache and closed his eyes. *Ratty*, they called him in the station canteen, though never, of course, to his face. On account of his tiny, dark eyes. That wasn't what she said, of course, his secret love. He'd been shocked when Aloysius Bent had skirted around the issue the other day, because if it became common knowledge Lestrade would be ruined, consorting with a woman like that. But he suspected Bent knew far less than he was intimating.

Like stars, she said. *Your eyes are like stars. Did you know that the light from some of those stars took so long to reach the Earth that sometimes the star was long dead?*

"Like ghosts, then," he'd pondered, as they had lain on their backs on a blanket on Clapham Common in the dead of night, the crowns of their heads touching as though they were telling the time, six o'clock, his feet to the south and hers to the north.

"The ghosts of stars." She'd laughed delightedly, rolling her body like the hand of a clock until she was alongside him, half past six. She kissed him. "That's what your eyes are like. The ghosts of dead stars."

"Sir?"

Lestrade blinked at the sound of Constable Ayres descending the cellar stairs with a heavy footfall. The sweet memory had forced away his headache; now it came flooding back, as though a stopper had been released from a bottle.

Ayres wrinkled his nose. "Pew. What's that smell, sir?"

Lestrade waved his hand at the smashed barometers. "Mercury, I dare say, Constable. Though if you are going to ask me why I think a man would smash up so many barometers, please do not. I have no idea."

"Gives a man a headache, that smell, in an unventilated place like this."

Lestrade smiled. "Shall we go back upstairs, Constable?"

The inspector followed Ayres up the narrow staircase, which ended in a wooden door that opened into the kitchen. The house in Kennington was spacious without being grand, functionally decorated—it lacked a woman's touch, in Lestrade's opinion, as had his own house until very recently, so he knew the signs—and well appointed. Probably worth a bit of cash. Ayres bobbed from foot to foot, as though it physically pained him to be standing on turf so far from the East End. Come to that, Lestrade wasn't quite sure why the constable was here at all. The inspector had been sent down because, suddenly and most unfortunately, the boundaries of his patch seemed to have been stretched out of all recognition. And it was all down to that bloody Jack the Ripper, and Professor Stanford Rubicon's dead maid. Killers who mutilated young women in the fog-wreathed streets of Whitechapel were not exactly a pleasant matter, but at least it was what he was used to. Now he'd been caught up in all this rather surprising business concerning Rowena Fanshawe, and the murder charge they had her up on. Lestrade would have been reluctant to admit it—especially to Aloysius Bent—but he had always been something of a secret aficionado of the penny bloods in general and *World Marvels & Wonders* in particular; he'd followed the adventures since the Captain Lucian Trigger days. Now Professor Miescher— Lestrade had known he was going to be trouble the minute he'd seen him—had somehow matched up the two lots of bloodstains. The ones found in Rubicon's laboratories after the break-in and before the maid had turned up dead were evidently the same as the blood from under the fingernails of one Edward Gaunt, who had been found murdered in this very house apparently at the hands of Rowena Fanshawe.

Which meant Rowena Fanshawe had for some reason been involved in the burglary at Professor Rubicon's rooms, which in turn meant that for reasons he didn't fully understand, she had now become Inspector Lestrade's problem.

"What brings you to Kennington, Constable?" asked Lestrade. "A social visit in the neighborhood?"

Ayres frowned. "No, sir. You said you were coming here, and I had something to tell you."

Lestrade sighed. Why did he have to be surrounded by such dullards? "Of course, Constable. Out with it, then."

Ayres withdrew his notebook from his overcoat. "We interviewed all the patrons of the Golden Ball who were present in the establishment on the night that Emily Dawson died. There were two gentlemen in particular who we were interested in, sir; they had propositioned Miss Dawson quite crudely as she passed the public house. We thought they might have been in-volved in her unfortunate fate. But we interviewed independent witnesses who confirmed that although the men had engaged Miss Dawson in ribald conversation and the girl had indeed appeared frightened at their behavior, they returned to the public house after speaking to her."

Lestrade shrugged. "Well, we knew we were dealing with a ripper."

"On that note, sir," said Ayres. "We have two independent witnesses who have given testimony about a person seen in the vicinity of the alley where Miss Dawson was found. Both report seeing an individual dressed completely in black with some kind of hood or cowl over their face."

Lestrade felt immediately cheered. This was the first time anyone had offered any kind of description of anyone possibly connected with the Ripper killings. Perhaps this was the break-through he had been waiting for.

"Get these witnesses into the station," said Lestrade. "And have the artist come down. Let's put together as near as dam-nation the best portrait of this masked man that we can."

"Something else, sir," said Ayres. "The morgue sent this in. It's a note they found clutched in Miss Dawson's hand. Only a scrap of paper, scribbled with what looks like a makeup pen-cil. One of those things the ladies use on their eyes." He mimed a flapping motion across his face.

"Yes, yes," said Lestrade. "What did it say?"

"They think she might have written it between being at-tacked and actually dying," said Ayres. "On account of the blood on it. Only trouble is, it doesn't make much sense."

Ayres withdrew a brown paper evidence bag from his in-side pocket and handed it over. Lestrade teased open the edges and peered in, twisting it until he could see the words scrawled on the tiny square of bloodstained paper.

"Lost yon toe," he said. "What on earth could that mean?"

"And ain't that an effing mystery!" boomed a jovial voice behind him.

Inspector Lestrade sighed. What was Aloysius Bent doing here?

⁜

"Why is it," said Inspector Lestrade, rubbing his eyes with his thumb and forefinger, "that whenever I attend a crime scene you are there, Mr. Bent? Perhaps I should have you arrested as a suspect."

"Suspected of what?" asked Bent.

"Everything," said Lestrade. "But chiefly, getting right on my nerves."

Bent guffawed. Truth to tell, he could have heard everything he needed to by lurking in the hallway outside the kitchen. If that fool constable was stupid enough to leave the front door swinging open behind him, it would have been positively rude of Aloysius Bent to ignore it. But even after listening at the kitchen door a good while—and what was all this about broken barometers? He'd not quite grasped that—he couldn't resist making an entrance to needle Lestrade. Having done so, he almost felt like giving old George a break; the inspector looked absolutely exhausted. All that Jack the Ripper business and now this. But at least Lestrade could clock off every night. With Rowena's trial underway, Bent couldn't see much rest in store this side of Christmas. And it would not be a very merry holiday if the Belle of the Airways ended up convicted of murder.

After the first morning in court, Bent had taken a carriage up to the East End to pay a little visit to Professor Stanford Rubicon.

The Professor of Adventure threw open the doors to his Bishopsgate complex himself; evidently, the Christmas season and the manner with which his former housekeeper had been dispatched had combined to ensure he had not yet procured a replacement maid.

"All right, Rubicon," said Bent, stamping his feet on the doorstep and blowing on his fingers. "You got a pot of coffee on, or maybe a decanter of whisky?"

Stanford, in his usual outfit of multi-pocketed overalls pushed into shiny leather boots, glared at Bent from the doorway, his beard bristling. "You! You're that damned journalist!"

"Calm down, Rubicon," he sighed. "It's me, Aloysius Bent. Saved your arse from the lost world a few months ago. Remember?"

Rubicon scrabbled in a breast pocket for a pair of wire-framed spectacles and hung them over his ears, scrutinizing the writer. "Ah! Bent! My apologies. I have a wonderful memory for names, but a shocking recollection of faces." He paused. "Or is that the other way around? No matter; come in, come in. I have a pot of coffee on the go, or I would have if I could get the blasted stove to work. You wouldn't have a look at it for me, would you?"

Like all men of academia—though once Bent had half-heartedly tried to source the provenance of Rubicon's so-called professorship, and was convinced it was merely bluster and fakery—the broad, bearded man had little knowledge of even the simplest domestic affairs. *It's a pity his housemaid got her head sliced off,* thought Bent as he fiddled with the stove. It was merely a gas tap not fully turned on, but he shook his head and rubbed his chin. "I can see the problem, Rubicon old chap. The, ah, flange has become uncoupled from the, erm, distressor. Going to take a professional." He smiled warmly. "Best just to break the scotch out, I'd say."

Over generous measures poured by Bent himself, he commiserated with the Professor of Adventure over the murder of Miss Emily Dawson. He took a deep drink and said, "Makes you wonder what she was doing out there on a Friday night. That Golden Ball is renowned as a rough-arse sort of place."

"She was coming to find me at my club," said Rubicon, staring into the honeyed depths of his whisky. "To inform me about the burglary."

"Ah, yes," said Bent, watching him closely over the rim of his glass. "I had heard something about that. Makes you wonder why she didn't alert the constabulary first before coming to find you. It was such a foul night into the bargain."

Rubicon harrumphed through his beard. "Yes, well, much of my work here is very secret, Mr. Bent. I daresay she thought she was doing the right thing. Poor girl."

"Speaking of poor girls," said Bent, "I spent the morning at the Old Bailey." He topped up Rubicon's glass. "Rowena Fanshawe is up on a murder charge."

"Terrible business," agreed the Professor. "Met the girl a few times myself on various escapades. Hard to imagine that she'd murder a fellow who'd done her no ill."

"Hmm," said Bent. "Odd thing is, though, they're saying she might have had something to do with the burglary here. Charged her with it, in fact. Now, where could they have gotten that idea?"

Rubicon finished his drink and Bent refilled his glass, waving away the Professor's halfhearted protestations. "Well, that is fascinating stuff. Old Lestrade at the Commercial Road station sent some fellow around here, German or Austrian, I think he said he was."

"Miescher, was it?"

"That's the one. You'll probably have heard about all this deoxyribo-doo-dah." He shook his head. "Amazing stuff."

"I had heard," said Bent. "Just remind me. . . ."

Rubicon took another long drink. "This Miescher fellow, he reckons we all have this . . . what did he call it . . . sort of a signature in our blood. He says from one drop of blood he can more or less match it with a sample taken from a living person."

Bent narrowed his eyes. "More or less match it?"

"It's not an exact science, the way he tells it," said Rubicon, accepting another drink without protest. "But if he, say, had a drop of claret from one of us two, our blood signatures are so different that he'd be able to tell who the drop had come from."

"Fascinating," agreed Bent. "And there was blood here, then, which he matched up to Rowena's?"

"Blood?" Rubicon laughed richly. "Oh, Mr. Bent, come and have a look at this."

There was indeed a large, heart-shaped stain the color of wine in the center of the rug on the floor of what seemed to be a huge square laboratory. "I'd have had it cleaned, but the constabulary said to leave it for a bit. Strictly speaking I'm not supposed to come in here, much less bring anyone else. I think a constable was meant to come around and take the rug away today. Evidence and all that."

But Bent's attention had been diverted to the large upright cage with strong steel bars against the wood-paneled wall, its hinged door hanging loose and mangled. "Now what on earth is that for?"

"Shark cage," said Rubicon brusquely. "They lower it down in the tropics so I can observe the predators. Now, we really shouldn't be here. . . ."

Bent raised an eyebrow. "A shark cage? With the lock on the outside? Doesn't seem very practical, Rubicon."

Rubicon opened his mouth then closed it again. "It's a foreign design," he said lamely.

Bent allowed himself a smile and threw down the last of his whisky. "And did you tell Inspector Lestrade that what the burglars had nicked was a real, live effing dinosaur? About . . . ooh, what would it be, now? Three months old?"

Rubicon frowned, looked as though he was about to shout at Bent, then slumped. "No, I haven't gotten around to telling them that yet. How did you know?"

"I was there, Rubicon. I was with Gideon Smith when he rescued you and Charles Darwin from that godforsaken rock in the middle of the Pacific Ocean. I saw those beasts, Rubicon. And I saw something else, as well."

"Oh?"

"You, in the engine room of the ship we sailed off in, the *Lady Jane*. And you had an egg, Rubicon. Did you know that bloody monster swam all the way to California looking for its stolen baby and nearly had us for supper? And all the while you were playing surrogate daddy back here in London, raising a baby effing tyrannosaur. Did you sit on the bloody egg yourself?"

"Of course not," mumbled Rubicon. "I used a heated incubator."

"And how big is a three-month-old tyrannosaur, anyway?"

"Seven, perhaps eight feet tall."

"Jesus effing Christ," said Bent. "And that thing's loose in London."

Rubicon forced a humorless smile. "If it were loose we'd have heard about it by now, Mr. Bent. Someone has stolen Tiddles and has hidden him away for nefarious purposes we can only guess at."

Bent stared at him, but not at the horrific possibilities of who had stolen an eight-foot Tyrannosaurus rex and what they planned to do with it. He said slowly, "You called it Tiddles?"

By rights, Bent should have told Lestrade about the dinosaur, but looking at him in the kitchen of Edward Gaunt's house in Kennington, he really didn't feel like adding to the inspector's woes. Besides, if the coppers had failed to work out what was stolen from Professor Rubicon's laboratories on Bishopsgate, then that was their problem. Bent wasn't about to do their job for them, not when he had so much else on his plate.

Instead he said, "She didn't do it, you know, George. Rowena. She didn't break into Rubicon's lab, and she didn't kill Edward Gaunt."

"That'll be for the jury to decide," sighed Lestrade.

There was a brisk knock at the door and the inspector said, "Who on earth is this, now? It's busier than the Victoria ziggurat here today."

Constable Ayres went off to answer the door, and Lestrade said, "For what it's worth, Bent, and just between us, I find it hard to believe that someone of Rowena Fanshawe's standing would be mixed up in such base criminality. But the prosecution would not have proceeded to trial if they did not believe there was a case to answer."

"What do you know of this Miescher fellow and his new blood techniques, George?"

Lestrade stroked his mustache. "Hmm. The judge has ruled that admissible, then?"

"He's considering it, going to decide tomorrow. What happened to good, old-fashioned, honest policing?"

"A very good question, Mr. Bent. Makes a good, old-fashioned, honest copper like myself wonder what his place is in this brave new world. To be quite honest, I don't even know why they've bothered me with this, considering all this Jack the Ripper business is set to blow like a powder keg."

Bent grinned. "Come around to my way of thinking, then, George?"

Lestrade nodded unhappily. "I thought this infernal Lizzie Strutter and her prostitutes' strike would be the best thing to happen to the East End. I was wrong and you were right, Bent." He lowered his voice. "Assaults of a sexual nature have doubled since Saturday. Trebled, even. And the populace is taking matters into its own hands. My officers found four men hanging from lampposts last night. Anyone who looks like an East Ender is being lynched, Bent." He held up his hand, his thumb and forefinger an inch apart. "We're this far from anarchy in Whitechapel."

Constable Ayres announced his return with a cough and said, "Sir? You won't want to hear this, but it's that Doctor Watson and his mental patient. . . ."

It was snowing again, and Doctor Watson stood under a wide, black umbrella, looking helplessly at Lestrade. "I am sorry, Inspector. My client was most insistent. At the Commercial Road station they said you were here. . . ."

"Wagging tongues at the station, George." Bent chuckled. "They told me you were here as well."

Lestrade put his head into his hands, and Bent watched the Great Detective with interest. A fruitcake, to be sure, but who was to say he hadn't had some insight into something everyone else had missed? After all, they'd said Aloysius Bent was mad when he kept trying to tell everyone there was something strange about the way Annie Crook had died.

The Great Detective was dancing again, standing straight one moment then lunging forward, his knee bent, then shuffling his feet in a most precise manner. Bent frowned; the movements definitely put him in mind of something.

"It's the footprints," explained Doctor Watson apologetically. "He says he's seen them at three Jack the Ripper crime scenes now. He's mimicking the movements that must have made them, he says."

Lestrade took a deep breath. "Doctor Watson. Please get him away from—"

Bent waved him down. "Hang on, George. There's something awfully effing . . . get him to do it again, Watson."

The Great Detective obliged, running through the almost graceful sequence, whispering to himself, "Pass . . . traverse . . . pivot . . . slope . . . pass . . . ha!"

"Eff!" yelled Bent as the Great Detective lunged forward on his final shout, his arm extended toward Bent's throat, glaring down the length of his sleeve and over his hand that seemed to clutch an invisible rod, or stick, or . . .

"Oh, eff," breathed Bent. "Of course."

15

TURNING NASTY

 She had gone to sleep Lottie the whore and awakened somewhere closer to Charlotte the lost girl, sitting bolt upright in the filthy blankets heaped upon the wooden bed frame. She had looked around wildly, the stench of the dark, cold room assaulting her senses, the scrabbling of vermin in the woodwork almost tearing a scream from her delicate mouth. The walls were bare, streaked with damp and mold and pocked with holes, and scurrying cockroaches climbed them with studied determination.

Where was she?

The sounds of life trickled through the shuttered window—which she noticed was fastened with a big iron padlock—though life she was unused to. The singsong voices of barrow boys, the shouts of flower girls, the raucous laughter of drunks. Thin daylight leaked through the slats of the shutters. What time was it? What day was it? There were seven other beds cheek-by-jowl in the tiny room, all of them neatly made, the blankets tucked in and turned down.

Lizzie Strutter likes to keep a tidy house, she remembered someone saying before she slept. But if others had slept in this freezing dormitory with her, they had long gone. She was alone.

Almost.

Charlotte pulled the blanket to her throat with a gasp as she realized there was a man sitting on a chair the wrong way around, leaning on the high back and watching her. With a small but glinting knife he carved slices from a red apple and deposited them in his wide, black mouth.

Henry, she remembered. *Henry Savage.* And with the recollection of his name the emerging presence of Charlotte

Elmwood was chased away, and the carefully constructed facade of Lottie was ascendant.

"What are you doing there?" she said, trying to hide her fear
behind effrontery. "Sitting there staring at me in my bed. You
quite gave me a fit of the vapors."

Henry Savage continued to stare at her and to eat his apple, slice by slice. Eventually he said, "Me and you got unfin-
ished business, girl."

She blanched as she remembered the night before, Henry
pushing himself against her in the alley, grabbing at her skirts,
planting his foul-smelling hot tongue in her mouth, scoring her
pale flesh with his razor-sharp chin stubble.

Lottie pushed away the nausea that threatened to have her
heaving her guts over the side of the bed. "You heard what Lizzie said she'd do to you," she warned. "We're having a strike,
don't you know?"

Henry licked the apple juice off his knife, keeping his eyes
on her, then folded the blade into the handle and secreted it
in his filthy jacket. "That we are, Lottie dear," he said, standing up from the chair. She tried not to look away in horror as
he brazenly rearranged the lump in the groin of his trousers,
squatting slightly to ease it into a more comfortable position.
He caught her looking and grinned. "And a strike means I've
been saving up all my pennies. Got quite a lot in my pot now.
And when this strike is over, which it will be soon . . ." He
grabbed at his crotch. "This'll be all yours, Lottie dear. And
that's a promise."

"Sun over the yardarm, is it, Lizzie?" said Henry Savage, letting himself into the kitchen as though he owned the place.

Lizzie Strutter placed a protective, gnarled hand on the
bottle of gin on the kitchen table. "We never see the sun on
Walden Street, even in July, but it's well past time for a drink,"
she said. Her eyes narrowed. "What you doing coming in that
door anyway, Henry? Where've you been?"

"Been to check out your new guest," he said, sitting at the

table and wiping the back of his hand across his nose. "There a spot of that gin going begging, Lizzie?"

She moved the bottle out of his reach and pointed at him across the table with a chipped red forefinger nail. "If you've laid a finger on that girl, Henry Savage, my earlier threat still stands. Nobody touches Lottie."

There was a tut from behind her. Rachel. Lizzie cast a look over her shoulder at where the girl was leaning on the sink, and raised an eyebrow. She knew the girls were curious about Lottie, knew they resented her for her smooth, unpocked skin and white teeth, her clean hair and her slim figure. Rachel more than most, perhaps; she'd always been Lizzie's favorite and maybe thought she was about to be supplanted. Lizzie would always like Rachel; she felt responsible for that scar on her face. Well, she should. She was the one who'd given it to her, after the girl had tried to hold back some money in the early days. She hadn't tried that again, and neither had anyone else. They were fast learners, Lizzie Strutter's girls.

Besides, she had bigger plans for little Lottie. Last night when she'd brought her back to Walden Street, she'd had old Mrs. Weatherbottom give her an examination, see if she had anything nasty. She didn't, but more than that, her maidenhood was intact.

The girl was a virgin.

Lizzie had no idea why a nice girl like that would be roaming around Whitechapel like a cat in heat, but to tell the truth she didn't rightly care. Lottie was going to be Lizzie Strutter's ticket to the big time. There were men who'd pay a whole lot of money to deflower a pretty little thing like that, and it wouldn't be Henry Savage who was sticking his cock in her. As soon as this Jack the Ripper was caught and the strike was called off, Lizzie was going big-time. She was going up west.

No, it wouldn't be Henry Savage who took her virginity, but there was more than one way to skin a cat, and more holes than the cunt. She said to Rachel, "Be a good girl and get me that jar of goose fat out of the pantry."

When Rachel handed it to her Lizzie slid it halfway across the table toward Henry. He looked at it quizzically. "I'd rather have a shot of gin."

Lizzie smiled. "How would you like to have a shot at Lottie? Not up the front, though. Around the back. Nicely slathered with this, mind. I don't want you hurting her too much."

Henry's eyes lit up. "Really?"

"Really. But you treat her nice, right? For every bruise on that girl's body I'll break one of your fingers."

He reached for the goose fat, but Lizzie snatched it away from him. "Not so fast. A treat like that don't come for free. You're going to have to do me a little favor first."

"Name it," he said, almost panting. Men were so weak and stupid. Give them the promise of a hole to pound away in for ten minutes and they'd pledge you the Earth.

"Do you know Salty Sylvia McMahon's bawdy house, off Houndsditch?"

Henry suddenly looked guilty. "No. You know I'm a loyal customer of yours, Lizzie."

"Oh, shut up with your wheedling, Henry. Salty Sylvia's refusing to take part in the strike. Without her I can't get to the tarts in Soho and the West End. I want you to get a few boys together, go and have a word. If you see what I mean."

Henry tugged on his bottom lip. "I don't know, Lizzie. You know Salty Sylvia's under the protection of Gruff Billy. He's a tough bloke, Lizzie."

She raised an eyebrow. "And you're scared of Gruff Billy? A big, strong feller like you? You could have him for supper."

Henry nodded, seemingly mollified. Weak, stupid men. Lizzie pressed the advantage of her flattery. "And you know what else you could have for supper? All I'm saying is that Salty Sylvia's is still open for business. Make sure by this time tomorrow it isn't, and I'll turn a blind eye to whatever you boys get up to while you're there. Do you understand me?"

Henry frowned, then smiled. "Oh, right. Yes, I get you, Lizzie."

"Good." She tapped her finger on top of the jar of goose fat. "Then tonight could be your lucky night."

Without so much as saying good-bye, Henry bolted from the kitchen. Rachel was still lurking by the pantry. Without turning around Lizzie said, "Out with it, girl. What you after?"

"Well, I was thinking . . . while we're not working some of the girls are getting a bit restless. Might be nice if we went out for a bit of entertainment, Mum. Take our minds off it. I've heard there's this German mind reader or some-such, over at the Britannia in Hoxton. . . ."

Lizzie sighed and dipped into the purse hanging from her skirts. "Oh, I suppose you've earned a bit of entertainment. But back by midnight, and no giving it away or coining it on the quiet. I'll hear about it if you do. And you know what I can do, Rachel."

Rachel touched her scar. "Yes, Mum. Do you want us to take the new girl?"

"You know full well she might be busy tonight, you cheeky brat," said Lizzie. "And no blabbering on about what you've heard in this kitchen today. I don't want it getting back to her before she's ready."

"Be a nice surprise for her, that," said Rachel, unable to keep the glee from her voice. "Henry Savage up the back." She took the coins from Lizzie's outstretched hand and danced out of the kitchen.

Henry Savage hand picked seven hard men to go with him to Houndsditch just as the light was beginning to fail. They walked the whole way in silence save for the rhythmic tapping of the blade of Henry's cleaver on his belt buckle. The cleaver was Henry's weapon of choice, and it always hung on a loop of twine from a button he'd sewed himself on the inside of his old overcoat. It had done him good service over the years, that cleaver. And with every outing it seemed to shine all the brighter. It liked blood, that cleaver. Thrived on it.

Salty Sylvia's was all shuttered up, in at least some mockery of deference to Lizzie Strutter's strike. But if Lizzie said the old girl was breaking the embargo, then who was Henry Savage to argue. He hammered on the door with his meaty fist.

It was flung open by Salty Sylvia herself, a rotund woman with heaving, liver-spotted breasts that a whalebone corset that had seen better days—better decades, probably—barely held in check. She frowned at him. "Henry Savage?"

"Can we come in, Sylvia?"

She looked up and down the snow-covered street. "There's a strike on, you know."

He roughly pushed inside, his men following him. "Not what I heard," he said. The last one in glanced around the street then quietly shut the door.

The parlor of the old house had been knocked through to what had once been the dining room to make one big room, lined with battered couches and chairs on which Sylvia's girls lounged, looking up with frightened eyes at the party that trooped in. Sylvia regarded Henry with eyes heavy with kohl. "You after doing business, Henry?"

"I'm here to talk business, Sylvia," he said. Salty Sylvia had once worked in Portsmouth before relocating to the capital. There was an old joke that the Royal Navy had named a ship after her, but it had gone down full of seamen. Henry Savage didn't rightly get it. He didn't do jokes. But he did violence very well. He reached into his jacket and pulled out his cleaver.

"Lizzie says you're to shut down. No more shagging until the strike's over."

Sylvia crossed her pockmarked arms over her vast bosom. "I think Gruff Billy might have something to say about that."

"Gruff Billy's not here," said Henry.

There was a noise behind him, a shuffle of feet, and the quiet click of a knife being opened.

"Oh yes he is, boyo."

Henry turned to look at Gruff Billy. The Welshman was as wide as a brick outhouse, and his hands were like shovels. His hair was black as the coal he'd once dug in the South Wales

Valleys. He held the knife out at Henry. "Take your boys and get out of here. Salty Sylvia's is under my protection."

Henry sighed. There was always the expectation of some measure of theater about these things. He could never be arsed. Quick as a dog after a rabbit, he brought his right arm up and across, the cleaver glinting in the low candlelight, a thick gout of blood leaping from Gruff Billy's throat. There was a collective gasp from the girls as the Welshman looked at Henry with what seemed to be mild annoyance, before the light dimmed in his eyes and he slumped to the bare floorboards.

Sylvia looked dispassionately down at her former bodyguard. "Well," she said finally. "You weren't here to mess about, were you, Henry?"

He leaned forward and wiped the cleaver on Gruff Billy's shirt. "There's a lot riding on this, Sylvia. Now, let's talk about the strike again."

"No business here," she sighed. "Tell Lizzie we're in."

He replaced his cleaver in his coat. "Good. Although . . ." He looked around. "I brought my boys all the way over here for nothing. They're all pumped up, and I went and spoiled their fun."

Sylvia sighed. "One on the house for everybody, Henry."

Henry's boys scrambled to get the girl of their choice, and there was a swift exodus to the stairs, some of the men already unbuttoning their breeches and hefting out their tackle before they'd even left the room.

"It's been a while for them." Henry smiled.

Sylvia moved in close, tugging down the front of her corset to show off her nipples, big as saucers. "What about you, Henry? I'm going to need a bit of protection now that Gruffy Billy's gone."

He pushed her away. "You'll get looked after, Sylvia, don't worry. But I'll say no, if you don't mind." She glared at him, pulling up her top. Henry smiled. "Nothing personal. I'm saving myself."

Bent had begged a lift in the constabulary steam-cab back to the Commercial Road station, Lestrade glaring at him all the way as Constable Ayres negotiated the blizzard that made the going slow in the darkness. "We'll all be traveling underground like moles if Parliament has its way." Bent chuckled. "Won't catch me going on a steam-train in a tunnel beneath the streets. I won't even get on the stilt-trains if I don't have to. My center of gravity's very low, you know. Need to be at ground level at all times."

"Are you going to share your insight with us, Mr. Bent?" said Lestrade testily.

Bent shook his head. "Not yet, George. It's only an idea. I need to do a bit of effing research first."

Lestrade harrumphed. "Withholding information from the police is a crime, Bent."

"It's not information at the moment, George. Just a hunch. Soon as I can stand it up, you'll be the first to know." He bit his lip. "There's something you can do for me, though."

Lestrade sighed. "What is it?"

"Gideon Smith. He went out on Saturday night, and as far as I know he hasn't come back yet."

"And you are worried about him?"

Bent shrugged in the tight cabin of the vehicle. "I don't know, George. He can look after himself, obviously. But it's not like him to go off like this without a word."

Constable Ayres let out a sigh of relief as he negotiated the cab into Commercial Road and brought it to a skidding stop outside the police station. There was another constable there, hopping about in the snow.

"So you want to file a missing persons report?" asked Lestrade, peering through the fogged-up side window at the policeman.

"Hmm, I don't think that would go down too well if my erstwhile colleagues in Fleet Street got hold of it. They'd have a bloody field day with that. The Hero of the Empire needs his arse wiped for him? No, I think I'd just appreciate it if your boys kept an eye out for him. He was last seen going to the Britannia on Hoxton Road, to see a show by Markus Mesmer, the hypnotist."

"Yes, I'll put the word out," said Lestrade. "I've never had the pleasure of meeting Mr. Smith—does he look like the illustrations in the penny bloods?"

"Pretty much," said Bent. "Dark curly hair, fit as a butcher's dog. Too handsome by half. He don't talk proper like me, though—he's a Yorkshireman." Bent paused. "Speaking of your boys, that lad out there seems keen to get your attention."

Constable Ayres eased himself out of the driver's seat into the snow and opened the door for Lestrade. The other constable, snow clinging to his helmet and making him look comically like a snowman, thought Bent, bobbed his head in.

"Been some trouble in Houndsditch, Inspector. Gruff Billy's turned up with his throat slashed. Found dumped in an alleyway. Word on the street is that Henry Savage's gang might be responsible."

"Uh oh," said Bent.

Lestrade looked at him. "What?"

"Henry Savage is the enforcer for Lizzie effing Strutter, ain't he? And Gruff Billy was known to frequent Salty Sylvia's. Last I heard, Salty Sylvia was refusing to take part in Lizzie Strutter's little strike. Sounds like things are turning nasty out there, and I don't mean the effing weather."

※

Bent let himself into 23 Grosvenor Square with a booming "Hello!" that fell on deaf ears. There was a fire in the parlor hearth, but the house was empty. He shucked off his overcoat and ventured into the kitchen, following the smells of cooking, but Mrs. Cadwallader was absent. She had left a note on the table, though.

Mr. Bent,
*   No sign of Master Gideon, I am afraid. Miss Maria went out on an errand of her own this afternoon, and I have not*

*heard from her. It is my night off tonight, and I am on a
social engagement. There is a lamb stew in the oven. Please
remember to turn the gas off when you have removed the
dish. I shall be back by ten.*

Mrs. Cadwallader

A social engagement? Where had Mrs. Cadwallader gone off
to? And where the eff was Maria? He remembered then that
he'd promised to go to the Britannia Theater with her, to see
if Gideon had indeed been to watch Markus Mesmer on Saturday night. Bent squinted at his pocket watch. It was after
seven already. He cursed and dithered near the stove, breathing in the wonderful smell of the lamb stew.

"Oh, eff it all!" he said, heading back into the hall and grabbing his coat. If Maria had gone to tackle Mesmer herself,
who knew what trouble she could be getting into? Pausing only
to dash into the parlor and take a swig of brandy straight from
the decanter, he headed out once more into the snow, hollering for a steam-cab to take him to Hoxton Road.

INTERMEDIO:
WEAVE, WARP, WEFT

Things were never what they seemed. Few knew that better than he. But perhaps ... perhaps there *was* a pattern to the killings. Perhaps he was too close to the pattern to see it properly, but he knew it was there. As surely as the warp and weft came together to make the weave, the pattern was there.

It had been cast off in the darkness, when a woman had been killed and her brain stolen. This much he knew. It wasn't until later that he had truly become part of the weave, that he had set to work to add his own design to the greater pattern. But he was a part of it, that much was sure.

And just as the pattern had a beginning, so it must have an end. And that end was close. He could almost sense it, like an ancient shaman divining the future from still-warm entrails.

The woman outside the theater troubled him. The way she had looked at him ... she could not know, of course. That was impossible. But there had been something in her eyes, a brief flash of connection. Less than a conscious recognition of his physical appearance, more an acknowledgment of kinship.

He resolved to go back to the theater and its masses, with half a mind to seek her out. Not for murder, no, because he felt deep inside him there was something special about her, something powerful even, perhaps even too powerful for him.

It was more that he needed some kind of ... validation, that it was all *real*. Because when he was in the intermedio, he gave up his knowledge of what was right and what was wrong, what was solid and what was make-believe. He was like a quiet berserker, such as the Norsemen used to have, a *hashishin* treading on shadows. He didn't know what was flesh and what was phantom.

Until he saw the blood.

But as each design came to an end, as each loose thread was tied off . . . what then? What came next? The pattern was near to its close.

What would become of him then?

For now his black soul had tasted blood, it hungered ever more. Even when this was finished, his soul would still cry out for that which fed it.

He would go to the theater again, because the intermedio seemed to connect him to the design, insert him into the weave. He was the warp and the weft, and connected as he was he felt . . . no, he *knew* that the design would begin to end there.

Perhaps the woman with shining black skin and bright eyes would be able to tell him what to do, or perhaps an answer would be forthcoming from elsewhere.

All he knew was that it would surely soon be time for a new pattern, a new design. A new weave, dyed with blood.

16

GLORIA MONDAY

Maria sat in the steam-cab for a long time, staring at the rag doll she still clutched in her hands. She should return it, but she couldn't face the Elmwoods again. Not when they'd confronted her with her own . . . not *mortality*, but lack of it. The driver waited a respectful few moments, then said softly, "Back home is it, miss? To Grosvenor Square?"

"No," she said, using the crook of her forefinger to wipe away the liquid leaking from her eyes. Damn Professor Einstein and his tinkering! Why did he have to make her so she could cry? She was a toy for the amusement of London's chattering classes, a machine that could do remarkable things.

Machines should not be able to cry.

"No," she said again, stuffing the doll into her skirt pockets. She would have it returned to the Elmwoods tomorrow. "Take me to the Britannia Theater on Hoxton Road."

"Very good, miss," said the driver, and with a hiss and a cloud of steam, the cab lurched forward, the steel wheel rims scrabbling for purchase in the slush, and they left not-quite-Winchmore Hill behind them.

It was fully dark when the cabbie let Maria out into the shelter of the canopy over the frontage of the Britannia, where the snow had redoubled its efforts, but it was still too early for Markus Mesmer's evening performance. There were lights on in the foyer of the theater but no crowds, save for a knot of figures some way down Hoxton Road, laughing and shouting.

Maria was considering whether she should inquire of the ushers whether Mesmer was inside, or perhaps buy a ticket and watch his performance, when louder shouts drew her attention back to what now appeared a ruckus of some description.

Through the swirling eddies of snow she could make out five, perhaps six men, gathered around a woman, her back to the shuttered window of a shop. Maria frowned as the wind snatched the voices and brought them closer.

"Come on, Gloria love, show us what's under your skirts."

Moving closer along the deserted road, Maria saw one of the men try to grab a handful of the woman's dress. She slapped his hand away, and they all laughed. Before she knew what she was doing, Maria began to stalk toward them, shouting, "What's going on! Leave her alone!"

"Leave her alone, she says," laughed the man who'd grabbed at the woman's skirts. He wore a derby pushed forward over his eyes, his high shirt collar frayed and grubby. In his hand he held a short club.

"This another Mary Ann?" said one of the other men. Maria counted six of them, young and cocky, their trousers tight and their jackets faded yet clinging to fashion.

"Well, well, well," said the ringleader, smacking the club in the palm of his hand as he turned to inspect Maria properly. "I think we've got a right proper little lady here."

Maria's eyes flicked toward the woman, still with her back against the shutters. "You leave her alone, you rowdy boys," she said, surprising Maria with the depth of her voice.

"Shut it, Mary Ann," said the man with the club. "Think we'll have a bit of fun with a real woman."

The man lunged at Maria, laughing. She stood firm and her hand snapped out, clamping on the club and wresting it from his grasp. He blinked and glared at her as his compatriots laughed even louder.

"Feisty one, eh?" he said, rubbing his hands together. Maria took his club in both hands and snapped it clean in half, throwing the pieces at his feet.

"Fucking hell," said one of the others.

When the ringleader looked up from his broken club, Maria smiled at him, drew back her fist, and smacked him hard on the chin. He staggered backward, falling on his backside in the slush, shaking his head. One of the others moved in toward her, and Maria gave him a swipe with the back of her hand, knocking him clean off his feet.

"Anyone else?" she said, looking at the others in turn.

"Fucking freak!" shouted the ringleader, scrabbling to his feet. "You're all fucking freaks."

Then he took off, his gang behind him, pelting through the snow until they were lost from sight. Maria turned to the woman, who was looking agog at her. She had on a fine dress with voluminous skirts, red curly hair flowing luxuriously over her shoulders. Maria said, "Are you all right, ma'am?"

"Yes. Thank you. My God, I've never seen anything like that."

Maria frowned at the unexpectedly deep voice again. Then she noticed the peppering of black whiskers forcing their way through the thick greasepaint on the woman's face like spring buds. Now Maria realized why those boys had been calling her "Mary Ann"—she had heard Aloysius bandy the term about when talking about men who dressed as women to satisfy the urges of those who liked to pay for such a thing.

"Oh," she said. "You're—"

"Not what you think, dear," said the other, pointing to a damp bill pasted to the wall. "Not what those lads were saying. I'm not a Mary Ann, not a chap who dresses up as a lady for attracting those men who likes that. This is what I'm about."

Maria looked at the bill. Two shows a day! It proclaimed. THE SENSATION OF SOHO! GLORIA MONDAY, BORN ON A SUNDAY, SHE'S BONNY AND BLITHE AND GOOD N'GAY!

"Gloria Monday?" said Maria.

"*Sic transit gloria mundi!*" said Gloria, curtseying with a flourish. "Thus passes the glory of the world. Now, there's a coffee shop around the corner, and I don't have a performance for another two hours. What say I buy you a drink to thank you for that rather amazing display of physical prowess?"

Gloria led Maria through throngs of loudly chattering people, gaily attired, who leaned on the counters ranged along the walls of the gaslit, cigarette smoke–wreathed coffee shop, until they found a snug booth in the shadows at the back. Gloria instructed Maria to save the table at all costs and disappeared into the crowd, returning moments later with two steaming white mugs of dark coffee.

"I got sugar," said Gloria. "Just the thing for shocks."

Maria stared into the chocolaty depths of the drink. "It must have been awful for you, those boys saying those terrible things."

Gloria watched Maria levelly over the coffee cup rim. "Those idiots? I get that all the time, though I am grateful to you for coming to my assistance like that. No, I meant you. It's always a shock for people when they first meet me."

Maria looked around the coffee shop. "They haven't given you a second glance in here."

Gloria shrugged. "Theater people. They get all sorts in here."

Maria sipped her coffee. "And what sort are you, Gloria? A man who dresses as a woman?"

Gloria smiled. "No. A woman in a man's body who dresses as a woman."

Maria raised an eyebrow. "Is that allowed, then? To be one thing and just decide to be another?"

"Ah, Maria, anything is allowed." Gloria laughed. "But I did not just choose to be what I am, on a whim. I chose to *not* be what I *wasn't*. Does that make sense?"

Maria shook her head. Gloria cupped her mug in her hands and gazed into the depths. "Almost as soon as I could think for myself, I knew I had been the victim of some divine joke, or perhaps hellish prank. With every fiber of my being I knew that I was a girl, with every single instinct. I would dream I was a girl, and be ever so disappointed when I awoke and found my soul was still imprisoned in the body of a boy." Gloria took a sip of the coffee. "School was hell. I was constantly in love with all the handsome boys. My father thought I was . . . distressingly unmanly, let us say. . . . When I was fifteen he found in my room women's clothing I had stolen from my mother, my sister, even from washing lines in the streets. He beat me until I was barely conscious and threw me bodily from the family home."

Maria looked curiously at Gloria. "And could that not have been it? What your father said? I know that it is, strictly speaking, against the law, two men loving each other, but . . . well. I knew Captain . . . I knew a man who loved another with as much vigor as any courting couple. There is no shame in it, whatever the courts say."

"That there isn't, Maria. But this wasn't really about sex, about loving other men. It was about loving *me*; about *me* loving me. Being happy with what I am." Gloria cocked her head, the curls falling over one shoulder. "Do you cook, Maria?"

"A little."

"You know the difference between scrambled eggs and an omelet? It is simply a matter of stirring. Leave your beaten eggs in the pan, and you have an omelet. Stir them, and you have scrambled eggs. It's the same with living things. Ten years ago, a German by the name of Boveri found this out with sea urchins. Chromosomes, they call it. Boys and girls are so close together, before they're born, Maria. There's nothing different about them for most of the time they're in the womb. Then, a stir here, you get a baby boy. No stirring, a baby girl." A sad, faraway look entered Gloria's eye. "My eggs got scrambled by mistake, Maria. I should have been an omelet."

"You are very well informed on such matters," said Maria.

Gloria laughed. "Such journals as I subscribe to do not make for very exciting reading, I admit, Maria. But when you are convinced God—or the devil—has played a trick on you . . . I searched out as much scientific evidence as I could find, to prove to myself, at least, that I was right."

Maria reached out and put a hand on Gloria's. "But your body, it is still . . . ?"

Gloria laughed. "Meat and two veg all present and correct

below." She dipped into the front of her frock and pulled out a half-sphere of stuffed cotton. "And these things won't sag, no matter how old I get. But . . . there's a doctor in Zurich I heard of. He can perform an operation . . . actually make a man into a woman. But it doesn't come cheap. That's why I do two shows a day here, to raise the money. That's why I parade my-self in front of idiots and sing music hall songs, and try not to mind when they jeer and throw cabbages."

"Then you'll be happier? After this . . . operation?"

Gloria considered. "I think so, yes. I'll look like what I feel." She dropped her voice. "And . . . I have a sweetheart. A more unlikely match you couldn't imagine. I can't tell you his name, but he's a copper. Loves me to high heaven. It would ruin him, if the top brass found out about us, but he doesn't care. I sneak into the police station to see him sometimes."

"Then you want to have the operation for him?"

"I cannot deny that I long for the day when we can have a proper tumble, for when I have my own pussy he can touch and kiss. But I am not doing it for him. I am doing it for me. He loves me just for what I am."

Maria smiled sadly and sighed. "Loves you for what you are."

"Because he knows as well as I do," said Gloria, pointing at the table, "what makes us what we are isn't down there, what we've got between our legs." She reached across the table and placed her hand on Maria's breast. "It's here, in our hearts." She tapped Maria's forehead. "And here, in our heads."

"You would be very surprised what I have in my heart and my head, Gloria." Maria felt wetness on her cheek and blinked away the tears. "I am sorry. This happens sometimes."

"Oh my darling," said Gloria, handing her a handkerchief. "Whatever is the matter?"

Maria looked down at herself. "I wish I were half of the woman you are. A hundredth of the woman."

Gloria laughed. "I would kill for tits like yours, love. And skin so smooth."

"I'm not real."

"You have a pretty mean right hook for a phantom."

Maria looked around. They were sheltered in the booth, and no one was looking their way. Swiftly she unlaced her bodice and opened her dress, baring her breasts. Gloria whistled softly. "Not real? You're beautiful, girl."

Wordlessly, Maria pressed her breastbone just so and a hairline crack appeared down the length of her chest and stomach. Gloria swore as the two halves of Maria's torso split and opened, revealing the array of pumps, pistons, gears, and pipes that powered her mechanical body.

"No, not real at all," said Maria, closing up her torso and rapidly lacing her corset. "I am an automaton. I have a human brain, true, but . . ."

Gloria continued to stare, then reached over and clasped Maria's hands in hers. "You're a miracle," she whispered.

"I'd rather be a woman."

"And do you feel like a woman? Do you know you're a woman, despite all this?"

"I sometimes forget I'm *not*," said Maria, her eyes overflowing with tears. "Then days like today happen, and I am somewhat brutally reminded."

Gloria smiled and squeezed her hands. "Look at us. A fine pair of . . ."

"What was it that boy said? Freaks?" said Maria.

"I was going to say 'women.'" Gloria raised her mug. "Here's to us."

Maria bit her lip and said, "I have a sweetheart, too."

"And he knows about all this? And he loves you for what you are?"

Maria nodded uncertainly. "He knows. And, yes, I think he does. I thought what I was stood between us, but I didn't realize until now that if that was the case, it was down to me, not him."

"Then you should go to him, girl. Now!"

"I was here to find him. Gloria . . . do you think you could get me inside the theater? I rather urgently need a word with Markus Mesmer."

※

The Britannia had just opened for business and to sell tickets, and crowds were already forming at the doors. Gloria took Maria's hand and pushed through, taking her past the rope barriers and nodding to the ushers. "She's with me."

Gloria led Maria up two flights of stairs to a dim corridor. "Artistes' dressing rooms. Mesmer is at the end. What do you want with him, anyway?"

"I think he can help me find Gideon."

"Your beau?"

"After a fashion."

Gloria scribbled an address in Soho on a scrap of paper and pushed it into Maria's hands. "Any time you wish to talk, or need any help, come and find me." She smiled, and the two embraced. "Us girls have to stick together."

Gloria let herself into her dressing room, and Maria padded softly along the corridor until she came to the door at the end. She paused, not knowing what she was meant to do. If Markus Mesmer was innocent, then she could not burst in and begin flinging around accusations. On the other hand, if he had indeed caused harm to Gideon . . . she would be walking into the lion's den.

Still, she had not come all this way for nothing. She rapped on the wooden door, and within seconds it was opened a crack, a suspicious pair of eyes set into a weather-lined face glaring at her. "*Sí?*"

She began to speak, then the eyes opened wide. "*La puta!*"

The man, a hulking beast with a striped, coarsely knitted sweater and a mop of shaggy black hair, flung open the door. Inside Maria could see three other men, attired in what she was sure was maritime dress—loose linen trousers, thick sweaters— and a fourth, slimmer and more groomed than the others, his hair greased and parted, his face angular and cruelly handsome.

He wore an immaculately cut gray suit, his shirt collar high and perfectly white. Markus Mesmer, she presumed.

Mesmer glanced up then looked again with interest, placing the device of lenses and lamps he had been scrutinizing onto a desk. "Ah," he said. "The Elmwood girl. What are you doing here?"

Maria said nothing. She should have anticipated this, after the Elmwoods' reaction to her. Mesmer said to the man who had opened the door, "Don't just stand there, bring her in."

Maria stepped inside and the door was closed and soundly locked behind her. What had Bent told her? Mesmer had hypnotized Charlotte Elmwood into believing she was a common streetwalker. But how should she behave, if she was to maintain the illusion that she was Charlotte? She dredged the recesses of her brain—of Annie Crook's brain—for memories of Cleveland Street and the folk who lived there. *Less demure,* she told herself. She put one hand on her hip. *More confident.* She looked Mesmer dead in his cold, blue eyes. *Not so obsequious.* She lifted her chin.

It felt good. All in all, perhaps the common women had it better than those who professed to be ladies. Perhaps Maria had been trying too hard to fit into polite London society. Perhaps there was a lot to be said for being herself.

Mesmer approached and returned her stare. "The hypnotism still holds, then? Have your parents sent you with the five thousand guineas I'd asked for? I confess, I'd quite forgotten all about you."

Maria sniffed. "I've left 'em, ain't I. Making my own way in the world now."

Mesmer made a half-amused, half-impressed face. "They were terrible prigs, anyway. You will be better off without them." He cocked his head and took a pinch of Maria's hair between his thumb and forefinger. "You are a very pretty thing. Too pretty for the streets of this sewer. Perhaps I should take you with me. How would you like to see the Austrian lakes, Charlotte? And then . . . French Louisiana!"

Maria pulled her head away, and he dropped her hair. She walked over to the desk and picked up the framework of lenses and wires. "Is this what you do your magic with?"

Mesmer laughed, moving behind her so closely that she could feel his breath on her neck. "No magic, dear Charlotte. Science! Technology! The natural power of man's mind!" He took the device gingerly from her. "That is my Hypno-Array. It aids me in my work. But the true power is within me."

"Those people who locked me up, my parents, they said you could turn me back," she said. "To how I was before. Would you use that to do it?"

He raised an eyebrow, amused. "Do you want to be 'turned back'?"

She considered then made a face. "Nah. I like myself just as I am."

He laughed and moved away from her. Her eyes fell on a leather wallet on the desk, one she had seen before. Gideon's wallet. Then he had been here. She turned to face Mesmer, leaning back on the desk. He watched her with a cool detachment, but she could discern a certain . . . hunger in his eyes. She gave him a coquettish look. "Come here."

He smirked. "It is Markus Mesmer who issues the orders." But he moved forward anyway, until he was standing right in front of her. "What do you want?"

Maria smiled and her hand darted out, grasping Mesmer by the throat. His eyes bulged, and his pale face reddened. The four sailors reached as one for guns hidden on their person, bringing up pistols to bear on Maria, but she said calmly, "I want to know what you've done with Gideon Smith. And if you don't tell your men to lay down their guns, I'll break your neck."

17

MARIA REVEALED

Rachel and the rest of Lizzie Strutter's girls departed for the theater not long after the residents of the bawdy house on Walden Street had gathered around the long table in the gloomy, candlelit kitchen for a communal meal of stale bread, cheese with a tough, shiny rind, and some thin, heavily salted slices of mottled ham. Although Lizzie had gladly handed over the coins for the show the girls wanted to attend in Hoxton, it didn't do them any harm to be reminded that their enforced holiday from earning their keep on their backs also meant that there wasn't any money coming in. Lizzie wasn't stupid, of course, and had salted away a few guineas here and there for when times were tougher than usual. And, she knew full well, the strike was all her doing, and while the girls might be enjoying some time off, if it dragged on for too long Lizzie would find the tide turning against her.

Still, it was early days, and she was confident it wouldn't come to that. Things were going her way for now and she'd heard not too long before that Salty Sylvia had indeed finally capitulated. Henry had done his job, which meant that he'd shortly be turning up to collect his payment.

The girl, Lottie, was staring wistfully at her diffuse reflection in the dark, grimy window over the cracked sink. "Couldn't I have gone with them, Mrs. Strutter?"

"It's Mum, love. My girls call me Mum." Lizzie cocked her head, looking at Lottie for a long moment. She was a mystery, this girl, no mistake. Talked the talk and walked the walk of a common whore, but she was clean as a whistle and had all her own teeth. And, strangest of all, her maidenhead was intact.

Either the girl was some medical miracle whose hymen grew back every night, or for reasons best known to herself she was some posh girl playing a part. Whatever the truth, she was Lizzie Strutter's now, body and soul, fallen like manna from heaven.

"Couldn't I have gone with them, then, Mum?"

"Bring me a glass and come and sit down," said Lizzie. A fat cockroach was tentatively scurrying over the remains of the cheese; Lizzie flicked her handkerchief at it and it sped into a cave of hollowed-out loaf. Lottie perched on the edge of a rickety chair and handed the cracked, oily shot glass to Lizzie, who filled it with gin and refilled her own glass.

"Do you drink, Lottie?" asked Lizzie, pushing the glass across the table.

The girl regarded the drink with a frown. "Gin, is it, Mum? I'm not rightly sure. . . ."

"Get it down your neck, girl, and then have a couple more. You're going to need 'em."

Lottie looked at her quizzically, and Lizzie felt suddenly almost sorry for her. "Look, Lottie, remember Henry?"

Her face darkened. "The man in the square? Who you saved me from?"

"That's the one. Thing is, Henry and me go way back. We're friends. We have an understanding. He looks out for me, and my girls, and in return . . . well, in return I let him avail himself of certain services."

Lottie looked blankly at her, and Lizzie sighed. "I want you to finish this gin and go up to the room. Henry will be up directly. Thing is, girl, he's done me something of a good turn, and that sort of thing don't come for free in Whitechapel. I've said Henry can have you."

Lottie said nothing but paled considerably. "Will—will he hurt me, Mum?"

Lizzie put her gnarled hand over the girl's soft one. "He might, love. I want to keep what you've got in your bloomers special, so I've said he can go up the Windward Passage."

Lottie's mouth wobbled, and tears filled her eyes. "You understand, girl? He's going to come knocking at the back door. He's a big man, but he never lasts long." Lizzie looked curiously at Lottie. "Have you any idea what I'm talking about?"

Lottie shook her head. Lizzie patted her hand. "Just as well, love. Now you go up to the room, make yourself comfortable. Henry will be here soon. Oh, and Lottie?"

The girl paused at the door, her cheeks shining in the flickering candlelight. "Yes, Mum?"

"Henry likes his girls to scream a bit. Thinks if he hears that, it makes him more of a man. Just think on it, eh?"

✳

"I mean it," said Maria, tightening her grip on Mesmer's throat until his pale face reddened to the follicles of his blond hair and his eyes bulged. "Drop your guns, or I will throttle him."

Mesmer waved his hand frantically and gasped, "Do it, you idiots."

Begrudgingly, the four henchmen slowly bent and laid their weapons on the rug, never taking their eyes from Maria.

"Good," she said, relaxing her grip enough for Mesmer to take a ragged breath. "Now, where is Gideon Smith?"

Part of Maria couldn't believe she had done this, marched into the lion's den and taken the villain by the throat. That part of her, that voice, was appalled, but a louder and ever-growing voice was drowning it out. She had rarely felt so exhilarated, save for when she took Apep into the wild blue, rarely felt so in control. It was as though Gloria Monday had thrown invisible switches and jabbed at unseen buttons, as though she had loosened bonds that Maria hadn't even known were suffocating her.

It was as though she had finally been given permission to be herself, whatever wondrous, fabulous collision of impossibilities that might be. Maria was Maria. She was a woman, though perhaps not the sort of woman the society she had blundered into considered acceptable. But she was a woman nevertheless. A woman who flew a dragon. No more would she

climb into the backseat to be driven by over-opinionated men
who thought they knew best.

"He came here, looking for you," said Mesmer. "I sent him
away."

Maria squeezed again. Mesmer's bulging eyes met hers.
"I hypnotized him. Made him forget who he was. He went
out into the night, and I never saw him again. But . . . Charlotte . . . I do not understand . . . from where do you get this
strength . . . ?"

Maria brought Mesmer closer to her. His breath smelled of
mint. Without taking her eyes from his, she whispered, "I am
not Charlotte Elmwood."

"Yes . . . yes, of course. . . . I can remove the hypnotism, I
can fix it. . . ."

Maria smiled. "No. I mean I am not Charlotte Elmwood
and have never been Charlotte Elmwood." For what seemed
the first time, she was assured of her own identity. "I am
Maria."

For a moment Mesmer stared at her, uncomprehending,
then his eyes widened. "Of course," he whispered. "Einstein's
automaton."

"You have been looking for me," she said, the Elmwoods'
words suddenly making sense. "You thought Charlotte Elmwood was me. That was why you were so angry when you discovered she was not, that was why you did what you did to
her, in a fit of pique." She redoubled her grip. "Why have you
been looking for me? Where is Professor Einstein? Who do you
serve?"

"Einstein is safe," gasped Mesmer. "Please . . . I cannot
breathe. . . ."

Maria loosened her hand only slightly. Mesmer said, "Professor Einstein has been . . . persuaded to work for us. We have
learned from him of the wonder that you carry in your head.
For many years we have been looking for you."

Maria raised an eyebrow. "Many years? But the Professor
only went missing a year ago."

Mesmer nodded. "We have known about the artifact for longer . . . three years now. Word reached us of Professor Einstein's experimentations . . . stories of an automaton, running amok in London. . . ."

Maria reeled slightly. Mrs. Elmwood's words came back to her. *They found you three hours later, on Cleveland Street, I believe. You had been terrorizing the locals.*

"Our intelligence was that the artifact was transplanted into the head of a prostitute. We dispatched an agent to find her. He has not had much success, though he has looked inside many heads," said Mesmer, his eyes narrowing. "He is a mewling, desperate, whining failure. I cannot wait to tell him that you have simply walked in here and presented yourself to us."

"But where is Professor Einstein?" asked Maria.

"I can take you to him, if you like," said Mesmer. Too late, Maria saw his hand emerge from his trouser pocket and lunge forward, piercing her side with a sharp blade. She looked down at it and blinked. It had done her no harm. But while she was distracted, she had failed to notice two of Mesmer's thugs circling behind her, cutting off her escape to the door. Suddenly the hypnotist wriggled free of her grasp and stepped back, producing a revolver from his jacket.

"Can guns hurt you? I'll bet they can slow you down, if nothing else."

She had lost the advantage, and before she had gleaned enough information from Mesmer. Or perhaps not . . . what had he said earlier? About seeing the Austrian lakes? And French Louisiana? Maria made a grab for Mesmer, allowing him to jerk out of her reach but instead grabbing the Hypno-Array he still clutched.

"I'll take that," she said. "Perhaps it will help me return Gideon and Charlotte to their normal selves."

"Unfortunately, you will be a long way from here by morning," said Mesmer with a smirk. "They will just have to fend for themselves." He nodded to the man behind her. "Tie her up."

She turned to the door, where the two men trained the guns they had retrieved on her. The other two thugs stood behind Mesmer. She could not be killed in the ordinary sense, but their weapons could still do damage. Maria thought about hollering for Gloria, but that would more than likely just get her new friend killed. She considered—briefly—allowing Mesmer to take her to Professor Einstein. But there was Gideon to consider. At least she knew what had happened to him. Now she just had to find him.

Finally deciding, Maria made a feint for the door, then changed direction, throwing herself across the room and toward the window. She cursed the skirts that slowed her down, almost tripping her as she dashed headlong toward the glass. Who on earth thought it was a good idea to dress in such unwieldy clothing? Finally, Mesmer realized what she was up to.

"Stop her!" he cried. "Shoot her! Bring her down! But not the head!"

Still clutching the Hypno-Array, Maria covered her face with her arm as she smashed through the window into the flurrying snow and a hail of bullets slammed into her back.

Maria hit a row of metal bins fortunately overflowing with rubbish that cushioned her landing, spilling her into the snow in a narrow alleyway empty of people—though as she rolled to a seated position she could see, far at the end, the main road in front of the Britannia, well lit and thronged with theatergoers. High above her, Mesmer leaned out of the window, shouting curses and drawing a bead on her with his revolver. She rolled into the deep shadows and stood.

And fell again. There was something wrong with her left leg. She tried to stand and stagger toward the street, but her leg would not cooperate, and she slumped against the brick wall. Mesmer was peering into the shadows but could not see her. Perhaps his cronies were already on their way. Maria put a hand to her back where the gang's bullets had hit her, and it came away slicked with thick, clear fluid. The guns had evidently done her some harm; one of the hydraulic pipes or tubes that helped operate her leg must have been severed. She cursed quietly; she needed to make repairs. If she could get to the main street . . . but as she looked along the alley she saw the bulky silhouettes of Mesmer's men gathered by the opening. She would have to go the other way. Her leg dragging behind her, Maria loped with as much stealth as she could into the darkness.

Another alleyway crossed hers, the high walls of shops and tenements sandwiching her in darkness. She struck out to the left, hoping to swing around to the main road, or at least shake off her pursuers. Then she pivoted on her good leg and stumbled against a gate; she needed to effect repairs, and quickly.

In America, Maria had been hit by a hail of bullets from a mechanical giant the Japanese on the West Coast had constructed to defend against possible incursions of the prehistoric beasts held on an island deep in the Pacific. Gideon and Maria had been tricked by the Governor of New York into believing this metal giant was a tool of war, not of defense, and in the brass dragon Apep they had attacked. But Maria had suffered terrible injuries, and it was only due to the skill of the Japanese engineer Haruki Serizawa that she had survived.

After that, Maria had made a point of learning as much engineering theory as she could. When she should have been reading books on etiquette and how to comport herself in polite society, she had been studying manuals of clockwork techniques and diagrams of hydraulic systems. It looked like she was going to need them.

Maria took a left turn into another alley. She was lost in a warren now, but hopefully that meant Mesmer's men were off her scent. There was another main road at the end of the passage, though this one seemed quieter and darker. Still, she would not want anyone to see what she was about to do. Waiting a moment in the shadows, until she was sure Mesmer's men had not followed, she staggered ahead to look at the main street. It was Hoxton Road, still; she could see the Britannia farther along. But the crowds that milled around the theater would not come here. She paused, leaning on a gas lamppost. Her head felt light all of a sudden. Perhaps the bullets had caused damage to the copper pipes that were connected to the Atlantic Artifact in her head, keeping her stolen brain alive. Maria ducked back into the alley and pulled herself along the wall until she was shrouded in darkness. Then she unbuttoned her serge shawl, unhooked her stiff white shirt, and, with some difficulty, unlaced her corset, exposing her naked torso.

Which she then opened.

Maria remembered the first time Gideon had seen her do that, back in Professor Einstein's house in the summer. It seemed so long ago. She had to remind herself that though he had been agog at the sight, he *had* seen her for what she really was . . . and it didn't seem to disturb him overly, nor dampen his shy, awkward, occasional proclamations of love.

Perhaps, like Gloria Monday's sweetheart, Gideon Smith really did love her for what she was.

Her chest opened like a set of double doors, revealing the tangle of pipework and tubes, the gears and pistons, the fly-wheels and pinions. She peered down, feeling at her bare back. She counted four bullet holes in her kid-leather skin—she would have to ask Mrs. Cadwallader to bring her invisible mending skills to bear on those. There was indeed a severed copper pipe in there, leaking fluid.

In the cotton bag she carried was a small set of tools she had asked Gideon to acquire for her. She stuffed the Hypno-Array she still carried into the bag and pulled out the tools in their linen pouch. The pipe would need welding, but she thought she could temporarily reconnect it with the pliers and the tube of plumber's adhesive, liberally applied and given time to harden. She worked the putty around the sev-ered pipe with her fingers until the leaking fluid slowed and halted; within minutes she felt her leg twitch as the hydrau-lics reconnected and fed her joints.

She sighed and closed her chest, the two halves sealing

themselves invisibly, and began to hook up her shirt. The corset could wait until she got home, she thought.

Then she saw him, looking at her.

He was standing a little way down the alley. How long he had been there, she had no idea. He was clothed in black from head to toe, scuffed boots to his knees, black, tight trousers, a dark woolen jacket over a black shirt. His eyes shone from the holes of a mask that fitted over his head, tied in a trailing knot at the back that fell over his shoulder and across his chest. Only his nose was visible, and his mouth, a thin mustache between them.

In his leather-gloved hand he held a long, thin sword.

Maria almost staggered with the familiarity of him.

He took a hesitant step toward her, his eyes wide beneath the mask. Maria quietly and slowly finished dressing. She tensed her leg; it still felt sluggish, not yet up to full power. And her head still swam, though whether from the attack by Mesmer's men or the fact that this grotesquely disguised man stood in front of her, she could not tell. Nor did she know if she had the strength to resist him. Could she have come so close to escaping Mesmer, to finding Gideon, for it all to end now?

He took another step in the crunching snow. Maria saw wetness glisten on his cheeks.

He was weeping.

At least I'll know, she thought. *At least I'll know that Gideon wasn't staying away from me through his own will.*

The masked man was just feet away. She met his eyes. Just a few more moments, and she would have felt strong enough to tackle him. But she could still barely stand on her own, still needed the support of the wall behind her.

Then he spoke.

"Por fin," he whispered, raising the sword. *"Por fin te he encontrado."*

18

Unforeseen Circumstances

There was a cry of consternation from the crowd outside the Britannia as the man in the livery of the theater's ushers presided over a workman in paint-spattered overalls who proceeded to paste rolls of paper bearing the legend CANCELED across the playbills for Markus Mesmer.

"Canceled?" called one man swaddled in a huge overcoat. "But I bought four bloody tickets for the show this afternoon."

"Refunds are available from the box office," said the usher. "The management of the Britannia is very sorry, but the run has been cut short at the request of the artiste. We hope you understand it is due to unforeseen circumstances beyond the theater's control."

Well, that's the end of that, thought Rachel. She jingled the coins Lizzie Strutter had given her and glanced at the other girls. They should go straight back to Walden Street, she supposed, but it was a shame to have come all this way for nothing.

"There's a gin shop down the street," she said. "I don't think Mum'd mind if we had a little warming beverage before we headed back."

As the grumbling crowd began to disperse from the front of the theater, a figure farther along Hoxton Road caught Rachel's eye, hobbling out of an alley, looking around somewhat furtively, then staggering rather unsteadily back into the shadows.

Rachel swore lightly. One of the other girls glanced at her. "What's up?"

She pressed half of the coins into the girl's hand. "You go and get a drink. I'll be down in a minute. And no flirting!"

Rachel headed down Hoxton Road in the direction of the alley, sloshing through the wet snow. Her stockings had more holes in them than a colander, and her boots were letting the wet in like the devil. She'd be lucky if she didn't have frost-bite by the time she got home. But that would be nothing com-pared to what Mum would do if Rachel had seen who she thought she'd seen.

She paused at the dark alley, hearing the murmur of voices within. She peered into the shadows, making out two figures, one against the wall, one little more than a smudge in the black-ness. Her eyes widened as she realized she'd been right.

✿✿

"Lottie! What the blazes are you doing? Mum'll have your guts for garters!"

Maria and the man looked up together. There was a woman framed in the diffuse lamplight and flurrying snow at the end of the alley—well, little more than a girl, really, shabbily dressed but pretty, aside from a cruel scar that ran the length of her face. There was the slightest movement on the periphery of Maria's vision, and when she looked back to her attacker, he had gone, melted into the shadows, the scuffing of his foot-prints in the snow the only evidence that he had been there at all.

"Lottie?" said the young woman again, stepping uncer-tainly into the shadows. "Who you with?"

"No one," said Maria shakily, and it was true. The man—whoever he truly was beneath that mask—had disappeared. "Who are you?"

The girl approached, looking around. "It's me, Rachel, you silly mare. I could have sworn you were down here with a feller. You know what Mum said. . . ."

Maria was about to thank the girl for coming to her aid but tell her that she had—fortuitously, of course—mixed her up with someone else, when something occurred to her. "What did you call me?" she asked.

The girl, Rachel, laughed. "Lottie, of course."

Lottie. *Charlotte.* Just as Mesmer had thought she was Charlotte Elmwood, so did this girl.

Which meant she knew where Charlotte Elmwood really was.

The girl cocked her head, the dim light shining off her scar. Her hair was ratty, and her dress was patched up and creased. She said, "I don't know why I'm being so nice to you."

"Why wouldn't you?" asked Maria.

The girl snorted. "Coming into our place with your soft skin and your white teeth, all lah-di-dah but talking like you's one of us. I don't know what you're up to, Lottie, I don't know what you're up to at all." Rachel narrowed her eyes. "Hey, you changed your clothes. Where did you get them?"

"I . . . brought them with me," said Maria. She could feel the strength coming back to her limbs, the fog lifting from her brain. She glanced around. But where was the man in black? Gone, or merely watching from the shadows?

"You looking for your feller? You know what Mum told us, we're not to do any business while the strike's on."

"He was . . . no one," said Maria. She looked at the girl. Business? Strike? She had read in the newspaper . . . then this girl was a prostitute. Charlotte had been taken into a bawdy house. But . . . "Mum?" she said.

"Has she not told you to call her Mum yet? Mrs. Strutter?"

"Oh, yes." Maria nodded. "Mum." Lizzie Strutter was the woman named in the newspaper, the one who had organized the prostitutes' strike. Jack the Ripper might have gone, and Gideon still eluded her, but if she could find out where Charlotte Elmwood was, then the evening had not been a total loss. If she could get the address from this girl, she could return with Bent and the police. She asked Rachel, "But why are you being nice to me? If you dislike me so much?"

Rachel shrugged. "Feel sorry for you, don't I?"

"Sorry for me?"

Rachel looked at her, something like pity in her eyes. "Did Mum not tell you what was going to happen tonight? I heard her talking to Henry Savage. She's giving you to him, as a favor." She shuddered. "Better you than me. None of the girls like Henry. He's rough and likes to hurt."

Distantly, a bell sounded seven times. Rachel's eyes widened. "Oh, lord. Seven o'clock already. If Henry turns up for his piece of tail and you're not there . . . Oh, bloody hell, I'd better get you back home straightaway. What the devil are you doing out here, anyway?" She put a hand on Maria's arm. "Did you see me and the girls heading out, and want to come with us?"

Maria nodded.

"Aw, that's sweet. Well, after tonight, you'll be one of the gang, eh? I'm sure Mum'll let you come out with us next time."

Maria bit her lip. She should go and find Aloysius, get the police . . . but it appeared that Charlotte Elmwood was in desperate peril. Who knew how long it would take to round up the constabulary and get them out to . . . She realized she didn't even know where the bawdy house was. There was nothing for it. She would rescue Charlotte Elmwood herself.

"How are we going to get there?" asked Maria. "Shall we find a steam-cab, or a horse-drawn . . . ?"

Rachel shrieked with laughter and linked arms with Maria. "What are you, made of money?" She leaned back and gave her a disapproving look. "You haven't been selling it, have you? Come on, lucky for you my show was canceled. Let's get you home. And we're walking."

Lottie sat in the darkness, the wind rattling the padlocked shutters, the other beds in the room cold and empty. She'd drawn her legs up to her chest, shivering from what she couldn't decide was cold or fear. Mum had sent her to the outhouse with a bar of carbolic soap and an old rag and told her to wash everywhere and do her hair as nice as she could. Then she'd told her to go to the dormitory and wait. She stared into the reflection of the pale flame from the lone candle on the bare floorboards.

Mum. There'd been another woman, one who wept a lot, who'd insisted Lottie call her "Mother." Those people who kept her locked up . . . she'd been desperate to escape them, but she'd just exchanged one prison for another, it seemed. And at least those other people were good to her. She pinched her nose between trembling fingers. Memories, or thoughts, or stories . . . she couldn't decide what they were, but they fluttered behind her eyes as insubstantial as gossamer threads, or the ghosts of butterflies.

At least there she had been safe and clean. Here . . . here she had no idea what was going on. It was as if she were playing a part at the theater, but she wasn't sure of her lines or her motivation. There was a veneer on her of Lottie, the streetwalker, the good-time girl. But it was cracking, and she was afraid to peel it off, because she didn't know what was underneath apart from a black, starless void.

If only she could remember who she was supposed to be.

If only she knew what she was supposed to do.

"Henry likes his girls to scream a bit. Thinks if he hears that, it makes him more of a man. Just think on it, eh?"

Lottie heard a soft tread on the creaking stairs and hugged her knees even tighter to her chest. She felt as though she might be sick—properly, violently sick. She began to shake uncontrollably, and tears began to cascade down her cheeks. As the handle twisted and a pale crack of light appeared at the door's edge, she thought she might scream with not very much encouragement at all.

Henry Savage felt as though his whole life had been leading up to this moment. His hand on the door handle, he paused for a moment to take a deep breath. Ever since he had seen that girl Lottie in the square, he had been obsessed. She was beautiful, of course, the sort of beautiful that Henry Savage had never really seen in the flesh before. Girls grew up quick in Whitechapel; the dirt was ingrained in them from an early age, the weight of poverty slumped their shoulders, the babies they popped out—more of them dead than alive, usually—wrecked their bodies, the sheer brutality of life battered their souls. Henry saw them sometimes just stop in the streets to watch an airship passing overhead, or to look at the smog-wreathed towers of the city, tantalizingly close but forever out of reach for Whitechapel's dirt-poor wretches. Henry never looked up. He didn't see the point. He'd never fly in an airship, never climb the towers of London. Better to keep your hand on your purse and your eyes in the back of your head, watching for whichever bastard had designs on it.

But Lottie was different. She was clean. Her body—as much as he'd felt it, for the brief, glorious moments he'd held it against her—was soft and curvy; her skin was clear and un-blemished. She smelled nice. She was like the airships or the towers . . . distant, unknowable, untouchable. She was what the rest of the world thought of as London itself, when the real London was here, in the rat-infested alleyways of the East End, the dark heart of the city beating more loudly in the shit-strewn streets than anywhere else. She was beautiful and pure.

Lottie was, in short, everything Henry hated, and what Henry Savage hated he fucked, one way or another. That was how you got to the top of the tree on these streets. Not by be-ing nice. But by fucking people, fucking them properly, like he had done on a nightly basis in this house before Lizzie Strut-ter had called her stupid strike; or fucking them over, with a knife between the ribs or a brick through the window, or a blade across the throat, like Gruff Billy'd gotten. And once Henry Savage had fucked somebody, they didn't fuck him back.

His head pounded as the blood deserted it and flooded to his groin. He clutched the jar of goose fat in his hand, trying not to think too much about what he was going to do. He wanted it to be new and fresh. He was going to fuck some Whitechapel into this pure, beautiful little thing, and he was going to enjoy every moment of it.

Henry was sweating when he finally opened the door, the light of one small candle illuminating the bed facing the door.

And there she was. Lottie, sitting with her legs drawn up. He felt a surge between his legs at the sight of her calves disappearing into the folds of her skirt. He stepped inside, the girl never taking her eyes off him, and closed the door quietly behind him.

"Lottie," he said. "Lizzie told you what I was going to do?"

She nodded, her blond hair shining in the candlelight. He said, "Stand up. Take off your clothes. Everything. I want a good look at you."

He stood at the bottom of the bed as she slid off it and walked primly around to him. She pointed at the jar in his hand. "What's that?"

Her voice was like honey. He smiled. "Bit of goose fat. Lizzie says I'm not to hurt you." He smiled, showing the rotten stumps of his teeth. "But it's no fun if it don't hurt a bit, is it?"

Lottie placed a hand on his chest, and he felt his heart pound. She took the jar from his hand. "Why don't I put that on for you?"

"You could. Get undressed."

"In a minute," she whispered.

Henry raised an eyebrow. He wasn't used to people going against him. Not really one for the alternative point of view, Henry Savage. But the way she said it, in her upper-crust voice . . . it excited him. He nodded, and her hand trailed down his chest to his trousers. Deftly, Lottie unbuttoned him, and he sighed as he felt himself spring forward. She slid her hand into his fly.

"Not too much," he gasped as her hand brushed past his thick member. "Don't make me come."

Lottie wriggled her hand into his shorts and cupped his balls. He put a hand out for a handful of skirts, and began to pull them up.

"Ow," he said. "Not so tight, girl." She was gripping his balls like she was trying to pull a pair of black puddings from a butcher's window.

Lottie continued to squeeze. "That's enough," said Henry

briskly. "Take off your dress and get on your hands and knees. I'm going to do you good, girl."

She continued to stare into his eyes and held on tighter, twisting. "Fuck!" he said. "You're hurting me! Lottie!"

She smiled at him, just as she twisted sharply and her nails dug into his flesh, and Henry Savage felt the blood that had filled his groin suddenly spill out into his trousers.

"My name's not Lottie," she whispered. "It's Maria."

Rachel had finally given in to Maria's demands for a horse-drawn cab at the very least, on the grounds that they had to get back to the bawdy house before Lizzie Strutter realized Lottie was missing. They had sneaked into a tumbledown, soot-blackened tenement on Walden Street, and Rachel had pushed her to the stairs, whispering, "Straight up, I'll go and distract Mum. You just hope Henry ain't already here."

"Which room?" hissed Maria.

Rachel looked at her quizzically. "Top of the stairs, you silly thing, same as before. Now *go*."

Maria climbed the dark, steep staircase, pausing at the door at the top of the stairs. The whole house seemed damp with shadows, and it was pungent with a musky, earthy stench that had seeped into the walls, the bowing ceilings, the few scraps of threadbare carpet. She turned the handle on the door, fearing what she would find. The door creaked open, the thin light from a single candle revealing . . .

"You're beautiful," Maria said eventually, after she and the girl on the bed had gaped at each other for long, silent, stock-still moments.

"You're . . . me?" said the girl.

Maria closed the door behind her and hurried to the bed where the girl sat with her legs drawn up to her chest, weeping quietly.

"Charlotte Elmwood," she said. "We have been looking for you."

The girl frowned. "My name is Lottie."

Maria cursed. Of course. Mesmer's hypnosis still held sway. Maria took the girl's shoulders in her hands and said, "Look at me. Your name is Charlotte Elmwood of Winchmore Hill. Your mind has been meddled with to make you forget who you are and think you are what you most certainly are not."

Charlotte met her eyes. She really was beautiful, even after several days of living rough on the streets. Maria could not believe she looked anything like this girl. It was like catching a glimpse of your reflection in a shop window and then realizing it was someone else in similar dress.

"How do you look like me?" asked Charlotte.

Maria sighed. "It is a story that will take longer to tell than we have time to waste. I must get you out of here now."

Charlotte shook her head violently. "No. Mum—Mrs. Strutter—says I'm to make Henry Savage happy on account of he's done her a big favor. He'll be here any minute." She looked at Maria sadly and began to cry. "She says he's going to hurt me."

"Do you not remember anything of who you are?" asked Maria fiercely. Charlotte shook her head and began to cry even harder, tears flowing down her filthy face. Maria dug in her pockets for a handkerchief. She needed the girl to be in a frame of mind to follow basic instructions if they were going to get out of this. Maria's hand fell on something soft, and she withdrew it from her pocket.

Charlotte stared at it for a long moment, the flow of tears dwindling, her eyes widening.

"Oh," she said. "Dolly."

Maria stared at the rag doll in her hand, the one that she had unwittingly taken from the Elmwoods' house when she fled. Charlotte Elmwood's favorite childhood toy. She handed it slowly over to the girl. "You remember Dolly?"

Charlotte took the doll and buried her face in it, closing her eyes tight and drinking in the memories imbued in the toy's faded gingham dress and woolen plaits. Eventually she opened her eyes, looked around in a panic, and asked, "Where am I? Who are you?"

"Welcome back, Charlotte," said Maria with a smile. She turned as she heard a heavy tread on the creaking stairs. "Now listen very carefully. We need to act quickly."

One hand gripping the front off his filthy shirt, the other tearing at his groin, Maria forced Henry Savage back against the door with a strength that caused surprise to flare up on his face, mingling with the pain. But mostly it was the pain. Maria didn't know Henry Savage from Adam, but in an instant he had become every man who had ever wronged every woman, from the despicable Crowe who had forced her to dance while he pleasured himself in Professor Einstein's tumbledown house to the ruffians who had abused Gloria Monday outside the Britannia Theater to, even, as her anger became a red fog that enveloped her mind, the idiot men who wrote those stupid etiquette books that dictated how a woman should walk and talk and wear her hair.

She could hear Henry Savage taking in a vast breath with which to issue a leviathanlike scream. She twisted once, twice, three times and dug her nails in even harder, until his scrotum split and gave up its pathetic little treasures, the cause of all womankind's problems since history began.

Her eyes met Henry's. He stared in uncomprehending horror for a split second, then started to release his bellow. Maria pulled her hand, soaked with gore, from Henry's trousers and pressed it against his open mouth, stuffing what felt like two hazelnuts deep into his throat, then clamping shut his foul lips with her hand. Henry went quiet, then purple in the dim candlelight, then still as Maria let go of him and he slid down the doorway to the floorboards.

Quickly, Maria crossed the room to the window shutters, the padlock she had broken off earlier hidden on the floor. She opened the shutters and peered out of the open window. There was no sign of Charlotte Elmwood. Good. Hopefully she would be on her way to 23 Grosvenor Square in a cab with the money Maria had given her before lowering her down to the street and taking her place in the bed.

With one slightly guilty look back at the body of Henry Savage slumped against the door, a spreading dark patch covering the front of his trousers, she swung out of the window and began to climb down.

19

El Hombre de Negro

Aloysius Bent had begun to think that through some bad fortune, conspiracy, or sheer carelessness he had lost everyone in the house. He had arrived at the Britannia Theater to find the place half-empty; there was some drag queen having cabbages hurled at her in the smaller of the theater's auditoria, and Bent suspected there were only as many people as there were watching the warbling renditions of popular music hall songs because the main attraction, Markus Mesmer's hypnotism show, had been canceled—"due to unforeseen circumstances" was all the theater management would say. A flower seller pushing her cart up and down Hoxton Road had said there'd been gunshots heard from the Britannia early in the evening, but she stank of cheap gin and Bent had thought her an unreliable witness, until he chuckled and remembered that before his luck had turned and he'd wound up in Grosvenor Square on Gideon's coattails, he'd largely stunk of cheap gin himself, and he had always been—in his own esteemed opinion—a very reliable witness indeed.

Still, there was nothing for it but to head home, where he found no sign of Gideon, which he'd been resigned to, of Maria, which he found worrying, or of Mrs. Cadwallader, which he found surprisingly perturbing. With a decanter of warming brandy by his side, he'd ventured into the study and began to haul books from the shelves until, two hours later, the volumes spread across the table, chairs, and most available floor space, he'd found what he was looking for.

"Destreza!" he said, laughing so loudly he didn't hear the front door bang open. "Gotcha! Effing gotcha!"

A sudden, bitingly cold wind riffled the pages of his books, and Bent looked up, realizing that someone had entered the house. Mrs. Cadwallader, back from her mysterious errand? Then Maria appeared at the open door to the study, and Bent's jaw dropped.

"Eff me, girl, what the bloody hell has happened to you?"

Bent helped Maria—her skirts torn and muddied, her right hand and arm covered in blood, her hair tousled and hanging out of its bun in thick wisps—into the armchair, where she reached for his snifter of brandy and downed it in one.

He stared at her. "You drink?"

She blinked at him. "It has a most pleasing effect on my human brain, I have discovered. And I believe people imbibe during times of stress. That seems entirely appropriate."

"Where have you been?"

She looked at the book open in front of her. There were pictures on the page, diagrams of a figure adopting different positions, holding out a thin sword. Of course. That was why it had seemed so familiar, the man's black costume in the alley.

Of course.

"Why are you looking at this, Aloysius?"

He gestured impatiently. "It's called *destreza*. It's a Spanish technique of swordplay, fencing. Something I picked up from that idiotic detective from Marylebone, maybe to do with the Jack the Ripper killings. It isn't really pertinent right now. For God's sake, girl, where have you been?"

She continued to stare at the diagrams. "Oh, I think it is pertinent, Aloysius. I think it is very pertinent indeed." She looked up. "I went to the theater. I found out what happened to Gideon. I rescued Charlotte Elmwood. And I think I might have been attacked by Jack the Ripper."

Bent opened his mouth, but all that came out was a tiny, strangled "eff." He cleared his throat, poured himself a large brandy, and said, "I think you'd better start from the beginning."

"So Charlotte Elmwood did not come here?" asked Maria with a groan after completing her summary of the evening's events. "I had her in the palm of my hand . . . had that horrible man not been at the door I would have escaped with her, but I feared if he found the room empty he would raise the alarm and we would be recaptured immediately."

Bent stared at her, his hand over his mouth. "You fed Henry Savage his own effing bollocks? Jesus Christ."

Maria met his eyes. "I fear I have killed him, Aloysius," she said levelly. "I was somewhat . . . enraged. I am afraid I might have made him a scapegoat for all the ills in modern society."

Bent shrugged. "Better than he deserved, Maria. He was a bad lot all around, Henry Savage. He was always going to meet a rough end." He chuckled. "Bet he wouldn't have seen that coming, though. Choked on his own balls. Dearie me. Nobody can say you've not got a sense of effing irony, love."

There was a noise from the hallway, and Mrs. Cadwallader appeared at the door, dropping her umbrella to the polished floor with a clatter and throwing her hands up in horror. "Land's sakes! Miss Maria! You're covered in blood!"

Maria smiled. "I also have a number of bullet holes in my back that could benefit from your invisible mending skills. And I really should give that broken pipe some more attention."

"I'll send a telegram to the Elmwoods, see if they've heard anything," said Bent. "I won't tell them we've seen her. Don't want to get their hopes up in case she hasn't made her way there. Then we need to share our information about Jack the Ripper." He held his forefinger and thumb half an inch apart. "We're this close, I can feel it. This effing close."

Maria stood. "I shall effect my repairs and clean up this blood, then we shall speak again." She picked up a scrap of paper from the table. "What does this mean?"

Bent looked up. "Hmm? Oh, that. Gobbledegook, I think. Apparently the final words of the Ripper's last known victim."

"Lost yon toe," said Maria, making a face. "Lost yon toe?"

Mrs. Cadwallader laughed. "*Lo siento*, more like. It means 'I'm sorry.' In Spanish."

The housekeeper frowned as Maria and Bent both stared at her. "What?" she said crossly.

Maria looked down at the book of Spanish fencing positions, thought of why the man in black's outfit seemed so familiar, remembered his final words to her in the alley, and met Bent's eyes.

"You speak Spanish, Sally?" said the journalist. "You speak effing Spanish?"

"Before I came to London," said Sally Cadwallader, "I harbored dreams of a more cultural life than the one I eventually fell into. Oh, do not get me wrong; I would not swap my time keeping house here at Grosvenor Square for all the tea in China." The housekeeper paused, gazing into the flames of the fire that crackled in the study hearth. "My family was by no means affluent, but my father always ensured there was enough money from his job down the pit so that I could attend an operatic society in Aberystwyth on Saturday afternoons. We used to put on all kinds of productions, and we went to see all the visiting professional operatic companies in Cardiff and Swansea."

Bent looked at her curiously. "Sally. I had no idea."

Mrs. Cadwallader blinked and waved her hands, as though flapping away the memories. "The point is, we spent a season one year doing *zarzuela*. That's like . . . Spanish opera. *Pan y Toros* was the production. It was my first big part. I learned a lot of Spanish. I liked the language. So . . . poetic. So passionate." Mrs. Cadwallader reddened and stared at the fire. "I kept my hand in, as they say. I know enough to get by. It's amazing where you can pick bits up. Why, in your former newspaper, Mr. Bent, there have been of late these rather odd advertisements. . . ."

"What was it he said to you?" Bent asked Maria. "Our evidently Spanish friend in the alley?"

Maria closed her eyes, putting herself back in Hoxton Road. *"Por fin te he encontrado,"* she said, opening her eyes and looking to Mrs. Cadwallader.

Mrs. Cadwallader frowned. *"Por fin* is 'at last.' At last . . . I found it? I have found you." She smiled. "At last, I have found you."

⚔

While Maria was in the corner of the basement armory that she had converted to a workshop, effecting her repairs—he didn't like to think too much about what that involved; it quite made him queasy—Bent had dragged out his carefully filed notebooks filled with shorthand notation, specifically the ones from their American adventure when they had all traipsed off to recover the brass dragon Apep from the Texan slaver-warlord to whom poor old Louis Cockayne had been trying to sell it—and Maria—for a quick profit.

By the time Maria and Mrs. Cadwallader emerged back into the study, the girl all cleaned up and in a fresh frock, Bent had spread out several sheets of plain foolscap paper on the table, on which he was rapidly writing names, dates, and places and connecting them with a spiderweb of lines and circles.

Mrs. Cadwallader tutted at the mess, but Bent shushed her. "I think I'm on to something here," he said, jamming a pencil behind his ear and standing up straight to admire his handiwork, rolling a cigarette between his nicotine-stained fingers. He patted his pockets for his matches and said to Maria, "What did it put you in mind of, this outfit Jack the Ripper was wearing?"

"If it truly was him," said Maria.

"Let's assume it was for a minute," said Bent, cupping the flaring match in his hands then sucking hard on his roll-up. "All in black, you said?"

"El hombre de negro," said Mrs. Cadwallader softly. "Will you excuse me for a moment?"

Maria shrugged. "Boots, up to his knees. Sturdy cotton trousers. A shirt, silk or expensive cotton, perhaps. A black woolen jacket. All in black."

"And the mask, of course," said Bent. He pushed a note-book toward her. "Like this?"

Maria glanced at the rough pencil sketch surrounded by notes. "Yes, exactly like that."

Bent sat down heavily in his chair. Maria said, "Exactly like the one Inez wore."

Mrs. Cadwallader reappeared with a tray of coffee and a folded newspaper. She said, "Inez?"

"Inez Batiste Palomo," said Bent. "She was the daughter of the governor of Uvalde, a one-horse town on the border be-tween New Spain and Texas. She fell in love with an Indian boy from the Yaqui tribe, and together they were instrumental in setting up the town of Freedom. She was also a pretty eff-ing nifty swordswoman. *Destreza,* she called it. It's more of an art than a way of fighting. I watched her at it . . . it was like bal-let. That's what got me thinking, with those footprints in the alleyway at the last Ripper killing, and that idiot Great Detec-tive prancing about, replicating them. I knew I'd effing seen them before."

Maria sat down at the table, looking at Bent's notes. "She took to wearing a black costume and a cowl," she said. "There had been some . . . masked champion of the downtrodden New Spanish border peoples."

"El Chupacabras," said Bent, reading from his notes. "Means 'goat-sucker,' if you can believe that. He'd defended the New Spanish against incursions by the Texan slaver-gangs. He was something of a folk hero. But he'd disappeared a few years before. Inez sort of took up the mantle."

Maria stared at him. "You don't think . . . Jack the Ripper is this El Chupacabras? But how did he get from New Spain to London? And why?"

Bent took a thoughtful drag of his cigarette. "Do you re-member, though, it turned out that Inez's father wasn't her real dad. She was the illegitimate daughter of the previous gover-nor of Uvalde." He consulted his notes. "Don Sergio de la Garcia. Her father had taken on the mother and de la Garcia's bastard as his own. And then . . ."

Maria gasped. "Sergio de la Garcia was called back to Madrid!"

Bent smiled. "About the same effing time that El Chupacabras hung up his mask, for reasons never really explained. I did wonder about that, but to be honest we were so knee-effing-deep in steam-powered warlords and mechanical giants and dinosaurs, I never gave it too much thought."

"You think Sergio de la Garcia was El Chupacabras?"

Bent shrugged. "Very coincidental, the masked champion disappearing at the same time as the governor is called back to the old country. And the way Inez handled a sword . . . maybe it was in the blood. And maybe it wasn't just de la Garcia's blood in her veins. Maybe it was El effing Chupacabras's, too." He stubbed out his cigarette on a saucer, ignoring Mrs. Cadwallader's gasps, and immediately began to roll another. "But as to how he got here, and why . . . I've no effing clue."

"I have," said Maria. "He's working for Markus Mesmer."

Bent gaped at her. "How the hell do you know that?"

It was Maria's turn to smile. "When I was . . . encouraging Mesmer to tell me what had happened to Gideon, and I revealed my true nature to him, he told me that his masters had dispatched an agent to find the Atlantic Artifact. He has not had much success, though he has looked inside many heads, he said."

Bent puffed hard on his cigarette. "But we can't be sure he was talking about Jack the Ripper. . . . It might have been a figure of speech."

"If I might interrupt?" said Mrs. Cadwallader. She brandished the newspaper she had brought in with the coffee. "I have been trying to tell you, Mr. Bent, about some advertisements that have been running in the *Illustrated London Argus* this past week."

"This isn't the time for talk of a new washing mangle, no matter how much of a bargain it is," said Bent, but when he caught her glare he said sheepishly, "Ah, sorry, Sally. Do go on."

"It's in Spanish," she said, arching an eyebrow at Bent. She passed it over and he looked at it.

El Hombre de Negro! Usted debe comunicarse con nosotros inmediatamente para que nos informe cómo sus ingresos de la misión. Tenemos que reunirnos con usted urgentemente. Puedes dejar un mensaje para nosotros en el teatro Britannia. Su compatriota, el señor Cerebro.

"Um, you couldn't read this for us, could you?"

She took the newspaper back. "Very roughly speaking . . . 'The Man in Black! You must contact us immediately to inform us how your mission proceeds. We must meet with you urgently. You can leave a message for us at the Britannia Theater. Your compatriot, Mr. Brain.'"

"Sally, you're a marvel," said Bent. "I could kiss you."

"Please don't, Mr. Bent," she said, making a face.

"Mr. Brain," said Bent, cackling. "He's not going to win any prizes for effing modesty, is he?"

"But undoubtedly Mesmer," said Maria.

Bent noisily pushed the coffee pot and cups to one side and spread out his sheets of paper on the table. "I have been trying to put a timeline together. But one thing I can't work out . . . Mesmer and his gang only kidnapped Professor Einstein a year ago. If de la Garcia is really Jack the Ripper, and it's all been a search for what's in your pretty little noggin, how come he's been slicing heads open since 1888? How did they know about you?"

Maria said quietly, "When I went to visit the Elmwoods, they told me something of which I have no real memory. Shortly after Professor Einstein installed Annie Crook's brain within me, he decided to show me off at a club of which

Mr. Elmwood was a member. I . . . in their words, I ran amok. I was found some time later, in Cleveland Street."

Bent put his hand to his mouth. "Then word could have gotten out, somehow," he said. "And with you fetching up on Cleveland Street, probably scaring the effing life out of people, claiming to be dead old Annie Crook . . . anyone who might have some prior knowledge of the Atlantic Artifact and what it did, coupled with an understanding of Professor Einstein's work . . . they might have put two and two together and come up with five, thinking that Einstein had put the Artifact in the brain of a street girl." He took a long slurp of coffee. "Jesus. All this time, they've been looking for you, Maria."

She met his eyes. "All those women dead, because of me."

Bent didn't know quite what to say to that. She was right, of course, but it was hardly her fault. "At least we know who he is, now. At least we can try to stop him."

"But we have no idea where he is," said Maria.

Bent stretched and yawned. "We'll come at it again in the morning." He slapped his head suddenly. "Oh, effing God! I almost bloody forgot about Rowena!" He looked at Maria. "I'm going to have to go to the Old Bailey tomorrow. Her trial's starting properly. I want you to stay indoors, do you hear? And if you have to go out, don't go anywhere near Whitechapel, for God's sake. Sally, can you watch the newspapers, look out for any more of these advertisements?"

Mrs. Cadwallader nodded. "I think we could all do with some sleep now." She smiled kindly. "Come, Miss Maria. Things will look better in the morning."

Maria nodded. "Perhaps," she said, with a smile Bent could see was forced. As he stood, stretched again, and headed for the door, he heard her say, in the tiniest of voices, "And perhaps not."

※

There were no steam-cabs, or horse-drawns, or anything that could get her away from that foul, accursed place. Charlotte Elmwood felt like sitting down in the filthy street and weeping.

But she knew she could not. She had no full understanding what had just happened, save that a woman who looked exactly like her had come in through the door and brought her back to her senses, with Dolly of all things. The last few days felt like some kind of fever dream; she could remember what she had done, what she had said—what was about to befall her—but it was as though it had all happened to someone else, as though it were a play unfolding on a stage, and she was merely a member of the audience.

This, though, was no production, these harsh, snow-filled streets no stage setting. Charlotte Elmwood was cold and alone and scared—and so hungry!—and on the streets of Whitechapel. Heaven knew what that strange woman was doing, after she had lowered Charlotte ungracefully down from the window of her prison. All she had said was to get away, find a cab or a policeman if need be, and get to 23 Grosvenor Square.

Charlotte kept repeating the address to herself under her breath. She had a home, she knew, and a loving mother and father, but the exact location seemed to bob around the periphery of her fogged brain. So all she could focus on was 23 Grosvenor Square, and the need for steam-cab or a policeman.

But there were no steam-cabs, and there were certainly no policemen. In fact, there was nothing in the supernaturally quiet Whitechapel alleys.

Nothing, save for the sudden crunch of boots on fresh snowfall.

Charlotte whirled around, but there was no one there. Then there was another sound, a soft whisper, and she turned quickly again, seeing nothing but her own shadow cast by a distant gas lamp. Panicked, she began to run, though she had no idea where. Another sound caused her to spin again, almost weeping. But the alley behind her was empty.

She turned, heaving a ragged sigh, and almost walked straight into the man blocking the alley. At first she thought it was Henry Savage or one of those horrible people from that house.

Then she saw that he was dressed all in black, a mask covering his face.

He smiled at her and held out his hand. In it he held a thin, cruel-looking sword. He said softly, *"Por fin. No voy a perder de nuevo."*

Charlotte Elmwood started to scream, though with a growing desperation that almost smothered her cries she knew that no one in Whitechapel would pay her much heed at all.

20

FERENG'S STORY

Deep down in the cavernous brick room where the shadows danced from the curiously smokeless fire, he had no idea what time of day it was. He knew he must have slept a long time, though, because he felt physically refreshed and rested, if no closer to piecing together his fractured mental state. Also, his bladder was full to bursting. Fereng and the four other men slumbered quietly on rolls alongside the walls of the room. At the entrance to the tunnel, the young dinosaur slept fitfully also. He noticed that the chain that kept it secured to the wall had been lengthened; the beast lay across the entrance to the room now, a nasty surprise for anyone who stumbled on it . . . or anyone who tried to escape.

As if sensing that he was awake, the others stirred also, and began to rise, yawning, from their beds. Fereng rolled up his mat and pulled a battered fob watch from his trouser pocket. "Seven o'clock," he said.

Smith rubbed the sleep from his eyes. "In the morning? I slept all night?"

"You were exhausted," said Fereng.

"I also need the lavatory," he said, gesturing to the tyrannosaur, which opened one yellow eye and grumbled loudly.

Fereng nodded. "Deeptendu. Distract the beast."

The Thuggee took up a hunk of meat from a large bowl and waved it at the dinosaur, until it got sluggishly to its feet, pushing itself up onto its powerful hind legs with its tiny arms. As it snapped at the meat with its powerful jaws, scar-faced Kalanath slid around the side of the room and began to turn a makeshift wheel set into the brickwork, pulling the chain that tethered the dinosaur tighter until it was close up against the wall, and Kalanath nimbly leaped out of its way. It was secured in the corner once again, and the tunnel entrance was clear.

"You thought I might flee in the night?" said Smith.

Fereng shrugged. "Would you have?"

Smith thought about it. "I don't know. I have no idea why I'm here, but then again I have no clue who I was up there anyway."

Phoolendu had set a kettle boiling above the hot embers of the fire, and he was preparing tin cups of sweet chai. Fereng said, "So you stay because you have nowhere else to go."

Smith said, "Perhaps. And perhaps I stay because I want to know what you are planning, and why."

Phoolendu was digging into the sack where the food was kept. "Crumpets!" He declared. "I will toast them now for our breakfast."

Fereng nodded to the tunnel. "Come. Let us piss."

Smith followed him into the cold shadows and they emerged into the stinking thoroughfare of the sewer. He held his breath as he loosed his bladder against the wall, Fereng doing the same.

"I'll tell you, if you like, some of what I am up to," said Fereng.

"Only some?" said Smith.

Fereng finished and rearranged his clothing. "Yes, some. I cannot trust you fully yet, Smith. But you deserve to know a little. Let us see if Phoolendu has managed to not completely ruin those crumpets." He sighed and looked a little longingly into the darkness. "It is a long time since I enjoyed a hot, buttered crumpet."

※

In the summer of 1870 (said Fereng, as they sat cross-legged around the fire, eating Phoolendu's not-too-ruined crumpets and drinking hot, sweet chai) my life was at something of a crossroads. I had enjoyed a career as an airshipman since I was young, first as an indentured pilot with some of the passenger and freight lines, followed by a spell in the Fleet Air Arm where

I earned my wings and came to the attention of other, more secret agencies working for the furtherance of the British Empire.

Not long after my military service I had married and started my own freight business. I was occasionally called upon—with increasing frequency—to fly covert missions for the British Government, largely ferrying agents and equipment to distant lands, sometimes taking a more active role in adventures and escapades.

But as thrilling as a life in the air was to me, it was not conducive to a happy domestic situation. My wife became increasingly concerned and frustrated with the government calling upon me for its secret journeys, and she issued me an ultimatum: If I wanted to remain married to her and a father to our young daughter, I would have to give up being an aerostat pilot.

I acceded to her request—I loved her, and she was fearful of what might happen to me on my increasingly dangerous missions—on the condition that I could continue to fly freight, as being a pilot was the only business I knew, the only way of providing for my family. But I found it a promise that was hard to keep. I was selfish. I maintained my business but continued to accept commissions from the government. Inevitably, my wife found out. When I should have been taking wool to Switzerland, I was getting shot at by spies in Shanghai. She said we must part, and divorce.

Thankfully, she did allow me to continue to see my daughter, and between the missions I flew for the government and the cargo commissions I continued to take to keep my business viable, I would spend wonderful yet brief days with my tiny girl.

Then, things subtly changed. The government wished me to take a more public role, and assigned me to missions that were widely reported in the press and the penny blood magazines. I was something of a hero; if I told you my name, Smith, I believe that you may have heard of me. It suited the government—or at least the department that gave me my orders—to have a familiar face the citizens could cheer on and follow.

Then I was given a most unusual job: a retrieval mission from an island in the Indian Ocean that was so tiny it did not appear on any maps. I was to fly there, alone, and obtain a . . . an artifact, I suppose you would call it, that had been lost for millennia but which I was assured would be there. I visited my former wife and child; this was in 1870, and my daughter was six years old. For reasons I still cannot explain, I felt troubled by the mission I was about to undertake. I hugged my daughter and asked her if she would like a present. She asked for a monkey. I begged my wife's forgiveness for my past behavior. She told me that it was too little, too late. While we had been apart she had been courted by another, a man with a stable position who was most unlike me, not about to dash off to the far corners of the world at the drop of a hat. They were to be married, and my daughter was to take his name.

It would be better for all concerned, she said, if I did not trouble my family again.

It is an understatement to say that it was with a heavy heart that I loaded up my 'stat and set off for the Indian Ocean. But a small part of me, one that I tried to suppress as I cast off my tethering cables and wept at the cruel blow I felt my wife had dealt me, exulted at the unfettered freedom I now enjoyed.

Oh, how ironic.

Whether it was recklessness at this newfound sense of utter freedom, or a lapse in concentration because of the cold way my wife had shut me out, or perhaps merely an unavoidable accident, I still do not fully know. But as I approached the point where my bearings and documentation said the unmapped, unnamed island should be, disaster struck.

It had been fine flying for the previous several hours, but I noticed the barometer showing an alarmingly steep fall in pressure, accompanied by the sudden swell of the sea below me and a brisk wind buffeting my 'stat. Too late I realized what was happening; I was flying right into a cyclone, such as often trap unwary sailors in that corner of the world. A hard rain began, and the winds rose to gale force, throwing my 'stat around. I struggled to keep altitude in the plummeting pressure and howling winds, and a tremendous cracking sound told me that the structure of my balloon frame had snapped in the onslaught. I went spiraling downward, thrown about by the cyclone, and it was only then that I saw the jagged black teeth rising from the sea, a ring of deadly rocks at the center of which was a small island, little more than a sea-bound hill crowned with a thick copse of trees and vegetation. This, I surmised, was my destination, but I had no time to check my documents and bearing before I smashed into the side of the hill.

When I came to, the cyclone had passed and the sky was blue once more. My 'stat was utterly wrecked; moreover, my leg was broken and severely gashed. I managed to crawl to the medical supplies in the wreckage of the 'stat and imbibed a dose of morphine while I tried to reset the broken bone and sew up the wound with fishing line. The effort and pain—despite the medicine—threw me into a black pit of unconscious despair, where I was beset by strange and terrifying visions.

What's that? The morphine? Yes, I am sure it played a part in my dreams. But more to open doors in my perception. As I lay there in the Stygian black, I was approached, with much pomp and music, by an elephant-headed god sitting on an open carriage drawn by four immense rats. He had four arms, in which he held an ax, a noose, one of his own broken tusks, and a handful of food.

When I awoke I, as you are, was convinced it was merely a fever dream brought on by the morphine and pain. But as my time on the island passed, I saw the vision for what it was: guidance from Ganesha, the remover of obstacles, the Lord of Beginnings.

Because although I lay there in the ruins of my airship, looking out at the vast circles of cruel rock that no ship could possibly navigate, lost on an uncharted island in vast waters, I felt as though I was on the cusp of something new. As I crawled from the wreckage, I was suddenly sure I was being reborn.

It was a rebirth that was likely to be short-lived, though. The debris and contents of my 'stat were scattered all across the small island—only a mile wide and perhaps two in length, but with my leg so agonizingly debilitated I had little hope of collecting it all in the short term. I had been lucky to find the medical kit; I was less so when it came to my stock of food and clean water. The glittering Indian Ocean lapped tantalizingly on the shore, only adding to my thirst.

After a day and a night I was sure I would die, when a small black-and-white shape appeared at the edge of my vision. It was a colobus monkey. My first thought was to catch it and eat it—even raw; I was so hungry I would have considered that. But it evaded my clumsy lunges, and watched me with almost human interest from a distance. After some hours it disappeared, my only hope of food gone.

But it returned, and astonishingly it brought food for me. Nuts and berries from the thick copse of trees that crowned the island. I managed to drag myself to the 'stat wreckage and tore a bowl-like chunk of steel from the framework, miming a drinking motion. The monkey seemed to understand, and it took the bowl. To my amazement, it appeared an hour later, carefully carrying the bowl filled with fresh, clear water.

Thus the monkey nursed me back to health over the course of the next few days. I named it Jip, after a dog my father once had. When I was stronger I fashioned a crutch from the timber in the ruined 'stat and Jip led me into the trees, where he showed me with chattering enthusiasm the trees from which it obtained the nuts and berries, and a spring flowing from the hill that rose at the center of the island.

My leg, however, had become infected, and gangrene had set in near the wounds. I had no option but to use the last of the morphine and amputate below the knee, cauterizing the wound in a blazing fire on the beach. You cannot imagine that pain, Smith. I knew that if I blacked out before the operation was complete, I would not wake up. I gripped a length of wood between my teeth, and even with the morphine, it took all my reserves to remain conscious. It was Jip who saved me, I think, dancing and chattering before me as though to try to distract me from the horrific agony. Still, I fancied they would hear my screams even in Delhi, but they brought no relief parties to investigate.

Jip and I became firm companions, he abandoning the company of his fellow colobus monkeys, none of which came close to me. I made a makeshift shelter on the beach from the fabric of my balloon, and collected as many of my supplies as I could. I fashioned a wooden leg and learned to walk anew on it. The stump of my leg I buried in the sand, marking it with a wooden cross. It felt symbolic, as though it were the last of England I was interring, or at least the last of my England. The ring of rocks around the island created a lagoon in which fish were abundant, and I speared them, cooking them over large fires which I hoped would attract the attention of the rescue party I was sure was coming from England. When I returned, I would present Jip to my daughter; a monkey, just as she had asked for.

But no rescue came. I saw no airships in the sky, could see no boats from the crest of the island. My original mission was all but forgotten, until one day Jip led me to the entrance of a cave hidden by hanging vines.

Inside was a box, like no box I had ever seen before. It was smooth and without joints, of some kind of strong metal I could not identify. It opened on invisible hinges, and I realized that this was what I had been dispatched from London to find.

A small glass half-sphere that fitted neatly into the palm of my hand.

I laughed heartily at the irony, that I had been sent all the way to a lost island for this, and almost forfeited my life. Also in the box was a thin sheet of the same metal that the box was made from, embossed with symbols that meant nothing to me.

At least I had the cave as a more permanent shelter, until they arrived for me.

And still, no rescue came. Days turned to weeks. I grew lean and brown in the sun, my hair long and gray. I spoke to Jip, but he never spoke back, and eventually I stopped speaking altogether, communing with Jip on a purely mental basis, or so it felt.

I tried to escape, obviously, but I knew how far from land my island was, and all rafts I attempted to build proved unable to pass the jagged rocks. Over time I forgot about escaping, indeed, forgot about my old life.

Then Jip died.

He had gone to sleep at the foot of my blankets, as he was wont to do, and in the morning he was cold and stiff. Curiously, I had dreamed of Ganesha again the previous night. New beginnings. In the absence of anything else to read, I had spent time trying to decode the strange symbols that accompanied the artifact, previously without any success. But then it suddenly became apparent.

The artifact was designed to encase a brain. A brain the size of Jip's. Feverishly working, and following the symbols that now read to me like some wordless instruction manual, I severed the top of Jip's head and connected the brain and spinal cord to the glass half-sphere. And he moved! He twitched and looked up at me! But my delight was short-lived; Jip's body was still cold and dead. Thus, over the next days, I worked to replace his joints and skeleton with discarded gears and cogs, pinions and flywheels, which had accumulated from the crash of my 'stat.

And, eventually, Jip lived again. His body was little more than a machine, but his brain was alive.

Smith? Are you well? You seem to be . . . no, of course. I shall go on. Not long after that—though I had long since given up trying to mark time—I saw the boat. It was an Indian fishing boat, several miles out at sea. I lit my fires and hollered and banged, but the boat did not turn to my island. I raged and shouted on the beach, wishing I could breach the walls of the rocks. Then Jip began to jump up and down excitedly, pointing to a smashed tabletop I used for gutting and cleaning fish. Of course! I could not pass the narrow gaps in the jagged rocks, but Jip could! I scribbled a note in half-remembered English, giving the bearing of the island as best as I could remember, and gave it to him. He mounted the tabletop, and I pushed it out into the lagoon, swimming with it to the rocks and pushing my friend through the narrow gaps until the swells of the ocean took him. Jip chattered a farewell, the note clutched in his hand, then he was lost in the rising waves.

By the time the second night had passed, I had resigned myself to the fact that rescue was not coming, and that I had also consigned my beloved Jip to a watery grave.

I was standing in the cave one morning, yawning and preparing for a day of fishing, when I saw the boat again. It was moored beyond the barrier, and the fishermen, in *lunghis* and sandals, were picking their way over the barnacle-encrusted rocks. Jip had found them, or they had found him. I was saved.

The fishermen took me back to their boat. They had been blown drastically off course by a cyclone themselves, and they were just finding their way back when they saw this amazing sight, a monkey on a table in the waves. They had rescued Jip, deciphered my note as best they could, and made for the island again. We were several hundred miles from India, but they were well stocked with food, and their boat had not been too damaged in the storm. They were fascinated by me, but I could barely even speak my gratitude. I managed to ask what month it was, so I could work out how many long weeks I had been lost.

It was September, he told me in singsong English. September 1877.

I had been on the island for seven years.

21

The Trial of Rowena Fanshawe

It was still dark when Bent stumbled down to the kitchen, but Sally Cadwallader was already busy, frying bacon and boiling water for the coffee. "I thought you would need a good breakfast," she said. "If you're going to be in that court all day, I imagine there isn't much to lunch on."

"Very good of you, Sally," said Bent, accepting a cup of coffee from her and slumping at the table. He watched her as she turned to the frying pan and began to pluck out thick, sizzling rashers of bacon. "So where did you get to last night?"

Mrs. Cadwallader turned with a frown. "Why, that's none of your—" She paused and took a deep breath. "Mr. Bent. I appreciate that this is a somewhat unorthodox household, but I feel it behooves me to remind you that I am the housekeeper here at 23 Grosvenor Square and that while you are under this roof you are in effect my employer. I would thank you to keep our relationship on a more professional footing."

She handed him a plate piled high with bacon sandwiches. "You make me sound all high-falutin', Sally."

"Mrs. Cadwallader, *please*."

He shrugged and bit into one of the sandwiches. "Where's Maria?"

"Still in her room, I suppose."

"Do you reckon she sleeps, then, her being an automaton and all?"

Mrs. Cadwallader wiped her hands on her apron. "She has a human brain. I suppose she must have to rest in the same way as everyone else."

Bent nodded. "Hadn't thought of it like that. You'll keep an eye on her today? I don't want her going out to Whitechapel

looking for Gideon, not after what she did last night. And any
trouble here, you go straight to the police. And don't let anyone in who you don't know." He shoved the last of the bacon
sandwich into his mouth. "Especially Spaniards."

Mrs. Cadwallader looked at him curiously. "You almost
seem quite . . . paternal around Miss Maria, Mr. Bent."

Bent smiled. "You never had kids, did you Sall—Mrs. Cadwallader?"

She looked at her hands. "No. Mr. Cadwallader and I were
never blessed, unfortunately."

"Me neither."

Mrs. Cadwallader stifled a sound that was half-laugh, half-
snort. Bent raised an eyebrow. "Would it surprise you to learn
I was once married?"

She blinked. "Why . . . yes. Yes, it would, Mr. Bent."

"I wasn't always like this," he said, pointing at himself. "I
didn't always look like ten pounds of horseshit in a five-pound
bag."

The housekeeper gave him a stern look for his language.
"So . . . when?"

Bent sighed. "Longer ago than I care to remember. It didn't
work out. I wouldn't let it work out. Daisy wanted children,
wanted a nice, quiet life. She should never have married a journalist. Money slipped through my fingers like water, but I
could hold my drink." He inspected his coffee. "Not a good
combination. Not for a happy domestic life."

They heard the gentle tread of footsteps above them and
both looked at the ceiling. "I'd have liked children, I think,"
said Bent thoughtfully. He shook his head. "Look at us. Like
that story, yeah? The one where the childless old couple bake
themselves a baby. Maybe Maria's our gingerbread girl."

He thought she was going to give him a lecture again, but
she just smiled. "I'll keep an eye on her, Aloysius. You get yourself off to the Old Bailey, make sure Miss Rowena comes out
of this safe and sound."

As he climbed into the steam-cab on the queue near the square, Bent wrestled with what he was going to do with the fact that they'd unmasked Jack the Ripper. He should go to the constabulary with it, but something held him back. For years he'd been on this case, pounding away at the streets of Whitechapel, combing over the particulars of every single murder, turning the evidence this way and that, trying to crack it. It had consumed him. It had been his obsession. He should go to the police, but he thought he might keep this to himself for a while. After all, if Sergio de la Garcia now knew that Maria was the one he wanted, he wasn't likely to go slicing up anyone else. No, this would be his secret, for a little bit longer.

He'd thought he might have been a bit happier about it all, though, after all this time. But he was distracted, couldn't properly focus.

Sally Cadwallader had called him Aloysius.

Bent twisted around in the leather seat, casting an eye back toward the square, just in time to see a tall figure walking with a wary gait along the frontage to number 23, some kind of conical parcel in his hand. Bent frowned. That man he'd seen lurking by the gate the other day, he was sure of it.

But then the driver joined the main road and the man was lost from sight, and Bent tried to devote his full attention to the trial of Rowena Fanshawe.

The Old Bailey was smog-bound when Bent arrived, graying the snow that still fell and obscuring the statue of Lady Justice far above. He hoped that wasn't some kind of omen. And was there ever going to be an end to this effing snow? The gawkers and ghouls were out early, jovially filling the foyer of the courthouse, laughing and joking as they waited for the trial to start. There were more hacks than Bent could count as well. He gave the press pack two fingers and shouted, "Sensation-hungry muckrakers!" before spying Willy Siddell flapping about in his robes by the courtroom door and ducking into the crowd toward him.

"Shine a light, Bent!" said Siddell, his eyes swiveling as though on stalks and his tattered wig askew. "Have you seen the size of this mob?"

"Hope you're not going to get stage fright, Willy," said Bent. "Have you been down to see Rowena?"

Siddell nodded. "She's not good, Bent. I don't think she favors being locked up."

"Well, she wouldn't, would she?" said Bent, rolling a cigarette between his cold, numb fingers. "She's the Belle of the effing Airways, ain't she?"

"Have you found Mr. Smith yet?" asked Siddell, struggling to keep his papers under control as a sudden breeze wafting through the marble and stone foyer snatched at them.

"Not yet," said Bent, and lit his cigarette. "I'm working on it."

Siddell's mustache drooped. "So just who the hell am I going to call as a witness for the defense?"

It was, Bent had to admit, a problem. Gideon was their best bet, and could have swung the jury with just a toss of his pretty curls. But with him out of the picture, and Walsingham exempting himself . . . well, everyone else who might have said anything nice about Rowena was dead. Lucian Trigger, Dr. John Reed, even Louis Cockayne . . . they could all have won the public over. Bent sucked hard on the cigarette. He must remind Gideon when he eventually effing saw him to be a bit more bloody careful what he did with his friends.

"The door's opening," said Siddell. "We're on." He looked around wildly. "Don't suppose there's time for me to go to the toilet, is there?"

❧

Squeezing onto the bench beside Siddell, with Scullimore and his assistants looking down their noses at them, Bent cast a glance around the courtroom. The galleries ranged around the upper story were packed with a jovial crowd, and he could hear the clink of bottles and the unwrapping of sandwiches. They were evidently here for a grand day out. The press bench was a scrum as well, familiar faces waving their pens at Bent and settling in for some good copy. The jury had been led in, twelve men good and true, a selection of London's citizenry that seemed to take in stiff-collared bankers, down-at-heel laborers, and keen-eyed ex-servicemen. As Bent struggled out of his overcoat, two court stewards with Rowena in between them emerged from the cells below and into the defendant's box.

"God, she looks awful," muttered Bent. And she did; Rowena's skin was pale and dark shadows hung beneath her eyes. Her hair was flat and greasy, her shoulders slumped. She managed a tremulous half-smile at Bent, and he did his best to give her an encouraging grin.

In truth, though—and he'd sat through enough cases in this very courtroom to have developed a keen sense of these things—he had a very bad feeling about this trial indeed.

The court clerk took his place below the judge's bench, and the court usher, a slow-moving, venerable gent, coughed and shouted with a surprisingly booming voice: "Silence in court and please rise for the Right Honorable Judge Stanger."

The catcalls and jocularity from the public gallery died to a muted muttering as Stanger, his robes flowing like black wings, entered from the offices at the rear of the courtroom and took his place on his aerie. He looked down at the clerk. "Has the jury been sworn in, Mr. Astin?"

"They have, sir," said the clerk.

"Very good, Mr. Astin," said Stanger, relaxing into his high-backed chair. "Gentlemen of the jury, you are here today to hear evidence put forward by Mr. Scullimore, who represents the Crown, which he hopes will convince you beyond reasonable doubt that the defendant, Miss Rowena Fanshawe, is guilty of one count of murder and a further count of burglary." He smiled. "Though if you reach a consensus that Miss Fanshawe is guilty of the former crime, the lesser charge is rendered almost moot." Stanger gazed at each of the jurors in turn. "Many, if not all, of you will be aware of Miss Rowena Fanshawe. It is very important that you put aside any prior knowledge you might think you have and concentrate upon the facts of the case as they are presented by Mr. Scullimore and Mr. Siddell, who speaks for the defense. You are to make up your mind purely on the evidence you hear in this court. Is that understood?"

The jurors nodded and murmured assent. Stanger glanced down at his papers. "Now, I must inform you that yesterday pleas were taken from the defendant, and she denies both charges. There is also a rather unusual request from the prosecution, which I have been considering overnight." He turned his gaze toward the lawyers. "Mr. Scullimore."

Scullimore leaped to his feet. "Your Honor."

"Mr. Scullimore, I have decided that your proposed evidence from your Dr. Miescher is too intriguing to ignore. I rule it admissible."

"Excellent, Your Honor," said Scullimore, smiling. Bent heard Siddell curse under his breath. "With that in mind, before I begin my opening speech, I would beg a further indulgence."

Stanger frowned. "What do you require now, Mr. Scullimore?"

"Blood, Your Honor."

The hacks' pens scribbled furiously, and the public gallery laughed, until silenced by a glare from Stanger. "Explain."

"Dr. Miescher would like to take a minuscule sample of blood from each of the jurors, Your Honor."

A gasp rolled around the courtroom. Bent nudged Siddell in the ribs and mouthed *What's he up to?* Siddell, his eyes manic, shrugged.

"To what purpose, Mr. Scullimore? It is a very gruesome request."

Scullimore inclined his head. "You have read the basics of Dr. Miescher's techniques, Your Honor. Think of the jurors' blood as a control sample, if you will. It will enable him to demonstrate beyond reasonable doubt"—and here he looked pointedly at the jury—"that Miss Fanshawe is guilty of the charge of murder."

Stanger ruminated for a moment and looked at Siddell. "You have no objection, Mr. Siddell?"

Siddell shot to his feet, scattering papers. "It is very unorthodox, Your Honor. But no, no objection."

"Hmm," said Stanger. He looked toward the jury. "This is a most unusual request, gentlemen, but I am inclined to indulge Mr. Scullimore. Having read Dr. Miescher's report, I think I can see the sense in this. Do you all agree?"

There was muttering and many glances passed between the jurors, and eventually the appointed chairman stood and said, "Your Honor, if it aids the course of true justice then we accept."

At Stanger's nod, the Swiss doctor hurried over to the jury bench with his black leather valise and took from it a number of glass vials and syringes. As he set about taking small samples of blood from the forearm of each of the twelve men, Bent whispered to Siddell, "You got advance disclosure of this? What's it all about?"

"I read this Miescher fellow's report," murmured Siddell back, "but to be quite honest, Bent, I couldn't make head nor tail of it. Shine a light, I'm a lawyer, not a bloody scientist."

When Miescher had finished Scullimore stood again and said, "I am going to ask the court to excuse my expert witness now; he must carry out certain procedures on the blood."

Stanger said, "Mr. Scullimore, how long will the doctor require for these processes?"

"I understand it is some hours' work," said Scullimore. "I am proposing to call most of my witnesses first; it may be tomorrow when we get to Dr. Miescher's evidence."

"Very well," said Stanger when Miescher had excused himself. "Let us have opening speeches."

Scullimore turned to the jury and smiled warmly at them. "Gentlemen. You will have heard that Miss Rowena Fanshawe is a heroine, that she has acquitted herself in the service of the British Empire most admirably on many occasions. We have all read her adventures in the penny dreadfuls. Miss Fanshawe's courage is not on trial here. Unfortunately, her disregard for human life—and the rule of English law—very much is. Gentlemen, by the time this trial is over you will be convinced beyond a shadow of a doubt that Rowena Fanshawe viciously murdered Edward Gaunt at his home in Kennington, south London. Heroine or not, Rowena Fanshawe is not above the law." He smiled again and turned to the judge. "Your Honor, I would like to call my first witness."

Stanger nodded and Scullimore said, "I call Rowena Fanshawe."

⚉

Rowena stood uncertainly in the dock. Scullimore said, "Your Honor, I crave another boon." He accepted from one of his assistants a length of thin rope. "I would like the defendant to tie me a knot."

Stanger raised an eyebrow. "There is something of the theater about this trial," he said mildly. "I do hope you are not playing to the gallery, Mr. Scullimore."

"Heaven forefend, Your Honor," said Scullimore. "If I may . . . ?" At Stanger's curt nod he gave the rope to the clerk, who passed it to Rowena's shaking hand. "Miss Fanshawe, are you familiar with the airman's knot?"

She nodded then said in a soft voice, "Of course."

Scullimore turned to the jury. "For the benefit of the earthbound among us, an airman's knot is commonly used by those who fly airships and dirigibles to tether their vessels. It is a very strong knot, though it can quickly be released by tugging a certain loop. Unless one knows which loop to pull, it is almost impossible to untie. Miss Fanshawe, would you . . . ?"

Rowena glanced at Bent, who made a face but nodded. She deftly tied the knot and handed it back to the clerk. Mr. Scullimore said, "Mr. Astin, would you pass that to the jury for them to examine?"

As the men passed the length of looped rope between them, Scullimore said, "Miss Fanshawe, why did you kill Edward Gaunt?"

"I didn't," she said quietly, then cleared her throat and said more strongly, "I did not kill Edward Gaunt."

Scullimore stroked his chin, as though contemplating that he might actually have gotten it all wrong. Bent had seen this many, many times before. "Though you were in the vicinity of his house on the night that he died."

Rowena looked at her hands. "Yes."

"For what purpose?"

"I was just passing."

Scullimore nodded. "Just passing. Mr. Astin, could I possibly have the bag marked Exhibit One?"

The clerk passed over a small hessian sack with a card label tied to it. Scullimore weighed it in his hands. "Edward Gaunt was found hanged in his house in Kennington. We know he did not commit suicide; there were signs of a struggle, and Mr. Gaunt had injuries to his face and body. There is also evidence that he caused some damage to his attacker, but not enough to prevent him being strung up from an exposed ceiling beam in the kitchen and left to die a most horrible death."

Scullimore paused, as though thinking hard, then untied the top of the hessian bag. "This is the very rope that was used to hang Edward Gaunt."

He pulled it out with a flourish, displaying a thick length of rope ending in a noose tied in what was unmistakably the very same airman's knot that Rowena had demonstrated to the court just moments before.

Scullimore waited until the excited chatter had died down, then smiled and said, "No further questions, Your Honor."

Stanger turned to Siddell. "You wish to cross-examine?"

Siddell stood and shook his head. "No, Your Honor, we shall be hearing Miss Fanshawe's evidence in chief later."

"Very good," said Stanger. "Miss Fanshawe, you may be seated. Mr. Scullimore, your next witness?"

Scullimore called a police constable, who took to the witness stand with his black helmet tucked under his arm and gave his name as Constable John Pryce, number 316, attached to the Kennington police station.

"Constable Pryce," said Scullimore, "thank you for taking time from your busy duties protecting London. Now, you were the officer who attended the offices of Fanshawe Aeronautical Endeavors at Highgate Aerodrome early on Sunday morning to arrest the defendant, is that correct?"

The constable nodded. "It is, sir."

"Can you tell us what you found, Constable?"

The policeman looked to the judge. "Might I refer to my notes, Your Honor?"

"You may, Constable Pryce," said Stanger.

The constable flipped through his black-bound notepad. "The offices of Fanshawe Aeronautical Endeavors is a small building on the edge of the commercial section of the aerodrome. I arrived with two other officers instructed to bring in Miss Rowena Fanshawe for questioning in relation to the death of Mr. Edward Gaunt in Kennington. The building is part workshop, part office, and also seems to be the place where the defendant actually lives."

Scullimore nodded. "Was Miss Fanshawe awake when you arrived?"

"No, sir. It was quite early, though. We knocked on the door and she answered, evidently having just risen from her bed. We informed her that she was under arrest in connection with an investigation into murder, and I formally cautioned her."

"And what did Miss Fanshawe say to that, Constable?"

Pryce looked uncomfortable, then said, "Uh, she responded 'I don't know who the fuck you are but get your fat arse off my property or I'll kick you in the bollocks.' Sir."

When the laughter that rang out from the public gallery died down, Scullimore smiled. "Somewhat colorful language from a young lady, and one who has been decorated by Queen Victoria herself for acts of bravery and heroism."

The constable shrugged. "We hear worse."

Scullimore's eyes narrowed. "From the criminal fraternity it is your duty to mingle with on a daily basis."

"I suppose."

Siddell leaped to his feet. "Objection! My learned friend is trying to insinuate into the jury's minds that the defendant's quite understandable reaction to being woken by the police somehow makes her guilty by spurious association with a criminal underclass."

"Sustained." Stanger nodded. "Please continue with more care, Mr. Scullimore."

"Of course, Your Honor." Scullimore leaned forward on the bench. "Constable Pryce, when you told Miss Fanshawe why you were so rudely disturbing her on a Sunday morning, what was her response?"

"Sir, she said, 'Who's dead?'"

"And your reply?"

"I told her that it was a Mr. Edward Gaunt of Kennington."

"And what did she say to that?"

Constable Pryce glanced at the judge, then at the jury, then made what was in Bent's opinion a highly choreographed show of checking his notes, clearing his throat, and saying loudly, "She said, *good*."

22

REIGN OF TERROR

"That was thirteen years ago," said Smith. Phoolendu poured hot water into a fresh pot of chai. "Why are you only returning to England now?"

Fereng stared into the flames of the fire, as though he were back beneath the hot Indian sun rather than the dank brick cavern in London's sewer system. Eventually he said, "What do you remember of the great famine that hit India between 1876 and 1878?"

Smith shrugged. "I do not remember much of anything."

Fereng grunted. "Of course. The truth is, Smith, even had you all your faculties about you, you would still be ignorant of it, unless you were particularly interested in global affairs. In the summer of 1876, there was a terrible drought that particularly affected the southwestern states—Madras, Bombay, and Mysore in particular. The crops failed. It was a crisis beyond all reckoning. I was brought ashore at Madras right in the middle of it. The fishermen, God bless them, shared with me their meager provisions; the only reason they had been so far out at sea when they were hit by the cyclone was desperation to find fuller fish stocks in deeper, unfished waters."

Fereng ruminated for a moment, then looked at Smith. "Hundreds of thousands of people died. From starvation, dysentery, malnutrition. And the British Government in India made it worse."

"Worse?"

Fereng nodded. "The fishermen did not know what to make of me at all, so they took me to a British garrison. They did not even know I was English, I had become so weather-burned and lean, so withdrawn. In truth, I barely knew who

I was myself, after seven years on that island. I tried to artic-
ulate to the authorities what had happened to me, but the
words would not come. All they saw was a brown man with
long hair and a monkey on his shoulder, raving at them as
though a lunatic. They immediately had me taken to a famine relief camp."

"Relief camp? That doesn't sound so bad."

Fereng laughed. "It was little more than an open-air prison.
A vast, sprawling shantytown riddled with disease and over-
run by rats, the dead lying festering in the heat until soldiers
could be bothered to periodically drive a cart through and pile
them up for burning elsewhere. The British Government had
appointed a famine relief commissioner called Sir Richard
Temple. He decreed that each man working in the relief camps
should have a daily 'wage' of one pound of rice a day." Fereng
looked at him. "That was half of what they gave to the criminals in the prisons."

"Working, though?" asked Smith. "Working on what?"

"A vast canal," said Fereng. "Even though the population
was half-starved and hundreds of thousands had already died,
it was decreed that a four hundred and twenty–mile canal
named for the Duke of Buckingham was still the top priority
of the British Raj."

Fereng spat into the fire. "And that wasn't the worst of it. I
was put to work digging the course of the canal with crowds of
Indians, and we would see carriages heading toward the docks,
carriages loaded with grain and rice. We salivated at the thought
of that food, wondered how many of our lives could be saved
by it. You know where it was bound?"

Smith shook his head, though he thought he might know
the answer.

"England. India starved, and the little food they could grow
was sent here. So it is hardly surprising that you would not have
heard of the great famine, Smith, because it didn't touch English lives one little bit."

"But your memory returned, eventually?"

Fereng nodded. "Not long into my incarceration in the relief camp."

"So why did you not present yourself to the authorities?
They would have surely freed you and sent you home."

Fereng's eyes shone. "Because I had no home anymore. I
had been abandoned by my masters, left to die on an uncharted
island. I could not call myself an Englishman, when England
had dealt with those around me so brutally. I forged new friend-
ships, new brotherhoods. Kalanath and Deeptendu were both
on my work detail. They were Thuggees, renowned for way-
laying travelers on the lonely roads, sending their souls to ap-
pease Kali. Rather than be imprisoned or executed when they
were arrested, they were sent into the camps. And at last, I
knew why Ganesha had appeared to me.

"The food he had carried in that vision was an omen, a por-
tent of the great famine. The snapped tusk represented the
irrevocably broken link between my homeland and myself.
The noose was the knot that would tie me to my new life, and
also the weapon of choice of the Thuggee assassin. And the
ax . . . the ax was a clear sign that I should make war."

"War?"

Fereng nodded. "War with the British Empire, the vast pig-
beast that befouls the world, treating entire countries as its
larders and enslaving populations in distant lands to do its bid-
ding. The Empire is corrupt and ruinous, Smith, a rapacious
machine that will not be content until it has flattened the entire world beneath its bootheel."

Smith shook his head. "Surely not . . ."

"You say that because you live in the comfort and embrace
of Victoria's Empire. The sun shall never set on Britannia, they
say, but the shadow she casts keeps the rest of the world in miserable, cold darkness."

"You said the famine lasted until 1878. You were freed from
the camps then?"

"No. I escaped, with Deeptendu and Kalanath. They
taught me the ways of the Thuggee, and one night we mur-

dered the guards and fled the camp, taking to the hills. There Deeptendu took me to a clan of Thuggees living in a vast network of caves, among them Phoolendu and Naakesh, who then was just a babe. I joined them, willingly, and thus began our reign of terror against the Raj. From our mountain hideaway we harried and attacked the British at every turn, overturning goods wagons and redistributing the rice and grain to starving villages. We fell upon garrisons of troops like shadows in the night, slaughtering them all. We burned the houses of the governors to the ground."

Smith straightened, shocked. "You are a villain, sir!"

Fereng smiled. "Perhaps. That is what they called me in the newspapers. The mysterious Fereng, leading his Thuggee assassins to commit terrorist atrocities. And all the while they had no idea, no notion, that it was an Englishman who waged war on them. You might call it villainy, Smith. I call it justice."

Smith stared at the fire for a long time. On the one hand, he felt he should flee, bring the police and the law down upon Fereng's head. On the other . . . something inside him burned and boiled at what he had been told. He looked at Fereng, who was keenly watching him. "In these camps . . ."

"Women. Children. Babies were born, and died very quickly. Men wasted away to nothing. And all for a canal, to be named after a duke, while we watched food grown by our brothers carried away across the sea to fill bellies in England."

"It is . . . appalling," agreed Smith eventually. "But why now? Why come home now?"

"Ah, that I must keep to myself until I am sure of you, Smith. What do you make of it all, though? Do you wish to join us?"

"To what end?"

Fereng shrugged. "Vengeance. Justice."

"Not for vengeance, no," said Smith slowly. "But perhaps for justice."

A test was to be arranged, to prove his loyalty. Smith would accompany Naakesh and the scar-faced Kalanath to the surface to obtain meat for the dinosaur. Fereng said, "It will be the last time it is fed. I need it hungry for what is to come."

"I won't be party to killing anyone," said Smith.

"You don't have to, today at least. Merely be party to theft."

"What if I try to escape?"

Fereng showed his teeth in a grin. "You are not our prisoner, Smith, you are our self-confessed compatriot. *For justice*, remember? Besides, Kalanath will see that you don't."

Kalanath met Smith's eyes and pulled taut the leather thong he held wrapped around his fists. "You betray us, I kill you."

"Then I am your prisoner," said Smith.

"Let us say you are . . . on a short leash," said Fereng. "For only two or three more days. I cannot risk you compromising my mission here. When my vengeance is satisfied, and there is no fear of you foiling me, then you may do as you wish. We will be leaving England, and I doubt we shall ever return." He smiled. "You might decide to come with us, Smith. After all, what is there for you here?"

What is there for me here? he thought. If only he could remember.

After what seemed like so long underground, the sudden sky—heavy with gray, snow-filled clouds and thick with smog as it was—almost overwhelmed him, buoying his spirits and weighing down upon him with its vastness all at the same time. With Kalanath going first and Naakesh bringing up the rear, Smith emerged with the two Thuggees from a manhole in an alleyway off a busy thoroughfare. The two men had taken him on a long and disorienting journey through the sewers before ascending to street level, he suspected so he could not find the way back to their lair with the authorities if he did somehow manage to evade them and abscond.

He took a deep lungful of air—not pure, of course, never pure in London, but of a dizzying freshness he thought he would never taste again down in the fetid sewers. It was early still, only just daylight, but the city roared with life and noise: steam-cabs and horse-drawns jostling for space on the slush-covered roads and tracks; people shouting from windows; barrow boys and flower girls flirting as they passed each other, calling their wares; distant, disembodied, singing; the sounds of anger and fighting; the relentless hammering of toil. Smith felt almost overwhelmed by something he could not remember if he had a name for.

And then he remembered Fereng's tale, the dreadful picture he had painted of the starving masses, brutalized and worked to death for the grandeur and glory of Britain, the food taken from their mouths to fill bellies in London.

And the thing that had flooded him, the unnamed thing he had just identified as love, or something like it, retreated and was replaced by the cold, ringing black abyss that he suddenly knew must fill Fereng's soul also, a cavernous, limitless void he thought might be hatred.

"I detest this place," said young Naakesh, spitting into the snow. "So many people! So little space! It suffocates me, all this brick and stone."

"And they want to dig beneath the streets, run their steam-trains through underground tunnels," said Kalanath, displaying the first sign of humor that Smith had seen from him. "As if it weren't enough living like rats, on top of one another, they want to run in tunnels like vermin, too!"

"We are living in tunnels," pointed out Naakesh. "Tunnels that stink of shit."

"Through necessity," said Kalanath. "And temporarily. When our work here is done we can leave this place with its rivers of shit and filthy snow."

"How did you get that scar?" asked Smith, suddenly angry with the Thuggee for his mockery, suddenly feeling defensive, suddenly wanting to needle the man.

Kalanath grinned at him. "An Englishman gave it to me. I killed him, and his father, his father's father, too. Then I killed his son, who was only seven years old. Four generations, gone! He lopped off his own lineage, just like that, when he gave me this wound."

"Can we get on?" said Naakesh, blowing into his hands. "It is positively freezing here. The sooner we can get food for the monster, the sooner we can get back down there. And the sooner we can all get home."

Kalanath nodded and led the way out of the alley, pausing only to buy a copy of the morning newspaper from a vendor on the slush-filled cobbled street. Naakesh said, "Fereng does like his newspaper. I think he feels he has a lot to catch up on, having been away so long."

"Quiet," said Kalanath, glaring at the younger man, and led them downhill, the smell of brine on the cold air. They were near the Wapping Dock, the gray skies filled with the shrieking shapes of gulls. Smith walked with the two Thuggees on either side of him, and no one gave them a second glance. London was a mélange of peoples at any time, but here on the docks its place as the hub of the vast British Empire was never more pronounced. Beyond the chimneys pumping out yellow-black smoke and the goods sheds that lined the wharves there was a swaying forest of ship masts and a chorus of hooting horns. Not everyone flew into London by airship to Highgate Aerodrome; nor did all freight come by air. Indeed, airship travel was for the moneyed few; Smith himself had never set foot on one until—

"Keep moving," said Kalanath with a hiss as Smith misstepped and lost his footing. *Until what? Until when?* But the tantalizingly close memory was snatched away as abruptly as it had arrived, leaving him with just a tickling sensation at the base of his neck.

Ranged along the quays, in front of the vast sheds with wheeled doors, were bales of cotton, barrels of ore, and foul-smelling bins of sulphur. They passed groups of sailors and dockers, the winter-pale native Londoners standing out against the crew of a Caribbean steamer huddled in big coats; a team of Chinese men unloading large lacquer boxes; tall, blond Germans smoking and laughing; two gangs of Spanish and French sailors being kept apart from a brewing fight by two harassed port watchmen. The cold morning air was thick with the smells of spices and coffee here, and Kalanath nodded toward the imminent trouble spilling over.

"We will take advantage of this. See that meat? Naakesh and I will take one each. Smith, you will add to the diversion." He pointed to a brick building a little way behind the quay. "We will make for that. There is some strange gathering there; we saw it yesterday. It will allow us to evade the authorities and escape onto the street beyond; there is a manhole into the sewers immediately to the left as you exit the front doors. Deeptendu and Phoolendu should have already removed the cover and be waiting for us beneath."

Smith looked at the racks of whole salted hogs being wheeled along a gangplank from a shabby steamer flying a German standard. Kalanath clapped him hard on the shoulder. "Now."

"But—" he began, but the two Thuggees were already barging into the dockers wheeling down the rack of meat. Smith swore then bent to snatch up a handful of gravel from the quay. He hurled it toward the nearest of the combative sailors, earning a volley of cursing in French as it hit home. The burly, unshaven sailor turned, grimacing at him, while the Spaniards began to heartily laugh. Smith grabbed another handful of gravel and tossed it into the closest laughing Spanish mouth. For good measure he then launched himself at the astonished port watchman, punching him in the nose, then, as the whole crew fell into shouting chaos, he ducked out of the melee and followed the two salted hogs being spirited away through the crowd on the shoulders of Kalanath and Naakesh.

Kalanath looked behind him to make sure Smith was following. "Get ahead of me," he grunted. "Up those steps."

The brick building was some kind of mission or union hall that was playing temporary host to, according to the white banner flapping over the double doors, The First Annual World Convention Devoted to the Appreciation of Printed Ephemera Concerned Chiefly with Fantastical, Scientific, and Swashbuckling Literature. Smith raced ahead to haul open the doors, looking beyond Kalanath and Naakesh to the scrapping crowd on the quay, where the skipper of the German steamer was dispatching heftily built sailors wielding sticks and knives in pursuit of his filched hogs.

Smith shouldered his way through the doors, holding them open for Kalanath and Naakesh and following them into the vast, lamplit space filled with ranks of what appeared to be market stalls, each of them festooned with the colorful covers of what he recognized as penny dreadful periodicals. More than recognized: as the two Thuggees barged through the outraged crowd of mainly middle-aged men in top hats and middling-to-well-to-do overcoats, Smith found himself slowing and gazing at the wares of the nearest stall with a growing pressure behind his eyes.

A whole rack was given over to *World Marvels & Wonders*, dating back from the year before to up to a decade earlier, most of them proclaiming the adventures of Captain Lucian Trigger, the Hero of the Empire. He reached up and touched the cover of one, which bore a line drawing of a strong face that was like a punch to his gut. Below it there was the legend, *Also inside: Captain Trigger finds treachery at the roof of the world in "The Golden Apple of Shangri-La"!*

Smith became aware of a kerfuffle beside him, and not related to the passage of Naakesh and Kalanath. A frowning, extravagantly-mustachioed man in a brown apron—the proprietor of the stall, Smith guessed—had a handful of grubby shirtfront belonging to a small, dirt-streaked boy.

"What's going on here?" Smith asked.

The man glared at him, as though it were anything but his business. "This little brat's trying to steal my goods!"

The boy, shivering in a shirt and ripped trousers, looked up at Smith with tearful eyes and a snotty nose. He did indeed have an armful of *World Marvels & Wonders*. Smith asked, "Is this true? How old are you?"

The boy nodded, his mouth quivering. "Ten, sir. Please, mister, I haven't got a ha'penny piece to my name, but I do so love the penny bloods. I know all my letters, and I love to read about Captain Trigger, and . . ." His voice trailed off, his eyes widening. "Is it you, sir? Is it really you?"

Smith thrust his hand into his pocket and found a handful of change nestled in the corners. He thrust it at the stall holder, who looked at it in contempt. "You are jesting with me, sir. You think these meager coins are fair recompense for these highly collectable and rare issues of—"

Smith put his face close to the man's. "They are, and you'll take them, gladly. And if I ever again find out you have been hurting small children who just want to read, you will be answerable to me."

Smith grabbed the boy by the shoulder and hauled him through the crowd, just as the German sailors burst through the doors, letting in a wind that riffled the magazines on the stall racks to the moans of the collectors and sellers. "Come on."

He dragged the boy to the far doors, where he could see the turbans of Kalanath and Naakesh. He knelt down in front of the boy, who just stared, slack jawed.

"I need you to run an errand for me," he said. The boy nodded. "You can keep all the magazines, but not this one—" he brandished the issue with the Shangri-La legend. "This you must take to . . ." Smith closed his eyes and pinched his nose viciously. He was on the verge of remembrance, but it danced away. "I can't remember his name, nor why I know him. He's a fat man. Lives in . . . lives in . . ." He snapped his fingers. "I don't know where he lives, but he works at the magazine! Fleet Street!"

The boy nodded again, his mouth still hanging open. "I'll take it to him. But what shall I tell him?"

Smith growled in frustration. "I don't know. I can't remember." There were shouts from Kalanath again, and the German sailors who were gaining on them. "Look, I have to go. But you promise you will do this?"

The boy nodded again, and Smith ruffled his hair then ran after the two Thuggees. As he burst through the doors he saw them lowering the pigs into a manhole, waving frantically at him. Just as the pursuing sailors piled through the doors after him, Smith slid into the manhole and pulled the cover over his head with an echoing clang.

The boy watched the Germans running around comically in the street, looking for the men who had stolen their cargo. His name was Tom, and he was still unsure what had happened, other than that he had in his arms a stack of *World Marvels & Wonders* that he'd be reading by candlelight until Easter. Apart from one, of course. He looked down at it, wondering why it was special. But he'd promised he'd take it to Fleet Street, though he'd never been there before, and he would. He'd find the fat man and give it to him, like he'd been told.

And he'd tell him that Gideon Smith had sent it.

23

GIDEON SMITH IS ALIVE!

Bent had watched his former colleagues furiously scribbling out their copy for the late editions with some measure of detached envy. He missed the days doing the real work of newsgathering. True, his life now was immeasurably more exciting and comfortable, but he still, on occasion, pined for the rush of excitement at getting a really good story, the scramble to write copy on the spot and have a waiting copyboy run with it back to Fleet Street to be set in hot metal for the next edition. If things had turned out differently, it would have been him elbowing the others out of the way for space in the pressroom, scrawling out in longhand the events of the morning's hearing.

And what copy it would be. "Good," Rowena Fanshawe had said upon being told of the fate of the deceased. And with that, thought Bent morosely, she might well have hanged herself. In the lunchtime break he had told Siddell that he needed to see Rowena in the cells, but the lawyer had shook his head wildly.

"Shine a light, Bent, you're the only bloody witness we've got at the moment, and you're hardly likely to win the jury over as it is, even just as a character witness." He paused, scratching his hot head under his wig. "No offense intended, of course."

"Every effing offense taken, you gog-eyed shag-bandit," growled Bent, but more out of frustration than slight. Siddell was right, of course; Gideon would only have to breeze in and he'd have the bloody jury eating out of his hand, but the Hero of the Empire had taken it upon himself to go missing at the worst possible time. But Bent was all they had, and if he started visibly mixing with the defendant before his own testimony, it would hardly be taken as impartial.

His stomach grumbling—he'd only managed to get a bag of hot chestnuts from a vendor who'd pitched up outside the Old Bailey to take advantage of the growing crowd of ghouls and bystanders here to watch Rowena's trial—Bent followed Siddell into the courtroom just as the usher called order and silence for Judge Stanger to return to his perch.

"Who are the prosecution dragging up next?" he whispered.

Siddell consulted his notes. "Inspector George Lestrade."

Lestrade gave Bent the merest of nods as he took the witness stand, swearing as to the truth of his evidence and waiting for Scullimore to begin his examination.

"Inspector Lestrade," said the prosecutor. "You are attached to the Commercial Road police station, that is correct?"

Lestrade said, "I am."

"And what is your involvement in this case? Commercial Road is a long way from Kennington."

"Certain aspects of the case came under my jurisdiction due to the linked charge of burglary at the premises belonging to Professor Stanford Rubicon," Lestrade said to the jury. "I have since been to examine the crime scene."

Scullimore looked at his notes. "Yes, the house in Kennington where Mr. Gaunt, the deceased, resided." He looked up at Lestrade. "Mr. Gaunt was a well-respected businessman, is that right, Inspector?"

Lestrade's mustache waggled. "He was a businessman, correct, sir. I believe he had been having some troubles lately in that regard."

Scullimore nodded. "Troubles upon troubles for Mr. Gaunt. Inspector, can you tell us the situation regarding Mr. Gaunt's domestic setup, including the sad news of which you have recently been informed."

Lestrade looked at the jury. "Mr. Gaunt was married to a

woman who has had to be confined to a sanatorium for some years."

Scullimore said, "That must have put an enormous strain upon him."

"I cannot say, sir."

"Of course not, Inspector. But there have been developments in that regard, I understand."

Lestrade nodded. "Yes. I am afraid that Mrs. Gaunt was found dead in her bed at the sanatorium where she resided on Monday morning."

There was a strangled cry from Rowena. Bent tried to catch her eye with a quizzical look but she had buried her face in her hands. Stanger leaned over his bench. "Miss Fanshawe? Are you quite all right?"

"Probably the defendant is only now realizing the full impact of her crime," said Scullimore, shrugging.

Siddell leaped to his feet. "Objection!"

Stanger nodded. "Sustained. Careful, Mr. Scullimore."

Scullimore nodded. "Poor Mrs. Gaunt. Died from a broken heart, no doubt."

Siddell shrieked, "Objection!"

Stanger smiled. "Sustained again, Mr. Siddell. Mr. Scullimore, such fripperies have no place in a court of law. Do we know of what Mrs. Gaunt actually did die?"

"I'm afraid not, Your Honor. Presumably related to her long-running illness—"

"Actually," said Lestrade, "I took the liberty of organizing a postmortem examination, and I had the results handed to me just before I came into court."

Scullimore frowned; evidently he had not been aware of this, thought Bent. The judge asked, "And those results, Inspector?"

"According to the coroner's report, Your Honor, it was mercury poisoning."

"I knew it!" shouted Rowena from the dock. "He did it! Gaunt killed her!"

"Objection!" shouted Scullimore. "The deceased is not on trial here!"

"Sustained," said Stanger. "Strike that from the record. Miss Fanshawe, you will be given ample opportunity to speak for yourself when your counsel examines you properly. Please refrain from such outbursts, or I'll hold you in contempt."

"It hardly matters," said Rowena quietly, and for a moment Bent saw the flare of the old fire in her eyes. "I'm on a murder charge, remember?"

Stanger stared down at her coldly. "How could I forget? Mr. Scullimore?"

"No further questions, Your Honor."

Stanger gestured at Lestrade. "Your witness, Mr. Siddell."

Before he could stand, Bent hauled on the back of Siddell's gown. Mercury poisoning! Mercury effing poisoning! Of course! He whispered urgently in Siddell's ear.

"Inspector Lestrade," said Siddell when Bent finally let go of him, "can you tell us what you found at the home of Edward Gaunt?"

Lestrade shrugged, though he kept his eyes on Bent. "You wish a full inventory of the house, sir?"

The gallery laughed, and Bent took the opportunity to whisper again in the ear of Siddell, who said, "No, Inspector. I am particularly thinking of the cellar of the property."

Was there a half-smile on Lestrade's face, directed at Bent? He couldn't be sure, but he sent up a silent prayer. This wasn't much, in the scheme of things, but it might buy them some time and a little sympathy from the jury, at least.

"The cellar," said Lestrade. "Yes, the cellar was full of a rather large quantity of smashed barometers."

Scullimore riffled through his notes, and Siddell said, "And what is the principal ingredient of a barometer, Inspector?"

"Objection," said Scullimore. "My witness is a police officer, not a meteorologist."

"Overruled," said Stanger. "You may answer, Inspector."

Lestrade looked to the jury. "Mercury, of course."

There was a loud gasp as the gallery and the jury finally caught up. Siddell said, "A huge number of broken barometers, Inspector Lestrade? Enough to obtain a considerable amount of mercury?"

Lestrade nodded. "I should say so."

Siddell smiled. "Enough to poison a person with?"

Lestrade said, "Yes."

Scullimore was on his feet again. "Objection, Your Honor! Once again, the deceased is not on trial here!"

"But he might have killed his wife," mused Stanger, steepling his fingers at his chin. "That could be pertinent, Mr. Scullimore. Continue, Mr. Siddell."

Siddell smiled broadly. "No further questions, Your Honor."

There followed another two police officers who had been first on the scene when Gaunt's body had been discovered, and a cab driver who had picked up Rowena Fanshawe a mile from Gaunt's house and taken her back to Highgate Aerodrome, on the night of the murder. Then Scullimore said, "I call Maud Richards."

Bent leaned forward as a young girl, dressed in her Sunday best, took the witness stand, barely peering over the wooden lip of the box with wide, terrified eyes. Stanger leaned forward and smiled with a kindness Bent would not have believed him capable of.

"Maud, is it? Hello, Maud."

"Hello, Mr. Judge," she said in a tiny voice. The gallery roared with laughter, quieted only by Stanger's baleful glare.

"You can call me Mr. Stanger, Maud. Now, Mr. Scullimore over there is going to ask you a few questions, and Mr. Siddell, who is sitting by the fat man"—the crowd guffawed again, and Bent snorted—"he might want to ask you some questions, too. Ignore everything else, Maud. But the most important thing is, you tell the truth. Do you understand that? You must tell the truth, whatever happens. Because you are in a court of law, before the eyes of God."

Maud nodded slowly, and haltingly repeated the oath the usher murmured to her, her hand on the Bible. Then Scullimore stood. "Maud," he asked, "how old are you?"

"Eleven, sir," she said.

"And you are a good girl, Maud? You do what your mother and father tell you?"

She nodded. "Yes, sir."

"And you always tell the truth?"

Maud bit her lip, scratching her head under the bonnet that was a shade too big on her. "Most of the time. Last year I knocked one of Mother's vases from the table in the parlor with my whip and top." She looked guiltily at a couple whom Bent surmised were her parents. "I wasn't supposed to play with my whip and top in the parlor. I told my mother that the dog knocked it off." She began to cry. "I'm sorry. Will I go to jail?"

The gallery laughed again, half of them making "Ah!" noises. Scullimore said, "No, no, Maud, I don't think you will go to jail for that, though your mother might have stern words with you afterward. However, I am not concerned with the vase. But I do need you to promise to tell the truth now."

She nodded, her eyes brimming with tears. Scullimore pointed at Rowena and said, "Do you remember ever seeing that lady before?"

Maud said, "Yes, sir. On Saturday night."

"And what was she doing, Maud?"

Maud looked at Rowena properly for the first time. "I don't want to get her into bother. She's in a lot of trouble, isn't she? I want to be Rowena Fanshawe when I grow up."

Scullimore scoffed. "There are better role models, child."

Rowena cleared her throat. "Maud," she said.

"Objection!" called Scullimore.

"Quiet," instructed Stanger. "Miss Fanshawe, you have something to say to the girl?"

"If you want to be like me, Maud, you must tell the truth," Rowena said, her eyes locked with the girl. "It's all right. Tell the truth."

Maud nodded. "I was getting ready to go home, because it was dark and cold, then I saw her on our street. I couldn't believe it. I read the penny dreadful, you see. *World Marvels & Wonders*. With the adventures of Mr. Gideon Smith. But I like Miss Fanshawe best. She's my favorite."

"On your street, Maud? Whereabouts exactly?"

Maud began to cry quietly. "Outside the house of that man who died, Mr. Gaunt. She had her hand on the latch, like she was about to go in."

"And did she go in?"

"I didn't see, sir. She said I should go home because it was late. She was still there when I left."

"What was she doing?"

Maud shrugged. "I turned around before I went into my house. She was just standing there with her hand on the gate, staring at the house."

Scullimore smiled and sat down. "No further questions."

As Maud Richards was the last of the prosecution witnesses, save for Miescher, Stanger decided that was a good point at which to halt proceedings for the day so they could approach all the new scientific evidence in the morning with sharp brains. As the reporters dashed off to file their copy, and Rowena was taken down to the holding cells, Bent said to Siddell, "Get down there before they cart her back off to Holloway for the night. Find out what Gaunt's wife meant to her. She was obviously effing distraught at the news the woman was dead."

"Is there any word of Gideon Smith?" asked Siddell, gathering his papers. "After this Miescher fellow has finished his evidence tomorrow, it will be our turn. And so far, all we've got is you."

"I'm working on it," muttered Bent. "But at the moment, no."

Siddell opened his mouth to speak, but Bent cut him off. "I know, I know. Shine an effing light, and all that."

This trial was costing him a small fortune in cab fares, thought Bent as he let himself into the warmth of 23 Grosvenor Square. But he couldn't face freezing his effing nuts off in a hansom, and he certainly wasn't hoofing it between the house and the Old Bailey. As soon as he was in the vestibule, Mrs. Cadwallader and Maria rushed at him, brandishing the late edition of the *Illustrated London Argus*.

"I know all about it. I was there, remember?" he said, looking at the latest report on Rowena's trial. They'd done well to get the latest happenings into the final edition, he had to concede. The headline read, DID MURDERED GAUNT KILL HIS WIFE WITH MERCURY, COURT ASKED. He smiled; that might take the heat off old Rowena for a bit. Though the deck beneath it read: *Belle of the Airways, upon being told the deceased had been hanged, retorts: "Good."*

"Not that," said Maria breathlessly—making Bent pause to wonder how a mechanical girl could quite rightly do anything *breathlessly*—and snatched the paper back from him. "Here, on page four."

She jabbed at an ad in the classified columns. Aha. It was in Spanish.

Señor Cerebro! Tengo la niña mecánica en mi poder! Finalmente mi exilio ha terminado! Por favor, asesorar en cuanto a cómo proceder. Atentamente, El Hombre de Negro

"From the Man In Black to Mr. Brain," said Bent. "That much I can read. What's the rest of it say?"

Mrs. Cadwallader removed a notepad from her apron pocket. "Very roughly, Mr. Bent, it says: 'I have the mechanical girl in my possession! Finally my exile is at an end! Please advise as to how to proceed.'"

Bent frowned. "He has the mechanical girl? But obviously he doesn't have—" He slapped his head. "Oh, effing hell, no."

Maria nodded excitedly. "He must have Charlotte Elmwood! He must have followed me to the bawdy house from

Soho, and when I effected Miss Elmwood's escape he must have captured her, thinking she was me."

Bent rubbed his chin. "Then she must still be alive, thank God, or he'd know he didn't have Maria if he'd already tried to slice her head off."

"But what shall we do?"

Bent shucked off his overcoat and patted his pockets for his tobacco. "Mesmer will have seen this and will be putting his response in tomorrow's edition, no doubt, telling Garcia where to take the girl." He snapped his fingers. "We need to intercept that advertisement."

"And put in our own in its place!" said Maria. "Diverting El Chupacabras and Charlotte to where we want them!"

"Brilliant!" roared Bent, dancing in the puddle of melted snow he was making. "Absolutely effing brilliant! But where can we tell him to go? Mesmer and his gang will merely beat us to him. We need to . . . to put it in code! A place that means something to only Garcia and ourselves, freezing Mesmer out in the effing cold. But what? Where?"

Mrs. Cadwallader smiled, crossing her arms in front of her ample bosom. "We've already thought of that."

Maria said, "What about something pertaining to Inez Batiste Paloma, who took the mantle of La Chupacabras after Garcia disappeared."

Bent snapped his fingers. "And she is Garcia's daughter. But he doesn't know that. . . ."

"Perhaps not," continued Maria. "But her mere existence, even as the daughter of his successor, a girl he watched grow up, is information we share with him, but a reference which Markus Mesmer is unlikely to understand."

"I like it, I like it," said Bent, finally finding his tobacco and papers and setting about rolling a cigarette. "But where would we find an 'Inez' in London which could be a meeting place? Or a 'Batiste'?"

They led Bent into the parlor where there was a welcome fire blazing in the hearth. On the table was a street map of

London unfurled. Mrs. Cadwallader said, "We have spent the afternoon pondering the same question. Then I remembered what the girl's surname, Palomo, means in English."

Bent poured himself a gin from the decanter. "And?"

She took up a pen, dipped it in ink, and scrawled a big circle around a portion of the Thames near Hammersmith.

"It means 'dove,' Aloysius," said Maria. "We scoured the map, and—"

"And you found the tavern the Dove, one of the oldest pubs in London," said Bent, breaking into a wide grin. "Now you're really talking my language. I could kiss you both. In fact, I think I effing will!"

For what seemed like the first time in days, shrieks of laughter rang out in the house on Grosvenor Square as Aloysius Bent enclosed the two women in his pungent embrace.

The reception desk of the London Newspaper and Magazine Publishing Company, publisher of Bent's current employer, *World Marvels & Wonders*, and his erstwhile one, the *Illustrated London Argus*, was just about to close when the steam-cab dropped Bent off at its grand marble facade that fronted onto Fleet Street. There was some snot-nosed child shivering in the snow; when he saw Bent, he said, "Excuse me, sir!"

"Not now, kid," said Bent, pushing past him. "Evening, Jug Ears." He nodded to the liveried doorman scowling at him in recognition before bursting through the glass doors and huffing over to the wide reception desk.

"Doris," he gasped, fighting for breath. "Thank eff I got here in time."

"Mr. Bent," said the receptionist, looking over her spectacles at him. "Why, we don't see much of you here since you transferred to the magazine. How is life treating you?"

"Tolerable. Listen, Doris, I'm in a rush. Have you had anybody bring in a notice for the *Argus* written in Spanish, by any chance?"

Doris blinked at him. "Why, yes, as it happens. I have it

here. Swarthy fellow brought it in. I thought it odd, because I could have sworn he was French, while the notice is, as you say, certainly Spanish."

Bent reached into his overcoat pocket for the advertisement Mrs. Cadwallader had drafted, purporting to be from Mesmer but in fact instructing Garcia to take Charlotte Elmwood to the Dove in Hammersmith tomorrow evening. "Hand it over, love, and put this one in instead, right?"

"I'm not sure I can—"

"Doris? Is there some problem here?"

Bent turned to see the frowning face of Bingley, his former news editor at the *Argus*, who said, "Aloysius Bent, as I live and breathe. What is all this commotion about?"

"Mr. Bent wants me to substitute his notice for a previously paid-for advertisement, Mr. Bingley," said Doris in a tone that indicated she disapproved most highly of even considering such a thing.

Bingley smirked. "And why would we do that, Mr. Bent?"

Bent smiled back. "Because it's going to catch Jack the eff-ing Ripper, Bingley."

Bingley opened his mouth to speak then narrowed his eyes. "Some trick of yours, no doubt."

Bent shrugged. "Can you afford to take the risk, Bingley old chap? Imagine what your bosses would say if you ruined the one chance we have to nail London's biggest mass murderer."

The news editor chewed his lip for a moment, then said, "Do as he says. But the *Argus* gets the story first, Bent, not your lurid little penny dreadful."

When he'd placed the advertisement, Bent stepped outside for a celebratory cigarette and contemplated a gin at Ye Olde Cheshire Cheese to go with it. The little brat was waiting for him outside.

"Mr. Aloysius Bent?"

Bent squinted at him in the flurrying snow. "You ain't one of the Fleet Street Irregulars. Who sent you?" His face fell. "This ain't about that effing bar tab at the Fleece, is it?"

The boy shook his head and handed over a rolled-up magazine. It was an old copy of *World Marvels & Wonders*. Bent chuckled. "Is it an autograph you're after, lad? Afraid this one's before my time. I only document the adventures of Gideon Smith."

The boy nodded enthusiastically. "That's who told me to bring it. He said, give it to the fat man at *World Marvels & Wonders*. I worked out after he must mean Mr. Aloysius Bent."

Bent dropped to his knees in front of the boy. "What? Gideon gave you this? Where? When?"

"This morning, sir. At Wapping Dock. He didn't seem right, sir, like he didn't really know who he was. Kept remembering things then forgetting them again. He was with two Indians in turbans. I think they'd been stealing sides of pork. But I knew it was him. I just knew it."

Bent stared at the periodical in his hand, rubbing his mouth. He said, "Pork?"

The boy said, "Are you well, Mr. Bent? Did I do right?"

Bent stood up. "Right? You did effing brilliantly, son." He dug into his pockets and drew out three shillings. He pushed them into the boy's hand and his grimy face lit up, but Bent barely noticed it.

All he could think was, *Gideon Smith is alive!*

24

THICKER THAN WATER

Smith pushed the vegetable dhal around the cracked bowl, but his appetite seemed to have deserted him, a combination of watching the beast tearing into the slabs of pig meat and, earlier, seeing Phoolendu gathering up the dinosaur's dung and slapping it into fat pancakes that he dried on the edges of the always-burning fire.

"Makes wonderful fire starters!" The plump Thuggee beamed. "Burns with practically no smoke at all! Wonderful for living underground."

Fereng, his clockwork monkey sitting on his shoulder, watched Smith intently. Smith held his gaze until the older man said, "You have passed the first test, then. You didn't run."

He shrugged. "Where would I go?"

"Where indeed?" said Fereng. "But you could have fled; you had opportunity. And you did not. So I surmise that you are with me."

Smith stared at the bowl of food. "Perhaps. You make a convincing argument against the British Empire. Your desire for vengeance seems . . . justified."

Fereng laughed. "And you do not yet know the half of it." He looked up and over Smith's shoulder. "Deeptendu. Kill him."

Instinctively, Smith began to climb from his cross-legged position, but the Thuggee was quicker, and he suddenly felt a constricting pressure around his throat. He tried to get a hand between the leather thong and his flesh, at the same time throwing his head backward until it connected with—he thought, given the grunt of pain that accompanied his action—Deeptendu's nose. Smith rammed an elbow back into the other man's ribs and finally dragged the leather thong away from his neck, rolling forward and twisting around. Deeptendu was on his knees, winded and holding his bleeding nose, but scar-faced Kalanath and young Naakesh were advancing on him with knives held aloft, and on the edge of his vision he saw Phoolendu, a garroting cord in his hands, sidling around the dancing shadows at the perimeter of the brick room. He risked a glance at Fereng, who was watching the proceedings with interest.

"What is the meaning of this betrayal?"

Fereng shrugged, just as Kalanath lunged forward with his knife. Smith—a tiny part of him marveling at his own instinctive, smooth moves—fell forward as though to perform a handstand, at the last moment swinging his legs out and around, the momentum carrying his boots into the chest of the Thuggee. He pushed himself up to his feet and ducked under a swipe from Naakesh, grabbing the wrist of the other man's knife hand until he dropped the weapon and, with his other fist, punching him hard, once, in the jaw. As the young man staggered back Smith snatched up the knife, but Deeptendu was rising to his feet, his face bloodied, his eyes narrowed.

"Insurmountable odds," said Fereng. "Four trained killers. What will you do, Smith?"

Smith gritted his teeth and lunged for Deeptendu but at the last second feinted away, tumbling forward and over and grabbing the front of Fereng's shirt. He pulled the old man toward him and twisted around, his arm across Fereng's throat and the knife pointed at his temple.

"Even those odds, somewhat," Smith said. He glared at each of the Thuggees in turn, indicating with a jerk of his head that Phoolendu, working his way around the shadows, should rejoin his brothers.

Then, Fereng began to clap.

"Excellent," he said, his applause ringing around the cavernous room. "Truly excellent."

Deeptendu dropped his garroting thong and smiled. "I think you might have broken my nose," he said. "Well done."

Smith looked, puzzled, from one man to another. Phoolendu joined in the applause. "Chai, I think, to celebrate!"

Even Kalanath gave Smith a curt, approving nod. Slowly, he released the pressure of the knife on Fereng's temple. He said, "This was . . . another test?"

Fereng gently removed Smith's arm from around his neck and turned to face him. "It was. To see how well you fight. And whether you have it in you."

"Have what in me?"

"Murder," said Fereng.

"No," said Smith. "I told you before. I shall be party to no killing." But even as he said the words, he could feel that they carried less conviction than they had the last time he had spoken them. He tried to imagine the millions starving in India while food was ferried to rich English tables. Tried to put himself on the remote, nameless island to which Fereng had been lost and abandoned. Thought of the small boy at the union hall, his belly rumbling from hunger, stealing magazines instead of an apple or bread, something approaching an education he and his family would never be able to afford. Smith met Fereng's eyes, and he felt something unspoken pass between them, but a message, a secret, an intention nevertheless.

Fereng snapped his fingers, and Naakesh handed him the newspaper they had bought that morning. There was a grainy printed photograph of a crowd of people milling outside the Old Bailey. The photograph accompanied a report of the case that had sent memories bouncing around his head the day before, a murder trial . . .

"Ignore the words," said Fereng. "Though I do admit the case in question is something of a coincidence. Look at this man."

He tapped his gnarled finger on a man to the left of the photograph, half-turning as though in the act of trying to avoid the flashpan of the photographer. He was tall and thin, with a black top hat and a cane in his gloved hand, a pale gray mustache beneath a hawkish nose.

"This is the man we are going to kill. His name is Walsingham."

They had taken it in turns to pore over the issue of *World Marvels & Wonders* that the boy, Tom, had given Bent outside the newspaper and magazine offices on Fleet Street. Bent had dashed into 23 Grosvenor Square, waving the periodical around like a flag and bellowing that Gideon was alive while Maria leaped up and down in excitement and Mrs. Cadwallader fanned her rapidly reddening face with a dish towel. Then they had repaired to the study, surrounded by glass cases containing the trophies and trinkets from Captain Trigger and John Reed's various adventures, and gathered around the coffee table while first Bent, then Maria, and finally the housekeeper examined each page of the penny dreadful for some mark or code, some hidden message or half-visible communication.

There was nothing, so they all surmised that Gideon must have meant for them to read something into the Captain Trigger adventure contained in the pages, "The Golden Apple of Shangri-La." Bent gave them a précis of the story—Dr. Reed (for it was he who carried out Mr. Walsingham's orders on behalf of Queen Victoria and the British Government, though the world was fooled into believing the hero was Captain Trigger, to allow Dr. Reed to remain in the shadows) had been taken by Rowena Fanshawe in the airship *Skylady* to the roof of the world, the distant Himalayas, where Reed had heard that his archenemy Von Karloff had been seen, with a colleague, Professor Reginald Halifax, in tow. Correctly thinking the Prussian adventurer with whom he had crossed swords many times was up to no good, Reed employed a local Tibetan mystic, Jamyang, to show him and Rowena the secret path to the hidden valley of Shangri-La, where it was summer all the time and the beautiful women who resided there did so eternally in the flower of youth.

It was only in Shangri-La, as Rowena had explained to them all one evening over dinner, that a truth most unpalatable to Dr. Reed had emerged, and one that contributed directly to Reed's later lapse of reason and decency that led him to attempt to firebomb Buckingham Palace. To wit, Von Karloff was in the employ of Walsingham also, and had been tasked with obtaining the legendary Golden Apple of Shangri-La, which kept the valley in eternal summer and removed the barriers of language between men.

Bent rose and stared beyond his own reflection in the glass of the trophy case to the golden apple, sitting on its velvet cushion after the adventures that almost saw it lost in America. "What's the boy trying to tell us?" he asked. "What's the relevance of the apple story?"

Mrs. Cadwallader was staring at the cover of the magazine, her hands framing the encouragement to turn inside to read the Captain Trigger adventure, above it the headline related to the main cover illustration in a somber, funereal font that read: LOST FOR FIFTEEN YEARS. She said, "Perhaps, if the boy you spoke to told the truth, it was merely happenstance that it was this particular magazine. Maybe Mr. Smith, his mind fogged by that dastardly Mesmer, simply wanted to send *some* message we would recognize as coming from him."

Bent shook his head. "Nah, the kid was certain that Gideon had said this particular issue was to come here." He glanced at the clock. "Look at the time. It's the last day of Rowena's trial in the morning, and we have a certain Jack the Ripper to catch tomorrow evening. It's going to be a long day. Bed, everyone!"

The first thing Bent did when he arrived at court was to find George Lestrade. He was under no illusions that the Grosvenor Square gang was going to apprehend Sergio de la Garcia themselves and rescue the Elmwood girl—there were limits to all this heroism business after all, especially with Gideon out of the picture. Bent elbowed his way into the foyer, already packed with people and the marble floor slick with snow and ice sloughed off their galoshes and umbrellas. As Bent skated awkwardly across the floor, grasping for his balance, he thought not for the first time in the last week that he couldn't wait for spring, was desperate for a bit of blue sky and warmth. Of course, he considered, Rowena might be watching spring from the inside of a cell at Holloway—if she was incredibly lucky and hadn't been hanged—and Gideon might be staring at the sun like an idiot from whichever gutter he'd fallen into, but . . . well, at least Aloysius Bent would have nabbed Jack the Ripper.

George Lestrade was looking insufferably pleased with himself, which gave Bent pause. The ferret-eyed policeman looked at Bent with something approaching glee. "Ah, Mr. Bent. I wondered when word would filter down to your social strata."

"Word, Lestrade? I've got *three* words for you—well, four really. Jack. The. Effing. Ripper."

"Precisely, Bent," said Lestrade with a thin smile. "Jack the Ripper. Walked into the Commercial Road police station not two hours ago and gave himself up."

Bent's mouth worked wordlessly, then he swallowed and said, "The Spaniard?"

Lestrade squinted at him. "Spaniard? What are you prattling on about, Bent?" The detective glanced from side to side. "Strictly speaking, this is all hush-hush at the moment, but while it's you . . . well, greengrocer from Balham. Confessed to the whole lot."

"You've got the wrong man," said Bent.

"He was wearing a leather apron," said Lestrade, as though explaining something terribly grown-up to a small child. "Covered in bloodstains." The policeman nodded toward the courtroom. "Speaking of which, there goes the Swiss fellow, Miescher. I think the final act is about to begin."

Judge Stanger gave a rare and indulgent smile as Dr. Miescher completed the setting up of his equipment in the space cleared for him in the courtroom. He glanced at the public gallery and asked, "Are we about to have a scientific demonstration, or is this some music hall conjuring act?"

Miescher, sweating in his high collar despite the cold, stood by a large wheeled apparatus, in the back of which a small furnace burned. Bursts of steam rose from the exhaust pipes at the side of the wood and brass box, and Miescher began to frantically wind a large crank handle set into the front of the device with a loud ratcheting sound.

Angus Scullimore leaned on the bench and said, "I appreciate the indulgence of the court in this matter. As the gentlemen of the press will no doubt be aware, this is a momentous scientific moment in the history of the English judicial process."

The juddering apparatus having settled into a rhythmic rumbling, Dr. Miescher turned his attention to a rack of glass vials each containing a straw-colored liquid. Behind the shaking box was a felt-covered wooden board with a small shelf at the base, on which he placed the wooden rack. The Swiss scientist nodded curtly at Scullimore.

The prosecuting counsel cleared his throat and addressed the judge. "Your Honor, I would like to call my final witness, Dr. Friedrich Miescher."

"I think that would be an eminently appropriate course of action," said Stanger with another smile.

Bent leaned over to Siddell and whispered in his ear, "The judge is in a tricky mood today. I'm not sure if that is a good or bad thing."

Dr. Miescher left his steaming machine and took to the witness box, allowing the clerk to swear him in. Scullimore said, "Dr. Miescher. In a moment I am going to ask you to use your techniques to prove without a shadow of a doubt that the defendant, Rowena Fanshawe, is guilty of the charge of murder most foul. But first, Doctor, could you tell us a little of what you are doing in London?"

The bearded Swiss nodded. "I have developed certain processes that aid greatly in the positive identification of individuals. My work came to the notice of the British Government, and Sir Edward Bradford, the Commissioner of your Metropolitan Police, gave me permission to visit crime scenes across the capital."

"And what were you looking for at these crime scenes, Doctor?"

Miescher nodded. "Blood, sir. It is my discovery that each of our blood contains a . . . a signature, if you will. If I mix blood with sodium sulfate, I am able to isolate a compound I call nuclein, and my device there is able to analyze the nuclein and measure the frequency and allocation of the nucleic acids present in the nuclein, with a different color each for cytosine, adenine, thymine, and guanine. . . ."

A hush had fallen over the courtroom, and Scullimore coughed. "I fear you have lost us, somewhat, Dr. Miescher. Perhaps a demonstration might aid our understanding. . . ."

Miescher left the witness box and stood behind the humming wheeled apparatus. He selected the first glass vial and held it up to the judge and jury. "This is the key to the whole mystery. I obtained samples of blood and skin from beneath the fingernails of Mr. Edward Gaunt, the deceased. I cross-matched the nuclein results with other samples from crime scenes across London. There was an exact match between the sample from Mr. Gaunt's fingernails and a patch of blood in the laboratory of Professor Stanford Rubicon."

Scullimore nodded. "So whoever killed Mr. Gaunt was the same person responsible for the burglary at Professor Rubicon's premises?"

Miescher said, "Yes, without a doubt. Allow me to demonstrate." From beneath the box he took two wooden tubes and extracted from them rolls of white paper, which he pinned side by side on the green felt board. The rolls of paper were inked with four-color rainbows, the sequence of blue, green, yellow, and red stripes identical on each. Dr. Miescher stepped back to admire them. "The different colors each represent one of the nucleic acids I mentioned earlier, and their sequence exactly as they appear in samples of nuclein extracted from blood. As you can see, the samples taken from Mr. Gaunt's attacker and Professor Rubicon's laboratory are undoubtedly the same."

Judge Stanger leaned forward to scrutinize the rolls of colored paper. "We need some kind of comparison for context, Doctor. And I still fail to see how this links the defendant to either crime scene."

Dr. Miescher took a further glass vial and held it up. "This is a sample taken from Miss Rowena Fanshawe upon her arrest. I am going to use it to demonstrate the nuclein machine in action. I have already run the blood samples I took from the members of the jury through it, but I have brought their nuclein extracts to court should you wish to verify any of my words."

Stanger invited him to continue and said, "That won't be necessary, Dr. Miescher. You are under oath and a man of science. Proceed."

Miescher took the glass vial and opened a hatch on the top of his apparatus, pouring the small measure of straw-colored liquid into it. Mr Stanger coughed and said, "Shouldn't that be red, if it is blood, Dr. Miescher?"

Miescher nodded and said, "This is the plasma, which constitutes a little over half of the content of our blood. It is the hemoglobin which gives blood its red color. It is the binding of iron and oxygen that—"

Stanger waved and said, "I think that is all, Dr. Miescher. Pray, continue with your work."

Miescher nodded then unraveled a dozen more rolls of paper and pinned them up side by side against the control sample of the suspected killer's nuclein signature. Bent leaned forward to study each in turn. He had to admit the spread of

colored lines was markedly different in each, and none was re-
motely similar to the murderer's nuclein.

Dr. Miescher took up a cane and indicated the first roll.
"Here you see a large grouping of blue lines, which represent
thymine. Then there are noticeable repeating sequences of cytosine, in purple. None of these patterns is evident in the
samples taken from the jury."

At that moment the shuddering machine began to spit out
a roll of paper from a slot in the front. "Ah," said Miescher.
"The nuclein signature of the blood sample taken from Miss
Fanshawe." He went to the front of the device and waited until
the paper had finished unspooling, then he tore it off and took
it to the felt board. He pinned the top of the roll next to the
murder sample and allowed it to unfurl.

"Bollocks," said Bent.

<hr/>

"These aren't quite identical, you know," said Bent, staring at
the striped rolls of paper. The court had broken for lunch, and
for the jury and judge to consider the new evidence. After the
break it was the defense's turn to examine witnesses. The only
problem was, they didn't have any. Bent kept looking to the
door, praying that at any moment Gideon would come bursting into the court to save the day.

Dr. Miescher joined him at the felt board in the otherwise
empty courtroom. He pointed to the clusters of colors and the
recurring sequences. "There are at least fifty percent of matching sequences in the same places. Here, here, here . . . The
other samples have between zero and two percent matches."

"You never get a complete match?"

Miescher nodded enthusiastically. "Oh, sometimes. But my
research has shown that a fifty percent match or above generally proves conclusive. The technology is still in its infancy. . . ."

Bent continued to stare at the colored lines. "So every single
one of us has a different one of these nuclein signatures?
Mine's different from yours and from hers and from the judge's?
From Scullimore's and . . . and my father's and—"

Miescher held up his hand. "Ah. There it becomes compli-cated. We are, you see, the product of our parents. Were you to sample my nuclein it would share half of the characteristics of my father's sample and half of my mother's signature."

It was Bent's turn to call a halt. "Hang on. Half? Fifty percent?" He pointed to the first roll on the board. "So the fifty percent match that occurs between this sample from the mur-derer and Rowena's signature . . . that could be explained by a family connection?"

"Well . . . kind of. Not necessarily. The familial fifty per-cent that matches Miss Fanshawe's could be the *other* fifty percent that she does not have in common with the killer sample. . . ."

Bent grabbed the surprised Miescher's elbows. "But there's a chance, right? There's an effing chance?"

"Yes," said the Doctor. "But I would need a sample from the parent to know for sure. . . ."

Glancing at his pocket watch, Bent ran as fast as his huff-ing body could carry him out of the courtroom.

Bent found Siddell halfway through a baked potato he'd ob-tained from one of the vendors who had been clustering in the foyer since the trial began. He snatched the cardboard tray and balsawood fork away from the lawyer.

"Shine a light, Bent!"

"You have to get me down to see Rowena. Now."

Siddell wiped his mouth on his sleeve. "If I do that, you'll be ruling yourself out of testifying. And do I need to remind you that you're all we've got?"

Nevertheless, Bent frog-marched Siddell down the staircase to the holding cells in the cellars beneath the Old Bailey and had him sign Bent an access pass. The dour-faced court atten-dant took him to a small, dark cell. Rowena, looking thinner, smaller, and paler than Bent had ever seen her, started as the door opened and ran to embrace him as the guard locked them in.

"Aloysius. Thank God. I thought you were never coming to see me."

"I couldn't, girl. Not while I was down as a character witness." He held her at arm's length, taking a good look at her. "How are you doing?"

She shook her head tightly. "You don't want to know, Aloysius. In Holloway . . . they know who I am. It's not good for me." She looked at him and brightened. "But you're here now! You've come to get me out!"

"Well . . . things have been a bit odd out there. Gideon had a run-in with Markus Mesmer and went missing. That's why he hasn't been in court."

"But he's back now?" Her voice fell to a low whisper. "What's the plan, Aloysius? An airship rescue? A tunnel through these cells?"

A pained look came across Bent's face. "Rowena . . . nothing like that, girl. We're at the mercy of the courts on this one."

Her eyes brimmed with tears. "I didn't do it, Aloysius. I didn't kill Gaunt."

He held her tight. "I know you didn't. But I'm going to find out who did. Rowena . . . I need to find your parents. And quickly."

She slumped in his arms. "If that's all that will save me, then I'm lost, Aloysius. They're both beyond us."

He felt his heart sink like a stone. "Both of them? In what way?"

She nodded, pulling back to meet his anguished gaze. "Edward Gaunt's wife? Catherine?"

"The one he killed with the mercury from the barometers?"

Rowena nodded sadly. "I knew he was doing something to her. If only I had acted earlier. I could have saved her. Saved my mother."

Bent stared at her. "Catherine Gaunt was your mother? Then Edward Gaunt . . . ?"

She shook her head vehemently. "No. Never. He married my mother after she divorced my father. . . ."

"Divorced him?" Bent exhaled in relief. "We must find your father, Rowena. Now. Tell me his name."

She smiled sadly. "It won't do any good, Aloysius." She looked at him levelly. "My father was Charles Collier."

25

LEARNING TO FLY

"I was twelve years old when I learned to fly," said Rowena. "I wasn't Rowena Fanshawe yet, though she was in the process of being born. Back then I was just plain Jane. Jane Collier, at first, then when she divorced my father and remarried, I became Jane Gaunt."

She looked beyond Bent, beyond the cool, musty air of the stone-lined cell, into the clean, blue sky of the past. She had been tiny when her mother told her that Father would not be living with them anymore. "He loves adventure more than his wife and child," her mother had said tremulously. "He cannot give up his perilous travels, even for us."

And little Jane Collier thought it must be a wonderful thing, to put adventure above everything else in the world, and did not blame him at all. Besides, he still visited most weekends and took her on days out, and on those weekends when his travels took him away he at least brought her presents: lumps of stone that floated on water, intricately carved jade statuettes, polished jet pendants. And then Charles Collier came to her and said he was going on a distant journey that would take him away from her for a long time, but he would bring her back a special present.

Jane had clapped her hands together. "A monkey!"

Charles Collier ruffled her hair with his big, callused hand and laughed. "A monkey."

But he never came back.

Catherine Collier was a handsome woman, and she had been courted in Charles Collier's absence by a man named Edward Gaunt, a businessman and entrepreneur. After a suitable period of mourning had elapsed, and Charles Collier had been legally declared dead, Edward Gaunt announced his intention to marry the Widow Collier, and she duly accepted. Jane Collier, who was twelve years old, was forced to change her name to that of her adoptive father, Edward Gaunt.

It was not long after the wedding that the arguments started. Jane would listen to them from the top of the staircase. They were invariably about money. Edward Gaunt was a businessman and an entrepreneur, but evidently not a particularly successful one. He constantly needed money to shore up his failing companies. Charles Collier had not been without money, and he had made a provision in his will for an allowance to be paid to his ex-wife. The bulk of his money, though, was put into a trust for his daughter, Jane, to pay for an education for her or, should she wish, a dowry for a marriage.

Jane Gaunt had no interest in marriage, at the age of twelve, and the only education she had any desire to pursue was the one she obtained from her father's old books. She had taken all his books on aeronautical engineering, the history of the flight pioneers from Jean-Pierre Blanchard onward, techniques of airship flying, and atlases and gazetteers of the world. She filled her head with all this knowledge and more, hiding in her room, away from the arguments below.

Which, she soon discovered, were not all about money.

Jane hated it when Edward Gaunt let himself into her room uninvited. She ignored him for as long as possible, taking pleasure from his rapidly rising anger as he stood in the doorway and watched her concentrating intently on a technical manual concerned chiefly with the maintenance and repair of altimeters. Eventually he closed the door behind him and crossed the space between them, slamming shut the book she was reading at her desk.

She glared at him, hating him intensely, but held her tongue, for her mother's sake. Gaunt swayed somewhat in the gaslight, and she could smell a cloud of brandy clinging to him. Her father, Charles Collier, had sometimes drunk (though never to excess, not in her presence) rum, which she considered an adventurous sort of liquor. Brandy, on Edward Gaunt, at least, was the perfume of desperation and gloom.

And, forever more after that night, the smell of something she would not be able to put a name to for many years, and when she finally did, it would end in death.

Gaunt had put a hand on her shoulder, making her flesh crawl. He said: "How old are you next birthday, Jane?"

"Thirteen."

"And what do you know of what occurs between a man and a woman, who are married and share a bed?"

Jane blushed furiously, staring at the leather cover of the book Gaunt had slammed shut. In truth she had no idea what he was talking about. Gaunt had insisted she be taught by the nuns at the nearby convent school, and such matters were not on the curriculum.

Gaunt left his hand on her shoulder. "Jane . . . a married man has certain rights. And your mother . . . well, she has been unwell recently. She has been unable to discharge her wifely duties. Therefore, I must exercise my rights in other ways." She felt his hand tighten on her bare flesh. Her throat was suddenly dry, and she thought there must have been a sudden heavy heat in the room, for when Edward Gaunt spoke next, his voice was thick and odd.

"Take off your dress and lie upon your bed."

* * *

"Jesus effing Christ," said Bent. "*Jesus*, Rowena."

She nodded. She felt as though she should cry, show some emotion. But she couldn't. "That first time, that was when I learned to fly. All the time he was . . . doing it, I was thinking about the construction, maintenance, and repair of altimeters. And the time after that I memorized the trade routes between London and North Africa. And then the correct inflation procedures for single, double, and four-celled rigid helium balloons. And the time—"

Bent held up a hand to stop her, then awkwardly placed it

upon hers, knotted together on the table surface. The action moved her more than anything else she could remember in years. He asked, "How long?"

Rowena gathered the memories like reeling in anchor lines. "It was inevitable, even at a convent school—or perhaps especially at a convent school—that conversation would turn at some point to matters of the heart, and the body. Whispered words, hushed questions, surreptitiously shared books on anatomy and magazines of pictures of women in states of undress. And every whisper, every query, every grainy photograph of white, bruised flesh, had made me want to throw up.

"I was sixteen. I went to my mother and asked her if she knew what Edward Gaunt had been doing to me since I was twelve years old. She looked at me as though she barely knew me. Now I know, of course, that even then Gaunt had started poisoning her, giving her doses of mercury to keep her compliant and eventually have her committed so he could begin the process of taking her money. She told me I was a liar and a fantasist, that I had my head in the clouds, and that I was just like my father."

"What did you do?" asked Bent.

Rowena took a deep, ragged breath. "I knew Gaunt would have designs on the money that was held in trust for me, and even then I feared he might harm me to get it. So I took matters into my own hands. I wrote a note that I posted through the next-door neighbor's door as I knew they would be out until teatime. Then I took a cab to the River Thames, weighed my dress pockets down with stones, and threw myself in."

Bent stared at her. "You tried to commit suicide?"

She smiled tightly. "Not suicide. Murder, after a fashion. I killed Jane Gaunt that day, let her weighted dress float to the bottom of the Thames, left a note saying my stepfather had been terribly abusing me, then floated downriver, hanging on to a piece of driftwood. I climbed out at Greenwich and waited, shivering, by the Lady of Liberty flood barrier for a courier to bring a trunk I had dispatched two days earlier. It was filled with clothing, my father's books, and all the money I could find in the house. It was addressed to a name I had plucked out of the air, like a passing dirigible. Jane Gaunt was gone, and I got my hair cut short then went to the Union Hall of the Esteemed Brethren of International Airshipmen and signed up. Despite much opposition I eventually managed to obtain a position as an apprentice aerostat first mate with a small cargo-running dirigible company flying out of Highgate Aerodrome. Rowena Fanshawe had arrived."

Bent was rubbing his face. "Jesus, Rowena. I had no idea."

Rowena smiled sadly. "So you see, Aloysius, that I have nothing but motives for killing Edward Gaunt, and I have no living relatives who can aid me in whatever eleventh hour legal challenge you had in mind."

But Aloysius Bent had taken a rolled magazine from the inside pocket of his overcoat and was staring at the cover. "I wouldn't be too sure, Rowena."

She raised a quizzical eyebrow at him, but he simply stuffed the periodical back into his coat and said, "You sit tight, girl, we're going to get you out of here. I just need a quick word with old Stanger. . . ."

Judge Stanger peered down with arched eyebrows at Willy Siddell, who sweated under his gaze in a courtroom still empty of the jury and public. Stanger said, "I am inclined to agree with Mr. Scullimore, Mr. Siddell. This is highly irregular."

Bent sighed and elbowed Siddell out of the way. "Look, Your Honor, while we're being highly irregular about everything, you might as well talk to the organ grinder as the monkey."

Siddell began to object, but Stanger waved him down. "Ah. Aloysius Bent. I have been used to seeing you on the press bench, but not so much with the defense counsel. Somewhat a case of poacher turned gamekeeper."

"Yeah, well, I'm a friend of Rowena Fanshawe, and I can tell you for a fact she didn't do it."

Stanger smiled. "A plea for clemency?"

Bent shook his head. "No, because I know that would do no good. It's a plea for time, Your Honor. New information has come to light. I know who killed Edward Gaunt. I just need to find him."

Stanger scrutinized Bent for a moment then took out his pocket watch. "Mr. Bent, given the defense case's sore lack of witnesses thus far, I am inclined to grant you this boon. You have until ten o'clock tomorrow morning to produce your new evidence." He leaned forward. "Take warning, though, Mr. Bent: If you fail I shall be sending out the jury to consider their verdicts. And should they return with a decision that Miss Fanshawe is guilty of murder . . . well, given the high-profile nature of this case I feel I shall be compelled to impose the most severe sentence for this crime that is open to me."

Bent gaped at him. "You'd give her the death penalty?"

The judge smiled without humor. "They call me Stanger the Hanger, do they not? Ten o'clock, Mr. Bent, and not a moment later."

Bent hurtled through the Old Bailey lobby, gathering people in his wake as a gale might snatch up leaves. Siddell followed, muttering over and over "shine a light" as Bent beckoned over Inspector Lestrade. "George. I'm going to need you. Your boys are going to have to comb London."

The protesting inspector fell in behind Bent as the journalist spied Walsingham and changed course to intercept him.

"You," he said, jabbing a finger at Walsingham's chest. "You have some explaining to do."

The thin secret service man used his cane to move Bent's finger from his chest. "I doubtless have much explaining to do, Mr. Bent, but none of it to you."

Bent brandished the magazine at him. "Did you know Charles Collier was still alive?"

Walsingham blinked, and Bent smiled. "I thought you'd be in that one up to your elbows. Now come on, time is short."

He pushed his way out of the Old Bailey, into the biting,

icy wind where crowds still milled on the pavements, not yet aware that the Fanshawe jury was at that moment being sent home for the day. Vendors and hawkers had gravitated toward the court, and Bent barged past a fat Indian in a black turban leaning on a hot chestnut stall before pushing a pin-striped banker out of the way and stepping into the horse-drawn cab he had just hailed. He held open the door for Walsingham and Lestrade and said to Willy Siddell, "Keep an eye on Rowena, and wait for news from me. I want you to subpoena Dr. Miescher in the meantime and take him back to your place. Make sure he's got his machine with him, and don't let him out of your sight."

Siddell nodded. "But where are you going?"

Bent slammed shut the cab door and told the driver to take them to 23 Grosvenor Square, then leaned out of the window to Siddell. "I'm off to find a corpse, see if I can't effing stop Rowena Fanshawe becoming one."

As the cab lurched away, Walsingham tapped his brass-tipped cane impatiently on the wooden floor of the vehicle. "Mr. Bent, would you care to explain yourself? Charles Collier has been dead for twenty years."

"He hasn't, and he's killed Edward Gaunt. I don't know where he's been, but he's well and truly back."

"Back?" said Walsingham. Was there a touch of something in his steely eyes that Bent hadn't seen before? Fear perhaps? "But why? And why now?"

"That," said Fereng, "is a very good question, Smith. Maybe you are ready for the answer."

The young tyrannosaur growled and grumbled in the dancing shadows of the underground room, but Fereng was standing by his decree that the beast was not to have any more food. Smith still had no idea how the monster fitted into Fereng's plans, save as some symbol of his desire for vengeance, stolen in an opportunistic moment. He had enjoyed a more restful night's sleep, used now to the towering presence of the beast and his new companions. After breakfast and dung gathering, Phoolendu had departed on a mission of his own, followed one by one by the other Thuggees, leaving Smith alone with Fereng and affording him the opportunity to ask why he had finally returned to England.

Fereng gazed into the dinosaur dung fire. "Do you know the name Charles Collier?"

Smith shrugged. "Perhaps. I can't say."

Fereng smiled. "Not so long ago, I felt the same way. Charles Collier, Hero of the Empire, was like a dream to me, a story. I almost forgot I used to be him. My new identity of Fereng, harrier of the British Raj, defender of the poor and weak, avenger of the dispossessed and downtrodden . . . it had subsumed all else. Charles Collier was an old coat, half-remembered, that I didn't wear any longer.

"But my new Thuggee brothers knew I had once been one of their enemies, knew I still clung, in a tiny corner of my soul, to my English roots. They used to bring me news from the Empire they picked up on their travels, and the occasional newspaper. Once, investigating an abandoned Colonial home, they found a huge stack of yellowing London newspapers, years old in some cases. They brought them back to me, and by degrees the old stories reconciled Fereng the revenge seeker with Charles Collier the hero, merging the two with each report from the London Stock Exchange, each court hearing at the assizes, each horse-racing result, each Parliamentary sketch.

"The newspapers were a disjointed collection, perhaps saved for starting fires or composting. They were dated from just a few months previously to twenty years or more before. Then, one morning just a few weeks ago, sheltering from the battering monsoon rains, I chanced upon a small piece in the *Illustrated London Argus*, from June 1880. It detailed how a young woman of just sixteen years old had died after throwing herself into the Thames. She had left a note implicating her stepfather, Edward Gaunt, in some manner of involvement in her suicide, but a resulting police investigation ruled there was no evidence. The girl's mother, Catherine Gaunt, told the inquest that the girl was given to flights of fancy and had never truly recovered from the death of her natural father."

Fereng locked eyes with Smith. "That was my little girl. My Jane. I was shocked back into myself, as though someone had thrown a bucket of iced water into my face. I had been snapping away at the British Empire on its fringes in India, like a small dog yapping at the heels of a giant. But now I had cause to bring the battle home to the heart of the Empire. I gathered my closest friends—Deeptendu, Naakesh, Kalanath, and dear Phoolendu—and we traveled to England. My vengeance was to be threefold, Smith, and almost as soon as we set foot on English soil we heard the rumors and whispers of the beast held captive in the laboratory of Professor Stanford Rubicon, and the key to our wrath was made clear to us."

"Threefold?"

Fereng nodded. "My first mission was to Kennington, just Saturday night. The home of Edward Gaunt, the man who sought to step into my shoes as husband and father. He failed miserably on both counts, confining my Catherine to a sanatorium and . . ." Fereng's lips drew back in a snarl. "He admitted everything, bloodied and battered, never taking his eyes from the noose I knotted there in front of him. How he abused and brutalized my darling Jane when she was little more than a child. How he drove her to take her own life. I made him pay, Smith. I restored the universal balance. A life for a life. Another thousand years' delay to Kali's return. He was my first vengeance.

"My second vengeance shall be Walsingham, the black heart of the British Empire, the shadowy soul of Albion, the darkness-stained core of Britannia. The man who dispatched me to my doom, and who knows how many besides."

"And your third vengeance?" asked Smith.

Fereng smiled. "One thing at a time, Smith."

The dinosaur growled, and there were echoing footsteps from the tunnel, Deeptendu leading the other Thuggees into the brick cavern. Fereng rose to meet them. "You have news?"

Phoolendu stepped forward. "Tsk, you let the fire burn low." He placed three bricks of dried tyrannosaur dung on the flames and turned back to Fereng. "But yes. News. I stationed myself outside the Old Bailey, and not long ago I saw him. Walsingham."

Fereng's eyes shone in the newly raging fire. "At last. You followed him?"

"He was in the company of a fat man, a journalist as far as I can understand, and a policeman, one of the kinds who does not wear a uniform. They took a horse-drawn cab outside the courts."

"You heard to where?"

Phoolendu nodded. "Grosvenor Square. Number 23."

Smith blinked and tried to speak, his mouth suddenly too dry to make sounds. Grosvenor Square? Number 23? Why that was . . . that was . . .

"A very exclusive address," said Fereng, suddenly dropping low and in one fluid movement whipping a knife from where it was tucked into his boot, flipping it into a whirling arc, and plucking it blade-first from the air, presenting it to Smith. "A very nice place to die."

26

Ghosts

Don Sergio de la Garcia had lived, for two and a half years, in a dark and cloying room on the third floor of a crammed tenement that straddled the border between Lambeth and Stockwell. He had seen three summers in this hellhole, the heat and stench from the streets rising to fill his dingy room, and was facing his third Christmas, the howling, icy winds rattling the windowpanes, the snow piling up on the sills. He had chosen the area because it was the haunt of many Portuguese immigrants, close enough in appearance to him that he could hide among them, but different enough in culture that he could live unbothered by attempts at friendship or conversation. He had never divulged his address to his masters, some nameless fear encouraging him to fog and blur his location, even from those who held all the cards. He had hinted at rooms in more salubrious locations on the rare occasions that they had sent envoys—Markus Mesmer chief among them—to check on his progress.

He had never felt so alone in his entire life. The summers in London were typified by thick, hot smog, through which the blue sky could be glimpsed only occasionally. He dreamed of the big country he had left behind, the far horizons, the endless skies, the air you could breathe deeply. The friends and family he had once had. There was none of that here, and he was alone.

Almost. For his dark and tiny room, paid for monthly with the bag of gold coins he had brought with him from New Spain—where he used to have coffers filled with such riches!—and which now lived beneath a loose floorboard under his bed, this room was never empty. It was always filled with young women.

Or, at any rate, their ghosts. The quiet ghosts of the women he had systematically murdered over the course of his two-and-a-half-year exile in London. They stood in pale battalions in the shadows of the room, crowding out the air, suffocating him, never speaking but always watching, each one with an accusing gash across her forehead, long-dried rivulets of black blood running into her eyes, her dead eyes that stripped away his soul, paper-thin layer by paper-thin layer.

His soul, and his sanity, too. Among the jostling ghosts he could swear he saw a more substantial spirit, a beautiful young woman with cascading blond hair, a rope wound tightly about her arms and torso, a filthy rag gagging her mouth. She had no telltale cut above her eyes, which implored him, tearful, beseeching. Then he remembered, half-giggling to himself. She wasn't a ghost at all. She was the mechanical girl, the automaton with treasure in her head.

Finally, Don Sergio de la Garcia could go home.

He looked again at the notice in the newspaper.

Congratulations, Man in Black! Meet us at the place that bears the family name of the girl you left behind! Eight o'clock tonight! It is almost over! Mr. Brain.

Garcia had puzzled over that for a good while. "What do you think this means?" he had asked the gagged automaton, who watched him with wild, tear-stained eyes. He paused to wonder at the workmanship that had gone into the mechanism, that it could weep so convincingly, then stalked up and down the tiny room. He still wore his black outfit, the cowl pulled back onto his shoulders, revealing his face with its high cheekbones and pencil-thin mustache. He had always been considered handsome back in New Spain, but now he knew he had acquired a sickly pallor beneath the London smog, and his

once-black hair was going gray, as if each murder he committed somehow drained a measure of color and vitality from
him. He was generally careful about hiding the El Chupacabras
costume away in the daylight hours, but he felt so close to the
end of it all that he allowed himself a little recklessness.

Garcia fell to his knees before the terrified-looking automaton. "I was a hero, back in New Spain. I fought for the poor
and the weak. I was a champion. Then they came for me. I
thought they were taking us to Madrid, at first: my wife, Julia,
my beautiful daughters Sophia and Eloise, and I. Important
business, they said. But it was not the Spanish Government. It
was . . . they took us to New Orleans. I had no idea those stories were true. I was given a mission." Garcia reached up and
stroked the hair of the flinching woman. "Find you. Find what
is in your head. They have your creator, you know. Professor
Einstein. They know that you escaped him in London, that
you have the brain of a whore in your head as well as the ancient treasure. Thus they sent me here, two years ago, more,
to begin slicing open the heads of whores, to find the treasure."

Garcia stood quickly and whirled around, hefting an imaginary rapier and dancing across the bare floorboards. "Jack the
Ripper they called me! Mary Ann Nichols!" He swiped his invisible sword. "Annie Chapman!" Parry. "Elizabeth Stride!"
Lunge. "Catherine Eddowes! Mary Jane Kelly!" He began to
slash and swipe furiously and wildly, falling to his knees once
again. He peered into the shadows, at the milling ghosts. "All
here. And more. I am sorry, I am so very sorry. *Lo siento.* But
now it is over. And I can finally see my beloved Julia and the
girls again."

He retrieved the newspaper from where he had tossed it.
"But . . . the girl I left behind? The family name? My Julia's
family name is Marcos, but I have scoured the maps and gazetteers and cannot . . ." He paused, squinting at the ghosts.
"You think? Teresa? But how could Mesmer know of that? We
were always so careful, and then she married Juan Batiste and
had her baby girl, Inez. . . ." He frowned. "Teresa died seven

years ago. Her name? Palomo." He scurried back to the maps, peering at them in the dull light. Then he straightened and turned back to the automaton. "The Dove."

In the suite of hotel rooms in Soho the party had commandeered, Markus Mesmer was sitting in the bay window, watching the gloom already gathering over London. He'd had the mechanical girl right in the palm of his hand, and she had escaped.

Thank God for El Chupacabras. Had he not captured the automaton, Mesmer would not have dared return to New Orleans. The swordsman might be half-mad, but he had finally come good. And that evening Mesmer would finally have Maria back in his custody, and he could take her to his paymaster.

Louis XVI, the Witch-King of New Orleans.

Markus Mesmer's long and varied career had led him to work for many masters, but he could safely say that his current one was the strangest by far. Still, Mesmer was a free agent, and while there was still much in New Orleans to interest him, when he had assuaged the hungers that the Witch-King's court fed so well, then the world in all its richness was still his oyster. There was a knock at the door of his room and the burly Spaniard, Alfonso, peered around it, bearing a folded newspaper.

"The notice is in?" said Mesmer.

Alfonso crossed the room to Mesmer's desk and handed over the newspaper. "*Sí, señor*, however . . ."

Mesmer snatched it from him and took a moment to decipher the advertisement in Spanish. He frowned at Alfonso. "I thought I said to have Garcia bring the automaton here. What is this *girl you left behind* nonsense?"

Sweat beaded on Alfonso's vast, shaved head. "I do not know. This is not the notice we placed at the newspaper office."

Mesmer screwed the paper up in his hands. "Someone is

playing us for fools. Either Garcia has switched allegiances and is in league with our enemies, or someone has intercepted our notice and means to divert Garcia and the mechanical girl to a meeting point of their choosing."

He tossed the newspaper back at Alfonso. "Try to find out what this means."

He did not have much faith in the ability of the motley gang of Frenchmen and Spaniards he had been saddled with to solve the riddle, though, and when Alfonso had left and closed the door behind him, Mesmer sat thoughtfully for a moment then took up his Hypno-Array and considered the framework of wires, lenses, and cogs, the one that he had used to convince that innocent shopkeeper that he was, in fact, Jack the Ripper. The man's confession—though delivered, no doubt, to the police with utter conviction—would not stand up to much scrutiny, but it would distract the constabulary sufficiently and buy Mesmer enough time to get away from London with Garcia and Maria. Or so he had supposed until this latest turn of events.

Mesmer's devices were complicated structures that took a long time to create. They were not the source of Mesmer's powers—that was deep within his head, nurtured and exercised over many, many years of training and development—but they did amplify and direct his talents. As such, his Hypno-Arrays were finely tuned with Mesmer's own mind. He had lost enough of them in the past to improve and modify each successive design, and now, though an array might be stolen, it was not necessarily lost . . . and it could still cause his foes harm.

The automaton had stolen his only other Hypno-Array, but the latest version he now placed over his head had a new function he had not had the opportunity to fully test yet. He closed his eyes and switched on the array, focusing his mind and funneling it into the lenses that turned and came together to create a telescope of sorts, which he trained upon the tumultuous hiss of millions of London minds suddenly turned on as though they were a gramophone disc and the Hypno-Array the needle. For many minutes he stood, turning on the spot, until somewhere amid the morass of white noise a pinprick of something else appeared. There. His missing Hypno-Array. But wait . . . a second signal? From exactly the same location? How was that possible?

Mesmer carefully triggered the mind signal he hoped would be received by these two stolen Hypno-Arrays, then watched with a satisfied smile as the pinpricks became flares of blinding light, and a location was revealed to him.

"The first thing you've got to understand," said Bent through a mouthful of cake provided by Mrs. Cadwallader, "is that the poor sap you've got locked up is most certainly not Jack the effing Ripper."

In the study, surrounded by the trophies and mementoes of Captain Trigger and John Reed's adventures, George Lestrade looked over the rim of his teacup with narrowed eyes. "How can you be so sure?"

Maria spoke up. "Because Jack the Ripper is a man from Uvalde in New Spain by the name of Sergio de la Garcia, who also had another identity as the masked champion of the oppressed, El Chupacabras."

"And we're going to nail him at eight o'clock tonight in Hammersmith, and get back Charlotte Elmwood before someone slices her bleeding head off, if they haven't already. We could probably use your help with that, George, seeing as we've also got until ten tomorrow morning to save Rowena Fanshawe from the noose by finding Charles Collier."

Mr. Walsingham placed his cup and saucer on the low table. "Ah. Charles Collier. The dead refuse to stay buried once again."

"He's not dead," said Bent. He placed the crumpled issue of *World Marvels & Wonders* on the table. "Gideon sent this as a message. At first I thought he was trying to tell us something about the Captain Trigger adventure in it. But he was being more obvious than that. Collier's on the effing cover. Perhaps you ought to tell us what you know about him."

"I suspect there is a spiderweb here that connects Collier to Markus Mesmer and your Sergio de la Garcia, however obliquely," said Walsingham.

"It takes a spider to know one," said Bent. "We know, thanks to Maria, that Mesmer and Garcia have the same boss, and that whoever that is also has Professor Einstein."

"And you said that Mesmer has both Spanish and French henchmen?" Walsingham said to Maria.

"Odd, that," said Bent. "You normally can't put a Spaniard and a Frenchie in the same room without one of them ending up dead."

"Strange bedfellows," agreed Walsingham. "But something I have come across in the past." He looked at Maria. "To do with the very artifact in your head."

"I'll get Mrs. Cadwallader to bring in a fresh pot of tea," said Bent. "Sounds like you're going to be doing a lot of talking."

"Many years ago, some very old pages extracted from a larger volume came into my possession," said Mr. Walsingham, after Mrs. Cadwallader had brought in a tray of fresh tea and seated herself on a footstool beside Bent's chair. "This was early in my career, and there were many strange and wonderful things in the world to come to grips with. These pages detailed just another enigma, another mystery, which I gave cursory attention to, not realizing just how important they were going to prove."

Walsingham steepled his fingers beneath his chin, as though considering how much to tell them. Bent said, "Come on, man!"

"The pages were old and concerned an account of rumors and stories about an ancient treasure, lost on an uncharted island in the Indian Ocean. They hinted that this treasure could have considerable, though not fully explained, power. I managed to extrapolate a possible location, and I dispatched one of the Empire's operatives to find it."

"Charles Collier," said Bent.

Walsingham nodded. "We never heard from him again."

Maria stared at him. "So you just abandoned him?"

"You must remember, young lady, that this was twenty years ago. Airship travel was not as sophisticated as it is today. We did not have the resources nor Collier's expertise in the air to send a rescue mission. Other matters and needs subsumed that particular endeavor." Walsingham took a sip of tea. "Then, some years later, the wider volume from which the pages had been extracted came into my possession. This was called the *Hallendrup Manuscript,* and it appeared to be the work of monks in Denmark in the mid-seventeenth century. It gathered oral and written reports from around the world of many similar, if not identical, ancient treasures that had surfaced at different times and locations. One of them had seemingly originated in ancient Egypt and had been lost, and found, and stolen, and regained, and ended up in the possession of the crew of a Viking longship which had been lost at sea somewhere off the Faroe Islands."

Maria gasped and touched her temple. Walsingham smiled and nodded. "Yes. The Atlantic Artifact that I gave to Professor Hermann Einstein and that ended up giving you your strange life."

"I must say," said Bent, "you're being awfully free and easy with your secrets today, Walsingham."

Walsingham spread his hands in an expression of innocence. "It is in all our interests that this Garcia is captured as soon as possible."

Bent made a harrumphing noise. "I don't believe you ever give anything away unless it benefits you."

Walsingham smiled. "Not me, Mr. Bent. The Empire."

"Let's say that's so," said Bent. "How did *you* come by the Atlantic Artifact?"

"Three years ago the Royal Navy had developed a proto-type submersible, an underwater boat. Captain James Palmer—who took you and Gideon to rescue Professor Rubicon and Charles Darwin from the Pacific this summer—and Dr. John Reed effected a retrieval mission. There were a number of un-related treasures rescued from the wreck of the longship, though the artifact was the only one to return to London. The others were stolen in a betrayal by Palmer's temporary crew, a strange—I thought at the time—alliance of French and Span-ish sailors, spies who had evidently infiltrated the *Lady Jane*."

"Deliberate treachery?" asked Bent. "But what does it mean? France and Spain have always been at each other's throats."

"Not always," said Walsingham. "At various points in his-tory the House of Bourbon has united French and Spanish ter-ritories to a greater or lesser extent. It is my belief that there are moves afoot to restore a Bourbon king to end the perpet-ual hostilities between France and Spain."

"To what end?" asked Bent.

"To challenge the British Empire," said Walsingham. "Apart, and warring, France and Spain are no threat to England. But united . . ."

Bent shook his head. "Neither France nor Spain would ca-pitulate to the other, even to form an alliance that could be more powerful than Britain."

"Perhaps not. But if a king came from outside those nations, a popular ruler who had the support and mandate of the people, then the current governments could conceivably be overthrown and a new House of Bourbon established to rule them both."

Bent laughed. "Ridiculous. Who would have the clout?"

Walsingham looked at him. "How about Louis the Six-teenth?"

Bent stared at him. "You don't mean those stories are true?"

"The most recent cause of the sustained hostilities between France and Spain dates back to 1781, when a fiery young Cor-sican named Napoleon Bonaparte marched into Paris to take control of a France that was in chaos," said Walsingham. "What the history books don't tell us is that Bonaparte was installed surreptitiously by Britain, who edged him into a war with Spain that he readily agreed to. France was in tatters following its support of the terrorists in the failed American rebellion of 1775; Britain punished France by forcibly taking most of its Canadian territories and with the help of our Prussian and Austrian allies forcing severe trade embargoes on the homeland."

"That is in the history books," said Bent. "It caused widespread starvation and suffering."

Walsingham nodded. "Exactly the right conditions for Bonaparte to take control. Before that, though, France was facing a revolution of its own, and fearing for his life Louis the Sixteenth and his court fled to America and the one territory the French still nominally held."

"Louisiana," said Maria. "When Mesmer thought I was Charlotte Elmwood he said he would take me there."

Walsingham smiled. "Then we know who Mesmer's paymaster is, and therefore who your Sergio de la Garcia works for. And, ultimately, who has Professor Hermann Einstein."

Lestrade spoke up at last. "You are talking of plots hatched by French kings who should have died a century ago." He shook his head. "This is madness."

Bent cackled. "Welcome to our world, George." He stood and started pacing the study. "All right . . . so three years ago Walsingham sends John Reed to the arsehole of the Atlantic Ocean to retrieve one of what might be many ancient artifacts, this one ending up in Maria's head. But the party is gate-crashed by agents of Louis the Sixteenth, who they say is kept alive by witchcraft in New Orleans. They've heard of these artifacts, too, we must surmise, though they don't get away with this one."

Maria said, "Not long after Professor Einstein . . . completed me, he showed me off at his club in London. The Elmwoods were there. He was a friend of theirs and had modeled me on Charlotte. But Einstein had not yet fully perfected me? . . . I am told I ran amok and ended up on Cleveland Street."

"Where Annie Crook lived and died," said Bent. "The poor girl whose brain you got."

Maria nodded. "I fear poor Annie must have thought she had been raised from the dead. I was said to have been terrorizing the local people until Professor Einstein turned up to retrieve me. Caused quite a stir."

Bent thumped his palm. "Which the Bourbons in Louisiana must, somehow, have heard about."

Walsingham said, "With the likes of Markus Mesmer on their payroll, who knows how far their influence and spy network reaches? We have ignored this simmering threat at our peril, I fear."

"So they go and get Sergio de la Garcia from Uvalde, evidently aware of his dual identity as El Chupacabras, the greatest swordsman in New Spain," said Bent. "And using some kind of leverage—his family, perhaps?—they send him to London. They've heard—mistakenly, through the grapevine—that the Atlantic Artifact is in the head of a whore. So they set Garcia to slicing open girls' heads in the East End. And thus the legend of Jack the Ripper is born."

"But they kidnapped Professor Einstein a year ago," said Maria. "And the killings continued."

Bent nodded. "What delicious effing irony. Imagine if they took Einstein from his house with you—the very thing they were looking for—upstairs in a room, clockwork wound down, a drop cloth over you. Einstein obviously kept his mouth shut."

"Mesmer knew it was an automaton he was looking for," said Maria.

"Then Einstein must have told them, or hinted, that when you had gotten loose in London and made your way to Cleveland Street, you were never recovered. They were convinced that they were looking for a machine, wandering the streets of Whitechapel for more than two years. A swift strike of El Chupacabras's sword, the top of a head cut off . . . then he would know he'd gotten the wrong girl. But for her, it would be too late."

"And you have arranged a meeting with this Garcia?" said Lestrade.

"Tonight, in Hammersmith," said Bent.

"Then I should arrange some support from my men," said the inspector, standing.

There was a shrill rattle of bells. "That'll be the door," said Mrs. Cadwallader. "I shall see to it." She rose from the footstool and left the study.

Walsingham clapped his hands together. "Bravo, Mr. Bent. Excellent deductive work all around."

Bent sighed. "Doesn't bring us any closer to getting Gideon back, though, nor finding Charles Collier, which we need to do if we're going to get Rowena off the hook by ten tomorrow morning."

There was a sudden shout of "Land sakes!" from the hallway, followed by a shriek. Bent looked up and moved quickly to the study door, calling, "Sally? Is everything—"

When he got to the hall he saw the front door wide open, the housekeeper sprawled against the wood-paneled wall. And bearing down on him was a figure that had evidently shoved Mrs. Cadwallader out of the way. Bent's eyes widened.

"Gideon, lad, you've come home!"

But Gideon Smith said nothing, just kept coming at him with a feral look in his eyes, the blade of a knife flashing in the gaslight.

27

HEARTS' DESIRES

 Smith was a fury, an avenging elemental force, a thing of muscle and bone fueled by a red mist and a roar of pounding blood in his ears.

And yet, even as he barged past the fat man in the doorway that led to a dimly lit study lined with glass trophy cases, even as he held aloft the knife given to him by Fereng, even as he spied his target, a tall, thin man dressed in black with a hawkish nose and piercing eyes, even as all this happened, something seemed to churn and boil within him.

I know this place.

Ignoring the other people in the room, he crossed the floor and grabbed the shirtfront of the white-haired man, pushing him hard against the mantelpiece and holding him fast there. He brandished the knife. "You are going to pay for your crimes."

The man, Walsingham, met his eyes with an ice-cold stare. "Crimes? I can see only one criminal here, Mr. Smith. Are you now a villain?"

"What if I convinced you that you were not the Hero of the Empire, but the enemy of Britain? Would you be able to fight that?"

Smith shook his head as though to clear away the sudden memories that clung to him. The fat man he had pushed out of the way said, "Gideon, what the eff are you doing?"

These people know me.

"The British Empire is the villain of the world," he spat, forcing the blade against the thin neck of Walsingham. "And you are its shadowy architect."

Walsingham raised an eyebrow. "You mean to kill me?"

He pressed the blade tighter, digging into the pale parchment flesh. "Yes. For justice. For vengeance."

"Gideon," said the fat man again, "this isn't you, lad. You're under Mesmer's spell. You're an effing hero!"

"What are you doing here, Herr Smith? Playing the hero?" He *paused for a moment. "But what is a hero? A man who does as he is told, or who finds his own way? And are heroes born or made, Herr Smith? Shall we find out?"*

His resolve slackened, as did the pressure he placed on the knife. Then he thought of Fereng's words, the pictures he painted of the starving hordes in India watching grain and rice transported to London, the island where he was abandoned by his government. He forced the knife harder against Walsingham's throat.

Then she spoke. He had barely noticed her in the room, but her words were honey, oozing into his head.

"Gideon. Gideon, it's me. Maria."

Maria?

"Yes, Herr Smith. Are heroes born or made? What if we took away all your heroic doings? What if we wiped the slate clean?"

"Maria?" he said uncertainly.

She moved into his sight line, and he gasped at her beauty.

She said, "When I brought Charlotte Elmwood out of Mesmer's influence, I used a doll she had loved since childhood. Look around you, Gideon. Here are the things you love, the trophies of Captain Trigger and John Reed. The heroism you have worshipped all your life."

But he couldn't look, couldn't tear away his eyes from Maria's perfection, the blond hair cascading over the knitted shawl on her shoulders, the flawless skin, the eyes that danced with bright intelligence.

No, he didn't love these trinkets in glass cases. He loved . . . he loved . . .

"Or," she said, "I can give you this."

He didn't protest as she moved toward him, felt the strength drain out of him and his knife fall away from Walsingham's throat as she took his face in her beautiful hands, and allowed her to turn him to face her.

He loved. He loved.

She kissed him.

He loved Maria.

He was . . .

He pulled away, and blinked. "I'm Gideon Smith," he said.

The fat man—no, Aloysius Bent—cheered. "Thank eff for that! Now lad, quickly, where's Charles Collier?"

Gideon looked at him. "Collier? Fereng? Why, he's outside."

Bent's eyes widened. "Lestrade!"

But the man with the mustache and pinprick eyes was already running toward the door.

§

Lestrade was out of the door like a ferret, and by the time Bent reached it the policeman was tearing across the square toward a figure limping near the railed-off garden at the center. The inspector's quarry was wiry and thin, hobbling on what looked like a wooden leg protruding from his right knee, with long, gray hair tied into a ponytail. Charles Collier? He looked a damn sight different than he had on the cover of the penny dreadful. What was it Gideon had called him? Fereng? But there was no time to ponder as Lestrade dove in a very effective rugby tackle at the fleeing man, bringing him down in a drift of blackening snow.

"Go on, George! Hit him!" called Bent, hurrying across the road just as a figure loomed out of the gathering dusk and slammed into him. Bent spun around and onto his backside, glaring at the thickset Indian in a black turban who had shoved him out of the way.

"Watch where you're going, fatty!" yelled Bent.

The man raised an eyebrow. "Hark at yourself, you elephantine fool!"

Bent tried to climb to his feet, but the man kicked him, hard, in the guts, and he fell back with a groan. He looked across the road to see Lestrade and Collier rolling in the snow, and three other turbaned shapes materializing out of the gloom.

Two of them made for where Collier and Lestrade fought, the other running up to the fat one who had felled him.

"Phoolendu?"

"It is all OK, Naakesh. This one is no threat."

"I'll give you no threat," said Bent, rolling onto his belly to push himself up. But the one called Phoolendu sat heavily on his back with a laugh.

"Irresistible force meets immovable object!"

"I will help Fereng," said the other, running across the road.

With Phoolendu on his back, Bent could only watch helplessly as the Indians hauled Lestrade off Collier and threw him against the railings, where he lay woefully still. They helped the one-legged man up and, one on each side of him, began to lope across the square.

"Gideon!" shouted Bent. "Gideon, where are you?"

"Time to leave!" said Phoolendu, jumping up and heading with remarkable fleetness of foot after the others. Bent pushed himself onto his knees just as Gideon emerged with Maria and Walsingham in his wake.

"George is down," said Bent as Gideon helped him up. "Your mate Collier . . . God effing knows."

They hurried across the square to Lestrade and Bent turned him over, drawing back in shock at the blossom of bright red blood that colored his shirtfront.

"Good God, George," said Bent. "Has he killed you . . . ?"

Lestrade stirred, evidently just stunned. His eyes widened as he looked at the blood on his shirt, and he patted himself down. "He had a knife, but . . . I don't think . . ." He pulled himself to his feet. "I think he must have stuck himself in the struggle. This is his blood."

Bent peered across the square. "No sign."

"They'll have gone into the sewers," said Gideon. "That's where they're hiding."

Lestrade straightened his coat and tie and said, "I shall get back to Commercial Road station immediately and organize some patrols."

"Bloody hell," said Bent, smacking his palms together. "Collier. We nearly had him. We nearly saved Rowena."

Gideon frowned. "Rowena? She needs saving?"

Bent looked at his watch. "A lot's happened while you've been away, son. We need to get ready to reel in Jack the Ripper." He wrinkled his nose. "You could probably do with a bath first. You don't half stink. Come on, I'll bring you up to date indoors."

※

Gideon stood on the landing on the upper story, looking out the picture window at Grosvenor Square and the rooftops of London beyond, while Mrs. Cadwallader drew a hot bath for him. He had been informed over a welcome pot of tea of everything that had happened while he had been in the sewers with Fereng.

"It's good to have you back, Gideon."

He hadn't heard Bent padding up the stairs. Without turning he said, "It's good to be back. I think. I feel . . . odd. Empty."

Bent joined him at the window. "Mesmer did a right number on you, by all accounts. Don't blame yourself for anything that's happened, lad. The hypnosis . . . it made you susceptible to Collier's poison."

Gideon shook his head vehemently. "It's not that, Aloysius. Not just that. It's . . ." He turned to look at his friend. "Despite everything, I can't condemn Fereng—Charles Collier—for what he's done. Not even murder. Not even sending me to kill Walsingham. The things he told me . . . It's as though all our enemies, their villainy is forged in the furnaces of Britain's relentless march across the globe."

"He has Tiddles, doesn't he?" said Bent. "I mean . . . he has a dinosaur. The baby tyrannosaur he nicked from Professor Rubicon's."

"So that's where it came from," said Gideon, nodding. "Yes, he does. But I have no idea what he plans to do with it."

"We'll have to find him," said Bent. "For Rowena's sake. I'm going to call George Lestrade at the Commercial Road station in a minute. Think you can remember where Collier's hiding out?"

Gideon shook his head. "I'm not sure. Underground, somewhere near Whitechapel." He gazed out the window and then said, "Do I really want to be a hero for this empire, Aloysius? Do I really want to work for Walsingham?"

Bent chuckled. "I remember asking you that way back when we were on the airship chasing the dragon from Egypt to London. I told you what governments are capable of. Especially ours. But . . ." He put a hand on Gideon's shoulder. "Look. Out there. At London. It's not Walsingham you work for, not really. It's *them*. There's good and bad out there, Gideon, angels and devils. But they're all just people, really, trying their best to get on with life in all the myriad ways they know how. And it's them you're the hero to, Gideon. It just so happens that most of the time their needs and the government's needs match up."

Gideon turned to look at him. "And when such time arrives that they don't?"

Bent smiled. "We'll cross that bridge when we come to it, eh? Now, I think your bath's ready." He wrinkled his nose. "You really do stink, you know?"

⁂

Bent found Mrs. Cadwallader in the study, righting the tables and potted plants that had been upended during the struggle. "Gideon in his bath?" he said.

She nodded, smiling a thank you as Bent took hold of the edge of a chair with her and stood it up. "Life doesn't get any less exhausting, does it?"

"Not around here, Sally. I mean—"

She smiled again, somewhat wearily. "It's all right, Mr. Bent. Aloysius, if you prefer." She paused. "You will be careful tonight? All of you?"

"Of course, Sally!" said Bent, his heart suddenly banging in his chest. "I . . ." He paused, cocking his head. "Did you hear that?"

They both turned to the glass cabinet in the corner, where a contraption of wires and lenses sitting on a velvet cushion had begun ticking like a clock.

"That's the old Hypno-Array of Markus Mesmer," said Bent, frowning. "From years ago, when Dr. Reed ran into him. . . ."

"But what is it doing?" asked Mrs. Cadwallader.

❧

The bath at least made Gideon feel more human again. He shaved the black whiskers from his cheeks and chin, staring at himself in the fogged mirror.

Who are you?

He wasn't sure he knew the answer any more than he had when he'd asked it of himself in the aftermath of Mesmer's hypnotic attack. But perhaps people never knew the answer to that question, not until they were on their deathbed. He was Gideon Smith. He was the Hero of the Empire.

"I'm the Hero of the Empire," he said aloud. The words felt hollow. Had Collier tricked him? Somehow, he felt not. Collier was what he was, the product of the British Empire. He had gone bad, in Britain's eyes. Just like John Reed had. But were there any villains, really? And if villainy was just a matter of perspective, did the same ring true for heroism?

Wrapped in a huge towel, Gideon padded out of the bathroom and made for his room. As he passed Maria's quarters, her door opened. He stopped, and they locked eyes for a moment. She wore a silk dressing gown, clutching it closed at her breast. He stood there, dripping water on the carpet, staring at her. She took a step toward him, reached out, and took hold of the towel bunched at his waist, dragging him with surprising force into her room.

"I've missed you," she whispered, closing the door and pushing him against it.

He was stirring beneath the towel, and he wrapped his arms around her neck, drawing her lips to his. She let go of the silk gown, letting it fall open to reveal her milk-white nakedness beneath.

"Touch me," she instructed, taking his hand and placing it between her legs. She gasped as he laid his fingers on her.

"You can feel that? It's nice?" he said.

"Yes," she said. "I can, and it is. I can feel more and more, day by day." She took his other hand. "And touch me here. And here."

He followed her instructions as she loosened the towel. He murmured, "Lie on the bed."

"No," she said. "*You* lie on the bed."

He blinked and smiled as she turned him around and steered him, backward, toward the bed. She smiled back. "While you have been away I have been learning how to be a lady. And how *not* to be."

The towel dropped away, and Gideon fell backward onto Maria's bed as she shucked off the dressing gown and began to sit astride him. Then she stopped. "Did you hear that?"

"No, I don't—" he began, then paused. He had heard something, a whirring and ticking as though . . .

"Oh," said Maria. Gideon followed her gaze to the bedside table, where there resided a mesh of wires, gears, and lenses that, too late, he recognized.

"It's the Hypno-Array I stole from Markus Mesmer," said Maria.

Then a silent rainbow explosion filled the room.

⁂

Markus Mesmer waited impatiently as Alain, who had been a burglar in Paris of some notoriety, picked the lock to the front door of 23 Grosvenor Square. When the thin Frenchman clicked his tongue and pushed the door open, Mesmer strode into the hall, his henchman Alfonso following close behind. He did not have much time. He had never tried to activate his Hypno-Arrays from a distance before, and guessed that the instructions he had mentally projected—to give anyone within sight of them their heart's desires—would not have a long-lasting effect.

He looked around the empty lower floors of the house. So this was where Einstein's automaton had been hiding all this time. She must have left the stolen Hypno-Array here before getting herself captured by Garcia. Above him he heard the rhythmic creaking of bedsprings; so the house was not empty, then, and someone was getting their heart's desire. He could hear voices, perhaps from a kitchen to the rear of the house, and stole across the hall as quietly as he could. He entered a room he guessed was a study, and a mystery was solved. Behind a pane of shattered glass in what appeared to be a trophy cabinet was a very old, early version of his Hypno-Array. He smiled. One taken from him by Dr. John Reed. So Maria had been hidden here, by his old foes Reed and Trigger? Their house inhabited after their deaths by their successor, Mr. Gideon Smith?

The creaking of the bedsprings continued above. In the parlor he found what he was looking for—a map of London spread out on a table, a ring inked around a location near the river at Hammersmith. Beside it was the original notice he had asked to be put into the newspaper—evidently Smith or his compatriots had intercepted it—and a sheet torn from a notepad.

The Dove, Hammersmith, 7 o'clock.

So that was where Garcia would be with the automaton. Mesmer snapped his fingers. "We leave now. We must pack our things and be ready to flee the country immediately after taking the mechanical girl. Our network is in place?"

Alfonso nodded. "We have a sympathizer on standby to take us by cargo dirigible to Malta, from whence we can make our way back to New Orleans. I shall have a message sent to him immediately to be ready."

Mesmer took one last look around. "Good. I shall be glad to be away from London. You would think, with half the world under their bootheels, they would seat their empire in a place where the weather is not so appalling."

The sun shone in through the window, waking Gideon. He felt in the bed beside him, but it was empty. She must be up already. The scent of cooking bacon drifted up the stairs. Gideon yawned and reached for his pocket watch on the bedside table. Seven o'clock. He started for a moment, thinking he should be out on the sea, but then remembered it was Sunday. He heard a whistle playing a jaunty melody, and tinkling laughter, and smiled. His father, Arthur, entertaining Gideon's son, while Maria, heavy with their second child, cooked breakfast.

Life was good. Breakfast, then church, then playing on the beach at Sandsend, and an early night in readiness for taking the *Cold Drake* out at dawn. Old Arthur would insist on coming, of course, but Gideon had decided this was going to be his father's last summer fishing the gearship. He deserved to retire and enjoy what was left of his life.

He heard a tread on the stair and the door opened, a tray bearing breakfast entering first. "Breakfast in bed?" he said. "What have I done to deserve this?"

His wife smiled at him, the sun catching in her short, auburn hair and giving her a flaming halo. Gideon tried to smile back, but failed, as the room began to shudder, crack, and shatter like a broken mirror.

"Rowena?" he said.

Maria was running, running for her life, or so it seemed. She fled through a dark forest, branches whipping her face, thorns grabbing at her skirts, tearing the skin of her arms, catching in her hair. And still she ran, whether to something or from something she couldn't quite tell.

She could stop, catch her breath, get her bearings. But she

didn't want to. Because every time she looked down at her hands, her arms, she could see the scratches there, leaking not oil or hydraulic fluid.

But blood.

Maria laughed joyously and plunged headlong into the thick trees, reveling in every drop of blood that was torn from her flesh.

Her *flesh*.

And she kept running. Running for her life.

※

Aloysius Bent wasn't quite sure how he'd found his way into his room, nor where he'd found the suit. He hadn't seen it since he was twenty-one, if not younger. A lovely check, it had, green and blue, with wide lapels. He turned this way and that, admiring his reflection in the full-length mirror.

He was a handsome bugger, was Aloysius Bent. Always effing had been. Straight back, strong arms, thin legs, a fine head of dark hair. A solid jaw and a smile that had made many a woman swoon.

From somewhere close he could hear music. Stirring, vibrant music. He gave himself a wink and went off to investigate, stepping out into the hall in shiny polished shoes. The music—opera, he thought, maybe Wagner—came from the next floor up, and it sounded louder and stronger as he climbed the stairs.

Mrs. Cadwallader's rooms. He paused outside the door, then knocked briskly and let himself in before he was asked.

What he saw took his breath away.

Mrs. Cadwallader was standing there by the bed, her gramophone vibrating from the loudness of the music. She wore a long blue dress with a plunging neckline, her magnificent breasts heaving in time to the tune. "Ride of the Valkyries," that was it. She held a spear in one hand and a shining shield in the other, and her hair hung in plaits on either side of her heavily made-up face. On her head was a horned helmet.

Bent shook his head in wonder. "Sally?"

The music seemed to hold its breath. She looked at him, her breasts rising as she inhaled deeply.

"Oh," she said, her lips full, her eyes half-closed. She flung her arms wide, the spear clattering against the light fixture, the shield knocking a vase from a chest of drawers. The music roared again. Sally Cadwallader threw back her head and cried, "Oh, take me, Aloysius! Take me!"

He didn't need effing telling twice.

28

Going Underground

This wasn't, conceded Lizzie Strutter to herself, going quite as planned. Christmas was looming, and the stock of money was getting low indeed. Perhaps she hadn't thought this through. The strike had gotten her name in the papers, of course, and focused some attention on the police's abject inability to capture Jack the Ripper, but still. There was a living to be made, and being made it most certainly wasn't.

There was an urgent rap at the door to her private room, and she swiftly pushed the few pound notes back into the wooden box on her lap, locked it, and slid it beneath the loose floorboard by her bed. The knock came again, louder, and a voice called, "Mum? Mum?"

She opened the door to Tess, a pockmarked girl with a thumb missing from her days working in the fish market, before Lizzie took her away from all that. The girl looked all of a flutter.

"Mum, come quick. There's a big mob in the square. They've got torches and sticks and everything. Salty Sylvia's with 'em."

Salty Sylvia? What was that old whore doing on Lizzie's manor? She wrapped her shawl around her shoulders and followed Tess downstairs and out of the house to the square at the head of Walden Street. The girl had been right. There were maybe forty or fifty of them, hard-looking men who appeared to be out for trouble. And they might just get it. Henry Savage's mob were pouring out of tenements and houses, throwing their shoulders back and facing up to the interlopers. This could get very ugly indeed.

Lizzie marched through the snow to the neutral ground between the two growing mobs, where Salty Sylvia stood by a fierce-looking meathead with a grubby patch over one eye.

"What's all this about, Sylvia?" she called.

It was the man who answered. "We're here for Henry Savage. He done Gruff Billy in and made Sylvia shut up shop. We're saying enough's enough."

Lizzie looked down her nose at him. "And who's we?"

The man jabbed his broad chest with his thumb. "One-Eyed Bob, they call me."

"Why's that?" asked Lizzie.

One-Eyed Bob frowned, as though unsure whether she was serious or not, then sniffed. "Me and the boys say it's gone too far now. We want Savage. Where is he?"

"Henry Savage is dead," said Lizzie. There was a wave of muttering from both sides. She'd had the girls wrap Henry's body up and dump him in the Thames in the dead of night, as far as possible from Walden Street. "Somebody cut off his balls and choked him on 'em."

One-Eyed Bob looked disconcerted. He glanced back at his gang, then at Lizzie again. "Then we'll take our pound of flesh from somebody else. Who's taken over his mob?"

Lizzie heard the rattle of weaponry being disgorged from pockets and shirtsleeves, knives clicking open. There was going to be bloodshed here.

"Mum!"

She looked up to see Rachel running across the square, between the two bristling factions. The scar-faced girl pelted through the snow, stopping in front of Lizzie to catch her breath. "Mum, I just heard. They've got Jack the Ripper."

A fresh wave of muttering swept through the ever-growing crowd. There must have been two hundred people in the square now, maybe more. Lizzie said, "You sure?"

Rachel nodded. "They've got him at the Commercial Road police station, so I heard. Does that mean the strike's off?"

Lizzie looked up at Salty Sylvia and One-Eyed Bob. She

was still Lizzie Strutter, and these people had come onto her turf looking for trouble. She couldn't back down so easily. She tapped her chin then said, "Why don't we all go down to the Commercial Road station, see for ourselves?"

One-Eyed Bob nodded. "Yeah. Maybe get them to hand him over to us, for a bit of street justice." He grinned, showing the stumps of his blackened teeth. "Whether they like it or not."

They had all emerged, cautiously and disoriented, from the effects of Markus Mesmer's attack, unsure what had happened, uncertain whether what they had seen and experienced had been real or imagined. The whole ordeal had taken twenty minutes, perhaps less. Gideon had awoken naked in Maria's room, her nowhere to be seen. He had wrapped the towel around him and ventured out into the hall, in time to see a confused-looking Bent descending the stairs from the top floor.

"What just happened, Gideon?" Bent had asked.

He shrugged helplessly. "Mesmer's Hypno-Array . . . a long-distance assault, of some kind. How do you feel?"

Bent made a face. "Tolerable. You?"

Then Maria emerged from the bathroom, wrapped in her silk dressing gown. She was jabbing a needle into her finger. She looked up, tearfully. "Nothing."

Bent looked at his pocket watch. "Four hours, give or take, before we nail Garcia and get Charlotte Elmwood back. I think that just gives us enough time to track down Charles Collier."

Gideon was thankful for him changing the subject. Mrs. Cadwallader, wiping her face with a damp cloth, came downstairs from her quarters then, refusing to meet anyone's eyes. Whatever had happened to them all, no one wished to disclose it. Gideon bit his lip. Rowena? What did that mean?

They dressed and decamped to the kitchen, where Bent had laid out a map of Bazalgette's sewers he had found in the study. "Have you any idea where Collier and his henchmen were camped out?"

Gideon studied the map. "I was in the East End when I went down into the sewers . . . but I've no idea how long I walked before I found the room. I was with . . ." He paused, then smiled. "What day is it?"

"Wednesday," said Maria, entering into the kitchen. She wore a rugged gray woolen dress and black ankle boots, leather gloves on her hands.

Gideon closed his eyes. *If it's Monday we're here, Tuesday over Holborn, Wednesday under Tottenham Court Road, Thursday up Highgate . . . regular as clockwork, ain't we, Mr. Tait?*

"Ropes, oil lanterns, and guns," said Gideon. "And Mrs. Cadwallader, can you organize us a steam-cab to take us to Tottenham Court Road as quickly as possible?"

The housekeeper put on her coat and went outside to hail a cab, while Bent went to the hall to use the telephone. Maria said, "Gideon? Before the Hypno-Array . . . were you shocked?"

He met her eyes. "No. Anything but."

She crossed the space between them, and he embraced her. "Tonight," he whispered into her hair. "Tonight you come to my room. And you can tell me more about how you've been learning not to be a lady. . . ."

Mrs. Cadwallader returned to say the cab was outside, and Bent dragged a knapsack of weapons and tools into the kitchen. "I got these from the armory. Tried to telephone Commercial Road, but the operator said all the lines are down. Do you want to swing by there first . . . ?"

"No time," said Gideon, taking a revolver from the bag and squinting along its barrel. "We'll have to do this without the police."

Mrs. Cadwallader wiped her hands on her apron and said, "Good luck, and take care."

Bent leaned in to her—*to kiss her?* Gideon thought with astonishment—but she turned away from him at the last moment. "Mr. Bent," she murmured. "Please . . ."

"Sorry, Sally," he said quietly. Then he looked up at Gideon and Maria. "Are we going to effing do this, or what?"

※

"Jesus effing Christ, it stinks down here," said Bent. "And I know that's a bit rich coming from me."

Gideon helped Maria down the ladder that led from the manhole cover they had pried free in an alley off Tottenham Court Road. As she stepped onto the brick ledge, the river of effluent running sluggishly beside him, she said, "I was real."

He looked quizzically at her. "You are real."

"No, in Mesmer's illusion. I bled. I was a real woman."

He took her face in his hands. "You are a real woman."

She met his gaze. "Do you love me for who and what I am?"

He nodded. Maria said, "What did you see?"

Gideon paused, still troubled over the vision. Carefully, he said, "I was in Sandsend. My father was still alive. I was married, and happy . . ."

Maria bit her lip. "To me?"

He had thought it was Maria cooking breakfast, hadn't he? Even as he knew it was impossible, one child playing in the garden, another on the way, he had thought it was Maria. So it wasn't really a lie.

"Yes," he said, and she embraced him even tighter. "Yes, it was you."

And a hollowness opened up within him, whether from the telling of the lie or the truth it masked, he wasn't quite sure.

"When you lovebirds have quite finished," said Bent, "there's rats as big as effing dogs down here. What are we looking for?"

"Ssh," said Gideon, holding up a hand. "That."

From the shadows that hid the curve of the sewer tunnel ahead of them came a low and sonorous singing.

※

"Miss Crotchety Quaver was sweet seventeen, and a player of excellent skill / she would play all the day, all the ev'ning as well / making all the neighborhood ill / and to keep her piano in tune she would have a good tuner constantly there / and he'd pull up the instrument three times a week, just to keep it in proper repair. . . ." Mr. Lyall

finished the verse with a belch that echoed around the narrow sewer tunnel. "Oh, I do apologize, Mr. Tait. It's that cat we had for dinner. Always gives me indigestion, cat."

Mr. Tait had stopped dead in his tracks, the pots and pans hanging from his pack jangling. Lyall ran into him. "I say, Mr. Tait, what's to do?"

"Speaking of dinners giving us indigestion, Mr. Lyall . . ."

Lyall glanced around his companion. "Ah," he said. "Smith. And he's brought friends."

Tait eyed up Smith's companions. "There's a lot of meat on that one there."

"My name is Gideon Smith, Hero of the Empire," said their errant meal, pulling back the safety of the revolver he was pointing at them. "And unless you want to end up as treats for the rats to gnaw on, you'd better do as I say."

⁂

"They were going to eat you?" asked Bent, looking at the shabby toshers with disgust. "Like, actually effing eat you?"

The short one, Lyall, put a grubby hand on his chest. "Man cannot live by bread alone."

"No hard feelings, Mr. Smith, eh?" said Tait. "No need for guns and all that malarkey."

"I hope not," said Gideon. "In fact, if you do what I tell you we can forget all about that unpleasantness."

"Name it, name it," said Tait, wringing his hands.

"I want you to take us to the place you last saw me."

Tait and Lyall exchanged glances. "See, that might not be possible." Gideon pushed the revolver closer, and Tait held up his hands. "On account of there being some kind of roaring monster there that we couldn't identify. Not for us, that sort of thing."

"Dinner for the rats it is, then," said Gideon.

"No need to be too hasty," said Lyall, nudging Tait in the ribs. "No need for guns. All that, as Mr. Tait says, malarkey. We'll take you there, won't we?"

"Oh yes, we'll take you." Tait nodded enthusiastically. "Not too close, though, eh? And you promise there'll be no further repercussions?"

Gideon indicated with the pistol that they should lead the way. As Tait brushed past Bent he squeezed his arm, making the journalist yelp.

"Nice bit of meat on that one," said Tait wistfully.

"No further repercussions, as long as you stop eyeing my friends and me up as though we were a buffet," said Gideon. "Move it."

Bent fell into line at the rear of the procession, looking around with his oil lamp held high. "Underground railways? They'll not catch me on one of those things."

Tait glanced back. "Underground railways, sir?"

"Parliament's debating it tonight," called Bent. "They want to build tunnels all over London, run steam-trains through them. Not for me."

Tait and Lyall looked at each other. "Oh, they don't want to be doing that. Not under London. Oh, dearie me, no," said Mr. Lyall.

"Move," said Gideon, pushing the barrel of the gun into Lyall's arm.

※

Bent was peering at his fob watch in the dim lamplight when Tait, at the front of the march, held up a hand. The tunnel forked in front of them, one side through what appeared to be a broken-down brick barrier. Gideon recognized it. "This is the place!" he said.

"Then we'll be taking our leave, having safely delivered you to the roaring monster that we can't identify," said Lyall.

"Not yet," said Gideon. "We might need you." He passed revolvers from his pack to Maria and Bent. "Keep the weapons on these two at all times. Come on."

Gideon pushed to the front and led the way until the tunnel widened and a sloping tunnel forked off to the right. He whispered, "This is it."

Gideon led them all into the tunnel, Tait whimpering. As

they turned the bend there was a faint glow, from the fire that Gideon remembered Phoolendu keeping burning at all times. He put a finger to his lips and then leaped around the corner, holding up his gun.

The room was empty.

Bent joined him, pushing the toshers ahead. "This was the place?"

Gideon tugged at the ring in the wall where the tyrannosaur had been tethered. There was a small pile of dung close by. "Yes. They're on the move. But where?"

"Collier did not tell you what his plan was for the monster?" asked Maria.

Gideon shook his head. "He spoke in riddles. His companions are Thuggees. They kill to keep the death-goddess Kali returning to destroy the world. Every life they take, they say, delays Kali's return for a thousand years."

Gideon walked to the abandoned camp, picking up that morning's newspaper scattered on the ground. The front-page story was about Parliament meeting that evening to debate the underground railway.

"All Fereng said was that what he had planned would keep Kali away from the world for six hundred and seventy thousand years. I thought that was odd, very . . . specific."

Bent frowned. "Six hundred and seventy thousand years? So . . . six hundred and seventy people would die?"

Gideon nodded, absently reading the front of the newspaper. "Where would there be precisely six hundred and seventy people in one place at one time?"

Bent stuck his lip out, thinking, then his eyes widened. "Six hundred and seventy? Jesus effing Christ, Gideon."

Gideon stared at him. "What?"

Bent pointed at the newspaper in his hands. "There are exactly six hundred and seventy Members of Parliament."

Gideon looked down at the front page again. "And they are all meeting right now." He looked up. "Collier's going to let loose the tyrannosaur in the House of Commons."

Bent looked at his watch and moaned. "We need to get to Hammersmith if we're going to nab Jack the Ripper." He swore loudly and long. "All we needed was a bit of Collier's blood to get Rowena off the bloody hook. One effing drop. What if he's not at Parliament? What if he's gone for good, left his Thuggees to do his dirty work? She's going to hang, Gideon."

Maria put a hand on Bent's arm. "Aloysius . . . did you say a drop of blood?"

He nodded. "For Miescher and his machine."

Maria looked at Gideon, and back to Bent. "Wasn't Inspector Lestrade's shirt covered in Charles Collier's blood?"

Bent's mouth fell open. "By eff, you're right, girl!"

"Right," Gideon said. "Aloysius, Maria, you get back up there, go to the Commercial Road police station, and get the shirt from Lestrade. You'll have time to get it to Miescher and then be at the Dove to catch Garcia. Alert Lestrade about the impending attack on Parliament, have him send the police, the bloody Duke of Wellington's Regiment."

"What are you going to do?" said Maria.

Gideon smiled tightly. "Mr. Tait and Mr. Lyall are going to show me the quickest way to the House of Commons, where I'll try to stop this insanity."

Bent put a hand on his shoulder. "Don't be reckless."

Gideon nodded. "Then don't be long."

As Bent helped Maria out of the manhole cover he had shouldered out of the way, she stepped up and cursed as the heel on her right ankle boot snapped clean off. "These clothes are quite impractical," she said.

Bent looked around to get his bearings. "That's what ladies wear, unfortunately. Ah, I think we're on Milk Street, off Cheapside. Had we better get a cab to Commercial Road?"

Maria hobbled off to the busy thoroughfare of Cheapside, Bent behind her, as a horse-drawn police carriage suddenly rounded the bend, siren wailing, and thundered up the street.

"Hold on!" shouted Bent, waving at the driver, who ignored

him. But running behind was a knot of constables on foot. Bent hailed the nearest one. "Where are you going? You need to get to Parliament, immediately!"

The policeman glared at him. "There's a bloody riot! They're attacking the Commercial Road police station! Going to burn it down! Every copper in London is on his way there."

As he ran to join his comrades, Bent turned to Maria. "Effing hell. We'll never get in there now. And we need George Lestrade's shirt."

Maria snapped her fingers. "How far are we from Soho?"

"Wrong bloody direction, girl! Why?"

"Because I think I know someone who can get us into the police station, riot or no riot."

※

"Who exactly are we here to see, again?" asked Bent, breathless after huffing up three flights of cramped stairs to the apartment above a gin palace on Manette Street. He'd gazed longingly through the window of the establishment, from where music and laughter emanated, until Maria hauled him up the stairs to the address she had written on a piece of paper. She banged on the door until it opened and a cautious face appeared, framed by unruly hair.

"Gloria Monday!"

"Maria!" said Gloria, opening the door wide. She glanced at Bent. "Who's your friend? If he's going to gawp at me like that, tell him to come back in the summer when he can at least catch the flies."

"This is Aloysius Bent, a journalist and a very good friend of mine," said Maria. "We need your help."

Bent nudged Maria and whispered, "It's a feller! Done up as a woman!"

Maria glared at him. "No, she's not. She's a woman."

Gloria, wearing a silk housecoat with embroidered dragons chasing each other along it, opened the door and let them into the small apartment, furnished with a bed in one corner and a small living area with cotton throws over moth-eaten sofas.

"Are you in trouble?" asked Gloria.

Maria limped in. "Gloria, you said you had a sweetheart? At Commercial Road?"

She narrowed her eyes. "What's this about? He's a journalist?"

Maria took hold of Gloria's arm. "You said you had a secret way in. The police station is under attack. Some kind of mob. We urgently need to get to—"

"George!" said Gloria, her hand flying to her mouth.

Maria blinked. "Why, yes. George Lestrade. How did—"

Gloria grabbed Maria's coat. "Is George hurt?"

Bent snapped his fingers. "You! You're Lestrade's secret love!"

Gloria sighed. "Not any longer, by all accounts. But yes, come, we must go. I can get us inside." She looked down at Maria's feet. "You have broken a heel. You need boots?"

"These blasted clothes are useless," said Maria. "I don't know why anyone would want to be a lady, Gloria, honestly. The outfits are no use at all for adventuring."

Gloria tapped her chin with a painted nail. "Quick, come with me. I was never a big man, and my old clothes probably would not look too amiss on you. If you really want something more . . . pragmatic . . ."

"Is this strictly necessary?" moaned Bent.

Gloria put her face against his. "Whatever your need at Commercial Road, mine is probably greater, Mr. Bent. But a woman cannot function properly without appropriate clothes. We shall be one minute."

They were ten seconds less than that, by Bent's watch. Gloria came first, dressed in a long, flowing dress and petticoats, boots laced to her knee, and a woolen shawl. Behind her came Maria.

"My old suit," said Gloria. "It was silly keeping it, but I hung on to it in case . . . well, I needed to make a sharp exit sometime, disguised as my old self. But I'm glad to let it go, let my old life go, at last. And I think you'll agree that Maria looks stunning."

Maria had tied her hair back in a loose ponytail and kept her ruffled-lapel white blouse on beneath the elegantly tailored two-piece suit in brown and sky-blue pinstripes, the trousers forced into a pair of black leather boots with a short heel.

"I'm ready," said Maria. "Now let's finish this."

29

FOR THE AVOIDANCE OF FURTHER DOUBT

 George Lestrade was searching through the uniform store looking vainly for a clean shirt when Constable Ayres found him.

"Crikey, sir. Are you injured?"

"No, the blood is not mine, Constable. I would quite like a clean shirt, though. Do we have any?"

Ayres coughed. "I think that might have to wait, Inspector. We have what you could call a situation."

Lestrade glared at him, inviting him to tell his superior officer what was more important than him getting out of a bloodstained shirt. Ayres said, "The station is under attack, sir. By a very angry mob."

Five minutes later Lestrade was on the steps of the station, flanked by two uniformed officers wielding revolvers.

Not that the peashooters would do much good. There were hundreds of them. Commercial Road was a sea of bodies, shouting and jostling, waving burning torches and jeering at him.

"I am Inspector George Lestrade," he shouted. The mob quieted somewhat. "Who is the leader here?"

A big man with an eye patch wielding a length of iron pipe waved at him from the front of the crowd. Beside him was a hatchet-faced woman with skin the color of rancid bacon, spilling out of a grubby dress. Lizzie Strutter.

Lestrade addressed the man but directed his narrow-eyed gaze at the woman. "What is the meaning of this?"

"You've got Jack the Ripper in there!" bellowed the man. The mob began to bay and cheer.

"Nobody of that name here," said Lestrade calmly.

"We know you've got him! Hand him over."

Lestrade took a deep breath. "If indeed we have anyone arrested in connection with any crimes, it will be a matter for the courts to decide—"

"Hand him over, or we burn the fucking place down!"

A stone smacked into the brickwork beside Lestrade's head, and he flinched as another and another rained on him.

"Inside," he hissed to the constables, then called, "Disperse now, or we shall be forced to arrest you for breaching the public peace."

Another stone narrowly missed his head. "All of us?" someone called back.

Lestrade decided that discretion was indeed the better part of valor, and he hurried inside as a hail of missiles began to pelt the frontage of the station.

"Constable Ayres," he said as the two officers secured the doors. "Call Scotland Yard and—"

"Tried, sir," said Ayres. "I think they've cut the telephone wires. And I've been on the roof, sir. They've got us surrounded. There are thousands of 'em, I should say."

Somewhere there was the sound of smashing glass. Lestrade said, "Then let us hope someone notices something is amiss and gets reinforcements here before things turn very nasty indeed."

※

"Who are you?" asked Lestrade.

The man in the cell in the basement looked miserably at him through the bars. "I told you. My name is James Woodcock, and I'm Jack the Ripper." But his words lacked conviction, and fear brimmed in his eyes.

"Have you ever met an Austrian called Markus Mesmer?"

"I'm Jack the Ripper," said the man quietly.

Lestrade sighed. "There are several hundred—perhaps thousands—of angry East Enders threatening to burn down my station unless I hand over Jack the Ripper. Perhaps I should comply with their wishes."

Constable Ayres spoke up. "Strictly speaking, sir, that would be against the regulations."

Lestrade ignored him. "Well, Woodcock?"

The man began to cry. Between his snotty sobs he said miserably, "I'm Jack the Ripper."

There was a sudden noise off to his left. A door led to a utility room, and in the floor was a trapdoor. . . . Had the mob found the secret tunnel? He glanced at Ayres and quietly drew his revolver as the handle rattled and then the door burst open, disgorging a lumpish gray figure into the basement. Lestrade raised his gun then gaped.

"Aloysius Bent," he said.

"Thank effing Christ," said Bent. "You've not changed your effing shirt."

Lestrade glanced at Ayres. "Lower your weapon, Constable. It's a friend."

"If I ever have to go down an effing sewer again within a century of tonight it'll be too soon," said Bent. He grinned at Lestrade and stepped to one side. "Look who brought us, George."

Lestrade felt the strength desert him as she stepped through the doorway. "Gloria," he said weakly. "You shouldn't have come here."

She stepped forward to him, Maria emerging behind her. "I know. I'm sorry, George, but it's an emergency." She glanced at Ayres. "I'm not trying to make things difficult, turning up uninvited."

"I didn't mean that," he said, opening his arms to embrace her. "It's not safe. The mob . . ."

Ayres was looking aghast at him, at Gloria. "Inspector Lestrade . . . ," he said slowly. "Unless I'm very much mistaken, that's a man. Do I need to remind you that according to section eleven of the Criminal Law Amendment Act 1885, commonly known as the Labouchere Amendment, gross indecency between two males is highly prohibited, and—"

"Constable Ayres," said Lestrade, still embracing Gloria Monday, "just fuck off, will you?"

Then he kissed her hard on the lips.

※

"I must say, George, you're a dark horse, aren't you," said Bent as they tramped the five hundred yards along the sewer from the long-forgotten service hatch that led into the bowels of the Commercial Road police station to the nearest manhole several streets away, beyond the rampaging mob.

Lestrade, shivering shirtless under his jacket and wool overcoat, his bloodstained garment safely bagged by Bent, shrugged. "From the moment I saw her onstage, I fell in love. Even when I found out what . . . *who* she was, I couldn't help myself. We didn't dare meet in public, not at first. I used to smuggle her into the station through here, in the dead of night. We'd sleep in the cells, if they were empty. Then I started to stop caring. Sometimes the heart is beyond even the law. I wouldn't expect you to understand."

"Don't be too sure," said Bent. "Even I've got a heart, George."

Gloria, walking a little way ahead with Maria, turned. "Oh, George, I've gone and ruined everything for you now."

"At least I'll go out with a bang, not a whimper," said Lestrade.

※

On the surface they could hear the sounds of running battle, the hand-cranked sirens on police carriages and fire carts sounding in the distance. Lestrade spied a phalanx of coppers making their way through the backstreets toward the station and went to hail them.

"You're sure you have Siddell's address?" asked Bent. "Miescher's staying with him, if the idiot hasn't managed to lose him."

Maria nodded and took the bag containing Lestrade's shirt from him. "I'll get it to him now and ensure he has the results ready for court tomorrow. Then I'll come and find you in Hammersmith."

"You don't have to," said Bent. "You can go home, wait for news from Gideon."

She shook her head. "I feel responsible for Charlotte Elmwood. I need to know she comes out of this safely."

Lestrade returned. "We need to move quickly. The mob's gone crazy, by all accounts, smashing up and burning anything and everything within sight. They're moving this way."

"Did you tell those coppers they need to get word out about Westminster?"

Lestrade nodded. "Every officer in London is on his way here, to try to contain the riot. I don't think they understood the gravity of the situation."

Maria bit her lip. "Gideon . . ."

"Let's get Garcia nabbed, then we'll get over to Parliament. Now go, Maria! And be careful!"

She nodded and disappeared into the night. Bent looked at Lestrade and Gloria. Perhaps not who he had expected to have at his back to rescue the Elmwood girl from the greatest swordsman in New Spain then stop a dinosaur chomping its way through the House of Commons. Still, beggars couldn't be choosers. He grinned. "Come on, you two. Hammersmith. Didn't I tell you a week ago we were going to nail Jack the Ripper, George?"

※

One disadvantage of being down in the sewers with his full faculties about him was that it was much more difficult to stave off his looming fear that he was about to be crushed by the tons of earth and stone pressing down on him from above. It was an irrational fear—there was much more to be afraid of than the possibility of being suffocated in a tunnel collapse, not least the pair of cannibalistic toshers he had co-opted as his guides and the ring of assassins and their pet dinosaur they were taking him to. That didn't stop the constricting feeling about his chest, though, nor the shortness of breath and the distant pounding in his ears.

Mr. Lyall was taking a deep breath and about to burst into song when Gideon slapped him suddenly in the chest then put a finger to his lips. Had he heard voices up ahead? It was difficult to tell. . . . Sometimes the rising and falling of the sewer ledges brought them tantalizingly close to the surface, and voices drifted down through the grates. And the gases Gideon was sure the putrid river of effluent gave off must affect a man's mind—how else did one account for Tait and Lyall? But no, there were definitely voices ahead. He indicated for the toshers to be quiet again, then crept forward to where the sewer split into a crossroads. Tait had said they were pretty much under the Palace of Westminster now, but Gideon had refused to let them go until he was sure.

Tait and Lyall had evidently decided that they had gone far enough, though, for Gideon hadn't gone more than a dozen steps when he heard a jangling of pans and sudden shouts, and looked over his shoulder to see Lyall running along the ledge back the way they had come, the taller Tait sloshing after him in the shallow channel of filth.

The element of surprise was lost in any case, so he shouted after his retreating guides, "And no eating anyone! I'll find out if you do, and I'll come for you."

He sighed and turned back, jumping despite himself at Kalanath's scarred visage, smiling viciously just two inches from his own. He felt a hand relieve him of his gun, Naakesh melting out of the darkness beside him, and the snap, snap, snapping of Phoolendu's leather garroting thong.

They led him forward toward dull but brightening lights, a ring of rusting oil lamps illuminating a shadowed alcove in which Deeptendu stood with Charles Collier, the monkey, Jip, sitting on his shoulder.

Gideon inclined his head slightly. "Fereng. I am relieved to see you are not injured. There was a lot of blood."

Collier kept his eyes locked with Gideon's. "A slight wound in the fleshy part of my thigh." He paused. "You killed Walsingham for me?"

Gideon raised an eyebrow. "You didn't stay around long enough to find out."

Fereng's eyes flickered for the first time. "No. I was not prepared for the response. I could not allow myself to be taken. Not so close to my vengeance being fulfilled."

"Where is the beast?" asked Gideon.

Fereng indicated upward with a nod of his head. Above him in the alcove Gideon realized there was a black shaft; iron rungs were inlaid into the slimy brick wall.

"Some kind of service tunnel, which accesses the space directly below the chamber of the House of Commons," said Gideon.

It was Fereng's turn to raise an eyebrow in surprise. "Who are you?"

"Gideon Smith. The Hero of the Empire."

Fereng shrugged. "Never heard of you. But I have been away a long time. And, you'll come to realize just as I did, heroes are ten a penny."

"How did you get the monster up there?" asked Gideon. "I'm genuinely interested."

"We drugged it. With opium. It should be waking up soon, with a fearful hunger on it. We trussed it up in a rope net and hauled it up there, the five of us. It is suspended beneath a service hatch hidden beneath a rug just in front of the speaker's seat. When the monster wakes, there is only one way for it to go. Up."

"Its name is Tiddles, would you believe?" said Gideon with a crooked smile.

Fereng's eyes narrowed. "Did you genuinely lose your memory, or was that merely a ruse to infiltrate us?"

"There was no plot, Fereng. I really had my mind wiped, by a man called Markus Mesmer. It was serendipity that brought me to you."

Collier bared his teeth. "That means 'happy accident.' I hardly think it was that, Smith."

"Oh, I don't know. You should have stayed at Grosvenor Square, Fereng. You might have learned something interesting."

"What, that the man I thought my ally was in fact my enemy, and now he has come to try to foil my plan?"

Gideon leaned in and peered up the pitch-dark shaft. Did he fancy he could hear the snuffling of the tyrannosaur, emerging from its slumber? He said, "I met one before, you know. That one's mother, in fact. Three times as big. I defeated that one without much trouble."

Though *with* a brass dragon that could spit fireballs, he neglected to add. And now he didn't even have a gun. Fereng, though, looked mildly impressed. "Is that why I should have stayed at Grosvenor Square? Would I have learned that you are a good little soldier who even throws himself into the jaws of long-extinct beasts for a pat on the head from his paymasters?"

That hurt Gideon enough for him to know for sure that it hadn't been Mesmer's hypnosis that had made him so ready to accept Fereng's words. Perhaps he did believe in the old hero; maybe on some level he did share his disgust and dismay at how his empire behaved. But it was just as Aloysius had said. . . .

"I don't do it for Walsingham. I do this for the people."

Fereng laughed. "Those who are not complicit are sheep. Either way, they are worthless."

"That's what John Reed thought," said Gideon. "He was wrong, too. And worthless, Fereng? All of them? Even your daughter?"

Charles Collier's brow darkened. "Don't even dare, Smith. Jane is dead."

Above, there was a creaking of ropes and the tentative growl of a hungry, disoriented beast waking up in the darkness. It was time to play his trump card.

"No, she isn't," said Gideon. "She isn't dead, Charles. Jane is alive."

For the first time in what felt like weeks, the dense white cloud that had smothered London thinned and parted, allowing the light of the full moon to break through and lend an eerie glow to the snow-covered streets. There was an alley alongside the Dove, a venerable tavern that backed on to the Thames, from where Aloysius Bent swore they drew the water with which they watered down the beer and whisky.

"Stuff that's in that water, it's kill or cure, a drink in the Dove. Either sees you off or gives you an iron constitution."

Bent, Lestrade, and Gloria had done a circuit around the busy pub and decamped outside to the mouth of the alley, unlit but possessed of a blue gloom as the slush reflected the moonlight. Bent watched Lestrade and Gloria hand in hand; a year ago he'd have been splashing them all across the *Argus*. Today . . . well, he privately found it did his old heart good. Either he was getting soft in his old age, or . . . He thought briefly of Mrs. Cadwallader, throwing her shield and spear aside with a clatter, tearing down her own dress.

Keep your mind on the job, Aloysius.

"Ssh," said Bent, suddenly alert. He peered down the alley. It was very narrow—wide enough for one person to pass comfortably along, or perhaps not so comfortably if that person was Aloysius Bent. He took out his watch. They were still an hour ahead of the appointed meeting time, but he'd seen some movement down the way.

He motioned for George to get out his gun and for the pair to follow him, then edged down the alley, calling softly, "*Señor Hombre de Negro! Señor Hombre de Negro!*"

There was silence, then Bent caught a sudden movement, and a deep voice said uncertainly, "Mesmer?"

Bent looked back at Lestrade, his eyes wide. At last. After all these years, he was going to nab Jack the Ripper.

He put out his hand to Gloria, who handed over the oil lantern, lit but shielded by hinged copper doors. Bent held it aloft and flipped open the shutters, flooding the alley with yellow light.

And there he was, Sergio de la Garcia, dressed from head to toe in black, his eyes white behind the holes cut into his cowl, his rapier point held at the throat of a terrified-looking Charlotte Elmwood, gagged and bound by many coils of thick rope around her arms and torso.

Bent held up a hand. "Don't panic, Garcia. Yes, we know who you are. And what you've done. Hand over the girl. It's not who you think it is. You're going to put the sword down and hand over the girl."

"Yes, indeed, you are," said a new voice from the alley behind George and Gloria. "But not to these people. As you were, El Chupacabras."

"Ah, those clipped Germanic tones. Mr. Mesmer, I presume," said Bent, glancing over his shoulder but not wanting to take his attention away from Garcia for too long.

"Mr. Aloysius Bent," said Mesmer. "And Inspector George Lestrade. And, how curious, the she-man who has been performing in the very same theater as myself. What an odd coincidence. I suggest you all lay down your weapons; I have five men, all armed."

Bent looked behind him again. He could indeed make out two or three shapes behind Mesmer, pointing guns over the shoulder of the Austrian, who Bent saw was carrying a heavy-looking leather valise. The others were lost to sight in the shadows. He said, "He's right, George. Put down your gun."

"I am an officer of the Metropolitan Police," said Lestrade, still aiming his gun over Bent's shoulder at Garcia. "And I am about to arrest that man."

"No, you're not," said Mesmer, "or the she-man is shot first."

Slowly, Lestrade lowered the gun and dropped it at his feet.

"Please," said Garcia. "I do not know who you people are, but Mesmer . . . take the automaton. I so dearly want to go home."

"That is what we are all going to do, Sergio," said Mesmer softly.

"Have you told him?" asked Bent, twisting around in the alley, putting the swordsman at his back. Had he just seen . . . ? He asked, "Have you told Garcia that his wife and kids are dead?"

There was a half-cry from behind him. "You lie! Mesmer, he lies!"

"Typhus, wasn't it?" said Bent coolly. "You going to tell him the truth, Mesmer?"

There it was again. He was sure this time. Bent pressed his advantage. "On top of all that, you've got the wrong girl, Garcia. That's Charlotte Elmwood."

"Mesmer! Tell me he is lying!" said Garcia.

"He's lying," said Mesmer. "How could he possibly know?"

"Same way as I know Garcia's got a daughter back in New Spain. Inez."

Garcia gasped. "How can you know that? It was a secret known only to myself and the girl's mother."

"And Don Juan Batiste, who took them in for you to stop you being ruined, as you had a wife and daughters already. He told her, by the way. Fed up of trying to live up to your shining example. She's even taken up the mantle of La Chupacabras, though I don't think she'd be too impressed to see you like this, skulking in an alley, the blood of God knows how many innocent women on your hands."

Bent looked at Garcia, whose sword was wavering. The Spaniard eyed Charlotte. "This is not the automaton?"

Mesmer sighed loudly. "Yet more penny dreadful melodrama. You must understand, Garcia, these people live their lives as though everything is a badly written adventure story. Unfortunately, I refuse to fit their stereotype of the villain. Yes, it is the automaton. Yes, your wife and children are dead. Yes, I am going to have everyone here shot. Even you, you crazy, sword-wielding Spaniard. Your usefulness is at an end. Alfonso, the rest of you, kill them."

Bent was just in time to see a black-gloved hand cover the face of the Spaniard behind Mesmer and drag the hefty hench-man back into the shadows. Just as he'd seen happen to each of the thugs in the narrow alley. One by one, Mesmer's hench-men had been silently and systematically taken out, and now the Austrian was alone.

Mesmer turned around. "Alfonso? Alain . . . ?"

But the thugs weren't there. Instead, her gloved fists on the hips of her trousers, her ponytail hanging down over the lapel of her jacket, was Maria. Bent broke out in a broad grin. Couldn't have timed it any effing better.

"They're out cold," said Maria, the lamplight illuminating her as though she were some avenging Greek goddess. "You're on your own."

Mesmer glanced back toward Charlotte Elmwood, frown-ing. "But which . . . ?"

Maria raised an eyebrow. "For the avoidance of any fur-ther doubt, Mesmer, you should be aware that never again will I deny what I am or pretend to be something I'm not. I'm Maria."

Then she drew back her fist and let loose a punch that knocked Markus Mesmer clean out. Lestrade bent down and scooped up his revolver, training it on Garcia while feeling around with his free hand for Mesmer's valise. "Drop that sword, matey, you are well and truly caught."

As the rapier clattered to the cobbles, Bent felt like crying. They'd done it. They'd gotten Jack the effing Ripper at last.

30

"A Lost Father Dies"

"You lie," said Collier, Jip chattering on his shoulder. "Some trick to turn me from my destiny. I must admit, I thought better of you, Smith."

"You know that Edward Gaunt was molesting your daughter. He admitted it to you. That's why you killed him."

Collier said, "He had been doing it since she was twelve years old. At the age of sixteen she decided enough was enough, and threw herself into the Thames."

Gideon looked at him curiously. "This is about guilt, isn't it? You feel guilty that you took the Indian Ocean mission over your own family. If you hadn't been wrecked on the island, you might have been able to stop what happened. Killing Edward Gaunt I can understand, perhaps even Walsingham for abandoning you. But this?" He waved his hand upward. "Letting the dinosaur loose in the House of Commons? It smacks of showmanship, Fereng. You are better than that."

"How can you know what I am better or worse than?"

Gideon smiled. "Because I cannot believe the father of my very good friend Rowena Fanshawe, Belle of the Airways, holder of the Conspicuous Gallantry Medal, could possibly be a true villain."

Collier stared at him for a moment, then looked upward. "I still do not believe you."

"Fereng. Rowena has been on trial this week for the murder of Edward Gaunt. The major plank of the prosecution's case is a new technique that matches up blood samples. Rowena's is a fifty percent match to samples obtained from under Gaunt's fingernails, samples he scratched from you when he fought back. Fifty percent. As similar as a child's blood might be to a parent's, apparently."

Collier stared up into the blackness. There was a distinct rumble from above. Deeptendu, beside Collier, said, "I think it is awake."

Collier looked at Gideon. "The girl who has been mentioned in the reports from the Old Bailey? You are saying . . . she is Jane?"

The rumble became a dull roar.

"I have always known her as Rowena Fanshawe," said Gideon. "But she told Aloysius Bent this very afternoon that she faked her death to begin a new life. She has followed in your footsteps. She is one of the finest airship pilots in the land. Your blood flows in her veins, Charles, or near as damn it. But the jury is set to consider their verdict tomorrow morning at ten, and the case against Rowena is strong, and she will hang without your testimony and your blood."

Now Collier's eyes were overflowing with tears. "If you are lying I will kill you."

"I'm not lying."

"Then take me to her. Tell me what I have to do."

A terrible, deafening roar was funneled down the hatch, echoing out and around the dank, curved sewer tunnel.

"No," said Gideon. "First we stop that thing."

Collier looked up then flinched as a shower of dust rained down on him. "Mr. Smith, I fear . . ." He stepped out of the alcove, dragging Deeptendu with him, as the dust became an avalanche of wood and brick debris, and the monster roared again. Collier met his eyes. "I fear we are too late."

✶

"I hope we're not too late," said Bent, tumbling out of the steam-cab at the steps to the Palace of Westminster. The faces of the clock tower, illuminated from within by gas lamps, said it was half past eight, and despite the brightness of the moon and the rows of lamps strung along Parliament Square, and the lights burning in almost every window in the stone walls of the Mother of Parliaments, the whole edifice felt deathly quiet, as though that little slice of London had been swallowed by the night.

Maria and Gloria followed Bent, and then Garcia, his hands bound behind his back by the same rope he had earlier used to tie up Charlotte Elmwood. Lestrade came after him, his revolver in his hand. Maria turned to the driver and said, "Winchmore Hill, and you stop for neither man nor beast. Understand?"

She turned back to the window of the cab, where Charlotte Elmwood sat, half-stunned still. "And that goes for you, too. Straight home, yes?"

The girl nodded tearfully. "Thank you for everything you have done, Maria. I will never forget you."

Maria smiled crookedly. "You will remember me every time you look in the mirror, Charlotte. Now go!"

"What should we do with him?" asked Lestrade, pointing his gun at Garcia.

"He'll have to come with us," said Bent. "No time to get him comfortable in an effing cell somewhere, George, and for all we know Commercial Road is burned to the ground."

They ran up the steps to the House of Commons, where a lone uniformed police officer before the vast double doors put his hand up uncertainly.

"I am Inspector George Lestrade," said Lestrade, digging in his pocket for his warrant card. "I'm sorry, it is somewhat bloodstained, but . . ."

The constable inspected it. "You are from Commercial Road? Every man is down there. They've got the army on their way, by all accounts. Is it bad?"

"Not as bad as it's going to effing get in here," said Bent, elbowing past him. "Has the underground railway debate started?"

"Half an hour ago," said the constable. "But you can't—"

The motley troupe marched into the marble foyer past the

protesting policeman and Bent led them to the doors of the main chamber, where a warden in the livery of Westminster Palace opened his mouth to challenge them.

"No effing time," said Bent, pushing him out of the way and leaning hard on the doors.

The chamber of the House of Commons was full to bursting, every seat on the four-tiered rows taken, the Liberal Members of Parliament facing the Conservatives, the Speaker, Viscount Arthur Peel, sitting resplendent on his thronelike perch between the two factions. William Hayes Fisher, the right honorable member for Fulham, was on his feet, waving papers across at the jeering Liberals.

"Progress, sirs! Progress! Would the honorable gentlemen opposite stand in the way of this, the greatest city upon God's Earth, becoming yet greater? The streets are choked with steam-cabs and omnibuses, horse-drawn carriages and stilt-trains. The skies are filled with dirigibles and aerostats. We have not a pennyworth of space left in London, so we must go down, underground!"

The Speaker nodded to a Liberal, and said, "Thomas Bolton for Derbyshire North East will respond."

The gentleman stood and hooked his thumbs in his waist-coat pockets. "And how much will this cost, sir? Once again the provinces are squeezed dry to pay for London's largesse. And, pray tell, what do we know of the subterranean world below our feet? Is it really safe? Can we be sure there are no . . ."

The MP tailed off at the sound of a huge crash, and all eyes turned to the doors, where Aloysius Bent, Maria, Gloria Monday, and George Lestrade, pushing the bound Sergio de la Garcia before him, burst through.

"Thank eff!" cried Bent. "We're in time!"

Then there was a shrieking of splintering wood, and the polished floor before the Speaker's chair buckled and erupted, the green head of the young Tyrannosaurus rex emerging and opening its mouth, lined with cruel rows of daggerlike teeth, to emit an earsplitting roar.

※

"Go," said Collier to Deeptendu. "Wait at our appointed meeting place for two days, then if I do not turn up you must make your way home. May Ganesha ease your passage."

"We will not abandon you, Fereng," said Deeptendu.

"Go!" hissed Collier. "I . . . I must see my daughter. I cannot have her remember me like this, the man who brought war to England. Gideon Smith is right. This is not the way. This is personal vengeance, not for the greater good."

The Thuggees all clapped Collier on his shoulder then melted into the shadows of the tunnel. He nodded at Gideon then began to climb, swiftly for a man with one wooden leg, up the iron rungs set into the brick service hatch.

They reached a wide but cramped space, light flooding in from the smashed trapdoor above them. Below it was a web of ropes where the Thuggees had slung the drugged dinosaur, its only escape to claw its way upward and through the hatch. From above rang the sounds of chaos and panic, shouts and screams providing a counterpoint to the rumbling roars of the tyrannosaur.

"You cannot have thought the beast would kill all six hundred and seventy Members of Parliament," said Gideon.

"It will kill enough," said Collier grimly. "Such a primal engine of destruction, such a forgotten force of nature, loose in the black heart of the most advanced empire on Earth."

"As my friend Aloysius Bent would say, the symbolism is not effing lost on me," said Gideon through gritted teeth. "Come on."

Then he began to climb the rope netting to the chamber of the House of Commons.

※

"Ouch," said Bent, wincing as the beast, standing between the opposing rows of seats on its powerful hind legs and casting this way and that with its massive head, eventually decided to lunge for a panicking front-bencher on the Conservative ranks trying to climb over the seat behind him. "Looks like they're going to be calling a special election in Dorset."

The chamber was a chaotic scramble of bodies fighting their way toward the double doors, but the sheer mass of them created a huge bottleneck behind the Speaker's chair.

"This way, this way!" cried Maria, waving them on. "But you must stop pushing and fighting!" She looked at Bent in despair. "They're like stampeding bulls."

Lestrade was trying to get a bead on the beast with his revolver but was constantly shoved and elbowed by screaming politicians. "Does anyone actually have a plan?" he shouted.

"Free me!" cried Garcia. "Take off my bonds!"

"Not now, there's a good chap," said Bent. "We've got our hands full."

"Free me!" said Garcia. "I can stop it!"

"Wait," said Maria. She looked at him. "What do you mean?"

His eyes met hers. "Please. I am going to die anyway, yes?"

Bent shrugged. "I imagine you'll hang for what you've done, yes."

"Then let me die a hero!" he cried. "My wife and children are dead; at least let Inez remember me for the right reasons."

Bent looked at Lestrade, who shrugged. Maria gripped the ropes binding Garcia's hands and tore them off. "My sword," he said.

She took the rapier from Gloria and handed it to him. He seemed to grow in stature, straighten, as though life flooded back into him. He looked at them each in turn and pulled his cowl over his head, holding the shaft of his sword in front of his face, his eyes shining.

"El Chupacabras!" he said, then turned and ran through the scrambling mob.

"And look!" cried Maria. "Gideon!"

"I must make this right," said Collier. "For Rowena." He drew his knife from his boot. The tyrannosaur had its back to them, the red-raw body of an MP before it, roaring in triumph.

Gideon put a hand on his arm. "A fortune-teller told me . . . 'a lost father dies' . . . don't you wish to see Rowena again?"

"Better she remembers me like this," said Collier.

Gideon held on to him. "Wait," he said. "Look."

Through the fleeing crowd a black shape was vaulting toward the beast, sword held high, crying, "El Chupacabras! El Chupacabras!"

"We need to get its attention," said Gideon. He ran, Collier behind him, straight for the beast, screaming and shouting until he was just feet from it. He began to stamp his boots on the wooden floor, and eventually it grunted and turned, its yellow eyes lighting upon him. It opened its mouth and roared, the chandeliers far above shaking in the roof. Then it lunged for Gideon.

Jip, the monkey, leaped from Collier's shoulder, screeching and waving its arms. It was a tiny, inconsequential thing compared to the dinosaur, but it was enough to distract the beast and buy enough time.

Garcia put one boot on the fallen Speaker's chair and launched himself into the air, holding the hilt of his rapier with both hands and pointing it downward, landing like a cat on the arched back of the reptile and calling out one last time "El Chupacabras!" before plunging the blade into the back of its neck.

The dinosaur roared, twisting around and swatting Jip across the room with its huge head. It took Garcia in its snapping jaws, worrying him to the ground in front of it and lifting its head to show its bloodred teeth, scraps of black hood hanging from them.

A lost father dies.

Then the beast's tiny brain finally received the messages of pain being sent by its nerve endings, and it howled and fell forward with a crash.

Gideon and Collier leaped out of the way as the beast fell. It lay silent for a moment, then raised its head and tried to claw its way to its feet, the rapier protruding from its neck. It fell again then pulled itself forward until it was near the splintered hatch, turning to regard Gideon with a baleful yellow eye, before dragging itself over the lip and into the shaft, and slithering out of sight.

Maria ran through the thinning crowds to embrace Gideon. "Is it dead?" she asked.

He held her tightly and looked down into the black shaft. "It's certainly gone," he said, looking up at Collier. "Though being gone and being dead are not necessarily the same thing."

Lizzie Strutter surveyed her room after packing her meager belongings into a battered trunk. Not much to show for a quarter of a century in the sex trade in London. It was her body that carried the main baggage, bore the memories, sported the scars. And speaking of scars . . . Lizzie looked up, frowning, as Rachel burst in unannounced.

"Mum, you'll never guess . . . ," said the girl, then stopped, looking at the trunk. "Mum? You off somewhere?"

"Manchester," said Lizzie.

Rachel gaped at her. "What for?"

Lizzie sighed. "I'm done with London. For a bit, anyway. We've wrung each other dry."

"But Mum, the riot . . . it's over. Haven't you heard? There's been some sort of monster attacking the Houses of Parliament. The *real* Jack the Ripper was there. He fought the monster and now he's dead. It's over, Mum."

Lizzie fastened the trunk. "Yes, it is." She looked at the girl. "Time for a clean break, love. There's too much bad blood for me here now. The police'll never leave me alone, not after starting that riot on Commercial Road."

"But what about me? And the rest of the girls?"

Lizzie tapped her finger against her chin, then dug in her apron pocket and fished out a set of keys. She tossed them to

Rachel. "Time for you to make a go of it, love. Give your cunt a rest."

"Me?" asked Rachel. "Run the house? Be a madam?"

"Yes." Lizzie smiled. "You've earned it."

Mr. Tait chewed the bone reflectively. A poodle, it had been, with a little ribbon in its curly fur. Wiry thing, not a lot of meat on it. He said, "Funny old thing, Mr. Lyall."

"The poodle, Mr. Tait?"

"No, all that business with Smith. And the one-legged chap. And this thing they had, what did he call it? Tyrannosaurus?"

"Tyrannosaurus rex, Mr. Tait. King of the dinosaurs, by all accounts."

Distantly there sounded an echoing roar, as if something were in pain, or angry, or perhaps both. They listened to it for a while, until it faded.

"Ever eaten lizard, Mr. Lyall?"

"Once or twice, Mr. Tait."

"Bet there'd be a bit of meat on a Tyrannosaurus rex."

They dampened the stove and packed away their pans and plates, hefting their packs onto their shoulders in the gloom of the sewer.

"Shall we, Mr. Lyall?"

"Well, you know what we always say down here, Mr. Tait. Eat or be eaten."

They began to trudge toward the ringing echo of the roars, and Mr. Lyall broke into song.

31

Scourge of the British Empire

"How . . . how was it, Rowena?"

She blinked and looked at him as though she hadn't heard. She was pale and thin, her hair dull and matted, and he immediately chided himself for the stupidity of his question. She had spent the best part of the week in Holloway and the Old Bailey, wrongly accused of murder, the death penalty looming over her.

She gazed into the depths of the fire. "I thought you would come for me, Gideon."

"I was lost," he began, but she put up a hand.

"I know. You would have come if you could have." She looked at him. "They formally dropped the charges this morning. At the same time they arrested my father. He admitted everything. He came back for revenge, Gideon. Came back to kill the man he thought had killed me long ago."

Gideon nodded; he remembered everything of his sojourn in the sewers. "He . . . his heart was in the right place, Rowena. I don't think he meant to cause harm, really."

She sighed. "I think you're wrong, Gideon. He knew what he was doing. The Empire treated him very badly."

Gideon said carefully, "But of course, you cannot condone his plan to attack Parliament. . . ."

Rowena raised an eyebrow. She had changed out of her prison shift and into her more usual clothes, but there still seemed something . . . trapped about her. She looked around the parlor at Grosvenor Square as though it were little better than her cell at Holloway. She said, "I still haven't seen him, you know."

Gideon poured her another cup of tea. "I'm sure that can be arranged. Mr. Walsingham will be able to sort out—"

Her lip curled viciously, unattractively, into a sneer. Gideon was taken aback. He'd never seen her like this. "Walsingham? Walsingham left my father to die. He would have watched me hang."

"He is as hidebound by the rule of law as the rest of us, Rowena."

She sneered again. "Law? We are above the law, Gideon."

He shook his head. "We are not."

She looked into the depths of her teacup, as though seeking her fortune there. "If not above it, then outside it. That has always been the way for me. The things I've seen, Gideon, the things I've done. And most of them at the behest of the Crown. Yet they would have hanged me like a dog for something I did not do."

He wasn't quite sure what to say, so he said, "What are your plans for Christmas? You are most welcome, of course, to join us."

She gave a wry grin. "I am planning to be out of the country for the season."

Gideon raised an eyebrow. "You are? Not working?"

She shook her head then met his gaze. "Gideon. I need to know something. You love Maria?"

He held her stare a long time before replying. He was back in the dream, the illusion created by Mesmer's Hypno-Array. The one where he lived a life of mundane happiness back in Sandsend, a life he had thought saw him married to Maria, until the door opened and his beloved walked through . . . and it was Rowena.

Illusion, misdirection, the mind playing tricks. Mesmer's mischief. Nothing more.

"Of course I do," he said. "Do you need to ask, after everything I've been through with her?"

Rowena pursed her lips and nodded, as though she had made up her mind about something. She said, "You do not have to be what they say you are, Gideon. The Empire owes you nothing, really. If you must be a hero, be a hero for Maria."

She placed her teacup in the saucer and stood. Gideon stood also. She said, "Will you say good-bye to Maria, and Aloysius, and Mrs. Cadwallader for me? I don't think I could bear to."

He raised an eyebrow. "You sound like you are not planning to return."

"I think once we are gone, we shall be away for some time. Perhaps, as you say, forever."

"*We*, Rowena?"

She smiled. "When Aloysius came to see me at court I asked him how I was to be freed. A tunnel? A daring escape over the prison walls? He told me that I was at the mercy of justice. I am Rowena Fanshawe, Gideon. The Belle of the Airways. When I drowned Jane Gaunt, I also killed the fetters of normal society. I will never be bound again, Gideon. No one clips Rowena Fanshawe's wings."

At last, it dawned on him. "Collier," he said. "You are going to break him out of Newgate Prison. I cannot allow this, Rowena."

She drew herself up to her full height and looked him square in the eye. Her pale skin flushed, the brightness returned to her eyes, and her auburn hair seemed to acquire a luster that had been absent.

Rowena Fanshawe was back.

She said, "I am. And so here we are. You are going to stop me, Gideon?"

He looked away first. How could he stop her, after all they had been through? Was he meant to wrestle her to the ground? Was he that sort of hero?

"No," he said quietly. "But I cannot let this go unchallenged."

She moved toward the parlor door. "Then do what you must, Gideon. But after what has happened to me, I doubt I shall be returning to England." She smiled, baring her teeth, and at that moment Gideon saw she was truly Charles Collier's flesh and blood. "Not as a friend, at any rate. Fair winds, Gideon. I'll see myself out."

"Fair winds," he said quietly as she closed the door behind her.

✦✦✦

"Gideon?" Maria let herself into the parlor, looking around. "Oh, Mrs. Cadwallader said that Rowena—"

"She has been, and gone," said Gideon. "I do not think we shall see her for some time, I fear."

Maria raised a quizzical eyebrow. "I had rather hoped she might spend Christmas with us."

Quickly, Gideon crossed the rug and gathered Maria in his arms. She yelped in surprise as he lifted her from the floor, holding her gaze fiercely.

"Maria. Tell me that you love me!"

She blinked. "Gideon, I do! I have told you many times. . . ."

"But always at moments of stress, or danger. Atop dragons high above London, amid Yaqui warriors baying for our blood! Tell me here, now, in the safety and comfort of our very own parlor, that you love me!"

There was urgency in his eyes, his voice, that infected her as well. "Put me down," she whispered, "and I shall tell you. I shall show you."

He lowered her to the rug, and she took his face in her hands. "Gideon Smith. Until I met you I thought I had no right to love, to hope that another could love me. I considered myself less than human, unable to enjoy the privileges of normal people. But Gloria Monday taught me, Gideon, that whatever I feel here"—she touched her head—"and here"—she placed his hand on her breast—"makes me what I am. And I feel that I am a woman, Gideon, despite outward—or rather inward— appearances. A woman who loves you very, very much."

He broke out into a huge smile, and she kissed him, hard and long and deep, until she felt his body stirring against hers. She broke away, planting a smaller kiss on his lips, and said, "And now I am going to take you upstairs to your room, and

I am going to show you how much of a woman I am, and how much I love you."

She led him by the hand from the parlor, and he paused in the hall. "Wait," he said. "I need to make one very quick call. . . ."

✠

Gloria Monday considered herself someone apart from the ordinary masses of London, but even she had to admit that the past few days had been somewhat unusual. Jack the Ripper, gigantic lizards, fleeing through the sewers . . . she sighed happily, and not a little forlornly, looking at her unmade-up face in the cracked mirror in her small room. Back to real life, performing for those cabbage-throwing Philistines to raise enough money to go to Zurich, with the added complication that her affair with George was now out in the open.

She started at a knock at her door. The landlord, probably, after the rent arrears. Or word was out about her and George, and it was someone from the Britannia Theater in Hoxton, telling her the rest of her run there had been canceled due to the scandal. Or . . . she sighed and went to open the door a crack, throwing it wide as she saw the figure standing on the other side.

"George!"

He stepped in and laid the leather bag he was carrying on the bare floorboards, allowing Gloria to plant a kiss upon his cheek. "Sorry," she said. "I haven't shaved yet."

Somewhat alarmingly, he withdrew a revolver from his overcoat pocket and began to check the chamber. "George . . . ?"

He smiled. "I have just received a telephone call from Mr. Gideon Smith, and there is some business to attend to at Highgate Aerodrome. I would like it if you could accompany me."

Gloria smothered him in kisses again until he playfully pushed her away. "So am I being deputized into the Metropolitan Police?"

"After a fashion. Are you ready?"

She fixed him with a hard stare. "I just told you I have not yet shaved, and I need my makeup. I'm not going *anywhere* like this."

Lestrade sighed and checked his pocket watch. "As quick as you can, dear."

There was nothing—nothing!—like the feeling of an airship pulling free of its tethers, nosing into the air with a sudden lurch, defying the gravity that had kept mankind earthbound for so many millennia. Rowena stood on the bridge of the *Skylady III*, her heart soaring higher and faster than the 'stat could rise in the sluggish, cold December air. How could they have thought to deny her this? Anger burned within her, flushing her cheeks. How *could* they?

She would never again put herself in the hands of men who thought to make the law. She should never have so meekly allowed herself to be taken from her offices, transported by policemen to Holloway Prison and then to the Old Bailey. She was Rowena Fanshawe. She was the Belle of the Airways. No longer would she pay lip service to empires, to nations, to laws. She had been betrayed, and no one betrayed Rowena Fanshawe twice.

As she left English soil for what could be the last time, she felt one final tug at her heart.

Gideon Smith. She could have loved him, if he'd loved her. It was best that she left. Not just for Gideon—he loved Maria, and she could never come between them—but for her. Gideon's love would have bound her as strongly as any prison cell, squeezed the life from her as much as any hangman's noose. It was like Louis Cockayne had always said . . . they were cut from the same cloth, him and her. Louis, Rowena, her father . . . the high winds flowed through their veins, not blood. You could cage them, as you could cage an eagle, but they'd die of that, eventually.

She shed a tear as she turned the *Skylady III* above the aerodrome, perhaps for Gideon Smith, perhaps for Louis Cockayne. She could have loved Louis, too, if he hadn't been a bastard. She was sorry he'd died back there at the Alamo, but perhaps that was for the best as well. Rowena Fanshawe didn't need any distractions. She'd thought her father dead all these years, and if she had any love to give, she had a lot of time to make up. Her heart was his, for now.

Newgate Prison nestled beside the Old Bailey. Its stone walls were bound by the blood of all those who had died there: from execution, from cruelty, from despair. As she nosed the *Skylady III* over central London, she smiled agreeably at the outraged fingers pointing her way from the snow-sodden streets. She shouldn't be flying so low over London, easing her way between the towers and ziggurats. The police blimps would already be mobilizing. She didn't have much time.

Locking the wheel, Rowena rushed out onto the observation deck, the biting cold air taking her breath away. The inmates were shuffling around the small exercise yard at the center of the prison, looking up at her. They had the same exercise routines at Newgate as at Holloway and, she supposed, at all the prisons across London. Nothing if not reliable, the English penal system.

She hoped her father was down there among the prisoners. She took position behind the Hotchkiss, already bolted to the deck. It would be a very big waste of some rather spectacular explosions if not.

And then, she saw him through the crosshairs of the Hotchkiss, unmistakable though she had not seen him for so many years. He stood apart from the others, as though even in prison he was afforded the respect she now knew was owed to him, merely for his refusal to conform.

Bringing the Hotchkiss lower, she let rip the first shell, and it exploded into the outer wall of Newgate with a shriek of splintering wood, smashing glass, and cracking stone.

###

They had been unable to bind Charles Collier's legs with irons because of his wooden stump, and had decided that it was enough to chain his wrists together on the supposition that he wasn't going to go very far with only one leg.

Idiots.

He gazed skyward as the airship hove into view above the narrow exercise yard, and he slowly began to smile as the first of the shells hit the front of the prison. The guards began to run toward the shattered frontage of Newgate, and the inmates began to lurch around in fear, hope, and panic. Only Charles Collier stood still, right in the center of the yard, alone.

"Good girl," he said softly to himself as another shell exploded on the roof in front of him.

Smoke billowed up from the prison and the inmates spied their chance, charging the wrecked walls. Collier remained where he was as the airship pulled up sharply, nosing over the walls, and a rope ladder unfurled. As it swung by he grabbed it in his chained hands, and he let out a cry of triumph as the 'stat, its pilot now back on the bridge, began to ascend sharply up and over the chaos, carrying him to his freedom.

⁂

"She's a fine 'stat, and no mistake," said Charles Collier as Rowena set to his chains with a pair of bolt cutters.

"She's what we call a tripler," said Rowena. "She's got a gear winder, some electric, and a light coal-powered steam engine. Came out of the Gefa-Flug factory in Aachen."

He looked out the window, behind the ship. "We're going to need it. I can already see the police airships."

Rowena smiled and pushed forward a lever on the bridge; the gondola lurched as the *Skylady III* thrust forward. Collier, his wrists free, hugged her. "I'm so proud of you, you know. I could not have spent another hour in that prison, shut off from the sky. I feel as though I have been delivered from hell."

Rowena felt tears prick her eyes. "We have lost so much time," she said. "We each thought the other dead."

"And here we are, both alive," said Collier. "Though we might as well be dead, at least as far as coming back to England is concerned. You know that, don't you? You have nothing to keep you here, I hope? For we are outlaws now, Jane."

She thought of Gideon again, then said softly, "No. Nothing to keep me here. Not anymore." She took her father by the hand. "And Jane, I'm very much afraid, is dead. You'll have to get used to calling me Rowena."

They ascended as they flew, the smog and clouds thinning. Collier said, "I was intending to take my punishment, you know. I deserve it. Mr. Smith was right; I was blinded by guilt. I mistook vengeance for justice. I still hate the British Empire and everything it has done, but that does not mean everyone who lives here is evil." He smiled again. "You live here."

"Not anymore," she said. "I'm done with England. Where shall we go first?"

There was a noise behind them, and they turned to see Inspector George Lestrade ascending the ladder to the bridge. Behind him came Gloria Monday, looking somewhat confused and carrying a large leather bag. Lestrade held a revolver, which he pointed directly at Rowena.

"I hope I don't have to use this gun," said Lestrade.

Rowena returned his stare. "You will if you expect me to land this ship on English soil. I presume Gideon alerted you?"

Lestrade helped Gloria onto the bridge, not lowering the revolver. "He did. He telephoned me at the Commercial Road police station."

"And you hid aboard the *Skylady III* to ambush us," said Collier. "Well done, Inspector. A good move." He appraised Gloria. "Though I thought you might have brought more . . . firepower."

Gloria looked at the gun, then to Collier, then to Lestrade. "I must confess, George, I'm not quite sure myself why you brought me here. . . ."

Lestrade took the bag from her, unlatched it with his free hand, and tossed it onto the bridge. He said, "I'm going to put the gun down now." He looked at Gloria, then at Rowena. "I'm not here to arrest you, Miss Fanshawe. In fact, I'm rather hoping you will take us with you."

Rowena stared at the money overflowing from the leather bag. There must have been thousands of pound notes.

"George?" said Gloria. "I thought you were here to stop them. . . . And where is all that money from?"

"Markus Mesmer's ill-gotten gains. I couldn't tell you before, Gloria, in case we failed. I did not wish to implicate you if I was stymied. I was going to log the money at the station, but before I could, and just before Mr. Smith called me . . . well, I have been relieved from my duties. Apparently my unblemished record with the force and my exemplary service is nothing compared to whom I choose to love. The law has abandoned me, Miss Fanshawe, much as I expect you feel it has abandoned you. Therefore, I have decided that I shall abandon the law." He looked at Gloria. "For love."

Gloria squealed and threw her arms around Lestrade. Rowena said, "Where would you have us take you, Inspector?"

"To Zurich, if you would. I believe there is a doctor there who can make my Gloria very happy. After that . . . who knows?" George Lestrade gave a rare smile. "It's all rather exciting, don't you think, Gloria?"

She began to smother him with kisses, and he added, "And please, Miss Fanshawe, it isn't Inspector any more. Just George, will do."

Rowena raised an eyebrow at her father. "Mr. Collier, would you set a course for Zurich?"

"Might I beg one stop before that?" he asked.

She nodded. "As you will, Mr. Collier."

He broke into a grin, saluted his daughter, and said, "Aye aye, Skipper," as the *Skylady III* broke through the clouds into clear blue sky.

⁂

"How long do we wait?" asked Kalanath, the scar on his face purple in the cold. "You read the newspapers, didn't you? They have captured Fereng. He is not coming for us."

"How far is it to India? And how are we to get there?" asked young Naakesh.

"A long way indeed," said Phoolendu, leaning on the gigantic statue that dominated Blanchard Square. It was a representation in bronze of the prototype powered balloon in which Jean-Pierre Blanchard had made the first powered flight in 1782, built in the place where he had landed in central London and not only astonished the Empire, but ushered in a new age of flight. It was the place where Fereng had said they should meet should they ever get separated. Phoolendu popped the last of the nuts into his mouth. "And we will need a lot of food."

There was a ripple of astonishment from the crowds around them, and the four Thuggees looked up. Deeptendu smiled and pointed at the huge dirigible bearing down on them, scattering the crowds from its shadow. The *Skylady III*. On the observation deck of the rapidly descending airship they could see the unmistakable shape of Fereng, scourge of the British Empire.

32

Delivered from Hell

"Now that," said Aloysius Bent as he poured himself out of the steam-cab that had just brought them home, "is what you call an adventure."

"Though not one to be repeated," said Gideon. They had been summoned to the Commercial Road police station to offer some explanation about what had happened at Newgate Prison. They had none. The new inspector, Abberline, had regarded them with suspicion.

"You might have gotten away with all sorts of things under George Lestrade, but he's shown his mettle now, and he's gone. There's a new guvnor in charge here. Just don't cross me, if you know what's good for you," he'd said, before curtly dismissing them.

"I cannot believe Rowena has gone," said Maria. "And in such spectacular fashion." Maria was still wearing the suit Gloria Monday had given her; she thought she might go shopping later, perhaps buy some more.

"Perhaps it's for the best," said Gideon, half to himself. "Though now she is considered a criminal . . . I rather hope our paths don't cross, not in the immediate future."

Bent nodded as he fished out his keys for the front door. "Everything tied up nicely, apart from one thing."

Gideon raised an eyebrow. "We have a mystery left unsolved?"

"That feller I saw hanging around here, two or three times now," said Bent, unlocking the door and pushing it in. "No idea who he—" He paused, openmouthed. "You!"

Bent launched himself at the man, dressed in a black suit and bowler, graying sideburns wobbling with astonishment on his face. He grabbed a handful of his lapels and pushed him against the wood-paneled wall. "Who are you working for? Walsingham? Are you one of Mesmer's?"

"Mr. Bent!" cried Mrs. Cadwallader stridently. "I shall thank you to leave Mr. Grayson be immediately!"

Bent blinked at her and slowly let go of the man. "Grayson?"

Mrs. Cadwallader sighed. "Mr. Bent. Might I have a moment in private with you in the study?"

Nonplussed, Bent followed her in and she closed the door. She said, "Mr. Grayson is in service with the Rogersons at number 17. He is a widower. We have been . . . spending some time together recently. When I went out the other night? We share a passion for opera, Mr. Bent."

Bent stared at her. "You and him? You're stepping out? But Sally . . . I thought . . . after yesterday . . ."

She closed her eyes. "Mr. Bent, please do not remind me of that. When those lights flooded the whole house . . . We were both under the influence of that dreadful Markus Mesmer. It should not have happened, would not have happened otherwise." She opened her eyes. "Please, Aloysius. I am very fond of Mr. Grayson. I am sorry if what occurred gave you the wrong idea of my feelings toward you. Now, as all the excitement is over, we are going for a walk to Hyde Park."

Bent followed her out and watched them depart. He looked at Gideon and Maria. "I need an effing drink. Pub?"

Gideon shook his head and placed his arm around Maria. "Rowena's experience with her father has taught us that opportunities must be seized, time must not be wasted."

"I am going to move my things into Gideon's room," said Maria.

As they began to climb the stairs, Bent snorted. "All right for some, I must say." He stood alone in the hallway. What the bloody hell was he supposed to do now? Then something occurred to him, and he broke out in a wide grin. The strike was over. The bawdy houses were open for business.

Whistling, he checked his wallet to make sure he was

well-off, then went out to find a cab to take him to Whitechapel. As Gideon Smith had so sagely said, opportunities must be seized. Time must not be wasted. Oh yes, time must not be effing wasted.

It was something of a subdued Christmas at 23 Grosvenor Square, the first one the house had seen without Captain Lucian Trigger and Dr. John Reed, and the absence of Rowena Fanshawe in the company weighed heavily. Gideon had written a long letter to Inez in the town of Freedom, hoping that enough traffic had built up between the British American enclaves and the burgeoning township to have it delivered.

"Perhaps we ought to have a little trip out there," said Bent, finishing off one of Mrs. Cadwallader's mince pies and washing it down with a gulp of sherry. "Be nice to see a bit of sun, after all this effing snow."

"No doubt our paymasters will have some other mission for us soon," said Gideon.

Bent sat back in the easy chair in the parlor, watching him. "Collier really got to you, didn't he? And it wasn't just the effects of Mesmer's hypnosis."

Gideon sighed. "I don't know, Aloysius. All my life I wanted to be a hero. I don't suppose I was anticipating that the fight between good and evil was going to be so lacking in defined black and white."

"Lots of gray." Bent nodded, smiling as Maria came into the room. She twirled around to show off her latest suit, an olive-green number, perfectly tailored for her. "You like your men's clothes, don't you, love?"

She shrugged. "Perhaps we place too much weight on what belongs to a man and what to a woman. Invariably, the men get the better deal."

The doorbell rang, and shortly Mrs. Cadwallader tapped on the parlor door. "Mr. Walsingham for you."

They all stood as Walsingham strode in, taking off his top

hat. Bent raised his glass. "Come to keep the season with us, Walsingham?"

"A glass of sherry, perhaps." He laid his hat on the ottoman. "But it is not merely a social visit."

"It never is, thank God," said Bent.

Walsingham accepted the glass from Mrs. Cadwallader and said, "I have news. Word has reached me from Munich, where reside Hermann Einstein's wife, Pauline, and their son, Albert. The apple has evidently not fallen far from the tree; the boy is something of a genius in most fields, perhaps displaying even at the early age of eleven yet more eccentricities than his father."

"They haven't been targeted by Bourbon agents?" said Gideon, sitting down again. "Mesmer and his crew managed to flee London after Garcia was apprehended."

"The boy is missing," said Walsingham. "Frau Einstein is beside herself with worry. It appears young Albert has taken himself off on a mission to find his father."

Bent said, "Not to bloody America?"

"Quite so, Mr. Bent. An eleven-year-old boy appears to be attempting to walk into the court of the Witch-King of New Orleans. This adds yet more urgency to our mission to find the professor. I humbly suggest you prepare to leave for America within the next few days."

"A pity Rowena isn't here to take us," said Maria.

Walsingham smiled. "The Crown has many agents at its disposal, Miss Maria. I will be in touch. In the meantime, enjoy what's left of Christmas."

When he'd gone, Bent belched and held up his glass. "And God bless us, every effing one."

Doctor Augustus returned to his laboratory at Rough Tor early after the Christmas holiday, to enjoy a day or two of solitude to study the data taken from his experiments with the automaton. There was only so far they could go with tests; he wondered whether Walsingham had been serious when he suggested there might have to be more *invasive* procedures. Even as a man of science, he felt a pang at the thought of decapitating Maria to get at the Atlantic Artifact. Despite himself, he had grown fond of her during their time together.

On his desk was a package wrapped in brown paper and string, addressed to him. He pulled it open to reveal a small, square box, and a note written in Walsingham's spidery hand.

> *Doctor Augustus, a belated Christmas present for you. It seems that Maria might keep her head, after all. For a while, at least. W.*

Doctor Augustus opened the box. Inside was the glassy-eyed, severed black-and-white head of what appeared to be a colobus monkey.

Spain had been on his mind. The memory of that childhood visit to Madrid had stayed with him all week, then the unmasking of Don Sergio de la Garcia, and the half-Spanish Bourbon plot. So when he ventured into the warren of Whitechapel streets, selected his victim, and set to her with the surgical instruments, he sat by her and cradled her head in his lap, singing *"Farewell and adieu, you fair Spanish ladies"* in a soft, crooning voice, even though neither she, nor of course he, were Spanish. She stared into the darkness, shuddering and growing colder as he sang, her entrails spread out on the snow as though for divining. In a way, he supposed, they were. And the future they told was red, like the blood staining the snow, and black, like his soul. When she had finally died he carefully extracted her kidney, wrapped it in newspaper, and set off for home.

It had been necessary for Garcia to be taken care of, certainly once his links to a much wider plot became apparent. Besides, the man was a half-hearted amateur, with no stomach for killing. He barely deserved the appellation of Jack the Ripper that the newspapers had given him.

There was a much more suitable candidate for that role.

He had been shadowing Garcia for some time, or at least, the masked man. He hadn't known who was beneath the black mask, hadn't thought to care while he was in the intermedio. He had observed Garcia's hesitant approaches to the women, the swordplay, the quick stroke across the forehead.

Sometimes the women Garcia had left behind were not even dead. Sometimes they were barely injured. He had seen to that. He had dispatched those Garcia hadn't the stomach to kill, creeping in the shadows as Garcia fled the scene, then finishing the job. And he'd added his own little flourishes, stabbing them in the gut to see how it felt when the knife went in, slashing their throats to see how much blood gouted out. He remembered the names of the ones he had killed, whom Garcia had left alive: Mary Ann Nichols, Annie Chapman, Elizabeth Stride, Catherine Eddowes, Mary Jane Kelly. Garcia was apparently so insane by the end, he barely knew how many he had killed.

He made his way home. Garcia was dead, and Jack the Ripper should die with him. Should. But he knew that the legend could not die as easily as the man. Not as long as he continued to slip into the intermedio, not as long as his black soul thirsted for blood.

He remembered the first time, watching Dr. Gull mutilating the body of Annie Crook on Cleveland Street, two and a half years ago now. The sight of Gull's clinical detachment as he set to work on the shopgirl had awakened something deep inside him.

In Mr. Walsingham. He shuddered at the thought, how he had stood over Gull while he worked on the girl, clasping his gloved hands behind his back and peering intently at every cut and slash, his soul slowly filling up with darkness.

He hadn't really known what to do about the hunger that consumed him, not until Jack the Ripper began to attack

women in London. Then he knew what he had to do, to feed
his shrieking soul, to ease the pressure in his brain.

Because it was pressure, being Mr. Walsingham. The safety
and security of the British Empire—threatened sometimes by
forces of which the populace could have scant understanding—
weighed upon his shoulders most heavily. He needed an outlet.
He needed his intermedio.

Walsingham let himself into his rooms and lit all the
candles, one by one. He eschewed gas lamps and electricity for
the guttering, dancing flames of the tallow; it comforted him
somehow, kept the modern world and all its horrors and marvels at bay. He washed his hands thoroughly in the sink, though,
like Lady Macbeth, he knew he would never wash the stain
from them or, ultimately, his soul. He would have to be careful, of course. . . . Aloysius Bent had already scented that there
was some other reason behind Walsingham's uncharacteristic
candor in his desire to see Garcia off the streets. Perhaps, Mr.
Walsingham considered, being so free with his secrets and
mysteries to guide Bent and his associates toward Garcia had
aroused the journalist's suspicions. He would have to watch
Mr. Bent. . . . He was shrewder than his foolish exterior would
suggest.

Walsingham extracted the soggy newspaper package from
his bag and laid it on the work surface. The girl's kidney. Perhaps he would fry it up with some onions and eat it later. For
now, while the intermedio was still upon him, he had the urge
to write. He sat at his desk and dipped his quill into the well,
which he had filled with red ink. He looked at it dripping from
the tip. Red ink, or blood, he didn't truly know. He would write
a letter to the constabulary. Inspector Lestrade had rather sen-
sationally left his position, but there was apparently a new inspector at the Commercial Road station now, a man by the
name of Abberline. Mr. Walsingham would write to him. He
began to scribble in a blocky, clumsy hand quite distinct from
his usual script. The writing of the intermedio. The hand of
Jack the Ripper.

Dear Boss,

I keep on hearing the police have caught me but they won't fix me just yet. I have laughed when they look so clever and talk about being on the right track. That joke about Leather Apron gave me real fits. I am down on whores and I shan't quit ripping them till I do get buckled. Grand work the last job was. I gave the lady no time to squeal. How can they catch me now? I love my work and want to start again. You will soon hear of me with my funny little games. I saved some of the proper red stuff in a ginger beer bottle over the last job to write with but it went thick like glue and I can't use it. Red ink is fit enough I hope ha, ha. The next job I do I shall clip the lady's ears off and send to the police officers just for jolly. My knife's so nice and sharp I want to get to work right away if I get a chance. Good Luck. Yours truly,

Jack the Ripper

Mr. Walsingham, or at least the thing he became when he surrendered to the intermedio, when he allowed his black soul to swell and consume him, sat back to admire the letter. He gave a thin smile, dipped his quill into the red ink, and with a flourish added at the top right, where the postmark would normally go, two words.

From Hell

Yes, he was so very far from home.

ABOUT THE AUTHOR

David Barnett is an award-winning journalist, currently multimedia content manager of the *Telegraph & Argus*, cultural reviewer for *The Guardian* and the *Independent on Sunday*, and he has done features for *The Independent* and *Wired*. He is the author of *Angelglass* (described by *The Guardian* as "stunning"), *Hinterland*, and *popCULT!*. His website can be found at davidbarnett.wordpress.com.